THE CONJURE WOMAN AND
OTHER CONJURE TALES

The Conjure Woman and Other Conjure Tales

Charles W. Chesnutt

Edited and with an Introduction by
Richard H. Brodhead

Duke University Press   Durham & London 1993

Second printing, 1994
© 1993 Duke University Press
All rights reserved
Printed in the United States of America
on acid-free paper ∞
Typeset in New Baskerville by Tseng Information Systems
Library of Congress Cataloging-in-Publication Data
appear on the last printed page of this book.

CONTENTS

THE CONJURE WOMAN AND
OTHER CONJURE TALES

INTRODUCTION

There are two reasons for presenting this edition of Charles W. Chesnutt's stories. The first is that *The Conjure Woman* has increasingly been recognized as a literary creation of remarkable interest and power. In the African-American tradition this book stands out as a major literary production from the period that Chesnutt named "Post-bellum–Pre-Harlem," and it helped pioneer a literary use of black vernacular culture important to many later writers. Within American literature at large, *The Conjure Woman* has a place in the line of distinguished short story collections that runs from Washington Irving's *Sketch Book* and Nathaniel Hawthorne's *Mosses from an Old Manse* to many more modern instances, making its own ingenious contributions to a well-established formal tradition.

But there is a second reason for this edition that is more particular to *The Conjure Woman,* and it has to do with the book's peculiar publication history. We customarily think of books as being conceived and created by their authors, then passing through a merely mechanical process—publication— that brings the writer's conception before readers. Whether the instruments of literature's public production ever play a wholly passive role in literary creation could be debated; but the common understanding certainly does not tell the story of this work's creation. What we have in *The Conjure Woman* is a work partly proposed by an author but also in significant part imagined by a publisher, then written by the author to the publisher's specifications. The publisher then chose the volume's contents from the batch of tales Chesnutt submitted, so that this book, apparently complete in itself, in fact embodies a selection, one version of Chesnutt's work carved from a much larger, and much more diverse, body of writing.

If this edition wished to be sensational it could call itself The Complete Conjure Woman or even The Unexpurgated Conjure Woman. For the first time it restores the tales printed in *The Conjure Woman* to the company of the unadopted works, the stories that were once equal candidates for inclusion but were chosen against. The reader now has a chance to see the whole array of related writings the published *Conjure Woman* was selected from; and just as important, the reader is put in the position to watch the process of the book's composition, to see the choices that were made in creating the volume we have known. Taken together, this collection significantly amplifies our knowledge of Chesnutt's early literary efforts that found eventual—and partial—expression in the *Conjure Woman* volume. With its full history displayed, the composition of *The Conjure Woman* also gives an extraordinarily vivid picture of the conditions that enabled and restricted African-American literary aspiration in late nineteenth-century America—the conditions that Chesnutt worked in, through, and against.

The tales contained in this volume largely follow a single formula, which might be labeled the plot of cultural tourism. Again and again a person who has traveled from afar meets a "native," a colorful yet characteristic denizen of a region remote from "civilization," and through him encounters the different ways of knowing and doing indigenous to that place. Since their different ways of talking are the most prominent sign of the larger difference between the two, we could also call the formula that produces John and Uncle Julius at the start of a Chesnutt story the plot of bilingualism. These tales are programmed to produce a display of standard, correct, literate speech that then calls up a different speaker, the bearer of a local dialect barbarously deviant from official literate English yet fully expressive on its own terms, who is invited to produce his vernacular for the other person's hearing.

This formula might be called the operative condition of authorship in Chesnutt's conjure stories, so fully does it govern the production of the tales. But to understand the nature of Chesnutt's work as an author it is essential to grasp that the formula he subscribes to here is by no means his own invention. It represents a convention already massively conventional when he adopted it, a formula fully established in the literary system of his time.

While the process did not begin or end then, the postbellum decades saw the United States rapidly transforming itself into a developed nation, a process that entailed the forceful intrusion of a nationally organized cultural economy upon once more autonomous and distinct local worlds. This transformation is witnessed in the large-scale national corporations that reorganized local enterprises into a translocal scheme of production in the late nineteenth century; in the railroads that brought previously separate regions into a national transportation—and market—network; in the telegraph and telephone lines that brought once-isolated communities into a national communication system; and in the postbellum constitutional amendments that placed national norms of citizenly rights over previously prevailing regional differences, differences most famously embodied in southern slavery.

Paradoxically, in the literary realm this process of delocalization helped produce a form of writing devoted to featuring local difference, so that the literature of local color emerged as the dominant American literary genre in the same decades as did the transcontinental railroad and Standard Oil. The relation of these apparently contradictory developments can be understood in several ways. This literary genre, we can speculate, took on prominence in the postbellum years because it performed a larger social work, the work of mourning ways of life being eradicated at this time. The elegaic remembrance of a premodern order now passing is often written into such works' titles, as in Harriet Beecher Stowe's *Oldtown Folks*, Thomas Wentworth Higginson's *Oldport Days*, and Mark Twain's "Old Times on the Mississippi." But this fiction itself fully participated in the new, delocalized cultural order that emerged in this time— these stories were published in nationally circulating journals for the highly literate like the *Atlantic Monthly* and *Harper's*

Monthly, and were certainly *not* written for the consumption of rustics or yokels. So instead of merely grieving for lost local cultures, this genre might be understood to have performed a mental rehearsal of the new order's triumph *over* the local, whose ways it fondly records, even celebrates, but also subjugates to its privileged point of view. (The local provides entertainment for the cosmopolitan in American local color fiction, never the reverse.) Serving as it did such complex cultural functions, a literary form pairing the sophisticated traveler with a vernacular-speaking indigene took on enormous popularity in late nineteenth-century America, and authors using this form produced a virtual survey of underdeveloped zones—Maine coastal villages in the work of Sarah Orne Jewett, the southern Appalachian hill country in the work of Mary Noailles Murfree, the Indiana backwoods in the work of Edward Eggleston, and so on.

Charles Chesnutt was born of free Negro parents from North Carolina just before the Civil War. At an early age he rose to a position of high eminence in North Carolina black education, but he also hungered to get out of the segregated South, and so he explored alternative careers. One of the careers that most profoundly appealed to him was that of the writer: "It is the dream of my life—to be an author!,"[1] he wrote in his journal at age twenty-three. But given that the centers of literary production in his time were located in cosmopolitan northern cities like Boston and New York, Chesnutt's will to authorship required him mentally to leave his local scene and to try to project himself into the literary culture of those distant centers where his authorship could be fully established. Looking out to northern literary cultures, then back at his home world through their eyes, is the means by which Chesnutt came to find southern black folk life as a possible literary subject. An early journal entry shows him taking an interest in collecting black spirituals because of the demand for them in the northern literary world: "I have thought, during the great revival which is going on, that a collection of the ballads or hymns which the

---

1. *The Journals of Charles W. Chesnutt,* ed. Richard H. Brodhead (Durham, N.C.: Duke University Press, 1993), p. 154.

4

colored people sing with such fervor, might be acceptable, if only as a curiosity, to people, literary people, at the North." A later entry shows him contemplating a novel on southern black life at the end of Reconstruction after he learns that this kind of work meets northern readers' interests, as evidenced in the reception of Albion Tourgée's best-seller *A Fool's Errand*. [2] Chesnutt did not follow through with these early plans, and he found another career path out of the South: in 1883 he left Fayetteville, North Carolina, for New York, then Cleveland, where he established himself and prospered as a legal stenographer. But when he achieved his first literary success, in the late 1880s, he did so by finding another northern/cosmopolitan literary form with potential relevance to his world of origin: the local color form discussed above.

Since the South became the American prototype of the "different," more backward zone after the Civil War, American regional writing had an active southern department almost from the first. By the mid-1870s George Washington Cable, Mark Twain, Constance Fenimore Woolson, and others were already supplying southern scenes and voices to feed the national hunger for regional fare. But with the official end of Reconstruction in 1877, southern regionalism spawned a specialized subgenre, a form with the more or less overt function of excusing the North's withdrawal from the plight of the freed southern slave. This subgenre, prefigured in Joel Chandler Harris's *Uncle Remus: His Songs and His Sayings* (1880) and perfected in Thomas Nelson Page's *In Ole Virginia* (1887), deployed a black rustic figure, an ex-slave but still-faithful retainer, to testify to his love of the old days and his lack of desire for equal social rights. Paradoxically, in order to deliver this reactionary message this form had to take a potentially progressive step. It handed the role of dialect speaker to a black character, and so made a literary place for an authentic-sounding black voice.

This literary-historical development set the precondition for Chesnutt's conjure stories in the most direct possible way. The accession of the black dialect tale in the mid-1880s placed literary value on something Chesnutt knew intimately, the life of

2. Ibid., pp. 121 and 124–26.

5

the black vernacular, and it established within the dominant culture's literary system a form that an outlander like Chesnutt was especially well equipped to produce, a fiction of black folk life. Seizing the opportunity for black authorship that this white-authored form had inadvertently created, Chesnutt embraced this genre, reimagined his Fayetteville (now Patesville) so as to supply its generic requirements, and so won a place for his writing in some of the most prestigious literary journals of his time.

To a person familiar with the black dialect tale of the 1880s, Chesnutt's first-written conjure tales are striking for their cool mastery of this form's conventions. In these works Chesnutt renders the set moves of a certain kind of story with suave perfection. He displays no resistance to these conventions, makes no visible effort to revise them or to struggle against their sway: all is compliance, so far as the surface appearance of these stories goes. Nevertheless Chesnutt makes his adopted form carry other messages than it had in other hands—messages always obliquely conveyed behind an elaborate show of conformity.

There is nothing at all original about the pair of speakers that organizes Chesnutt's tales, for instance. No effort is made to individualize John or Uncle Julius or to naturalize the relation between them. Stock characters, they are given to us virtually *as* stock characters, as standard-issue figures of the local color form. This lightly emphasized conventionality already communicates the ironic message that dialect stories deal in stereotypes or stand-ins for reality, not the thing itself; but as usual this message is left completely implicit, available to those who have ears to hear it. But if Chesnutt does not deviate from the formulaic in creating this pair, he does convey the sense that the relation between them is one of conflict, not the cross-cultural harmony the genre typically evokes.

The social interest that John belongs to is thus clearly if lightly marked. Everything about him links him to the American haute bourgeoisie of the post–Civil War years. His speech, correctly written and featuring a rather learned Latinate vocabulary (words like "sabbatic," "desuetude," "equable," and "sojourn" come naturally to him), identifies him at every point

6

as a member of the educated classes. His wife's poor health ties him to the contemporary social group in which women are leisured, unproductively employed, and given to neurasthenia. His family doctor, whose opinion he shares "from an unprofessional standpoint," groups him with the still relatively new part of American society in which medical care has become the office of professional experts, and in which others are downgraded into nonprofessionals or amateurs. His Sundays spent attending "the church of our choice" and "occupying ourselves with the . . . contents of a fairly good library" tie him to the decorous, nonenthusiastic Protestantism of the contemporary upper orders and to their high-minded literary culture.

But the character who has these social affiliations also belongs to a distinctive economic interest, the culture of northern capitalism, and he is present on the scene not through cultural curiosity but through the action of this economic interest. John instinctively believes that everything is a potential commodity and that all commodities should be exploited for maximum profit. When he sees sandy soil, he sees grapes and melons that could be grown and marketed; when he sees a swamp, he sees ground that could be cleared and made productive; when he sees clay, he sees bricks that could be manufactured and sold. This entrepreneurialism is what brings him to the McAdoo plantation. He finds in the postwar South a Third World, a place where "labor was cheap, and land could be bought for a mere song," and so where investment in development will yield the greatest profit. As he puts it, his grape-growing business displays "the opportunities open to northern capital in the development of southern industries."

The figure Chesnutt stations over against this outsider, Uncle Julius, is at first glance a completely stock creation. Chesnutt has not troubled even to change the full name of Julius's literary original, Harris's Uncle Remus. But as he did with John, Chesnutt takes pains unobtrusively to evoke the whole organized world or *culture* that a freed slave of the postbellum period might inhabit. Julius thus has his own system of medical expertise, administered not by professional men but by conjure women. He has his own version of religion, involving not decorous Sabbath observance but life-charms, ghosts, and the magical control of natural vitality. He has his own version of literature, consisting not of books written by others but of oral tales he himself remembers and performs. He has his own system of language, a locally accented *spoken* language that looks monstrous in print (John's element) but makes perfect sense once we learn to sound it. In addition, as a further extension of this coherent world of mutually supporting practices, Julius has his own relation to the place where he lives, based on a sense not of abstract interchangeability but of the particularizing history that attaches people to scenes; and he brings his own precapitalist economics to bear on his world—exploiting it to be sure, but always within the context of his lived attachment to it and aiming for limited practical gains instead of infinite, abstract returns.

When John follows his investment strategy to the McAdoo plantation he enters on a note of bland noncompetitiveness and coexistence: "Don't let us disturb you. . . . There is plenty of room for us all." But Julius sizes John up for the threat that he is: "Is you de Norv'n gemman w'at's gwine ter buy de ole vimya'd?" For as Chesnutt develops the regionalist formula, contact between different cultures must always entail conflict, the struggle to control the space these groups share. Chesnutt's stories take place where John's and Julius's conflicting outlooks collide, at the point where one set of inhabitants meets the incursion of another group's way of owning and managing the world. At this site, Julius defends himself against John's superior power—the surplus capital that lets him buy the new McAdoo plantation—with the weapon he has in endless supply: the countless stories he knows about the land that John knows as mere property.

Julius's stories deal with the threat of John's new-style mastery by shifting back to the old one of "slabery days." In Chesnutt, unlike Harris or Page, the ex-slave's account of the old days has no element of nostalgic longing. Uncle Julius knows slavery simply as a system of domination and subjugation—a system this unsentimental narrator for the most part accepts as a historical given or fact of life (the total absence of righteous moralizing is one of the beauties of Julius's tales) except when it issues in an unbearable excess. Such an excess, an exercise of power so extreme as to threaten the very humanity of the slave, occurs toward the start of almost every tale here, as when a mother has her child taken from her to complete a deal between slaveowners ("Sis' Becky's Pickaninny"), or a slave is so generously loaned out to his master's children that he loses control of his own location ("Po' Sandy"), or an overseer is allowed to whip his slaves toward the goal of infinite labor and productivity ("Mars Jeems's Nightmare").

In such extremity, Chesnutt's slaves resort to conjure. The practice of conjure is complexly characterized in these tales, where it combines the occult properties of magic with the this-worldly, even businesslike properties of a social administration system. Conjure figures in these tales as a way to control property and settle property disputes, a way to regulate love conflicts, and, in "A Victim of Heredity," even as a bank, and it is used by both whites and blacks. But above all conjure figures as a recourse, a form of power available to the powerless in mortally intolerable situations.

One of the most moving features of Chesnutt's work lies in his suggestion that the oppressed are never absolutely oppressed, and their domination is never total. Because the slaves once shared a coherent way of life together in Africa, elements of their own distinctive culture—like the African-derived practice of conjure—accompany them into slavery and take on new life as a means of resistance. The "monst'us strong" work of conjure exerts real power in *The Conjure Woman*, power sometimes almost unlimited—as in "Sis' Becky's Pickaninny," where conjure can make whole the family bonds the slave system regularly violates. But if domination's power is never total in Chesnutt, neither is the power of resistance; and these tales more typically trace the qualified strength—the combination of power and limitations—of the force slaves call conjure. Spells that are cast defy their makers' efforts to undo them; spells go only partly right and do harms they did not intend; slaves escape from slavery via conjure by becoming immovable things like trees, but the master turns out to own the tree as much as he did the slave; conjure makes a master suffer the experience of his own harsh rule, but this experience leads him only to mitigate his demands, not to renounce his mastery: "De nex' day atter he come back, he tol' de han's dey neenter wuk on'y fum sun ter sun."

Uncle Julius's tales plot the range of outcomes that can be

reached when two groups collide, neither of which has an absolute monopoly of power, but whose powers are also never simply equal. And while slavery is their apparent referent, the play of power within Julius's tales has an obvious relevance to the situation in which he tells his tales. In the scene of their telling Julius's stories confront a new subjugation, the subjection of former slaves to the mastery not of plantation owners but of new-style capitalist developers. (To get some sense of the reality of this force we could remember that North Carolina went from being the poorest to the most highly developed of the former Confederate states between 1860 and 1900.) Julius tells his tales in the face of this historical force, which John rather obliviously incarnates, and Julius's tales embody his own indigenous resistance to this force—a resistance that shows traditional cultural resources taking on new uses in a new historical situation.

Traditional possessions, the embodiments of a quintessentially local knowledge ("eve'ybody roun' heah knows it"), Julius's tales are another part of the vernacular culture of which conjure is one expression, and in their telling his tales perform a conjure of a second order. Like the conjure woman working her roots or distributing her goopher mixtries, Julius's storytelling creates a zone of reality under his imaginative control, the space of a fictional reality. Casting his own kind of spell, the persuasion of his telling relocates his hearers' imaginations within this mind-managed world, where he can subject them to the counterforce of his different understanding. Through his fictions he shows John things that John takes for granted in a different light: in "The Goophered Grapevine" he shows this believer in the naturalness of private property the process by which naturally growing things (grapes *and* men) get made over into private property, and their vitality made into the source of someone else's profit; in "Mars Jeems's Nightmare" he shows the apparent good of highly disciplined productivity as a violation of more fundamental human needs. Julius is trying to protect his economic interests through his storytelling—Chesnutt knows that fiction in Julius's culture is not mere "art," a dysfunctional aesthetic product made for disinterested aesthetic contemplation, but an instrument, a means to worldly ends—and his fictional conjure, like the conjure within his tales, is by no means unavailing. An audit would reveal the many benefits Julius extracts by subjecting his hearers to his narrative powers: free hams, sinecure jobs for shiftless relatives, protection of his honey monopoly, and so on.

But here again Chesnutt is careful to note that if dominated people are not powerless, neither is their power limitless. Julius is always winning little advantages within an order that stays under someone else's control, and his very need to extract concessions repeatedly testifies to the fact that someone else is in charge. Like the story swappers in Zora Neale Hurston's *Mules and Men* and William Faulkner's *Hamlet,* this virtuoso tells his tales on the porch, but this piazza belongs to the white owner; it is a communal space the owner controls. Julius's tales win rewards from his hearers, but each reward carries the message that it was in his employers' power to give or withhold that benefit.

If there are limits to what storytelling can accomplish, we should also not rush to the conclusion that telling itself is a cost-free activity. The economy associated with Julius (not a cash economy) is based on bargaining, striking deals in which one gives up something another wants in order to get something the other has. Aunt Peggy exchanges her services for kerchiefs, pecks of potatoes, and other suitable goods; the slaveowners swap slaves for horses and horses for slaves; and Chesnutt strongly suggests that Julius's storytelling itself functions within another such economy of exchange. Julius has something his hearers need. Chesnutt makes their need plain in the figure of Annie. Annie is ill, but her malaise is not physical. She is afflicted with a depression at times almost fatal in its intensity. The stories clearly indicate that the cause of her depression is boredom—a boredom induced by her way of life. It is almost always Sunday in *The Conjure Woman,* yet another day when there is nothing to do. Reading is this couple's resource to fill the dead space of their empty leisure, but their entertainment merely intensifies their *tedium vitae:* Annie almost dies as John reads aloud to her in "Sis' Becky's Pickaninny." This is to say that John and Annie inhabit an organized way of life whose very decencies and "superiorities"—its refined manners, feminine leisure, and literary culture—afflict them with a sense of experiential deprivation. Julius appears before this audience as the bearer of a better entertainment. ("A story will be a godsend to-day," says the wife sick unto death of her husband's reading.) And by telling his tales, Julius gives Annie what she needs: "greater interest," "delightful animation," the chance to live vicariously, through the narrated experience of black slaves, a life richer in passion, sorrow, and delight—a life richer in *life*—than the devitalized, civilized one she leads. She gives Julius benefits in exchange for this gain, but the logic of exchange suggests that he too must be giving something in return. This price is never stated but can be surmised: he is giving up his people's life as other people's entertainment. Like a long line of black show business successes in American white culture he wins an enhanced social place for himself by making African-American expressive forms and "soul" available to others' imaginative participation and consumption.

Chesnutt had his own reasons for being hyperconscious of the mixture of powers and constraints that characterize this asymmetrical exchange. His own writing in these stories, after all, embodies a further act of negotiation between a residual folk culture and a dominant order—in his case, the literary establishment of his time. Nothing was clearer to Chesnutt than that this system *was* dominant. High-cultural literary institutions so fully monopolized the machinery of literary prestige in the United States in the 1880s and 1890s that to be established as an author at this time one had to establish oneself through these institutions, and Chesnutt strongly felt this. All through the decade of the conjure stories Chesnutt was concerned to be published by the *Atlantic Monthly* and its parent company, Houghton Mifflin, the great high-literary organs of his time. His very adoption of the dialect tale formula in the conjure tales can be read as a tribute to the power of this literary system. The dialect tale was a specialty of the high-cultural journals in these years, and in writing it Chesnutt took pains to speak the language of a dominant literary order.

But if Chesnutt, like Julius, worked in a communication situation not under his control, he too was no mere passive victim. Conjure tales from southern black vernacular culture gave him a form of power, too. By writing such tales he could cast a literary spell of his own, and so could work his own worldly advancement: his supplying of a literary genre in strong demand won him access to the pages of the *Atlantic* in 1887–89, a reward, in his terms, worth more than any ham. Chesnutt appeared in these pages in the company of America's most prestigious authors, including Henry James. ("Po' Sandy" was first printed together with James's "The Aspern Papers," and "Dave's Neckliss" appeared with James's *Tragic Muse*.) Yet as Chesnutt already anticipated and was increasingly to learn, his power in this position was in no sense unqualified.

Admirers of the conjure stories will be surprised to learn that once Chesnutt got his "in" to the literary system his almost immediate wish was to cease working in this genre. "I think I have about used up the old Negro who serves as mouthpiece, and I shall drop him in future stories, as well as much of the dialect,"[3] he wrote in an 1889 letter, after placing his first four Uncle Julius tales ("The Goophered Grapevine," "Po' Sandy," "Dave's Neckliss," and "The Conjurer's Revenge"). His reasons for wanting to drop these devices can be guessed. However cunningly an author manipulated it, the local color story or dialect tale remained a genre of strong conventions, offering a highly stereotypical rendering of the cultural actualities it purported to convey. Chesnutt would have been supremely aware of just how little of actual black life was registered through the Old Uncle formula. Chesnutt was not a citizen of black vernacular culture. A well-educated person who wrote exquisitely correct English from a young age and who taught himself French, German, and Latin in his teens, Chesnutt not only did not speak like Julius, he spent his early career trying to teach black children out of dialect speech and folk superstition in the schools of North Carolina. Educated as he was, Chesnutt would have been extraordinarily well equipped to recognize how the dialect fiction formula made illiterate rural blacks seem to be The Black for the white reading audience of his time, and how this formula helped put other contemporary forms of black

3. Chesnutt to Albion W. Tourgée, September 26, 1889, cited in William L. Andrews, *The Literary Career of Charles W. Chesnutt* (Baton Rouge: Louisiana State University Press, 1980), p. 21.

experience—that of his own educated, professional class, for instance—out of social sight. (One of the more curious ironies of *The Conjure Woman* is that in social and cultural terms Chesnutt himself was considerably closer to John's position than to Julius's. To identify Chesnutt with Julius's black vernacular, as is commonly done, is to fall into this genre's trap of identifying all blacks with a single image of black culture.) The black dialect speaker of regional fiction also failed to tell other stories southern blacks of this time would have known all too well. The real-life Uncle Julius would have been much more likely to be a tenant farmer—a new economic position the local color formula does nothing to explore—than a coachman. The 1890s were also the heyday of disenfranchisement acts, segregation laws, and the vicious breed of racial phobia that found issue in the lynching of black men. Seen against this reality, the cultural preference for the reminiscences of old black Uncles was a preference for a *fiction* of racial history.

Equipped by a lifetime of prejudice to know the enduring power of stereotypes, Chesnutt would also not have overestimated his ability to undo the racial stereotyping intrinsic to his form. A letter from 1890 shows him still wary of the social message inscribed in black dialect fiction and doubtful of his readers' ability to pick up ironic variations: "I notice that all of the many Negroes . . . whose virtues have been given to the world in the magazine press recently, have been blacks, full-blooded, and their chief virtues have been their dog-like fidelity to their old master, for whom they have been willing to sacrifice almost life itself. Such characters exist. . . . But I can't write about those people, or rather I won't write about them."[4]

What Chesnutt attempted to do, after his initial success with his first conjure tales, was to turn to a noncomic, nondialect-based form of literary writing that would address the social problems of people of mixed race. (This "black" author himself had white ancestry on both sides and was the product of a racial mixing the John/Julius dualism implicitly denies.) He embodied his new hopes in the work known through many drafts

---

4. Chesnutt to George Washington Cable, June 5, 1890, cited in Helen M. Chesnutt, *Charles Waddell Chesnutt: Pioneer of the Color Line* (Chapel Hill: University of North Carolina Press, 1952), pp. 57–58.

as "Rena Walden," the source of the later novel *The House behind the Cedars*. But when he approached publishers with this work, he found no comparable welcome to what the conjure tales had enjoyed. Editors refused this work on at least four separate submissions in the 1890s, and the author who had got so strong a start in the late 1880s dropped out of literary sight.

After these "years of silence" (as he called them) Chesnutt got two more stories placed in the *Atlantic* in 1897, and his fortunes began to change.[5] The new editor of the *Atlantic*, North Carolina–born Walter Hines Page, raised the question whether "a skillfully selected list of your short stories might make a book," then requested Chesnutt to "send us all the short stories, both published and unpublished, and let our readers take the whole collection up and see whether by selecting judiciously from them a selection can be made which seems likely to make a book of sufficient unity to put upon the market."[6] In October 1897 Chesnutt bundled up the manuscripts of twenty miscellaneous stories and sent them off. On December 15 Page wrote the exhilarating news that "your stories are undergoing a rather unusual experience here; because they are being read, I believe, by our whole staff of readers, and I hope to have in a very little while definite word to send you."[7] A very little while passed, then a longer while; finally, on March 30, 1898, Page wrote Chesnutt this devastating message: "The unpleasant task (for I assure you it is an unpleasant one) falls to my lot to write to you, saying that the firm [of Houghton Mifflin] is sorry that they do not see a way to make you an offer to publish either a book made up of your short stories or the longer story, 'A Business Career,' the manuscript of which you were kind enough to send at my suggestion a little while ago." Page's letter proceeds to expatiate on the reasons why Chesnutt's work could not be accepted—the literary field is overcrowded with novels; on the other hand, books of short stories have become "harder

5. See Helen Chesnutt, *Charles Waddell Chesnutt*, p. 73.
6. Walter Hines Page to Charles W. Chesnutt, October 2 and 20, 1897, cited in ibid., pp. 82–83. The Page-Chesnutt letters, the originals of which are on deposit in the Charles W. Chesnutt Collection in the Fisk University Library, are reprinted at length in Helen Chesnutt's biography of her father, which offers the first full narrative of the birth of *The Conjure Woman*.
7. Page to Chesnutt, December 15, 1897, ibid., p. 87.

and harder to market." Then, quite unexpectedly, he offers this thought:

> There is yet a possibility of Messrs. Houghton, Mifflin and Company's doing something for you along this line—if you had enough "conjure" stories to make a book, even a small book. I cannot help feeling that that would succeed. All the readers who have read your stories agree on this—that "The Goophered Grapevine" and "Po' Sandy," and the one or two others that have the same original quality that these show, are stories that are sure to live—in fact, I know of nothing so good of their kind anywhere. For myself, I venture unhesitatingly the prediction of a notable and lasting success with them, but the trouble at present is there are only about three of these stories which have this quality unmixed with other qualities. If you could produce five or six more like these, I think I am safe in making you a double promise—first, of magazine publication, and then the collection, I think would make a successful book. This last opinion concerning the publication of them in a volume I make on my own responsibility, for the firm has not warranted me definitely to promise so much; but we are all so impressed with them that I think there would be no doubt about it.[8]

Spurred by this request, Chesnutt in the spare hours left over from his full-time job wrote six new conjure stories in the next six weeks—"A Victim of Heredity," "The Gray Wolf's Ha'nt," "Mars Jeems's Nightmare," "Sis' Becky's Pickaninny," "Tobe's Tribulations," and "Hot-Foot Hannibal"—and sent them off to Page. Two of these stories were dropped, the remaining four were rejoined with three tales now a decade old ("The Goophered Grapevine," "Po' Sandy," and "The Conjurer's Revenge"), and *The Conjure Woman* was at last completed. It was published in March 1899.

This publishing history supplies a crucial later chapter in the story of Chesnutt's negotiations with a dominant literary order. It shows that the author who accepted a conventional form, then

---

8. Page to Chesnutt, March 30, 1898, ibid., pp. 91–92.

exploited it in his own ways and to his own advantage, did not thereby escape from the power of the socially established literary order. In Page's letter that order, through one of its most prominent official representatives, tells Chesnutt that he cannot be an author—or that he can be one, but only on terms of their, not his, devising. More particularly, Chesnutt is told that he can be published on the condition that he write in one form: the vernacular dialect tale he had long since chosen against.

The Chesnutt-Page correspondence makes clear that *The Conjure Woman* was partly the work of its author, but partly too of an institutional context that controlled the terms of this author's appearance. But what we are to make of this external "aid" is not altogether easy to say. Many readers studying the evidence will feel that Chesnutt was lucky to find Page as his editor and that this *miglior fabbrio* helped Chesnutt to a strong literary version of himself. It would be hard to dispute that in "The Goophered Grapevine" and "Po' Sandy" Page identified the best of the stories Chesnutt sent him, and it would be easy to argue that Page's letter helped Chesnutt envision the whole, coherent work these splendid pieces could form the foundation of. (He shows no signs of having envisioned it on his own.) The four conjure tales written to Page's orders do not read like alienated labor, and the book they helped round out is a marvelous volume: beautifully modulated in tone, subtly in control of its cumulative implications, well balanced between repetition and variation.

On the other hand, if a publisher helped Chesnutt to *The Conjure Woman*, there was surely an element of disciplinary control in the process. Page's editorial proposals enforce a canon of artistic coherence ("the practical trouble presented is the miscellaneous quality of these stories," he wrote) that is backed up by literary market imperatives (he seeks "a book of sufficient unity to put upon the market"). A reading of the excluded miscellany could easily lead to the conclusion that these market/aesthetic norms covertly enforced other agendas. "Dave's Neckliss," for instance, was apparently left out of *The Conjure Woman* because it lacked the recourse to conjure. But the rule that enforced uniformity on this point threw out more than a misfitting tale. "Dave's Neckliss," one of his most powerful works from any phase of his career, shows Chesnutt projecting both a more dignified, more capable black figure than elsewhere in the Uncle Julius tales—a fully literate black—and a grislier picture of the enduring harm slavery did to blacks, imaged in the intentional manufacture, by a lower-class white overseer envious of the slave's manifest superiority, of a punitively damaged identity. Made to wear a ham as the public emblem of his alleged theft, Dave comes to take this outward designation as his selfhood, to have no identity except through his identification with his stigma. Like those who have said I AM a slave or I AM a member of an inferior race, the man who says I AM a ham fiercely embraces the subhumanity an official degradation system assigns to him—and Chesnutt here implies that Julius too, and by possible extension the bulk of freedmen in the postemancipation generation, continues to be the bearer of the damaged selfhood slavery helped him compose.

The editorial protocol that ruled out "Dave's Neckliss" denied expression to Chesnutt's darkest assessment of the power of official orders and so functioned as a virtual censorship. The case of "The Dumb Witness" would raise the same charge. The norms Page erected put this piece with neither conjure elements nor a vernacular speaker wholly out of the question for the published volume. But again his apparently purely aesthetic criteria of formal unity purged Chesnutt's book of one of its darkest, most accusatory social messages. White masters appear in this tale as greed-driven figures who brutalize their slaves, wounding them specifically in their power of expression. (Julius cannot write but he can talk; the injured heroine of this tale can only babble—unless she is speaking a non-European language that sounds like babble to white folk, an issue the tale leaves wholly enigmatic.) Blacks appear here, with similar grimness, as the vindictive nemesis white authoritarianism creates for itself. Like Babo in Melville's "Benito Cereno," Viney shows the slave become her master's master by play-acting a lack of power that is in fact only feigned. That such visions were unwelcome to the nineteenth-century public that loved the works of Thomas Nelson Page hardly needs to be added.

But if Chesnutt's fiction has anything to teach us, it is to beware of one-sided visions of the play of power; and a theory that sees him as a mere victim of omnipotent censors falls into melodramatic simplifications. To read the whole of his conjure fiction will lead to a mixed evaluation of both his and his editor's contributions, and sometimes into ambiguities beyond any sort of secure evaluation. To cite one instance, some of the rejected conjure tales show Chesnutt flirting fairly unironically with demeaning racial stereotypes—the image of the Negro as natural chicken thief in "A Victim of Heredity," as watermelon thief in "A Deep Sleeper," or as more concerned with his stomach than his freedom in "Tobe's Tribulations" are conspicuous examples. Such tales raise extremely difficult questions about Chesnutt's intentions. Does the author of these stories unknowingly subscribe to racist stereotypes of his own? Or are these strategic pieces of self-advancement, knowingly insincere attempts to produce the formulaic belittlements of blacks that seem to be the price of literary admission? Or does an even slyer author present these stereotypes as a tacit test for the reader: grotesque caricatures that the wise will recognize as caricatures and the ignorant accept, as usual, as "the truth"? "The Deep Sleeper" provides a fairly overt critique on such stereotypes, unfolding the notion that the apparent moral failings of blacks are in fact defense mechanisms erected against their dehumanization. In this story Skundus becomes a deep sleeper not out of laziness but to avoid feeling the grief of his violated union. "Lonesome Ben"—a story that approaches "Dave's Neckliss" in its sense of what slavery does to identity—makes the same kind of overtly revisionary suggestion: Ben's compulsive clay eating is shown as an eating disorder, what a slave does when stuck between an escape from slavery he is too ill educated to carry off and a reintegration into slavery he is no longer equipped to manage. But no such help is forthcoming in the other tales. The policy that rejected them may have censored some of Chesnutt's more overtly subversive visions, but it is arguable that it also kept Chesnutt from a racial self-caricaturing that he was too willing to engage in. All we can say here is that any simple reading of the case is likely to be a wrong one.

To mention another perplexity, Robert Stepto, the critic who has most thoughtfully considered the sequence of Uncle Julius stories in the order of their composition, has argued that the tales excluded from *The Conjure Woman* show John growing into a fuller understanding of Julius, a growth marked by his emerging ability to become the narrator of the story, as he is in "The Dumb Witness." The omission of such tales, Stepto contends, negates Chesnutt's suggestion that whites who listen to blacks long enough can be brought to enter into their point of view, and even to become critics of white oppression: another official curtailment of Chesnutt's subversive meanings.[9] This is a very suggestive reading, and interpretation will always have to contend with it, but it is by no means clear that it is right. A striking passage in "The Dumb Witness" strongly supports the theory of a John grown more liberal and self-critical (he has not, of course, entirely escaped from assumptions of Anglo-Saxon superiority): "We like to speak of Negro cunning, of Indian revengefulness, of the low morality of the inferior races, when, alas! our own race excels them all, when it wishes, because it lends to evil purpose a higher intelligence and a wider experience than inferior races can command." But how are we to explain the fact that in a revision of the story Chesnutt cut this passage? Is this an act of self-censorship, a concession in advance to expected editorial disfavor, or did Chesnutt himself come to regard it as a mistake for John to seem so enlightened? After all, if there is profundity in the imagining of John's possible education, there is a different profundity in the notion that others' points of view are not so easily entered into by outsiders, and that those who "appreciate" others do not cease to occupy their own different social positions. This is a logic that an editorially assisted selection process helped build into Chesnutt's conjure volume, so that outside forces either strengthened or weakened the work, depending on what we want it to mean.

This new edition will make it possible for Chesnutt's readers to take the place of his original editor and choose their own preferred version of his work. More interestingly, rather than

---

9. Robert B. Stepto, "Charles W. Chesnutt: The Uncle Julius Stories" (typescript). A shorter version of this argument is published in Stepto's "'The Simple but Intensely Human Inner Life of Slavery': Storytelling and the Revision of History in Charles W. Chesnutt's 'Uncle Julius Stories,'" in *History and Tradition in Afro-American Culture*, ed. Gunter H. Lenz (Frankfurt: Campus, 1984), pp. 29–55.

just enabling us to enforce a new "judicious selection" upon his writing, it allows us to enter into the whole field of possibilities that that writing once unfolded, to see the many different intentions Chesnutt brought to the conjure formula and the different significations he pushed that form toward. Whatever version of these stories we end up preferring, there will be no escaping the fact that it is a collaborative product—the result of cooperating and competing pressures brought to bear by the author, his first publisher, and his later readers, ourselves included. But this outcome is in the spirit of *The Conjure Woman,* a work that suggests that cultural events always have more than one party to them and unfold through the interactions of competing interests.

RICHARD H. BRODHEAD

CHRONOLOGY OF COMPOSITION

This book prints the seven tales of *The Conjure Woman* in the order in which they appear in the published volume; the seven related tales appear in the apparent order of their composition. The following list arranges the tales according to the chronology of their writing as far as that chronology can be determined.

1887   "The Goophered Grapevine" published in the *Atlantic Monthly*.

1888   "Po' Sandy" published in the *Atlantic*.

1889   (June) "The Conjurer's Revenge" appeared in the *Overland Monthly*.

       (October) "Dave's Neckliss" printed in the *Atlantic*.

1893   "A Deep Sleeper" published in *Two Tales*.

1897   (February) "Lonesome Ben" submitted to Walter Hines Page, editor of the *Atlantic*, and turned down.

       (October 2) "The Dumb Witness" tentatively accepted by Page.

       (October 20–22) Page asks to see all Chesnutt's work, and Chesnutt sends twenty stories.

1898   (March 30) Page proposes a book of conjure stories.

       (May 20) Chesnutt sends six new tales: "A Victim of Heredity; or Why the Darkey Loves Chicken," "The Gray Wolf's Ha'nt," "Mars Jeems's Nightmare," "Sis' Becky's Pickaninny," "Tobe's Tribulation," and "Hot-Foot Hannibal."

1899   *The Conjure Woman* published by Houghton Mifflin.

1924   "The Marked Tree," apparently a late reprise of the conjure formula, printed in *The Crisis*.

A NOTE ON THE TEXT

The seven stories that appeared in *The Conjure Woman* are reprinted from the first edition, published by Houghton Mifflin in 1899.

Six other stories are reprinted as they were first published in the following sources:

"Dave's Neckliss," *Atlantic Monthly* 64 (October 1889): 500–508.

"A Deep Sleeper," *Two Tales* 5, no. 53 (March 11, 1893): 1–8.

"Lonesome Ben," *Southern Workman* 29 (March 1900): 137–45.

"A Victim of Heredity; or Why the Darkey Loves Chicken," *Self-Culture Magazine* 11 (July 1900): 404–409.

"Tobe's Tribulations," *Southern Workman* 29 (November 1900): 656–64.

"The Marked Tree," *The Crisis* 29 (December 1924, and January 1925): 59–64 and 110–13.

"The Dumb Witness," which was never separately published during Chesnutt's lifetime, presents special editorial problems. It survives in the Charles Waddell Chesnutt Papers at the Fisk University Library in two manuscript versions, a twenty-one-page typescript of which the second page is missing, and a second typescript version of which only eight pages survive. The second typescript is obviously a revision of the first, and so must be regarded as the more considered version of the story; but since it is incomplete, we have no idea how Chesnutt intended to revise the pages it fails to include. This edition follows the text of the second typescript wherever it exists, filling in the

missing pages with the version in the first typescript. Some unusually interesting passages included in the first version but
later deleted are also printed here in notes.

A third version of "The Dumb Witness," revised to fit into
the context of a novel, can be found in Chesnutt's later book
The Colonel's Dream.

Acknowledgments

I owe thanks to Beth Howse, of the Special Collections at the
Fisk University Library, for help in consulting the typescripts
of Chesnutt's stories, and to David Southward for aid in estab-
lishing the texts of "A Victim of Heredity" and "The Dumb
Witness."

SELECTED BIBLIOGRAPHY

Andrews, William L. *The Literary Career of Charles W. Chesnutt,* pp. 17–74. Baton Rouge: Louisiana State University Press, 1980.

Baker, Houston A., Jr. *Modernism and the Harlem Renaissance,* especially pp. 41–47. Chicago: University of Chicago Press, 1987.

Brodhead, Richard H. *Cultures of Letters: Scenes of Reading and Writing in Nineteenth Century America,* pp. 177–210. Chicago: University of Chicago Press, 1993.

Chesnutt, Charles W. "Superstitions and Folk-Lore of the South." *Modern Culture* 13 (May 1901): 231–35. Reprinted in Alan Dundes, ed., *Mother Wit from the Laughing Barrel.* Englewood Cliffs, N.J.: Prentice-Hall, 1973.

Fienberg, Lorne. "Charles W. Chesnutt and Uncle Julius: Black Storytellers at the Crossroads." *Studies in American Fiction* 15 (1987): 161–73.

Hemenway, Robert. "The Functions of Folklore in Charles Chesnutt's *The Conjure Woman.*" *Journal of the Folk Institute* 13 (1976): 283–309.

Lauter, Paul. *Canons and Contexts,* pp. 60–71. New York: Oxford University Press, 1991.

Mackethan, Lucinda. "Plantation Fiction, 1865–1900." In *The History of Southern Literature,* ed. Louis D. Rubin et al., pp. 209–18. Baton Rouge: Louisiana State University Press, 1985.

Sollers, Werner. "The Goopher in Charles Chesnutt's Conjure

Tales: Superstition, Ethnicity, and Modern Metamorphosis." *Letterature d'America* 6 (1985): 107–29.

Stepto, Robert B. "'The Simple but Intensely Human Inner Life of Slavery': Storytelling and the Revision of History in Charles W. Chesnutt's 'Uncle Julius Stories.'" In *History and Tradition in Afro-American Culture,* ed. Gunter Lenz, pp. 29–55. Frankfurt: Campus, 1984.

Sundquist, Eric J. *To Wake the Nations: Race in the Making of American Literature,* pp. 271–454. Cambridge, Mass.: Harvard University Press, 1993.

Wideman, John Edgar. "Charles Chesnutt and the WPA Narratives: The Oral and Literate Roots of Afro-American Literature." In *The Slave's Narrative,* ed. Charles T. Davis and Henry Louis Gates, Jr., pp. 59–78. New York: Oxford University Press, 1985.

THE CONJURE WOMAN

The Goophered Grapevine

Some years ago my wife was in poor health, and our family doctor, in whose skill and honesty I had implicit confidence, advised a change of climate. I shared, from an unprofessional standpoint, his opinion that the raw winds, the chill rains, and the violent changes of temperature that characterized the winters in the region of the Great Lakes tended to aggravate my wife's difficulty, and would undoubtedly shorten her life if she remained exposed to them. The doctor's advice was that we seek, not a temporary place of sojourn, but a permanent residence, in a warmer and more equable climate. I was engaged at the time in grape-culture in northern Ohio, and, as I liked the business and had given it much study, I decided to look for some other locality suitable for carrying it on. I thought of sunny France, of sleepy Spain, of Southern California, but there were objections to them all. It occurred to me that I might find what I wanted in some one of our own Southern States. It was a sufficient time after the war for conditions in the South to have become somewhat settled; and I was enough of a pioneer to start a new industry, if I could not find a place where grape-culture had been tried. I wrote to a cousin who had gone into the turpentine business in central North Carolina. He assured me, in response to my inquiries, that no better place could be found in the South than the State and neighborhood where he lived; the climate was perfect for health, and, in conjunction with the soil, ideal for grape-culture; labor was cheap, and land could be bought for a mere song. He gave us a cordial invitation to come and visit him while we looked into the matter. We accepted the invitation, and after several days of leisurely travel, the last hundred miles of which were up a river on a sidewheel steamer, we reached our destination, a quaint old town, which I shall call Patesville, because, for one reason, that is not its name. There was a red brick market-house in the public square, with a tall tower, which held a four-faced clock that struck the hours, and from which there pealed out a curfew at nine o'clock. There were two or three hotels, a court-house, a jail, stores, offices, and all the appurtenances of a county seat and a commercial emporium; for while Patesville numbered only four or five thousand inhabitants, of all shades of complexion, it was one of the principal towns in North Carolina, and had a considerable trade in cotton and naval stores. This business activity was not immediately apparent to my unaccustomed eyes. Indeed, when I first saw the town, there brooded over it a calm that seemed almost sabbatic in its restfulness, though I learned later on that underneath its somnolent exterior the deeper currents of life—love and hatred, joy and despair, ambition and avarice, faith and friendship—flowed not less steadily than in livelier latitudes.

We found the weather delightful at that season, the end of summer, and were hospitably entertained. Our host was a man of means and evidently regarded our visit as a pleasure, and we were therefore correspondingly at our ease, and in a position to act with the coolness of judgment desirable in making so radical a change in our lives. My cousin placed a horse and buggy at our disposal, and himself acted as our guide until I became somewhat familiar with the country.

I found that grape-culture, while it had never been carried on to any great extent, was not entirely unknown in the neighborhood. Several planters thereabouts had attempted it on a commercial scale, in former years, with greater or less success; but like most Southern industries, it had felt the blight of war and had fallen into desuetude.

I went several times to look at a place that I thought might suit me. It was a plantation of considerable extent, that had formerly belonged to a wealthy man by the name of McAdoo. The estate had been for years involved in litigation between disputing heirs, during which period shiftless cultivation had well-nigh exhausted the soil. There had been a vineyard of some extent on the place, but it had not been attended to since the war, and had lapsed into utter neglect. The vines—here partly supported by decayed and broken-down trellises, there twining themselves among the branches of the slender saplings which had sprung up among them—grew in wild and unpruned luxuriance, and the few scattered grapes they bore were the undisputed prey of the first comer. The site was admirably adapted to grape-raising; the soil, with a little attention, could not have been better; and with the native grape, the luscious scuppernong, as my main reliance in the beginning, I felt sure that I could introduce and cultivate successfully a number of other varieties.

One day I went over with my wife to show her the place. We drove out of the town over a long wooden bridge that spanned a spreading mill-pond, passed the long whitewashed fence surrounding the county fair-ground, and struck into a road so sandy that the horse's feet sank to the fetlocks. Our route lay partly up hill and partly down, for we were in the sand-hill country; we drove past cultivated farms, and then by abandoned fields grown up in scrub-oak and short-leaved pine, and once or twice through the solemn aisles of the virgin forest, where the tall pines, well-nigh meeting over the narrow road, shut out the sun, and wrapped us in cloistral solitude. Once, at a crossroads, I was in doubt as to the turn to take, and we sat there waiting ten minutes—we had already caught some of the native infection of restfulness—for some human being to come along, who could direct us on our way. At length a little negro girl appeared, walking straight as an arrow, with a piggin full of water on her head. After a little patient investigation, necessary to overcome the child's shyness, we learned what we wished to know, and at the end of about five miles from the town reached our destination.

We drove between a pair of decayed gateposts—the gate itself had long since disappeared—and up a straight sandy lane, between two lines of rotting rail fence, partly concealed by jimson-weeds and briers, to the open space where a dwelling-house had once stood, evidently a spacious mansion, if we might judge from the ruined chimneys that were still standing, and the brick pillars on which the sills rested. The house itself, we had been informed, had fallen a victim to the fortunes of war.

We alighted from the buggy, walked about the yard for a while, and then wandered off into the adjoining vineyard. Upon Annie's complaining of weariness I led the way back to the yard, where a pine log, lying under a spreading elm, afforded a shady though somewhat hard seat. One end of the log was already occupied by a venerable-looking colored man. He held on his knees a hat full of grapes, over which he was smacking his lips with great gusto, and a pile of grapeskins near him indicated that the performance was no new thing. We approached him at an angle from the rear, and were close to him before he perceived us. He respectfully rose as we drew near, and was moving away, when I begged him to keep his seat.

"Don't let us disturb you," I said. "There is plenty of room for us all."

He resumed his seat with somewhat of embarrassment. While he had been standing, I had observed that he was a tall man, and, though slightly bowed by the weight of years, apparently quite vigorous. He was not entirely black, and this fact, together with the quality of his hair, which was about six inches long and very bushy, except on the top of his head, where he was quite bald, suggested a slight strain of other than negro blood. There was a shrewdness in his eyes, too, which was not altogether African, and which, as we afterwards learned from experience, was indicative of a corresponding shrewdness in his character. He went on eating the grapes, but did not seem to enjoy himself quite so well as he had apparently done before he became aware of our presence.

"Do you live around here?" I asked, anxious to put him at his ease.

"Yas, suh. I lives des ober yander, behine de nex' san'-hill, on de Lumberton plank-road."

"Do you know anything about the time when this vineyard was cultivated?"

"Lawd bless you, suh, I knows all about it. Dey ain' na'er a man in dis settlement w'at won' tell you ole Julius McAdoo 'uz bawn en raise' on dis yer same plantation. Is you de Norv'n gemman w'at's gwine ter buy de ole vimya'd?"

"I am looking at it," I replied; "but I don't know that I shall care to buy unless I can be reasonably sure of making something out of it."

"Well, suh, you is a stranger ter me, en I is a stranger ter you, en we is bofe strangers ter one anudder, but 'f I 'uz in yo' place, I wouldn' buy dis vimya'd."

"Why not?" I asked.

"Well, I dunno whe'r you b'lieves in cunj'in' er not,—some er de w'ite folks don't, er says dey don't,—but de truf er de matter is dat dis yer ole vimya'd is goophered."

"Is what?" I asked, not grasping the meaning of this unfamiliar word.

"Is goophered,—cunju'd, bewitch'."

He imparted this information with such solemn earnestness, and with such an air of confidential mystery, that I felt somewhat interested, while Annie was evidently much impressed, and drew closer to me.

"How do you know it is bewitched?" I asked.

"I wouldn' spec' fer you ter b'lieve me 'less you know all 'bout de fac's. But ef you en young miss dere doan' min' lis'nin' ter a ole nigger run on a minute er two w'ile you er restin', I kin 'splain to you how it all happen'."

We assured him that we would be glad to hear how it all happened, and he began to tell us. At first the current of his memory—or imagination—seemed somewhat sluggish; but as his embarrassment wore off, his language flowed more freely, and the story acquired perspective and coherence. As he became more and more absorbed in the narrative, his eyes assumed a dreamy expression, and he seemed to lose sight of his auditors, and to be living over again in monologue his life on the old plantation.

"Ole Mars Dugal' McAdoo," he began, "bought dis place long many years befo' de wah, en I 'member well w'en he sot out all dis yer part er de plantation in scuppernon's. De vimes growed monst'us fas', en Mars Dugal' made a thousan' gallon er scuppernon' wine eve'y year.

"Now, ef dey's an'thing a nigger lub, nex' ter 'possum, en chick'n, en watermillyums, it's scuppernon's. Dey ain' nuffin dat kin stan' up side'n de scuppernon' fer sweetness; sugar ain't

35

a suckumstance ter scuppernon'. W'en de season is nigh 'bout ober, en de grapes begin ter swivel up des a little wid de wrinkles er ole age,—w'en de skin git sof' en brown,—den de scuppernon' make you smack yo' lip en roll yo' eye en wush fer mo'; so I reckon it ain' very 'stonishin' dat niggers lub scuppernon'.

"Dey wuz a sight er niggers in de naberhood er de vimya'd. Dere wuz ole Mars Henry Brayboy's niggers, en ole Mars Jeems McLean's niggers, en Mars Dugal's own niggers; den dey wuz a settlement er free niggers en po' buckrahs down by de Wim'l'ton Road, en Mars Dugal' had de only vimya'd in de naberhood. I reckon it ain' so much so nowadays, but befo' de wah, in slab'ry times, a nigger didn' mine goin' fi' er ten mile in a night, w'en dey wuz sump'n good ter eat at de yuther een'.

"So atter a w'ile Mars Dugal' begin ter miss his scuppernon's. Co'se he 'cuse' de niggers er it, but dey all 'nied it ter de las'. Mars Dugal' sot spring guns en steel traps, en he en de oberseah sot up nights once't er twice't, tel one night Mars Dugal'—he 'uz a monst'us keerless man—got his leg shot full er cow-peas. But somehow er nudder dey couldn' nebber ketch none er de niggers. I dunner how it happen, but it happen des like I tell you, en de grapes kep' on a-goin' des de same.

"But bimeby ole Mars Dugal' fix' up a plan ter stop it. Dey wuz a cunjuh 'oman livin' down 'mongs' de free niggers on de Wim'l'ton Road, en all de darkies fum Rockfish ter Beaver Crick wuz feared er her. She could wuk de mos' powerfulles' kin' er goopher,—could make people hab fits, er rheumatiz, er make 'em des dwinel away en die; en dey say she went out ridin' de niggers at night, fer she wuz a witch 'sides bein' a cunjuh 'oman. Mars Dugal' hearn 'bout Aun' Peggy's doin's, en begun ter 'flect whe'r er no he couldn' git her ter he'p him keep de niggers off'n de grapevimes. One day in de spring er de year, ole miss pack' up a basket er chick'n en poun'-cake, en a bottle er scuppernon' wine, en Mars Dugal' tuk it in his buggy en driv ober ter Aun' Peggy's cabin. He tuk de basket in, en had a long talk wid Aun' Peggy.

"De nex' day Aun' Peggy come up ter de vimya'd. De niggers seed her slippin' 'roun', en dey soon foun' out what she 'uz doin' dere. Mars Dugal' had hi'ed her ter goopher de grapevimes. She sa'ntered 'roun' 'mongs' de vimes, en tuk a leaf fum dis

one, en a grape-hull fum dat one, en a grape-seed fum anudder
one; en den a little twig fum here, en a little pinch er dirt fum
dere,—en put it all in a big black bottle, wid a snake's toof en
a speckle' hen's gall en some ha'rs fum a black cat's tail, en den
fill' de bottle wid scuppernon' wine. W'en she got de goopher
all ready en fix', she tuk 'n went out in de woods en buried it
under de root uv a red oak tree, en den come back en tole one
er de niggers she done goopher de grapevimes, en a'er a nigger
w'at eat dem grapes 'ud be sho ter die inside'n twel' mont's.

"Atter dat de niggers let de scuppernon's 'lone, en Mars Dugal'
didn' hab no 'casion ter fine no mo' fault; en de season wuz mos'
gone, w'en a strange gemman stop at de plantation one night
ter see Mars Dugal' on some business; en his coachman, seein'
de scuppernon's growin' so nice en sweet, slip 'roun' behine
de smoke-house, en et all de scuppernon's he could hole. Nobody didn' notice it at de time, but dat night, on de way home,
de gemman's hoss runned away en kill' de coachman. W'en we
hearn de noos, Aun' Lucy, de cook, she up 'n say she seed
de strange nigger eat'n' er de scuppernon's behine de smoke-
house; en den we knowed de goopher had b'en er wukkin'. Den
one er de nigger chilluns runned away fum de quarters one day,
en got in de scuppernon's, en died de nex' week. W'ite folks say
he die' er de fevuh, but de niggers knowed it wuz de goopher.
So you k'n be sho de darkies didn' hab much ter do wid dem
scuppernon' vimes.

"W'en de scuppernon' season 'uz ober fer dat year, Mars
Dugal' foun' he had made fifteen hund'ed gallon er wine; en
one er de niggers hearn him laffin' wid de oberseah fit ter kill,
en sayin' dem fifteen hund'ed gallon er wine wuz monst'us good
intrus' on de ten dollars he laid out on de vimya'd. So I 'low ez
he paid Aun' Peggy ten dollars fer to goopher de grapevimes.

"De goopher didn' wuk no mo' tel de nex' summer, w'en 'long
to'ds de middle er de season one er de fiel' han's died; en ez dat
lef' Mars Dugal' sho't er han's, he went off ter town fer ter buy
anudder. He fotch de noo nigger home wid 'im. He wuz er ole
nigger, er de color er a gingy-cake, en ball ez a hoss-apple on
de top er his head. He wuz a peart ole nigger, do', en could do
a big day's wuk.

"Now it happen dat one er de niggers on de nex' plantation,

one er ole Mars Henry Brayboy's niggers, had runned away de day befo', en tuk ter de swamp, en ole Mars Dugal' en some er de yuther nabor w'ite folks had gone out wid dere guns en dere dogs fer ter he'p 'em hunt fer de nigger; en de han's on our own plantation wuz all so flusterated dat we fuhgot ter tell de noo han' 'bout de goopher on de scuppernon' vimes. Co'se he smell de grapes en see de vimes, an atter dahk de fus' thing he done wuz ter slip off ter de grapevimes 'dout sayin' nuffin ter nobody. Nex' mawnin' he tole some er de niggers 'bout de fine bait er scuppernon' he et de night befo'.

"W'en dey tole 'im 'bout de goopher on de grapevimes, he 'uz dat tarrified dat he turn pale, en look des like he gwine ter die right in his tracks. De oberseah come up en axed w'at 'uz de matter; en w'en dey tole 'im Henry be'n eatin' er de scuppernon's, en got de goopher on 'im, he gin Henry a big drink er w'iskey, en 'low dat de nex' rainy day he take 'im ober ter Aun' Peggy's, en see ef she wouldn' take de goopher off'n him, seein' ez he didn' know nuffin erbout it tel he done et de grapes.

"Sho nuff, it rain de nex' day, en de oberseah went ober ter Aun' Peggy's wid Henry. En Aun' Peggy say dat bein' ez Henry didn' know 'bout de goopher, en et de grapes in ign'ance er de conseq'ences, she reckon she mought be able fer ter take de goopher off'n him. So she fotch out er bottle wid some con-juh medicine in it, en po'd some out in a go'd fer Henry ter drink. He manage ter git it down; he say it tas'e like whiskey wid sump'n bitter in it. She 'lowed dat 'ud keep de goopher off'n him tel de spring; but w'en de sap begin ter rise in de grape-vimes he ha' ter come en see her ag'in, en she tell him w'at e's ter do.

"Nex' spring, w'en de sap commence' ter rise in de scuppernon' vime, Henry tuk a ham one night. Whar'd he git de ham? *I* doan know; dey wa'n't no hams on de plantation 'cep'n' w'at 'uz in de smoke-house, but *I* never see Henry 'bout de smoke-house. But ez I wuz a-sayin', he tuk de ham ober ter Aun' Peggy's; en Aun' Peggy tole 'im dat w'en Mars Dugal' begin ter prune de grapevimes, he mus' go en take 'n scrape off de sap whar it ooze out'n de cut een's er de vimes, en 'n'int his ball head wid it; en ef he do dat once't a year de goopher wouldn' wuk agin 'im long ez he done it. En bein' ez he fotch her de ham, she fix' it so he kin eat all de scuppernon' he want.

"So Henry 'n'int his head wid de sap out'n de big grapevime des ha'f way 'twix' de quarters en de big house, en de goopher nebber wuk agin him dat summer. But de beatenes' thing you eber see happen ter Henry. Up ter dat time he wuz ez ball ez a sweeten' 'tater, but des ez soon ez de young leaves begun ter come out on de grapevimes, de ha'r begun ter grow out on Henry's head, en by de middle er de summer he had de bigges' head er ha'r on de plantation. Befo' dat, Henry had tol'able good ha'r 'roun' de aidges, but soon ez de young grapes begun ter come, Henry's ha'r begun to quirl all up in little balls, des like dis yer reg'lar grapy ha'r, en by de time de grapes got ripe his head look des like a bunch er grapes. Combin' it didn' do no good; he wuk at it ha'f de night wid er Jim Crow,[1] en think he git it straighten' out, but in de mawnin' de grapes 'ud be dere des de same. So he gin it up, en tried ter keep de grapes down by havin' his ha'r cut sho't.

"But dat wa'n't de quares' thing 'bout de goopher. When Henry come ter de plantation, he wuz gittin' a little ole an stiff in de j'ints. But dat summer he got des ez spry en libely ez any young nigger on de plantation; fac', he got so biggity dat Mars Jackson, de oberseah, ha' ter th'eaten ter whip 'im, ef he didn' stop cuttin' up his didos en behave hisse'f. But de mos' cur'ouses' thing happen' in de fall, when de sap begin ter go down in de grapevimes. Fus', when de grapes 'uz gethered, de knots begun ter straighten out'n Henry's ha'r; en w'en de leaves begin ter fall, Henry's ha'r 'mence' ter drap out; en when de vimes 'uz bar', Henry's head wuz baller 'n it wuz in de spring, en he begin ter git ole en stiff in de j'ints ag'in, en paid no mo' 'tention ter de gals dyoin' er de whole winter. En nex' spring, w'en he rub de sap on ag'in, he got young ag'in, en so soopl en libely dat none er de young niggers on de plantation couldn' jump, ner dance, ner hoe ez much cotton ez Henry. But in de fall er de year his grapes 'mence' ter straighten out, en his j'ints ter git stiff, en his ha'r drap off, en de rheumatiz begin ter wrastle wid 'im.

"Now, ef you'd 'a' knowed ole Mars Dugal' McAdoo, you'd 'a' knowed dat it ha' ter be a mighty rainy day when he couldn' fine sump'n fer his niggers ter do, en it ha' ter be a mighty

---

1. A small card, resembling a currycomb in construction, and used by negroes in the rural districts instead of a comb.

39

little hole he couldn' crawl thoo, en ha' ter be a monst'us cloudy night when a dollar git by him in de dahkness; en w'en he see how Henry git young in de spring en ole in de fall, he 'lowed ter hisse'f ez how he could make mo' money out'n Henry dan by wukkin' him in de cotton-fiel'. 'Long de nex' spring, atter de sap 'mence' ter rise, en Henry 'n'int 'is head en sta'ted fer ter git young en soopl, Mars Dugal' up 'n tuk Henry ter town, en sole 'im fer fifteen hunder' dollars. Co'se de man w'at bought Henry didn' know nuffin 'bout de goopher, en Mars Dugal' didn' see no 'casion fer ter tell 'im. Long to'ds de fall, w'en de sap went down, Henry begin ter git ole ag'in same ez yuzhal, en his noo marster begin ter git skeered les'n he gwine ter lose his fifteen-hunder'-dollar nigger. He sent fer a mighty fine doctor, but de med'cine didn' 'pear ter do no good; de goopher had a good holt. Henry tole de doctor 'bout de goopher, but de doctor des laff at 'im.

"One day in de winter Mars Dugal' went ter town, en wuz santerin' 'long de Main Street, when who should he meet but Henry's noo marster. Dey said 'Hoddy,' en Mars Dugal' ax 'im ter hab a seegyar; en atter dey run on awhile 'bout de craps en de weather, Mars Dugal' ax 'im, sorter keerless, like ez ef he des thought of it,—

"'How you like de nigger I sole you las' spring?'

"Henry's marster shuck his head en knock de ashes off'n his seegyar.

"'Spec' I made a bad bahgin when I bought dat nigger. Henry done good wuk all de summer, but sence de fall set in he 'pears ter be sorter pinin' away. Dey ain' nuffin pertickler de matter wid 'im—leastways de doctor say so—'cep'n' a tech er de rheumatiz; but his ha'r is all fell out, en ef he don't pick up his strenk mighty soon, I spec' I'm gwine ter lose 'im.'

"Dey smoked on awhile, en bimeby ole mars say, 'Well, a bahgin's a bahgin, but you en me is good fren's, en I doan wan' ter see you lose all de money you paid fer dat nigger; en ef w'at you say is so, en I ain't 'sputin' it, he ain't wuf much now. I 'spec's you wukked him too ha'd dis summer, er e'se de swamps down here don't agree wid de san'-hill nigger. So you des lemme know, en ef he gits any wusser I'll be willin' ter gib yer five hund'ed dollars fer 'im, en take my chances on his livin'.'

"Sho 'nuff, when Henry begun ter draw up wid de rheumatiz en it look like he gwine ter die fer sho, his noo marster sen' fer Mars Dugal', en Mars Dugal' gin him what he promus, en brung Henry home ag'in. He tuk good keer uv 'im dyoin' er de winter,—give 'im w'iskey ter rub his rheumatiz, en terbacker ter smoke, en all he want ter eat,—'caze a nigger w'at he could make a thousan' dollars a year off'n didn' grow on eve'y huckleberry bush.

"Nex' spring, w'en de sap ris en Henry's ha'r commence' ter sprout, Mars Dugal' sole 'im ag'in, down in Robeson County dis time; en he kep' dat sellin' business up fer five year er mo'. Henry nebber say nuffin 'bout de goopher ter his noo marsters, 'caze he know he gwine ter be tuk good keer uv de nex' winter, w'en Mars Dugal' buy him back. En Mars Dugal' made 'nuff money off'n Henry ter buy anudder plantation ober on Beaver Crick.

"But 'long 'bout de een' er dat five year dey come a stranger ter stop at de plantation. De fus' day he 'uz dere he went out wid Mars Dugal' en spent all de mawnin' lookin' ober de vimya'd, en atter dinner dey spent all de evenin' playin' kya'ds. De niggers soon 'skiver' dat he wuz a Yankee, en dat he come down ter Norf C'lina fer ter l'arn de w'ite folks how to raise grapes en make wine. He promus Mars Dugal' he c'd make de grapevimes b'ar twice't ez many grapes, en dat de noo winepress he wuz a-sellin' would make mo' d'n twice't ez many gallons er wine. En ole Mars Dugal' des drunk it all in, des 'peared ter be bewitch' wid dat Yankee. W'en de darkies see dat Yankee runnin' 'roun' de vimya'd en diggin' under de grapevimes, dey shuk dere heads, en 'lowed dat dey feared Mars Dugal' losin' his min'. Mars Dugal' had all de dirt dug away fum under de roots er all de scuppernon' vimes, an' let 'em stan' dat away fer a week er mo'. Den dat Yankee made de niggers fix up a mixtry er lime en ashes en manyo, en po' it 'roun' de roots er de grapevimes. Den he 'vise Mars Dugal' fer ter trim de vimes close't, en Mars Dugal' tuck 'n done eve'ything de Yankee tole him ter do. Dyoin' all er dis time, mind yer, dis yer Yankee wuz libbin' off'n de fat er de lan', at de big house, en playin' kya'ds wid Mars Dugal' eve'y night; en dey say Mars Dugal' los' mo'n a thousan' dollars dyoin' er de week dat Yankee wuz a-ruinin' de grapevimes.

"W'en de sap ris nex' spring, ole Henry 'n'inted his head ez yuzhal, en his ha'r 'mence' ter grow des de same ez it done eve'y year. De scuppernon' vimes growed monst's fas', en de leaves wuz greener en thicker dan dey eber be'n dyoin' my rememb'ance; en Henry's ha'r growed out thicker dan eber, en he 'peared ter git younger 'n younger, en soopler 'n soopler; en seein' ez he wuz sho't er han's dat spring, havin' tuk in consid'able noo groun', Mars Dugal' 'cluded he wouldn' sell Henry 'tel he git de crap in en de cotton chop'. So he kep' Henry on de plantation.

"But 'long 'bout time fer de grapes ter come on de scuppernon' vimes, dey 'peared ter come a change ober 'em; de leaves withered en swivel' up, en de young grapes turn' yaller, en bimeby eve'ybody on de plantation could see dat de whole vimya'd wuz dyin'. Mars Dugal' tuk 'n water de vimes en done all he could, but 't wa'n' no use: dat Yankee had done bus' de watermillyum. One time de vimes picked up a bit, en Mars Dugal' 'lowed dey wuz gwine ter come out ag'in; but dat Yankee done dug too close under de roots, en prune de branches too close ter de vime, en all dat lime en ashes done burn' de life out'n de vimes, en dey des kep' a-with'in' en a-swivelin'.

"All dis time de goopher wuz a-wukkin'. When de vimes sta'ted ter wither, Henry 'mence' ter complain er his rheumatiz; en when de leaves begin ter dry up, his ha'r 'mence' ter drap out. When de vimes fresh' up a bit, Henry'd git peart ag'in, en when de vimes wither' ag'in, Henry'd git ole ag'in, en des kep' gittin' mo' en mo' fitten fer nuffin; he des pined away, en pined away, en fine'ly tuk ter his cabin; en when de big vime whar he got de sap ter 'n'int his head withered en turned yaller en died, Henry died too,—des went out sorter like a cannel. Dey didn't 'pear ter be nuffin de matter wid 'im, 'cep'n' de rheumatiz, but his strenk des dwinel' away 'tel he didn' hab ernuff lef' ter draw his bref. De goopher had got de under holt, en th'owed Henry dat time fer good en all.

"Mars Dugal' tuk on might'ly 'bout losin' his vimes en his nigger in de same year; en he swo' dat ef he could git holt er dat Yankee he'd wear 'im ter a frazzle, en den chaw up de frazzle; en he'd done it, too, for Mars Dugal' 'uz a monst'us brash man w'en he once git started. He sot de vimya'd out ober ag'in, but it wuz th'ee er fo' year befo' de vimes got ter b'arin' any scuppernon's.

"W'en de wah broke out, Mars Dugal' raise' a comp'ny, en went off ter fight de Yankees. He say he wuz mighty glad dat wah come, en he des want ter kill a Yankee fer eve'y dollar he los' 'long er dat grape-raisin' Yankee. En I 'spec' he would 'a' done it, too, ef de Yankees hadn' s'picioned sump'n, en killed him fus'. Atter de s'render ole miss move' ter town, de niggers all scattered 'way fum de plantation, en de vimya'd ain' be'n cultervated sence."

"Is that story true?" asked Annie doubtfully, but seriously, as the old man concluded his narrative.

"It's des ez true ez I'm a-settin' here, miss. Dey's a easy way ter prove it: I kin lead de way right ter Henry's grave ober yander in de plantation buryin'-groun'. En I tell yer w'at, marster, I wouldn' 'vise you to buy dis yer ole vimya'd, 'caze de goopher's on it yit, en dey ain' no tellin' w'en it's gwine ter crap out."

"But I thought you said all the old vines died."

"Dey did 'pear ter die, but a few un 'em come out ag'in, en is mixed in 'mongs' de yuthers. I ain' skeered ter eat de grapes, 'caze I knows de old vimes fum de noo ones; but wid strangers dey ain' no tellin' w'at mought happen. I wouldn' 'vise yer ter buy dis vimya'd."

I bought the vineyard, nevertheless, and it has been for a long time in a thriving condition, and is often referred to by the local press as a striking illustration of the opportunities open to Northern capital in the development of Southern industries. The luscious scuppernong holds first rank among our grapes, though we cultivate a great many other varieties, and our income from grapes packed and shipped to the Northern markets is quite considerable. I have not noticed any developments of the goopher in the vineyard, although I have a mild suspicion that our colored assistants do not suffer from want of grapes during the season.

I found, when I bought the vineyard, that Uncle Julius had occupied a cabin on the place for many years, and derived a respectable revenue from the product of the neglected grape-vines. This, doubtless, accounted for his advice to me not to buy the vineyard, though whether it inspired the goopher story I am unable to state. I believe, however, that the wages I paid him for his services as coachman, for I gave him employment in that capacity, were more than an equivalent for anything he lost by the sale of the vineyard.

Po' Sandy

On the northeast corner of my vineyard in central North Carolina, and fronting on the Lumberton plank-road, there stood a small frame house, of the simplest construction. It was built of pine lumber, and contained but one room, to which one window gave light and one door admission. Its weather-beaten sides revealed a virgin innocence of paint. Against one end of the house, and occupying half its width, there stood a huge brick chimney: the crumbling mortar had left large cracks between the bricks; the bricks themselves had begun to scale off in large flakes, leaving the chimney sprinkled with unsightly blotches. These evidences of decay were but partially concealed by a creeping vine, which extended its slender branches hither and thither in an ambitious but futile attempt to cover the whole chimney. The wooden shutter, which had once protected the unglazed window, had fallen from its hinges, and lay rotting in the rank grass and jimson-weeds beneath. This building, I learned when I bought the place, had been used as a school-house for several years prior to the breaking out of the war, since which time it had remained unoccupied, save when some stray cow or vagrant hog had sought shelter within its walls from the chill rains and nipping winds of winter.

One day my wife requested me to build her a new kitchen. The house erected by us, when we first came to live upon the vineyard, contained a very conveniently arranged kitchen; but for some occult reason my wife wanted a kitchen in the back yard, apart from the dwelling-house, after the usual Southern fashion. Of course I had to build it.

To save expense, I decided to tear down the old schoolhouse, and use the lumber, which was in a good state of preservation, in the construction of the new kitchen. Before demolishing the old house, however, I made an estimate of the amount of material contained in it, and found that I would have to buy several hundred feet of lumber additional, in order to build the new kitchen according to my wife's plan.

One morning old Julius McAdoo, our colored coachman, harnessed the gray mare to the rockaway, and drove my wife and me over to the sawmill from which I meant to order the new lumber. We drove down the long lane which led from our house to the plank-road; following the plank-road for about a mile, we turned into a road running through the forest and across the swamp to the sawmill beyond. Our carriage jolted over the half-rotted corduroy road which traversed the swamp, and then climbed the long hill leading to the sawmill. When we reached the mill, the foreman had gone over to a neighboring farmhouse, probably to smoke or gossip, and we were compelled to await his return before we could transact our business. We remained seated in the carriage, a few rods from the mill, and watched the leisurely movements of the mill-hands. We had not waited long before a huge pine log was placed in position, the machinery of the mill was set in motion, and the circular saw began to eat its way through the log, with a loud whir which resounded throughout the vicinity of the mill. The sound rose and fell in a sort of rhythmic cadence, which, heard from where we sat, was not unpleasing, and not loud enough to prevent conversation. When the saw started on its second journey through the log, Julius observed, in a lugubrious tone, and with a perceptible shudder:—

"Ugh! but dat des do cuddle my blood!"

"What's the matter, Uncle Julius?" inquired my wife, who is of a very sympathetic turn of mind. "Does the noise affect your nerves?"

"No, Mis' Annie," replied the old man, with emotion, "I ain' narvous; but dat saw, a-cuttin' en grindin' thoo dat stick er timber, en moanin', en groanin', en sweekin', kyars my 'memb'ance

back ter ole times, en 'min's me er po' Sandy." The pathetic in-
tonation with which he lengthened out the "po' Sandy" touched
a responsive chord in our own hearts.

"And who was poor Sandy?" asked my wife, who takes a
deep interest in the stories of plantation life which she hears
from the lips of the older colored people. Some of these stories
are quaintly humorous; others wildly extravagant, revealing the
Oriental cast of the negro's imagination; while others, poured
freely into the sympathetic ear of a Northern-bred woman, dis-
close many a tragic incident of the darker side of slavery.

"Sandy," said Julius, in reply to my wife's question, "was a
nigger w'at useter b'long ter ole Mars Marrabo McSwayne. Mars
Marrabo's place wuz on de yuther side'n de swamp, right nex'
ter yo' place. Sandy wuz a monst'us good nigger, en could do
so many things erbout a plantation, en alluz 'ten' ter his wuk so
well, dat w'en Mars Marrabo's chilluns growed up en married
off, dey all un 'em wanted dey daddy fer ter gin 'em Sandy fer a
weddin' present. But Mars Marrabo knowed de res' wouldn' be
satisfied ef he gin Sandy ter a'er one un 'em; so w'en dey wuz
all done married, he fix it by 'lowin' one er his chilluns ter take
Sandy fer a mont' er so, en den ernudder for a mont' er so, en
so on dat erway tel dey had all had 'im de same lenk er time; en
den dey would all take him roun' ag'in, 'cep'n' oncet in a w'ile
w'en Mars Marrabo would len' 'im ter some er his yuther kin-
folks 'roun' de country, w'en dey wuz short er han's; tel bimeby
it go so Sandy didn't hardly knowed whar he wuz gwine ter stay
fum one week's een' ter de yuther.

"One time w'en Sandy wuz lent out ez yushal, a spekilater
come erlong wid a lot er niggers, en Mars Marrabo swap'
Sandy's wife off fer a noo 'oman. W'en Sandy come back, Mars
Marrabo gin 'im a dollar, en 'lowed he wuz monst'us sorry fer
ter break up de fambly, but de spekilater had gin 'im big boot,
en times wuz hard en money skase, en so he wuz bleedst ter
make de trade. Sandy tuk on some 'bout losin' his wife, but he
soon seed dey want no use cryin' ober spilt merlasses; en bein'
ez he lacked de looks er de noo 'oman, he tuk up wid her atter
she'd be'n on de plantation a mont' er so.

"Sandy en his noo wife got on mighty well tergedder, en de
niggers all 'mence' ter talk about how lovin' dey wuz. W'en Tenie

46

wuz tuk sick oncet, Sandy useter set up all night wid 'er, en den go ter wuk in de mawnin' des lack he had his reg'lar sleep; en Tenie would 'a' done anythin' in de worl' for her Sandy.

"Sandy en Tenie hadn' be'n libbin' tergedder fer mo' d'n two mont's befo' Mars Marrabo's old uncle, w'at libbed down in Robeson County, sent up ter fin' out ef Mars Marrabo couldn' len' 'im er hire 'im a good han' fer a mont' er so. Sandy's marster wuz one èr dese yer easy-gwine folks w'at wanter please eve'ybody, en he says yas, he could len' 'im Sandy. En Mars Marrabo tol' Sandy fer ter git ready ter go down ter Robeson nex' day, fer ter stay a mont' er so.

"It wuz monst'us hard on Sandy fer ter take 'im 'way fum Tenie. It wuz so fur down ter Robeson dat he didn' hab no chance er comin' back ter see her tel de time wuz up; he wouldn' 'a' mine comin' ten er fifteen mile at night ter see Tenie, but Mars Marrabo's uncle's plantation wuz mo' d'n forty mile off. Sandy wuz mighty sad en cas' down atter w'at Mars Marrabo tol' 'im, en he says ter Tenie, sezee:—

"'I'm gittin' monst'us ti'ed er dish yer gwine roun' so much. Here I is lent ter Mars Jeems dis mont', en I got ter do so-en-so; en ter Mars Archie de nex' mont', en I got ter do so-en-so; den I got ter go ter Miss Jinnie's: en hit's Sandy dis en Sandy dat, en Sandy yer en Sandy dere, tel it 'pears ter me I ain' got no home, ner no marster, ner no mistiss, ner no nuffin. I can't eben keep a wife: my yuther ole 'oman wuz sol' away widout my gittin' a chance fer ter tell her good-by; en now I got ter go off en leab you, Tenie, en I dunno whe'r I'm eber gwine ter see you ag'in er no. I wisht I wuz a tree, er a stump, er a rock, er sump'n w'at could stay on de plantation fer a w'ile.'

"Atter Sandy got thoo talkin', Tenie didn' say naer word, but des sot dere by de fier, studyin' en studyin'. Bimeby she up'n' says:—

"'Sandy, is I eber tol' you I wuz a cunjuh 'oman?'

"Co'se Sandy hadn' nebber dremp' er nuffin lack dat, en he made a great 'miration w'en he hear w'at Tenie say. Bimeby Tenie went on:—

"'I ain' goophered nobody, ner done no cunjuh wuk, fer fifteen year er mo'; en w'en I got religion I made up my mine I wouldn' wuk no mo' goopher. But dey is some things I doan

47

b'lieve it's no sin fer ter do; en ef you doan wanter be sent roun' fum pillar ter pos', en ef you doan wanter go down ter Robeson, I kin fix things so you won't haf ter. Ef you'll des say de word, I kin turn you ter w'ateber you wanter be, en you kin stay right whar you wanter, ez long ez you mineter.'

"Sandy say he doan keer; he's willin' fer ter do anythin' fer ter stay close ter Tenie. Den Tenie ax 'im ef he doan wanter be turnt inter a rabbit.

"Sandy say, 'No, de dogs mought git atter me.'

"'Shill I turn you ter a wolf?' sez Tenie.

"'No, eve'ybody's skeered er a wolf, en I doan want nobody ter be skeered er me.'

"'Shill I turn you ter a mawkin'-bird?'

"'No, a hawk mought ketch me. I wanter be turnt inter sump'n w'at'll stay in one place.'

"'I kin turn you ter a tree,' sez Tenie. 'You won't hab no mouf ner years, but I kin turn you back oncet in a w'ile, so you kin git sump'n ter eat, en hear w'at's gwine on.'

"Well, Sandy say dat'll do. En so Tenie tuk 'im down by de aidge er de swamp, not fur fum de quarters, en turnt 'im inter a big pine-tree, en sot 'im out 'mongs' some yuther trees. En de nex' mawnin', ez some er de fiel' han's wuz gwine long dere, dey seed a tree w'at dey didn' 'member er habbin' seed befo'; it wuz monst'us quare, en dey wuz bleedst ter 'low dat dey hadn' 'membered right, er e'se one er de saplin's had be'n growin' monst'us fas'.

"W'en Mars Marrabo 'skiver' dat Sandy wuz gone, he 'lowed Sandy had runned away. He got de dogs out, but de las' place dey could track Sandy ter wuz de foot er dat pine-tree. En dere de dogs stood en barked, en bayed, en pawed at de tree, en tried ter climb up on it; en w'en dey wuz tuk roun' thoo de swamp ter look fer de scent, dey broke loose en made fer dat tree ag'in. It wuz de beatenis' thing de w'ite folks eber hearn of, en Mars Marrabo 'lowed dat Sandy must 'a' clim' up on de tree en jump' off on a mule er sump'n, en rid fur ernuff fer ter spile de scent. Mars Marrabo wanted ter 'cuse some er de yuther niggers er heppin' Sandy off, but dey all 'nied it ter de las'; en eve'ybody knowed Tenie sot too much sto' by Sandy fer ter he'p 'im run away whar she couldn' nebber see 'im no mo'.

48

"W'en Sandy had be'n gone long ernuff fer folks ter think he done got clean away, Tenie useter go down ter de woods at night en turn 'im back, en den dey'd slip up ter de cabin en set by de fire en talk. But dey ha' ter be monst'us keerful, er e'se somebody would 'a' seed 'em, en dat would 'a' spile' de whole thing; so Tenie alluz turnt Sandy back in de mawnin' early, befo' anybody wuz a-stirrin'.

"But Sandy didn' git erlong widout his trials en tribberlations. One day a woodpecker come erlong en 'mence' ter peck at de tree; en de nex' time Sandy wuz turnt back he had a little roun' hole in his arm, des lack a sharp stick be'n stuck in it. Atter dat Tenie sot a sparrer-hawk fer ter watch de tree; en w'en de woodpecker come erlong nex' mawnin' fer ter finish his nes', he got gobble' up mos' 'fo' he stuck his bill in de bark.

"Nudder time, Mars Marrabo sent a nigger out in de woods fer ter chop tuppentime boxes. De man chop a box in dish yer tree, en hack' de bark up two er th'ee feet, fer ter let de tuppentime run. De nex' time Sandy wuz turnt back he had a big skyar on his lef' leg, des lack it be'n skunt; en it tuk Tenie nigh 'bout all night fer ter fix a mixtry ter kyo it up. Atter dat, Tenie sot a hawnet fer ter watch de tree; en w'en de nigger come back ag'in fer ter cut ernudder box on de yuther side'n de tree, de hawnet stung 'im so hard dat de ax slip en cut his foot nigh 'bout off.

"W'en Tenie see so many things happenin' ter de tree, she 'cluded she'd ha' ter turn Sandy ter sump'n e'se; en atter studyin' de matter ober, en talkin' wid Sandy one ebenin', she made up her mine fer ter fix up a goopher mixtry w'at would turn herse'f en Sandy ter foxes, er sump'n, so dey could run away en go some'rs whar dey could be free en lib lack w'ite folks.

"But dey ain' no tellin' w'at's gwine ter happen in dis worl'. Tenie had got de night sot fer her en Sandy ter run away, w'en dat ve'y day one er Mars Marrabo's sons rid up ter de big house in his buggy, en say his wife wuz monst'us sick, en he want his mammy ter len' 'im a 'oman fer ter nuss his wife. Tenie's mistiss say sen' Tenie; she wuz a good nuss. Young mars wuz in a tarrible hurry fer ter git back home. Tenie wuz washin' at de big house dat day, en her mistiss say she should go right 'long wid her young marster. Tenie tried ter make some 'scuse fer ter git away en hide 'tel night, w'en she would have eve'ything fix' up

49

fer her en Sandy; she say she wanter go ter her cabin fer ter git her bonnet. Her mistiss say it doan matter 'bout de bonnet; her head-hankcher wuz good ernuff. Den Tenie say she wanter git her bes' frock; her mistiss say no, she doan need no mo' frock, en w'en dat one got dirty she could git a clean one whar she wuz gwine. So Tenie had ter git in de buggy en go 'long wid young Mars Dunkin ter his plantation, w'ich wuz mo' d'n twenty mile away; en dey wa'n't no chance er her seein' Sandy no mo' 'tel she come back home. De po' gal felt monst'us bad 'bout de way things wuz gwine on, en she knowed Sandy mus' be a wond'rin' why she didn' come en turn 'im back no mo'.

"W'iles Tenie wuz away nussin' young Mars Dunkin's wife, Mars Marrabo tuk a notion fer ter buil' 'im a noo kitchen; en bein' ez he had lots er timber on his place, he begun ter look 'roun' fer a tree ter hab de lumber sawed out'n. En I dunno how it come to be so, but he happen fer ter hit on de ve'y tree w'at Sandy wuz turnt inter. Tenie wuz gone, en dey wa'n't nobody ner nuffin fer ter watch de tree.

"De two men w'at cut de tree down say dey nebber had sech a time wid a tree befo': dey axes would glansh off, en didn' 'pear ter make no progress thoo de wood; en of all de creakin', en shakin', en wobblin' you eber see, dat tree done it w'en it commence' ter fall. It wuz de beatenis' thing!

"W'en dey got de tree all trim' up, dey chain it up ter a timber waggin, en start fer de sawmill. But dey had a hard time gittin' de log dere: fus' dey got stuck in de mud w'en dey wuz gwine crosst de swamp, en it wuz two er th'ee hours befo' dey could git out. W'en dey start' on ag'in, de chain kep' a-comin' loose, en dey had ter keep a-stoppin' en a-stoppin' fer ter hitch de log up ag'in. W'en dey commence' ter climb de hill ter de sawmill, de log broke loose, en roll down de hill en in 'mongs' de trees, en hit tuk nigh 'bout half a day mo' ter git it haul' up ter de sawmill.

"De nex' mawnin' atter de day de tree wuz haul' ter de saw-mill, Tenie come home. W'en she got back ter her cabin, de fus' thing she done wuz ter run down ter de woods en see how Sandy wuz gittin' on. W'en she seed de stump standin' dere, wid de sap runnin' out'n it, en de limbs layin' scattered roun', she nigh 'bout went out'n her min'. She run ter her cabin, en got her goopher mixtry, en den follered de track er de timber waggin ter de sawmill. She knowed Sandy couldn' lib mo' d'n a minute er so ef she turnt him back, fer he wuz all chop' up so he'd 'a' be'n bleedst ter die. But she wanted ter turn 'im back long ernuff fer ter 'splain ter 'im dat she hadn' went off a-purpose, en lef' 'im ter be chop' down en sawed up. She didn' want Sandy ter die wid no hard feelin's to'ds her.

"De han's at de sawmill had des got de big log on de kerridge, en wuz startin' up de saw, w'en dey seed a 'oman runnin' up de hill, all out er bref, cryin' en gwine on des lack she wuz plumb 'stracted. It wuz Tenie; she come right inter de mill, en th'owed herse'f on de log, right in front er de saw, a-hollerin' en cryin' ter her Sandy ter fergib her, en not ter think hard er her, fer it wa'n't no fault er hern. Den Tenie 'membered de tree didn' hab no years, en she wuz gittin' ready fer ter wuk her goopher mixtry so ez ter turn Sandy back, w'en de mill-hands kotch holt er her en tied her arms wid a rope, en fasten' her to one er de posts in de sawmill; en den dey started de saw up ag'in, en cut de log up inter bo'ds en scantlin's right befo' her eyes. But it wuz mighty hard wuk; fer of all de sweekin', en moanin', en groanin', dat log done it w'iles de saw wuz a-cuttin' thoo it. De saw wuz one er dese yer ole-timey, up-en-down saws, en hit tuk longer dem days ter saw a log 'en it do now. Dey greased de saw, but dat didn' stop de fuss; hit kep' right on, tel fin'ly dey got de log all sawed up.

"W'en de oberseah w'at run de sawmill come fum breakfas', de han's up en tell him 'bout de crazy 'oman—ez dey s'posed she wuz—w'at had come runnin' in de sawmill, a-hollerin' en gwine on, en tried ter th'ow herse'f befo' de saw. En de oberseah sent two er th'ee er de han's fer ter take Tenie back ter her marster's plantation.

"Tenie 'peared ter be out'n her min' fer a long time, en her marster ha' ter lock her up in de smoke-'ouse 'tel she got ober her spells. Mars Marrabo wuz monst'us mad, en hit would 'a' made yo' flesh crawl fer ter hear him cuss, 'caze he say de speki-later w'at he got Tenie fum had fooled 'im by wukkin' a crazy 'oman off on him. W'iles Tenie wuz lock up in de smoke-'ouse, Mars Marrabo tuk 'n' haul de lumber fum de sawmill, en put up his noo kitchen.

"W'en Tenie got quiet' down, so she could be 'lowed ter go 'roun' de plantation, she up'n' tole her marster all erbout Sandy en de pine-tree; en w'en Mars Marrabo hearn it, he 'lowed she wuz de wuss 'stracted nigger he eber hearn of. He didn' know w'at ter do wid Tenie: fus' he thought he'd put her in de po'-house; but fin'ly, seein' ez she didn' do no harm ter nobody ner nuffin, but des went 'roun' moanin', en groanin', en shakin' her head, he 'cluded ter let her stay on de plantation en nuss de little nigger chilluns w'en dey mammies wuz ter wuk in de cotton-fiel'.

"De noo kitchen Mars Marrabo buil' wuzn' much use, fer it hadn' be'n put up long befo' de niggers 'mence' ter notice quare things erbout it. Dey could hear sump'n moanin' en groanin' 'bout de kitchen in de night-time, en w'en de win' would blow dey could hear sump'n a-hollerin' en sweekin' lack it wuz in great pain en sufferin'. En it got so atter a w'ile dat it wuz all Mars Marrabo's wife could do ter git a 'oman ter stay in de kitchen in de daytime long ernuff ter do de cookin'; en dey wa'n't naer nigger on de plantation w'at wouldn' rudder take forty dan ter go 'bout dat kitchen atter dark,—dat is, 'cep'n' Tenie; she didn' 'pear ter min' de ha'nts. She useter slip 'roun' at night, en set on de kitchen steps, en lean up agin de do'-jamb, en run on ter herse'f wid some kine er foolishness w'at nobody couldn' make out; fer Mars Marrabo had th'eaten' ter sen' her off'n de plantation ef she say anything ter any er de yuther niggers 'bout de pine-tree. But somehow er 'nudder de niggers foun' out all erbout it, en dey all knowed de kitchen wuz ha'nted by Sandy's sperrit. En bimeby hit got so Mars Marrabo's wife herse'f wuz skeered ter go out in de yard atter dark.

"W'en it come ter dat, Mars Marrabo tuk en to' de kitchen down, en use' de lumber fer ter buil' dat ole school'ouse w'at you er talkin' 'bout pullin' down. De school'ouse wuzn' use' 'cep'n' in de daytime, en on dark nights folks gwine 'long de road would hear quare soun's en see quare things. Po' ole Tenie useter go down dere at night, en wander 'roun' de school'ouse; en de niggers all 'lowed she went fer ter talk wid Sandy's sperrit. En one winter mawnin', w'en one er de boys went ter school early fer ter start de fire, w'at should he fin' but po' ole Tenie, layin' on de flo', stiff, en col', en dead. Dere didn' 'pear ter be nuffin pertickler de matter wid her,—she had des grieve' herse'f ter def fer her Sandy. Mars Marrabo didn' shed no tears. He thought Tenie wuz crazy, en dey wa'n't no tellin' w'at she mought do nex'; en dey ain' much room in dis worl' fer crazy w'ite folks, let 'lone a crazy nigger.

"Hit wa'n't long atter dat befo' Mars Marrabo sol' a piece er his track er lan' ter Mars Dugal' McAdoo,—*my* ole marster,— en dat's how de ole school'ouse happen to be on yo' place. W'en de wah broke out, de school stop', en de ole school'ouse be'n stannin' empty ever sence,—dat is, 'cep'n' fer de ha'nts. En folks sez dat de ole school'ouse, er any yuther house w'at got any er dat lumber in it w'at wuz sawed out'n de tree w'at Sandy wuz turnt inter, is gwine ter be ha'nted tel de las' piece er plank is rotted en crumble' inter dus'."

Annie had listened to this gruesome narrative with strained attention.

"What a system it was," she exclaimed, when Julius had finished, "under which such things were possible!"

"What things?" I asked, in amazement. "Are you seriously considering the possibility of a man's being turned into a tree?"

"Oh, no," she replied quickly, "not that"; and then she murmured absently, and with a dim look in her fine eyes, "Poor Tenie!"

We ordered the lumber, and returned home. That night, after we had gone to bed, and my wife had to all appearances been sound asleep for half an hour, she startled me out of an incipient doze by exclaiming suddenly,—

"John, I don't believe I want my new kitchen built out of the lumber in that old schoolhouse."

"You wouldn't for a moment allow yourself," I replied, with some asperity, "to be influenced by that absurdly impossible yarn which Julius was spinning to-day?"

"I know the story is absurd," she replied dreamily, "and I am not so silly as to believe it. But I don't think I should ever be able to take any pleasure in that kitchen if it were built out of that lumber. Besides, I think the kitchen would look better and last longer if the lumber were all new."

Of course she had her way. I bought the new lumber, though not without grumbling. A week or two later I was called away from home on business. On my return, after an absence of several days, my wife remarked to me,—

"John, there has been a split in the Sandy Run Colored Baptist Church, on the temperance question. About half the members have come out from the main body, and set up for themselves. Uncle Julius is one of the seceders, and he came to me yesterday and asked if they might not hold their meetings in the old schoolhouse for the present."

"I hope you didn't let the old rascal have it," I returned, with some warmth. I had just received a bill for the new lumber I had bought.

"Well," she replied, "I couldn't refuse him the use of the house for so good a purpose."

"And I'll venture to say," I continued, "that you subscribed something toward the support of the new church?"

She did not attempt to deny it.

"What are they going to do about the ghost?" I asked, somewhat curious to know how Julius would get around this obstacle.

"Oh," replied Annie, "Uncle Julius says that ghosts never disturb religious worship, but that if Sandy's spirit *should* happen to stray into meeting by mistake, no doubt the preaching would do it good."

MARS JEEMS'S NIGHTMARE

We found old Julius very useful when we moved to our new residence. He had a thorough knowledge of the neighborhood, was familiar with the roads and the watercourses, knew the qualities of the various soils and what they would produce, and where the best hunting and fishing were to be had. He was a marvelous hand in the management of horses and dogs, with whose mental processes he manifested a greater familiarity than mere use would seem to account for, though it was doubtless due to the simplicity of a life that had kept him close to nature. Toward my tract of land and the things that were on it—the creeks, the swamps, the hills, the meadows, the stones, the trees—he maintained a peculiar personal attitude, what might be called predial rather than proprietary. He had been accustomed, until long after middle life, to look upon himself as the property of another. When this relation was no longer possible, owing to the war, and to his master's death and the dispersion of the family, he had been unable to break off entirely the mental habits of a lifetime, but had attached himself to the old plantation, of which he seemed to consider himself an appurtenance. We found him useful in many ways and entertaining in others, and my wife and I took quite a fancy to him.

Shortly after we became established in our home on the sand-hills, Julius brought up to the house one day a colored boy of about seventeen, whom he introduced as his grandson, and for whom he solicited employment. I was not favorably impressed by the youth's appearance,—quite the contrary, in fact; but mainly to please the old man I hired Tom—his name was Tom—to help about the stables, weed the garden, cut wood and bring water, and in general to make himself useful about the outdoor work of the household.

My first impression of Tom proved to be correct. He turned out to be very trifling, and I was much annoyed by his laziness, his carelessness, and his apparent lack of any sense of responsibility. I kept him longer than I should, on Julius's account, hoping that he might improve; but he seemed to grow worse instead of better, and when I finally reached the limit of my patience, I discharged him.

"I am sorry, Julius," I said to the old man; "I should have liked to oblige you by keeping him; but I can't stand Tom any longer. He is absolutely untrustworthy."

"Yas, suh," replied Julius, with a deep sigh and a long shake of the head, "I knows he ain' much account, en dey ain' much 'pen'ence ter be put on 'im. But I wuz hopin' dat you mought make some 'lowance fuh a' ign'ant young nigger, suh, en gib 'im one mo' chance."

But I had hardened my heart. I had always been too easily imposed upon, and had suffered too much from this weakness. I determined to be firm as a rock in this instance.

"No, Julius," I rejoined decidedly, "it is impossible. I gave him more than a fair trial, and he simply won't do."

When my wife and I set out for our drive in the cool of the evening,—afternoon is "evening" in Southern parlance,—one of the servants put into the rockaway two large earthenware jugs. Our drive was to be down through the swamp to the mineral spring at the foot of the sand-hills beyond. The water of this spring was strongly impregnated with sulphur and iron, and, while not particularly agreeable of smell or taste, was used by us, in moderation, for sanitary reasons.

When we reached the spring, we found a man engaged in cleaning it out. In answer to an inquiry he said that if we would wait five or ten minutes, his task would be finished and the spring in such condition that we could fill our jugs. We might have driven on, and come back by way of the spring, but there was a bad stretch of road beyond, and we concluded to remain where we were until the spring should be ready. We were in a cool and shady place. It was often necessary to wait awhile in North Carolina; and our Northern energy had not been entirely proof against the influences of climate and local custom.

While we sat there, a man came suddenly around a turn of the road ahead of us. I recognized in him a neighbor with whom I had exchanged formal calls. He was driving a horse, apparently a high-spirited creature, possessing, so far as I could see at a glance, the marks of good temper and good breeding; the gentleman, I had heard it suggested, was slightly deficient in both. The horse was rearing and plunging, and the man was beating him furiously with a buggy-whip. When he saw us, he flushed a fiery red, and, as he passed, held the reins with one hand, at some risk to his safety, lifted his hat, and bowed somewhat constrainedly as the horse darted by us, still panting and snorting with fear.

"He looks as though he were ashamed of himself," I observed.

"I'm sure he ought to be," exclaimed my wife indignantly. "I think there is no worse sin and no more disgraceful thing than cruelty."

"I quite agree with you," I assented.

"A man w'at 'buses his hoss is gwine ter be ha'd on de folks w'at wuks fer 'im," remarked Julius. "Ef young Mistah McLean doan min', he'll hab a bad dream one er dese days, des lack 'is grandaddy had way back yander, long yeahs befo' de wah."

"What was it about Mr. McLean's dream, Julius?" I asked. The man had not yet finished cleaning the spring, and we might as well put in time listening to Julius as in any other way. We had found some of his plantation tales quite interesting.

"Mars Jeems McLean," said Julius, "wuz de grandaddy er dis yer gent'eman w'at is des gone by us beatin' his hoss. He had a big plantation en a heap er niggers. Mars Jeems wuz a ha'd man, en monst'us stric' wid his han's. Eber sence he growed up he nebber 'peared ter hab no feelin' fer nobody. W'en his daddy, ole Mars John McLean, died, de plantation en all de niggers fell ter young Mars Jeems. He had be'n bad 'nuff befo', but it wa'n't long atterwa'ds 'tel he got so dey wuz no use in libbin' at all ef you ha' ter lib roun' Mars Jeems. His niggers wuz bleedzd ter slabe fum daylight ter da'k, w'iles yuther folks's didn' hafter

wuk 'cep'n' fum sun ter sun; en dey didn' git no mo' ter eat dan
dey oughter, en dat de coa'ses' kin'. Dey wa'n't 'lowed ter sing,
ner dance, ner play de banjo w'en Mars Jeems wuz roun' de
place; fer Mars Jeems say he wouldn' hab no sech gwines-on,—
said he bought his han's ter wuk, en not ter play, en w'en night
come dey mus' sleep en res', so dey'd be ready ter git up soon
in de mawnin' en go ter dey wuk fresh en strong.

"Mars Jeems didn' 'low no co'tin' er juneseyin' roun' his plantation,—said he wanted his niggers ter put dey min's on dey
wuk, en not be wastin' dey time wid no sech foolis'ness. En he
wouldn' let his han's git married,—said he wuzn' raisin' niggers,
but wuz raisin' cotton. En w'eneber any er de boys en gals 'ud
'mence ter git sweet on one ernudder, he'd sell one er de yuther
un 'em, er sen' 'em way down in Robeson County ter his yuther
plantation, whar dey couldn' nebber see one ernudder.

"Ef any er de niggers eber complained, dey got fo'ty; so co'se
dey didn' many un 'em complain. But dey didn' lack it, des de
same, en nobody couldn' blame 'em, fer dey had a ha'd time.
Mars Jeems didn' make no 'lowance fer nachul bawn laz'ness,
ner sickness, ner trouble in de min', ner nuffin; he wuz des
gwine ter git so much wuk outer eve'y han', er know de reason w'y.

"Dey wuz one time de niggers 'lowed, fer a spell, dat Mars
Jeems mought git bettah. He tuk a lackin' ter Mars Marrabo
McSwayne's oldes' gal, Miss Libbie, en useter go ober dere eve'y
day er eve'y ebenin', en folks said dey wuz gwine ter git married
sho'. But it 'pears dat Miss Libbie heared 'bout de gwines-on
on Mars Jeems's plantation, en she des 'lowed she couldn' trus'
herse'f wid no sech a man; dat he mought git so useter 'busin'
his niggers dat he'd 'mence ter 'buse his wife atter he got useter
habbin' her roun' de house. So she 'clared she wuzn' gwine ter
hab nuffin mo' ter do wid young Mars Jeems.

"De niggers wuz all monst'us sorry w'en de match wuz bust'
up, fer now Mars Jeems got wusser 'n he wuz befo' he sta'ted
sweethea'tin'. De time he useter spen' co'tin' Miss Libbie he put
in findin' fault wid de niggers, en all his bad feelin's 'ca'se Miss
Libbie th'owed 'im ober he 'peared ter try ter wuk off on de po'
niggers.

"W'iles Mars Jeems wuz co'tin' Miss Libbie, two er de han's
on de plantation had got ter settin' a heap er sto' by one ernud-

der. One un 'em wuz name' Solomon, en de yuther wuz a 'oman
w'at wukked in de fiel' 'long er 'im—I fe'git dat 'oman's name,
but it doan 'mount ter much in de tale nohow. Now, whuther
'ca'se Mars Jeems wuz so tuk up wid his own junesey dat he
didn' paid no 'tention fer a w'ile ter w'at wuz gwine on 'twix'
Solomon en his junesey, er whuther his own co'tin' made 'im kin'
er easy on de co'tin' in de qua'ters, dey ain' no tellin'. But dey's
one thing sho', dat w'en Miss Libbie th'owed 'im ober, he foun'
out 'bout Solomon en de gal monst'us quick, en gun Solomon
fo'ty, en sont de gal down ter de Robeson County plantation,
en tol' all de niggers ef he ketch 'em at any mo' sech foolishness, he wuz gwine ter skin 'em alibe en tan dey hides befo' dey
ve'y eyes. Co'se he wouldn' 'a' done it, but he mought 'a' made
things wusser 'n dey wuz. So you kin 'magine dey wa'n't much
lub-makin' in de qua'ters fer a long time.

"Mars Jeems useter go down ter de yuther plantation sometimes fer a week er mo', en so he had ter hab a oberseah ter look
atter his wuk w'iles he 'uz gone. Mars Jeems's oberseah wuz a
po' w'ite man name' Nick Johnson,—de niggers called 'im Mars
Johnson ter his face, but behin' his back dey useter call 'im Ole
Nick, en de name suited 'im ter a T. He wuz wusser 'n Mars
Jeems ever da'ed ter be. Co'se de darkies didn' lack de way Mars
Jeems used 'em, but he wuz de marster, en had a right ter do ez
he please'; but dis yer Ole Nick wa'n't nuffin but a po' buckrah,
en all de niggers 'spised 'im ez much ez dey hated 'im, fer he
didn' own nobody, en wa'n't no bettah 'n a nigger, fer in dem
days any 'spectable pusson would ruther be a nigger dan a po'
w'ite man.

"Now, atter Solomon's gal had be'n sont away, he kep' feelin'
mo' en mo' bad erbout it, 'tel fin'lly he 'lowed he wuz gwine
ter see ef dey couldn' be sump'n done fer ter git 'er back,
en ter make Mars Jeems treat de darkies bettah. So he tuk a
peck er co'n out'n de ba'n one night, en went ober ter see ole
Aun' Peggy, de free-nigger cunjuh 'oman down by de Wim'l'ton
Road.

"Aun' Peggy listen' ter 'is tale, en ax' him some queshtuns, en
den tol' 'im she'd wuk her roots, en see w'at dey'd say 'bout it,
en ter-morrer night he sh'd come back ag'in en fetch ernudder
peck er co'n, en den she'd hab sump'n fer ter tell 'im.

"So Solomon went back de nex' night, en sho' 'nuff, Aun'

Peggy tol' 'im w'at ter do. She gun 'im some stuff w'at look' lack it be'n made by poundin' up some roots en yarbs wid a pestle in a mo'tar.

"'Dis yer stuff,' sez she, 'is monst'us pow'ful kin' er goopher. You take dis home, en gin it ter de cook, ef you kin trus' her, en tell her fer ter put it in yo' marster's soup de fus' cloudy day he hab okra soup fer dinnah. Min' you follers de d'rections.'

"'It ain' gwineter p'isen 'im, is it?' ax' Solomon, gittin' kin' er skeered; fer Solomon wuz a good man, en didn' want ter do nobody no rale ha'm.

"'Oh, no,' sez ole Aun' Peggy, 'it's gwine ter do 'im good, but he'll hab a monst'us bad dream fus'. A mont' fum now you come down heah en lemme know how de goopher is wukkin'. Fer I ain' done much er dis kin' er cunj'in' er late yeahs, en I has ter kinder keep track un it ter see dat it doan 'complish no mo' d'n I 'lows fer it ter do. En I has ter be kinder keerful 'bout cunj'in' w'ite folks; so be sho' en lemme know, w'ateber you do, des w'at is gwine on roun' de plantation.'

"So Solomon say all right, en tuk de goopher mixtry up ter de big house en gun it ter de cook, en tol' her fer ter put it in Mars Jeems's soup de fus cloudy day she hab okra soup fer dinnah. It happen' dat de ve'y nex' day wuz a cloudy day, en so de cook made okra soup fer Mars Jeems's dinnah, en put de powder Solomon gun her inter de soup, en made de soup rale good, so Mars Jeems eat a whole lot of it en 'peared ter enjoy it.

"De nex' mawnin' Mars Jeems tol' de oberseah he wuz gwine 'way on some bizness, en den he wuz gwine ter his yuther plantation, down in Robeson County, en he didn' 'spec' he'd be back fer a mont' er so.

"'But,' sezee, 'I wants you ter run dis yer plantation fer all it's wuth. Dese yer niggers is gittin' monst'us triflin' en lazy en keerless, en dey ain' no 'pen'ence ter be put in 'em. I wants dat stop', en w'iles I'm gone erway I wants de 'spenses cut 'way down en a heap mo' wuk done. Fac', I wants dis yer plantation ter make a reco'd dat'll show w'at kinder oberseah you is.'

"Ole Nick didn' said nuffin but 'Yas, suh,' but de way he kinder grin' ter hisse'f en show' his big yaller teef, en snap' de rawhide he useter kyar roun' wid 'im, made col' chills run up and down de backbone er dem niggers w'at heared Mars Jeems a-talkin'. En dat night dey wuz mo'nin' en groanin' down in de qua'ters, fer de niggers all knowed w'at wuz comin'.

"So, sho' 'nuff, Mars Jeems went erway nex' mawnin', en de trouble begun. Mars Johnson sta'ted off de ve'y fus' day fer ter see w'at he could hab ter show Mars Jeems w'en he come back. He made de tasks bigger en de rashuns littler, en w'en de niggers had wukked all day, he'd fin' sump'n fer 'em ter do roun' de ba'n er som'ers atter da'k, fer ter keep 'em busy a' hour er so befo' dey went ter sleep.

"About th'ee er fo' days atter Mars Jeems went erway, young Mars Dunkin McSwayne rode up ter de big house one day wid a nigger settin' behin' 'im in de buggy, tied ter de seat, en ax' ef Mars Jeems wuz home. Mars Johnson wuz at de house, and he say no.

"'Well,' sez Mars Dunkin, sezee, 'I fotch dis nigger ober ter Mistah McLean fer ter pay a bet I made wid 'im las' week w'en we wuz playin' kya'ds te'gedder. I bet 'im a nigger man, en heah's one I reckon'll fill de bill. He wuz tuk up de yuther day fer a stray nigger, en he couldn' gib no 'count er hisse'f, en so he wuz sol' at oction, en I bought 'im. He's kinder brash, but I knows yo' powers, Mistah Johnson, en I reckon ef anybody kin make 'im toe de ma'k, you is de man.'

"Mars Johnson grin' one er dem grins w'at show' all his snaggle teef, en make de niggers 'low he look lack de ole debbil, en sezee ter Mars Dunkin:—

"'I reckon you kin trus' me, Mistah Dunkin, fer ter tame any nigger wuz eber bawn. De nigger doan lib w'at I can't take down in 'bout fo' days.'

"Well, Ole Nick had 'is han's full long er dat noo nigger; en w'iles de res' er de darkies wuz sorry fer de po' man, dey 'lowed he kep' Mars Johnson so busy dat dey got along better 'n dey'd 'a' done ef de noo nigger had nebber come.

"De fus' thing dat happen', Mars Johnson sez ter dis yer noo man:—

"'W'at 's yo' name, Sambo?'

"'My name ain' Sambo,' 'spon' de noo nigger.

"'Did I ax you w'at yo' name wa'n't?' sez Mars Johnson. 'You wants ter be pa'tic'lar how you talks ter me. Now, w'at is yo' name, en whar did you come fum?'

"'I dunno my name,' sez de nigger, 'en I doan 'member whar I come fum. My head is all kin' er mix' up.'

"'Yas,' sez Mars Johnson, 'I reckon I'll ha' ter gib you sump'n fer ter cl'ar yo' head. At de same time, it'll l'arn you some manners, en atter dis mebbe you'll say "suh" w'en you speaks ter me.'

"Well, Mars Johnson haul' off wid his rawhide en hit de noo nigger once. De noo man look' at Mars Johnson fer a minute ez ef he didn' know w'at ter make er dis yer kin' er l'arnin'. But w'en de oberseah raise' his w'ip ter hit him ag'in, de noo nigger des haul' off en made fer Mars Johnson, en ef some er de yuther niggers hadn' stop' 'im, it 'peared ez ef he mought 'a' made it wa'm fer Ole Nick dere fer a w'ile. But de oberseah made de yuther niggers he'p tie de noo nigger up, en den gun 'im fo'ty, wid a dozen er so th'owed in fer good measure, fer Ole Nick wuz nebber stingy wid dem kin' er rashuns. De nigger went on at a tarrable rate, des lack a wil' man, but co'se he wuz bleedzd ter take his med'cine, fer he wuz tied up en couldn' he'p hisse'f.

"Mars Johnson lock' de noo nigger up in de ba'n, en didn' gib 'im nuffin ter eat fer a day er so, 'tel he got 'im kin'er quiet' down, en den he tu'nt 'im loose en put 'im ter wuk. De nigger 'lowed he wa'n't useter wukkin', en wouldn' wuk, en Mars Johnson gun 'im anudder fo'ty fer laziness en impidence, en let 'im fas' a day er so mo', en den put 'im ter wuk ag'in. De nigger went ter wuk, but didn' 'pear ter know how ter han'le a hoe. It tuk des 'bout half de oberseah's time lookin' atter 'im, en dat po' nigger got mo' lashin's en cussin's en cuffin's dan any fo' yuthers on de plantation. He didn' mix' wid ner talk much ter de res' er de niggers, en couldn' 'pear ter git it th'oo his min' dat he wuz a slabe en had ter wuk en min' de w'ite folks, spite er de fac' dat Ole Nick gun 'im a lesson eve'y day. En fin'lly Mars Johnson 'lowed dat he couldn' do nuffin wid 'im; dat ef he wuz his nigger, he'd break his sperrit er break 'is neck, one er de yuther. But co'se he wuz only sont ober on trial, en ez he didn' gib sat'sfaction, en he hadn' heared fum Mars Jeems 'bout w'en he wuz comin' back; en ez he wuz feared he'd git mad some time er 'nuther en kill de nigger befo' he knowed it, he 'lowed he'd better sen' 'im back whar he come fum. So he tied 'im up en sont 'im back ter Mars Dunkin.

"Now, Mars Dunkin McSwayne wuz one er dese yer easy-gwine gent'emen w'at didn' lack ter hab no trouble wid niggers er nobody e'se, en he knowed ef Mars Ole Nick couldn' git 'long wid dis nigger, nobody could. So he tuk de nigger ter town dat same day, en sol' 'im ter a trader w'at wuz gittin' up a gang er lackly niggers fer ter ship off on de steamboat ter go down de ribber ter Wim'l'ton en fum dere ter Noo Orleens.

"De nex' day atter de noo man had be'n sont away, Solomon wuz wukkin' in de cotton-fiel', en w'en he got ter de fence nex' ter de woods, at de een' er de row, who sh'd he see on de yuther side but ole Aun' Peggy. She beckon' ter 'im,—de oberseah wuz down on de yuther side er de fiel',—en sez she:—

"'W'y ain' you done come en 'po'ted ter me lack I tol' you?'

"'W'y, law! Aun' Peggy,' sez Solomon, 'dey ain' nuffin ter 'po't. Mars Jeems went away de day atter we gun 'im de goopher mix-try, en we ain' seed hide ner hair un 'im sence, en co'se we doan know nuffin 'bout w'at 'fec' it had on 'im.'

"'I doan keer nuffin 'bout yo' Mars Jeems now; w'at I wants ter know is w'at is be'n gwine on 'mongs' de niggers. Has you be'n gittin' 'long any better on de plantation?'

"'No, Aun' Peggy, we be'n gittin' 'long wusser. Mars Johnson is stric'er 'n he eber wuz befo', en de po' niggers doan ha'dly git time ter draw dey bref, en dey 'lows dey mought des ez well be dead ez alibe.'

"'Uh huh!' sez Aun' Peggy, sez she, 'I tol' you dat 'uz monst'us pow'ful goopher, en its wuk doan 'pear all at once.'

"'Long ez we had dat noo nigger heah,' Solomon went on, 'he kep' Mars Johnson busy pa't er de time; but now he's gone erway, I s'pose de res' un us'll ketch it wusser 'n eber.'

"'W'at's gone wid de noo nigger?' sez Aun' Peggy, rale quick, battin' her eyes en straight'nin' up.

"'Ole Nick done sont 'im back ter Mars Dunkin, who had fotch 'im heah fer ter pay a gamblin' debt ter Mars Jeems,' sez Solomon, 'en I heahs Mars Dunkin has sol' 'im ter a nigger-trader up in Patesville, w'at 's gwine ter ship 'im off wid a gang ter-morrer.'

"Ole Aun' Peggy 'peared ter git rale stirred up w'en Solomon tol' 'er dat, en sez she, shakin' her stick at 'im:—

"'W'y didn' you come en tell me 'bout dis noo nigger bein' sol' erway? Didn' you promus me, ef I'd gib you dat goopher, you'd come en 'po't ter me 'bout all w'at wuz gwine on on dis plantation? Co'se I could 'a' foun' out fer myse'f, but I 'pended on yo' tellin' me, en now by not doin' it I's feared you gwine spile my cunj'in'. You come down ter my house ter-night en do w'at I tells you, er I'll put a spell on you dat'll make yo' ha'r fall out so you'll be bal', en yo' eyes drap out so you can't see, en yo teef fall out so you can't eat, en yo' years grow up so you can't heah. W'en you is foolin' wid a cunjuh 'oman lack me, you got ter min' yo' P's en Q's er dey'll be trouble sho' 'nuff.'

"So co'se Solomon went down ter Aun' Peggy's dat night, en she gun 'im a roasted sweet'n' 'tater.

" 'You take dis yer sweet'n' 'tater,' sez she,—'I done goophered it 'speshly fer dat noo nigger, so you better not eat it yo'se'f er you'll wush you hadn',—en slip off ter town, en fin' dat strange man, en gib 'im dis yer sweet'n' 'tater. He mus' eat it befo' mawnin', sho', ef he doan wanter be sol' erway ter Noo Orleens.'

" 'But s'posen de patteroles ketch me, Aun' Peggy, w'at I gwine ter do?' sez Solomon.

" 'De patteroles ain' gwine tech you, but ef you doan fin' dat nigger, *I'm* gwine git you, en you'll fin' me wusser 'n de patteroles. Des hol' on a minute, en I'll sprinkle you wid some er dis mixtry out'n dis yer bottle, so de patteroles can't see you, en you kin rub yo' feet wid some er dis yer grease out'n dis go'd, so you kin run fas', en rub some un it on yo' eyes so you kin see in de da'k; en den you mus' fin' dat noo nigger en gib 'im dis yer 'tater, er you gwine ter hab mo' trouble on yo' han's 'n you eber had befo' in yo' life er eber will hab sence.'

"So Solomon tuk de sweet'n' 'tater en sta'ted up de road fas' ez he could go, en befo' long he retch' town. He went right 'long by de patteroles, en dey didn' 'pear ter notice 'im, en bimeby he foun' whar de strange nigger was kep', en he walked right pas' de gyard at de do' en foun' 'im. De nigger couldn' see 'im, ob co'se, en he couldn' 'a' seed de nigger in de da'k, ef it hadn' be'n fer de stuff Aun' Peggy gun 'im ter rub on 'is eyes. De nigger wuz layin' in a co'nder, 'sleep, en Solomon des slip' up ter 'im, en hilt dat sweet'n' 'tater 'fo' de nigger's nose, en he des nach'ly retch' up wid his han', en tuk de 'tater en eat it in his sleep, widout knowin' it. W'en Solomon seed he'd done eat de 'tater, he went back en tol' Aun' Peggy, en den went home ter his cabin ter sleep, 'way 'long 'bout two o'clock in de mawnin'.

64

"De nex' day wuz Sunday, en so de niggers had a little time ter deyse'ves. Solomon wuz kinder 'sturb' in his min' thinkin' 'bout his junesey w'at 'uz gone away, en wond'rin' w'at Aun' Peggy had ter do wid dat noo nigger; en he had sa'ntered up in de woods so's ter be by hisse'f a little, en at de same time ter look atter a rabbit-trap he'd sot down in de aidge er de swamp, w'en who sh'd he see stan'in' unner a tree but a w'ite man.

"Solomon didn' knowed de w'ite man at fus', 'tel de w'ite man spoke up ter 'im.

"'Is dat you, Solomon?' sezee.

"Den Solomon reco'nized de voice.

"'Fer de Lawd's sake, Mars Jeems! is dat you?'

"'Yas, Solomon,' sez his marster, 'dis is me, er w'at's lef' er me.'

"It wa'n't no wonder Solomon hadn' knowed Mars Jeems at fus', fer he wuz dress' lack a po' w'ite man, en wuz bare-footed, en look' monst'us pale en peaked, ez ef he'd des come th'oo a ha'd spell er sickness.

"'You er lookin' kinder po'ly, Mars Jeems,' sez Solomon. 'Is you be'n sick, suh?'

"'No, Solomon,' sez Mars Jeems, shakin' his head, en speakin' sorter slow en sad, 'I ain' be'n sick, but I's had a monst'us bad dream,—fac', a reg'lar, nach'ul nightmare. But tell me how things has be'n gwine on up ter de plantation sence I be'n gone, Solomon.'

"So Solomon up en tol' 'im 'bout de craps, en 'bout de hosses en de mules, en 'bout de cows en de hawgs. En w'en he 'mence' ter tell 'bout de noo nigger, Mars Jeems prick' up 'is yeahs en listen', en eve'y now en den he'd say, 'Uh huh! uh huh!' en nod 'is head. En bimeby, w'en he'd ax' Solomon some mo' queshtuns, he sez, sezee:—

"'Now, Solomon, I doan want you ter say a wo'd ter nobody 'bout meetin' me heah, but I wants you ter slip up ter de house, en fetch me some clo's en some shoes,—I fergot ter tell you dat a man rob' me back yander on de road en swap' clo's wid me widout axin' me whuther er no,—but you neenter say nuffin 'bout dat, nuther. You go en fetch me some clo's heah, so nobody won't see you, en keep yo' mouf shet, en I'll gib you a dollah.'

"Solomon wuz so 'stonish' he lack ter fell ober in his tracks, w'en Mars Jeems promus' ter gib 'im a dollah. Dey su't'nly wuz a change come ober Mars Jeems, w'en he offer' one er his niggers dat much money. Solomon 'mence' ter 'spec' dat Aun' Peggy's cunj'ation had be'n wukkin' monst'us strong.

"Solomon fotch Mars Jeems some clo's en shoes, en dat same eb'nin' Mars Jeems 'peared at de house, en let on lack he des dat minute got home fum Robeson County. Mars Johnson was all ready ter talk ter 'im, but Mars Jeems sont 'im wo'd he wa'n't feelin' ve'y well dat night, en he'd see 'im ter-morrer.

"So nex' mawnin' atter breakfus' Mars Jeems sont fer de oberseah, en ax' 'im fer ter gib 'count er his styoa'dship. Ole Nick tol' Mars Jeems how much wuk be'n done, en got de books en showed 'im how much money be'n save'. Den Mars Jeems ax' 'im how de darkies be'n behabin', en Mars Johnson say dey be'n behabin' good, most un 'em, en dem w'at didn' behabe good at fus' change dey conduc' atter he got holt un 'em a time er two.

"'All,' sezee, ''cep'n' de noo nigger Mistah Dunkin fotch ober heah en lef' on trial, w'iles you wuz gone.'

"'Oh, yas,' 'lows Mars Jeems, 'tell me all 'bout dat noo nigger. I heared a little 'bout dat quare noo nigger las' night, en it wuz des too redik'lus. Tell me all 'bout dat noo nigger.'

"So seein' Mars Jeems so good-nachu'd 'bout it, Mars Johnson up en tol' 'im how he tied up de noo han' de fus' day en gun 'im fo'ty 'ca'se he wouldn' tell 'im 'is name.

"'Ha, ha, ha!' sez Mars Jeems, laffin' fit ter kill, 'but dat is too funny fer any use. Tell me some mo' 'bout dat noo nigger.'

"So Mars Johnson went on en tol' 'im how he had ter starbe de noo nigger 'fo he could make 'im take holt er a hoe.

"'Dat wuz de beatinis' notion fer a nigger,' sez Mars Jeems, 'puttin' on airs, des lack he wuz a w'ite man! En I reckon you didn' do nuffin ter 'im?'

"'Oh, no, suh,' sez de oberseah, grinnin' lack a chessy-cat, 'I didn' do nuffin but take de hide off'n 'im.'

"Mars Jeems lafft en lafft, 'tel it 'peared lack he wuz des gwine ter bu'st. *Tell* me some mo' 'bout dat noo nigger, oh, *tell* me some mo'. Dat noo nigger int'rusts me, he do, en dat is a fac'.'

"Mars Johnson didn' quite un'erstan' w'y Mars Jeems sh'd make sich a great 'miration 'bout de noo nigger, but co'se he want' ter please de gent'eman w'at hi'ed 'im, en so he 'splain' all 'bout how many times he had ter cowhide de noo nigger, en how he made 'im do tasks twicet ez big ez some er de yuther han's, en how he'd chain 'im up in de ba'n at night en feed 'im on co'n-bread en water.

" 'Oh! but you is a monst'us good oberseah; you is de bes' oberseah in dis county, Mistah Johnson,' sez Mars Jeems, w'en de oberseah got th'oo wid his tale; 'en dey ain' nebber be'n no nigger-breaker lack you roun' heah befo'. En you desarbes great credit fer sendin' dat nigger 'way befo' you sp'ilt 'im fer de market. Fac', you is sech a monst'us good oberseah, en you is got dis yer plantation in sech fine shape, dat I reckon I doan need you no mo'. You is got dese yer darkies so well train' dat I 'spec' I kin run 'em myse'f fum dis time on. But I does wush you had 'a' hilt on ter dat noo nigger 'tel I got home, fer I'd 'a' lack ter 'a' seed 'im, I su't'nly should.'

"De oberseah wuz so 'stonish' he didn' ha'dly know w'at ter say, but fin'lly he ax' Mars Jeems ef he wouldn' gib 'im a riccommen' fer ter git ernudder place.

" 'No, suh,' sez Mars Jeems, 'somehow er 'nuther I doan lack yo' looks sence I come back dis time, en I'd much ruther you wouldn' stay roun' heah. Fac', I's feared ef I'd meet you alone in de woods some time, I mought wanter ha'm you. But layin' dat aside, I be'n lookin' ober dese yer books er yo'n w'at you kep' w'iles I wuz 'way, en fer a yeah er so back, en dere's some figgers w'at ain' des cl'ar ter me. I ain' got no time fer ter talk 'bout 'em now, but I 'spec' befo' I settles wid you fer dis las' mont', you better come up heah ter-morrer, atter I's look' de books en 'counts ober some mo', en den we 'll straighten ou' business all up.'

"Mars Jeems 'lowed atterwa'ds dat he wuz des shootin' in de da'k w'en he said dat 'bout de books, but howsomeber, Mars Nick Johnson lef' dat naberhood 'twix' de nex' two suns, en nobody roun' dere nebber seed hide ner hair un 'im sence. En all de darkies t'ank de Lawd, en 'lowed it wuz a good riddance er bad rubbage.

"But all dem things I done tol' you ain' nuffin 'side'n de change w'at come ober Mars Jeems fum dat time on. Aun' Peggy's goopher had made a noo man un 'im enti'ely. De nex' day atter he come back, he tol' de han's dey neenter wuk on'y fum sun ter sun, en he cut dey tasks down so dey didn' nobody hab ter stan' ober 'em wid a rawhide er a hick'ry. En he 'lowed ef de niggers want ter hab a dance in de big ba'n any Sad'day night, dey mought hab it. En bimeby, w'en Solomon seed how good Mars Jeems wuz, he ax' 'im ef he wouldn' please sen' down ter de yuther plantation fer his junesey. Mars Jeems say su't'nly, en gun Solomon a pass en a note ter de oberseah on de yuther plantation, en sont Solomon down ter Robeson County wid a hoss en buggy fer ter fetch his junesey back. W'en de niggers see how fine Mars Jeems gwine treat 'em, dey all tuk ter sweethea'tin' en juneseyin' en singin' en dancin', en eight er ten couples got married, en bimeby eve'ybody 'mence' ter say Mars Jeems McLean got a finer plantation, en slicker-lookin' niggers, en dat he 'uz makin' mo' cotton en co'n, dan any yuther gent'eman in de county. En Mars Jeems's own junesey, Miss Libbie, heared 'bout de noo gwines-on on Mars Jeems's plantation, en she change' her min' 'bout Mars Jeems en tuk 'im back ag'in, en 'fo' long dey had a fine weddin', en all de darkies had a big feas', en dey wuz fiddlin' en dancin' en funnin' en frolic'in' fum sundown 'tel mawnin'."

"And they all lived happy ever after," I said, as the old man reached a full stop.

"Yas, suh," he said, interpreting my remarks as a question, "dey did. Solomon useter say," he added, "dat Aun' Peggy's goopher had turnt Mars Jeems ter a nigger, en dat dat noo han' wuz Mars Jeems hisse'f. But co'se Solomon didn' das' ter let on 'bout w'at he 'spicioned, en ole Aun' Peggy would 'a' 'nied ef she had be'n ax', fer she'd 'a' got in trouble sho', ef it 'uz knowed she'd be'n cunj'in' de w'ite folks.

"Dis yer tale goes ter show," concluded Julius sententiously, as the man came up and announced that the spring was ready for us to get water, "dat w'ite folks w'at is so ha'd en stric', en doan make no 'lowance fer po' ign'ant niggers w'at ain' had no chanst ter l'arn, is li'ble ter hab bad dreams, ter say de leas', en dat dem w'at is kin' en good ter po' people is sho' ter prosper en git 'long in de worl'."

"That is a very strange story, Uncle Julius," observed my wife, smiling, "and Solomon's explanation is quite improbable."

"Yes, Julius," said I, "that was powerful goopher. I am glad, too, that you told us the moral of the story; it might have escaped us otherwise. By the way, did you make that up all by yourself?"

The old man's face assumed an injured look, expressive more of sorrow than of anger, and shaking his head he replied:—

"No, suh, I heared dat tale befo' you er Mis' Annie dere wuz bawn, suh. My mammy tol' me dat tale w'en I wa'n't mo' d'n knee-high ter a hopper-grass."

I drove to town next morning, on some business, and did not return until noon; and after dinner I had to visit a neighbor, and did not get back until supper-time. I was smoking a cigar on the back piazza in the early evening, when I saw a familiar figure carrying a bucket of water to the barn. I called my wife.

"My dear," I said severely, "what is that rascal doing here? I thought I discharged him yesterday for good and all."

"Oh, yes," she answered, "I forgot to tell you. He was hanging round the place all the morning, and looking so down in the mouth, that I told him that if he would try to do better, we would give him one more chance. He seems so grateful, and so really in earnest in his promises of amendment, that I'm sure you'll not regret taking him back."

I was seriously enough annoyed to let my cigar go out. I did not share my wife's rose-colored hopes in regard to Tom; but as I did not wish the servants to think there was any conflict of authority in the household, I let the boy stay.

THE CONJURER'S REVENGE

Sunday was sometimes a rather dull day at our place. In the morning, when the weather was pleasant, my wife and I would drive to town, a distance of about five miles, to attend the church of our choice. The afternoons we spent at home, for the most part, occupying ourselves with the newspapers and magazines, and the contents of a fairly good library. We had a piano in the house, on which my wife played with skill and feeling. I possessed a passable baritone voice, and could accompany myself indifferently well when my wife was not by to assist me. When these resources failed us, we were apt to find it a little dull.

One Sunday afternoon in early spring,—the balmy spring of North Carolina, when the air is in that ideal balance between heat and cold where one wishes it could always remain,—my wife and I were seated on the front piazza, she wearily but conscientiously ploughing through a missionary report, while I followed the impossible career of the blonde heroine of a rudimentary novel. I had thrown the book aside in disgust, when I saw Julius coming through the yard, under the spreading elms, which were already in full leaf. He wore his Sunday clothes, and advanced with a dignity of movement quite different from his week-day slouch.

"Have a seat, Julius," I said, pointing to an empty rocking-chair.

"No, thanky, boss, I'll des set here on de top step."

"Oh, no, Uncle Julius," exclaimed Annie, "take this chair. You will find it much more comfortable."

The old man grinned in appreciation of her solicitude, and seated himself somewhat awkwardly.

"Julius," I remarked, "I am thinking of setting out scuppernong vines on that sand-hill where the three persimmon-trees are; and while I'm working there, I think I'll plant watermelons between the vines, and get a little something to pay for my first year's work. The new railroad will be finished by the middle of summer, and I can ship the melons North, and get a good price for them."

"Ef you er gwine ter hab any mo' ploughin' ter do," replied Julius, "I 'spec' you'll ha' ter buy ernudder creetur, 'ca'se hit's much ez dem hosses kin do ter 'ten' ter de wuk dey got now."

"Yes, I had thought of that. I think I'll get a mule; a mule can do more work, and doesn't require as much attention as a horse."

"I wouldn' 'vise you ter buy no mule," remarked Julius, with a shake of his head.

"Why not?"

"Well, you may 'low hit's all foolis'ness, but ef I wuz in yo' place, I wouldn' buy no mule."

"But that isn't a reason; what objection have you to a mule?"

"Fac' is," continued the old man, in a serious tone, "I doan lack ter dribe a mule. I's alluz afeared I mought be imposin' on some human creetur; eve'y time I cuts a mule wid a hick'ry, 'pears ter me mos' lackly I's cuttin' some er my own relations, er somebody e'se w'at can't he'p deyse'ves."

"What put such an absurd idea into your head?" I asked.

My question was followed by a short silence, during which Julius seemed engaged in a mental struggle.

"I dunno ez hit's wuf w'ile ter tell you dis," he said, at length. "I doan ha'dly 'spec' fer you ter b'lieve it. Does you 'member dat club-footed man w'at hilt de hoss fer you de yuther day w'en you was gittin' out'n de rockaway down ter Mars Archie McMillan's sto'?"

"Yes, I believe I do remember seeing a club-footed man there."

"Did you eber see a club-footed nigger befo' er sence?"

"No, I can't remember that I ever saw a club-footed colored man," I replied, after a moment's reflection.

"You en Mis' Annie wouldn' wanter b'lieve me, ef I wuz ter 'low dat dat man was oncet a mule?"

"No," I replied, "I don't think it very likely that you could make us believe it."

"Why, Uncle Julius!" said Annie severely, "what ridiculous nonsense!"

This reception of the old man's statement reduced him to silence, and it required some diplomacy on my part to induce him to vouchsafe an explanation. The prospect of a long, dull afternoon was not alluring, and I was glad to have the monotony of Sabbath quiet relieved by a plantation legend.

"W'en I wuz a young man," began Julius, when I had finally prevailed upon him to tell us the story, "dat club-footed nigger —his name is Primus—use' ter b'long ter ole Mars Jim McGee ober on de Lumbe'ton plank-road. I use' ter go ober dere ter see a 'oman w'at libbed on de plantation; dat's how I come ter know all erbout it. Dis yer Primus wuz de livelies' han' on de place, alluz a-dancin', en drinkin', en runnin' roun', en singin', en pickin' de banjo; 'cep'n once in a w'ile, w'en he'd 'low he wa'n't treated right 'bout sump'n ernudder, he'd git so sulky en stubborn dat de w'ite folks couldn' ha'dly do nuffin wid 'im.

"It wuz 'gin' de rules fer any er de han's ter go 'way fum de plantation at night; but Primus didn' min' de rules, en went w'en he felt lack it; en de w'ite folks purten' lack dey didn' know it, fer Primus was dange'ous w'en he got in dem stubborn spells, en dey'd ruther not fool wid 'im.

"One night in de spring er de year, Primus slip' off fum de plantation, en went down on de Wim'l'ton Road ter a dance gun by some er de free niggers down dere. Dey wuz a fiddle, en a banjo, en a jug gwine roun' on de outside, en Primus sung en dance' 'tel 'long 'bout two o'clock in de mawnin', w'en he start' fer home. Ez he come erlong back, he tuk a nigh-cut 'cross de cotton-fiel's en 'long by de aidge er de Min'al Spring Swamp, so ez ter git shet er de patteroles w'at rid up en down de big road fer ter keep de darkies fum runnin' roun' nights. Primus was sa'nt'rin' 'long, studyin' 'bout de good time he'd had wid de gals, w'en, ez he wuz gwine by a fence co'nder, w'at sh'd he heah but sump'n grunt. He stopped a minute ter listen, en he heared sump'n grunt ag'in. Den he went ober ter de fence whar he heard de fuss, en dere, layin' in de fence co'nder, on a pile er pine straw, he seed a fine, fat shote.

"Primus look' ha'd at de shote, en den sta'ted home. But somehow er 'nudder he coudn' git away fum dat shote; w'en he tuk one step for'ards wid one foot, de yuther foot 'peared ter take two steps back'ards, en so he kep' nachly gittin' closeter en closeter ter de shote. It was de beatin'es' thing! De shote des 'peared ter cha'm Primus, en fus' thing you know Primus foun' hisse'f 'way up de road wid de shote on his back.

"Ef Primus had 'a' knowed whose shote dat wuz, he'd 'a' man-age' ter git pas' it somehow er 'nudder. Ez it happen', de shote b'long ter a cunjuh man w'at libbed down in de free-nigger sett'ement. Co'se de cunjuh man didn' hab ter wuk his roots but a little w'ile 'fo' he foun' out who tuk his shote, en den de trouble begun. One mawnin', a day er so later, en befo' he got de shote eat up, Primus didn' go ter wuk w'en de hawn blow, en w'en de oberseah wen' ter look fer him, dey wa' no trace er Primus ter be 'skivered nowhar. W'en he didn' come back in a day er so mo', eve'ybody on de plantation 'lowed he had runned erway. His marster a'vertise' him in de papers, en offered a big reward fer 'im. De nigger-ketchers fotch out dey dogs, en track' 'im down ter de aidge er de swamp, en den de scent gun out; en dat was de las' anybody seed er Primus fer a long, long time.

"Two er th'ee weeks atter Primus disappear', his marster went ter town one Sad'day. Mars Jim was stan'in' in front er Sandy Campbell's bar-room, up by de ole wagon-ya'd, w'en a po' w'ite man fum down on de Wim'l'ton Road come up ter 'im en ax' 'im, kinder keerless lack, ef he didn' wanter buy a mule.

"'I dunno,' says Mars Jim; 'it 'pen's on de mule, en on de price. Whar is de mule?'

"'Des 'roun' heah back er ole Tom McAllister's sto',' says de po' w'ite man.

"'I reckon I'll hab a look at de mule,' says Mars Jim, 'en ef he suit me, I dunno but w'at I mought buy 'im.'

"So de po' w'ite man tuk Mars Jim 'roun' back er de sto', en dere stood a monst'us fine mule. W'en de mule see Mars Jim, he gun a whinny, des lack he knowed him befo'. Mars Jim look' at de mule, en de mule 'peared ter be soun' en strong. Mars Jim 'lowed dey 'peared ter be sump'n fermilyus 'bout de mule's face, 'spesh'ly his eyes; but he hadn' los' naer mule, en didn' hab no recommemb'ance er habin' seed de mule befo'. He ax' de po' buckrah whar he got de mule, en de po' buckrah say his brer raise' de mule down on Rockfish Creek. Mars Jim was a little s'picious er seein' a po' w'ite man wid sech a fine creetur, but he fin'lly 'greed ter gib de man fifty dollars fer de mule,—'bout ha'f w'at a good mule was wuf dem days.

"He tied de mule behin' de buggy w'en he went home, en put 'im ter ploughin' cotton de nex' day. De mule done mighty well fer th'ee er fo' days, en den de niggers 'mence' ter notice some quare things erbout him. Dey wuz a medder on de plantation whar dey use' ter put de hosses en mules ter pastur'. Hit was fence' off fum de corn-fiel' on one side, but on de yuther side'n de pastur' was a terbacker-patch w'at wa'n't fence' off, 'ca'se de beastisses doan none un 'em eat terbacker. Dey doan know w'at's good! Terbacker is lack religion, de good Lawd made it fer people, en dey ain' no yuther creetur w'at kin 'preciate it. De darkies notice' dat de fus' thing de new mule done, w'en he was turnt inter de pastur', wuz ter make fer de terbacker-patch. Co'se dey didn' think nuffin un it, but nex' mawnin', w'en dey went ter ketch 'im, dey 'skivered dat he had eat up two whole rows er terbacker plants. Atter dat dey had ter put a halter on 'im, en tie 'im ter a stake, er e'se dey wouldn' 'a' been naer leaf er terbacker lef' in de patch.

"Ernudder day one er de han's, name' 'Dolphus, hitch' de mule up, en dribe up here ter dis yer vimya'd,—dat wuz w'en ole Mars Dugal' own' dis place. Mars Dugal' had kilt a yearlin', en de naber w'ite folks all sont ober fer ter git some fraish beef, en Mars Jim had sont 'Dolphus fer some too. Dey wuz a wine-press in de ya'd whar 'Dolphus lef' de mule a-stan'in', en right in front er de press dey wuz a tub er grape-juice, des pressed out, en a little ter one side a bairl erbout half full er wine w'at had be'n stan'in' two er th'ee days, en had begun ter git sorter sha'p ter de tas'e. Dey wuz a couple er bo'ds on top er dis yer bairl, wid a rock laid on 'em ter hol' 'em down. Ez I wuz a-sayin', 'Dolphus lef' de mule stan'in' in de ya'd, en went inter de smoke-house fer ter git de beef. Bimeby, w'en he come out, he seed de mule a-stagg'rin' 'bout de ya'd; en 'fo' 'Dolphus could git dere ter fin' out w'at wuz de matter, de mule fell right ober on his side, en laid dere des' lack he was dead.

"All de niggers 'bout de house run out dere fer ter see w'at wuz de matter. Some say de mule had de colic; some say one thing en some ernudder; 'tel bimeby one er de han's seed de top wuz off'n de bairl, en run en looked in.

"'Fo' de Lawd!' he say, 'dat mule drunk! he be'n drinkin' de wine.' En sho' 'nuff, de mule had pas' right by de tub er fraish grape-juice en push' de kiver off'n de bairl, en drunk two er th'ee gallon er de wine w'at had been stan'in' long ernough fer ter begin ter git sha'p.

"De darkies all made a great 'miration 'bout de mule gittin' drunk. Dey never hadn' seed nuffin lack it in dey bawn days. Dey po'd water ober de mule, en tried ter sober 'im up; but it wa'n't no use, en 'Dolphus had ter take de beef home on his back, en leabe de mule dere, 'tel he slep' off 'is spree.

"I doan 'member whe'r I tol' you er no, but w'en Primus disappear' fum de plantation, he lef' a wife behin' 'im,—a monst'us good-lookin' yaller gal, name' Sally. W'en Primus had be'n gone a mont' er so, Sally 'mence' fer ter git lonesome, en tuk up wid ernudder young man name' Dan, w'at b'long' on de same plantation. One day dis yer Dan tuk de noo mule out in de cotton-fiel' fer ter plough, en w'en dey wuz gwine 'long de tu'n-row, who sh'd he meet but dis yer Sally. Dan look' 'roun' en he didn' see de oberseah nowhar, so he stop' a minute fer ter run on wid Sally.

"'Hoddy, honey,' sezee. 'How you feelin' dis mawnin'?'

"'Fus' rate,' 'spon' Sally.

"Dey wuz lookin' at one ernudder, en dey didn' naer one un 'em pay no 'tention ter de mule, who had turnt 'is head 'roun' en wuz lookin' at Sally ez ha'd ez he could, en stretchin' 'is neck en raisin' 'is years, en whinnyin' kinder sof' ter hisse'f.

"'Yas, honey,' 'lows Dan, 'en you gwine ter feel fus' rate long ez you sticks ter me. Fer I's a better man dan dat low-down runaway nigger Primus dat you be'n wastin' yo' time wid.'

"Dan had let go de plough-handle, en had put his arm 'roun' Sally, en wuz des gwine ter kiss her, w'en sump'n ketch' 'im by de scruff er de neck en flung 'im 'way ober in de cotton-patch.

W'en he pick' 'isse'f up, Sally had gone kitin' down de tu'n-row, en de mule wuz stan'in' dere lookin' ez ca'm en peaceful ez a Sunday mawnin'.

"Fus' Dan had 'lowed it wuz de oberseah w'at had cotch' 'im wastin' 'is time. But dey wa'n't no oberseah in sight, so he 'cluded it must 'a' be'n de mule. So he pitch' inter de mule en lammed 'im ez ha'd ez he could. De mule tuk it all, en 'peared ter be ez 'umble ez a mule could be; but w'en dey wuz makin' de turn at de een' er de row, one er de plough-lines got under de mule's hin' leg. Dan retch' down ter git de line out, sorter keerless like, w'en de mule haul' off en kick him clean ober de fence inter a brier-patch on de yuther side.

"Dan wuz mighty so' fum 'is woun's en scratches, en wuz laid up fer two er th'ee days. One night de noo mule got out'n de pastur', en went down to de quarters. Dan wuz layin' dere on his pallet, w'en he heard sump'n bangin' erway at de side er his cabin. He raise' up on one shoulder en look' roun', w'en w'at should he see but de noo mule's head stickin' in de winder, wid his lips drawed back over his toofs, grinnin' en snappin' at Dan des' lack he wanter eat 'im up. Den de mule went roun' ter de do', en kick' erway lack he wanter break de do' down, 'tel bimeby somebody come 'long en driv him back ter de pastur'. W'en Sally come in a little later fum de big house, whar she'd be'n waitin' on de w'ite folks, she foun' po' Dan nigh 'bout dead, he wuz so skeered. She 'lowed Dan had had de nightmare; but w'en dey look' at de do', dey seed de marks er de mule's huffs, so dey couldn' be no mistake 'bout w'at had happen'.

"Co'se de niggers tol' dey marster 'bout de mule's gwines-on. Fust he didn' pay no 'tention ter it, but atter a w'ile he tol' 'em ef dey didn' stop dey foolis'ness, he gwine tie some un 'em up. So atter dat dey didn' say nuffin mo' ter dey marster, but dey kep' on noticin' de mule's quare ways des de same.

"'Long 'bout de middle er de summer dey wuz a big camp-meetin' broke out down on de Wim'l'ton Road, en nigh 'bout all de po' w'ite folks en free niggers in de settlement got 'ligion, en lo en behol'! 'mongs' 'em wuz de cunjuh man w'at own' de shote w'at cha'med Primus.

"Dis cunjuh man wuz a Guinea nigger, en befo' he wuz sot free had use' ter b'long ter a gent'eman down in Sampson

County. De cunjuh man say his daddy wuz a king, er a guv'ner, er some sorter w'at-you-may-call-'em 'way ober yander in Affiky whar de niggers come fum, befo' he was stoled erway en sol' ter de spekilaters. De cunjuh man had he'ped his marster out'n some trouble ernudder wid his goopher, en his marster had sot him free, en bought him a trac' er land down on de Wim'l'ton Road. He purten' ter be a cow-doctor, but eve'ybody knowed w'at he r'al'y wuz.

"De cunjuh man hadn' mo' d'n come th'oo good, befo' he wuz tuk sick wid a col' w'at he kotch kneelin' on de groun' so long at de mou'ners' bench. He kep' gittin' wusser en wusser, en bimeby de rheumatiz tuk holt er 'im, en drawed him all up, 'tel one day he sont word up ter Mars Jim McGee's plantation, en ax' Pete, de nigger w'at tuk keer er de mules, fer ter come down dere dat night en fetch dat mule w'at his marster had bought fum de po' w'ite man dyoin' er de summer.

"Pete didn' know w'at de cunjuh man wuz dribin' at, but he didn' daster stay way; en so dat night, w'en he'd done eat his bacon en his hoe-cake, en drunk his 'lasses-en-water, he put a bridle on de mule, en rid 'im down ter de cunjuh man's cabin. W'en he got ter de do', he lit en hitch' de mule, en den knock' at de do'. He felt mighty jubous 'bout gwine in, but he was bleedst ter do it; he knowed he couldn' he'p 'isse'f.

"'Pull de string,' sez a weak voice, en w'en Pete lif' de latch en went in, de cunjuh man was layin' on de bed, lookin' pale en weak, lack he didn' hab much longer fer ter lib.

"'Is you fotch' de mule?' sezee.

"Pete say yas, en de cunjuh man kep' on.

"'Brer Pete,' sezee, 'I's be'n a monst'us sinner man, en I's done a power er wickedness endyoin' er my days; but de good Lawd is wash' my sins erway, en I feels now dat I's boun' fer de kingdom. En I feels, too, dat I ain' gwine ter git up fum dis bed no mo' in dis worl', en I wants ter ondo some er de harm I done. En dat's de reason, Brer Pete, I sont fer you ter fetch dat mule down here. You 'member dat shote I was up ter yo' plantation inquirin' 'bout las' June?'

"'Yas,' says Brer Pete, 'I 'member yo' axin' 'bout a shote you had los'.'

"'I dunno whe'r you eber l'arnt it er no,' says de cunjuh man, 'but I done knowed yo' marster's Primus had tuk de shote, en I wuz boun' ter git eben wid 'im. So one night I cotch' 'im down by de swamp on his way ter a candy-pullin', en I th'owed a goopher mixtry on 'im, en turnt 'im ter a mule, en got a po' w'ite man ter sell de mule, en we 'vided de money. But I doan want ter die 'tel I turn Brer Primus back ag'in.'

"Den de cunjuh man ax' Pete ter take down one er two go'ds off'n a she'f in de corner, en one er two bottles wid some kin' er mixtry in 'em, en set 'em on a stool by de bed; en den he ax' 'im ter fetch de mule in.

"W'en de mule come in de do', he gin a snort, en started fer de bed, des lack he was gwine ter jump on it.

"'Hol' on dere, Brer Primus!' de cunjuh man hollered. 'I's monst'us weak, en ef you 'mence on me, you won't nebber hab no chance fer ter git turn' back no mo'.'

"De mule seed de sense er dat, en stood still. Den de cunjuh man tuk de go'ds en bottles, en 'mence' ter wuk de roots en yarbs, en de mule 'mence' ter turn back ter a man,—fust his years, den de res' er his head, den his shoulders en arms. All de time de cunjuh man kep' on wukkin' his roots; en Pete en Primus could see he wuz gittin' weaker en weaker all de time.

"'Brer Pete,' sezee, bimeby, 'gimme a drink er dem bitters out'n dat green bottle on de she'f yander. I's gwine fas', en it'll gimme strenk fer ter finish dis wuk.'

"Brer Pete look' up on de mantel-piece, en he seed a bottle in de corner. It was so da'k in de cabin he couldn' tell whe'r it wuz a green bottle er no. But he hilt de bottle ter de cunjuh man's mouf, en he tuk a big mouff'l. He hadn' mo' d'n swallowed it befo' he 'mence' ter holler.

"'You gimme de wrong bottle, Brer Pete; dis yer bottl 's got pizen in it, en I's done fer dis time, sho'. Hol' me up, fer de Lawd's sake! 'tel I git th'oo turnin' Brer Primus back.'

"So Pete hilt him up, en he kep' on wukkin' de roots, 'tel he got de goopher all tuk off'n Brer Primus 'cep'n' one foot. He hadn' got dis foot mo' d'n half turnt back befo' his strenk gun out enti'ely, en he drap' de roots en fell back on de bed.

"'I can't do no mo' fer you, Brer Primus,' sezee, 'but I hopes you will fergib me fer w'at harm I done you. I knows de good Lawd done fergib me, en I hope ter meet you bofe in glory. I sees de good angels waitin' fer me up yander, wid a long w'ite robe en a starry crown, en I'm on my way ter jine 'em.' En so de cunjuh man died, en Pete en Primus went back ter de plantation.

"De darkies all made a great 'miration w'en Primus come back. Mars Jim let on lack he didn' b'lieve de tale de two niggers tol'; he sez Primus had runned erway, en stay' 'tel he got ti'ed er de swamps, en den come back on him ter be fed. He tried ter 'count fer de shape er Primus' foot by sayin' Primus got his foot smash', er snake-bit, er sump'n, w'iles he wuz erway, en den stayed out in de woods whar he couldn' git it kyoed up straight, 'stidder comin' long home whar a doctor could 'a' 'tended ter it. But de niggers all notice' dey marster didn' tie Primus up, ner take on much 'ca'se de mule wuz gone. So dey 'lowed dey marster must 'a' had his s'picions 'bout dat cunjuh man."

My wife had listened to Julius's recital with only a mild interest. When the old man had finished it she remarked:—

"That story does not appeal to me, Uncle Julius, and is not up to your usual mark. It isn't pathetic, it has no moral that I can discover, and I can't see why you should tell it. In fact, it seems to me like nonsense."

The old man looked puzzled as well as pained. He had not pleased the lady, and he did not seem to understand why.

"I'm sorry, ma'm," he said reproachfully, "ef you doan lack dat tale. I can't make out w'at you means by some er dem wo'ds you uses, but I'm tellin' nuffin but de truf. Co'se I didn' see de cunjuh man tu'n 'im back, fer I wuzn' dere; but I be'n hearin' de tale fer twenty-five yeahs, en I ain' got no 'casion fer ter 'spute it. Dey's so many things a body knows is lies, dat dey ain' no use gwine roun' findin' fault wid tales dat mought des ez well be so ez not. F' instance, dey's a young nigger gwine ter school in town, en he come out heah de yuther day en 'lowed dat de sun stood still en de yeath turnt roun' eve'y day on a kinder axletree. I tol' dat young nigger ef he didn' take hisse'f 'way wid dem lies, I'd take a buggy-trace ter 'im; fer I sees de yeath stan'in' still all de time, en I sees de sun gwine roun' it, en ef a man can't b'lieve w'at 'e sees, I can't see no use in libbin'— mought 's well die en be whar we can't see nuffin. En ernudder thing w'at proves de tale 'bout dis ole Primus is de way he goes on ef anybody ax' him how he come by dat club-foot. I axed 'im one day, mighty perlite en civil, en he call' me a' ole fool, en got so mad he ain' spoke ter me sence. Hit's monst'us quare. But dis is a quare worl', anyway yer kin fix it," concluded the old man, with a weary sigh.

"Ef you makes up yo' min' not ter buy dat mule, suh," he added, as he rose to go, "I knows a man w'at's got a good hoss he wants ter sell,—leas'ways dat's w'at I heared. I'm gwine ter pra'rmeetin' ter-night, en I'm gwine right by de man's house, en ef you'd lack ter look at de hoss, I'll ax 'im ter fetch him roun'."

"Oh, yes," I said, "you can ask him to stop in, if he is passing. There will be no harm in looking at the horse, though I rather think I shall buy a mule."

Early next morning the man brought the horse up to the vineyard. At that time I was not a very good judge of horse-flesh. The horse appeared sound and gentle, and, as the owner assured me, had no bad habits. The man wanted a large price for the horse, but finally agreed to accept a much smaller sum, upon payment of which I became possessed of a very fine-looking animal. But alas for the deceitfulness of appearances! I soon ascertained that the horse was blind in one eye, and that the sight of the other was very defective; and not a month elapsed before my purchase developed most of the diseases that horse-flesh is heir to, and a more worthless, broken-winded, spavined quadruped never disgraced the noble name of horse. After worrying through two or three months of life, he expired one night in a fit of the colic. I replaced him with a mule, and Julius henceforth had to take his chances of driving some metamorphosed unfortunate.

Circumstances that afterwards came to my knowledge created in my mind a strong suspicion that Julius may have played a more than unconscious part in this transaction. Among other significant facts was his appearance, the Sunday following the purchase of the horse, in a new suit of store clothes, which I had seen displayed in the window of Mr. Solomon Cohen's store on my last visit to town, and had remarked on account of their striking originality of cut and pattern. As I had not recently paid Julius any money, and as he had no property to mortgage, I was driven to conjecture to account for his possession of the means to buy the clothes. Of course I would not charge him with duplicity unless I could prove it, at least to a moral certainty, but for a long time afterwards I took his advice only in small doses and with great discrimination.

SIS' BECKY'S PICKANINNY

We had not lived in North Carolina very long before I was able to note a marked improvement in my wife's health. The ozone-laden air of the surrounding piney woods, the mild and equable climate, the peaceful leisure of country life, had brought about in hopeful measure the cure we had anticipated. Toward the end of our second year, however, her ailment took an unexpected turn for the worse. She became the victim of a settled melancholy, attended with vague forebodings of impending misfortune.

"You must keep up her spirits," said our physician, the best in the neighboring town. "This melancholy lowers her tone too much, tends to lessen her strength, and, if it continue too long, may be fraught with grave consequences."

I tried various expedients to cheer her up. I read novels to her. I had the hands on the place come up in the evening and serenade her with plantation songs. Friends came in sometimes and talked, and frequent letters from the North kept her in touch with her former home. But nothing seemed to rouse her from the depression into which she had fallen.

One pleasant afternoon in spring, I placed an armchair in a shaded portion of the front piazza, and filling it with pillows led my wife out of the house and seated her where she would have the pleasantest view of a somewhat monotonous scenery. She was scarcely placed when old Julius came through the yard, and, taking off his tattered straw hat, inquired, somewhat anxiously:—

"How is you feelin' dis afternoon, ma'm?"

"She is not very cheerful, Julius," I said. My wife was apparently without energy enough to speak for herself.

The old man did not seem inclined to go away, so I asked him to sit down. I had noticed, as he came up, that he held some small object in his hand. When he had taken his seat on the top step, he kept fingering this object,—what it was I could not quite make out.

"What is that you have there, Julius?" I asked, with mild curiosity.

"Dis is my rabbit foot, suh."

This was at a time before this curious superstition had attained its present jocular popularity among white people, and while I had heard of it before, it had not yet outgrown the charm of novelty.

"What do you do with it?"

"I kyars it wid me fer luck, suh."

"Julius," I observed, half to him and half to my wife, "your people will never rise in the world until they throw off these childish superstitions and learn to live by the light of reason and common sense. How absurd to imagine that the fore-foot of a poor dead rabbit, with which he timorously felt his way along through a life surrounded by snares and pitfalls, beset by enemies on every hand, can promote happiness or success, or ward off failure or misfortune!"

"It is ridiculous," assented my wife, with faint interest.

"Dat's w'at I tells dese niggers roun' heah," said Julius. "De fo'-foot ain' got no power. It has ter be de hin'-foot, suh,—de lef' hin'-foot er a grabe-ya'd rabbit, killt by a cross-eyed nigger on a da'k night in de full er de moon."

"They must be very rare and valuable," I said.

"Dey is kinder ska'ce, suh, en dey ain' no 'mount er money could buy mine, suh. I mought len' it ter anybody I sot sto' by, but I wouldn' sell it, no indeed, suh, I wouldn'."

"How do you know it brings good luck?" I asked.

"'Ca'se I ain' had no bad luck sence I had it, suh, en I's had dis rabbit foot fer fo'ty yeahs. I had a good marster befo' de wah, en I wa'n't sol' erway, en I wuz sot free; en dat 'uz all good luck."

"But that doesn't prove anything," I rejoined. "Many other

people have gone through a similar experience, and probably more than one of them had no rabbit's foot."

"Law, suh! you doan hafter prove 'bout-de rabbit foot! Eve'y-body knows dat; leas'ways eve'ybody roun' heah knows it. But ef it has ter be prove' ter folks w'at wa'n't bawn en raise' in dis naberhood, dey is a' easy way ter prove it. Is I eber tol' you de tale er Sis' Becky en her pickaninny?"

"No," I said, "let us hear it." I thought perhaps the story might interest my wife as much or more than the novel I had meant to read from.

"Dis yer Becky," Julius began, "useter b'long ter ole Kunnel Pen'leton, who owned a plantation down on de Wim'l'ton Road, 'bout ten miles fum heah, des befo' you gits ter Black Swamp. Dis yer Becky wuz a fiel'-han', en a monst'us good 'un. She had a husban' oncet, a nigger w'at b'longed on de nex' plantation, but de man w'at owned her husban' died, en his lan' en his niggers had ter be sol' fer ter pay his debts. Kunnel Pen'leton 'lowed he'd 'a' bought dis nigger, but he had be'n bettin' on hoss races, en didn' hab no money, en so Becky's husban' wuz sol' erway ter Fuhginny.

"Co'se Becky went on some 'bout losin' her man, but she couldn' he'p herse'f; en 'sides dat, she had her pickaninny fer ter comfo't her. Dis yer little Mose wuz de cutes', blackes', shiny-eyedes' little nigger you eber laid eyes on, en he wuz ez fon' er his mammy ez his mammy wuz er him. Co'se Becky had ter wuk en didn' hab much time ter was'e wid her baby. Ole Aun' Nancy, de plantation nuss down at de qua'ters, useter take keer er little Mose in de daytime, en atter de niggers come in fum de cotton-fiel' Becky 'ud git her chile en kiss 'im en nuss 'im, en keep 'im 'tel mawnin'; en on Sundays she'd hab 'im in her cabin wid her all day long.

"Sis' Becky had got sorter useter gittin' 'long widout her hus-ban', w'en one day Kunnel Pen'leton went ter de races. Co'se w'en he went ter de races, he tuk his hosses, en co'se he bet on 'is own hosses, en co'se he los' his money; fer Kunnel Pen'leton didn' nebber hab no luck wid his hosses, ef he did keep hisse'f po' projeckin' wid 'em. But dis time dey wuz a hoss name' Light-nin' Bug, w'at b'longed ter ernudder man, en dis hoss won de sweep-stakes; en Kunnel Pen'leton tuk a lackin' ter dat hoss, en ax' his owner w'at he wuz willin' ter take fer 'im.

"'I'll take a thousan' dollahs fer dat hoss,' sez dis yer man, who had a big plantation down to'ds Wim'l'ton, whar he raise' hosses fer ter race en ter sell.

"Well, Kunnel Pen'leton scratch' 'is head, en wonder whar he wuz gwine ter raise a thousan' dollahs; en he didn' see des how he could do it, fer he owed ez much ez he could borry a'ready on de skyo'ity he could gib. But he wuz des boun' ter hab dat hoss, so sezee:—

"'I'll gib you my note fer 'leven hund'ed dollahs fer dat hoss.'

"De yuther man shuck 'is head, en sezee:—

"'Yo' note, suh, is better 'n gol', I doan doubt; but I is made it a rule in my bizness not ter take no notes fum nobody. Howsomeber, suh, ef you is kinder sho't er fun's, mos' lackly we kin make some kin' er bahg'in. En w'iles we is talkin', I mought's well say dat I needs ernudder good nigger down on my place. Ef you is got a good one ter spar', I mought trade wid you.'

"Now, Kunnel Pen'leton didn' r'ally hab no niggers fer ter spar', but he 'lowed ter hisse'f he wuz des bleedzd ter hab dat hoss, en so he sez, sezee:—

"'Well, I doan lack ter, but I reckon I'll haf ter. You come out ter my plantation ter-morrer en look ober my niggers, en pick out de one you wants.'

"So sho' 'nuff nex' day dis yer man come out ter Kunnel Pen'leton's place en rid roun' de plantation en glanshed at de niggers, en who sh'd he pick out fum 'em all but Sis' Becky.

"'I needs a noo nigger 'oman down ter my place,' sezee, 'fer ter cook en wash, en so on; en dat young 'oman'll des fill de bill. You gimme her, en you kin hab Lightnin' Bug.'"

"Now, Kunnel Pen'leton didn' lack ter trade Sis' Becky, 'ca'se she wuz nigh 'bout de bes' fiel'-han' he had; en 'sides, Mars Dugal' didn' keer ter take de mammies 'way fum dey chillun w'iles de chillun wuz little. But dis man say he want Becky, er e'se Kunnel Pen'leton couldn' hab de race hoss.

"'Well,' sez de kunnel, 'you kin hab de 'oman. But I doan lack ter sen' her 'way fum her baby. W'at'll you gimme fer dat nigger baby?'

"'I doan want de baby,' sez de yuther man. 'I ain' got no use fer de baby.'

"'I tell yer w'at I'll do,' 'lows Kunnel Pen'leton, 'I'll th'ow dat pickaninny in fer good measure.'

"But de yuther man shuck his head. 'No,' sezee, 'I's much erbleedzd, but I doan raise niggers; I raises hosses, en I doan wanter be both'rin' wid no nigger babies. Nemmine de baby. I'll keep dat 'oman so busy she'll fergit de baby; fer niggers is made ter wuk, en dey ain' got no time fer no sich foolis'ness ez babies.'

"Kunnel Pen'leton didn' wanter hu't Becky's feelin's,—fer Kunnel Pen'leton wuz a kin'-hea'ted man, en nebber lack' ter make no trouble fer nobody,—en so he tol' Becky he wuz gwine sen' her down ter Robeson County fer a day er so, ter he'p out his son-in-law in his wuk; en bein' ez dis yuther man wuz gwine dat way, he had ax' 'im ter take her 'long in his buggy.

"'Kin I kyar little Mose wid me, marster?' ax' Sis' Becky.

"'N-o,' sez de kunnel, ez ef he wuz studyin' whuther ter let her take 'im er no; 'I reckon you better let Aun' Nancy look atter yo' baby fer de day er two you'll be gone, en she'll see dat he gits ernuff ter eat 'tel you gits back.'

"So Sis' Becky hug' en kiss' little Mose, en tol' 'im ter be a good little pickaninny, en take keer er hisse'f, en not fergit his mammy w'iles she wuz gone. En little Mose put his arms roun' his mammy en lafft en crowed des lack it wuz monst'us fine fun fer his mammy ter go 'way en leabe 'im.

"Well, dis yer hoss trader sta'ted out wid Becky, en bimeby, atter dey'd gone down de Lumbe'ton Road fer a few miles er so, dis man tu'nt roun' in a diffe'nt d'rection, en kep' goin' dat erway, 'tel bimeby Sis' Becky up 'n ax' 'im ef he wuz gwine ter Robeson County by a noo road.

"'No, nigger,' sezee, 'I ain' gwine ter Robeson County at all. I's gwine ter Bladen County, whar my plantation is, en whar I raises all my hosses.'

"'But how is I gwine ter git ter Mis' Laura's plantation down in Robeson County?' sez Becky, wid her hea't in her mouf, fer she 'mence' ter git skeered all er a sudden.

"'You ain' gwine ter git dere at all,' sez de man. 'You b'longs ter me now, fer I done traded my bes' race hoss fer you, wid yo' ole marster. Ef you is a good gal, I'll treat you right, en ef you doan behabe yo'se'f,—w'y, w'at e'se happens'll be yo' own fault.'

"Co'se Sis' Becky cried en went on 'bout her pickaninny, but co'se it didn' do no good, en bimeby dey got down ter dis yer man's place, en he put Sis' Becky ter wuk, en fergot all 'bout her habin' a pickaninny.

"Meanw'iles, w'en ebenin' come, de day Sis' Becky wuz tuk 'way, little Mose 'mence' ter git res'less, en bimeby, w'en his mammy didn' come, he sta'ted ter cry fer 'er. Aun' Nancy fed 'im en rocked 'im en rocked 'im, en fin'lly he des cried en cried 'tel he cried hisse'f ter sleep.

"De nex' day he didn' 'pear ter be as peart ez yushal, en w'en night come he fretted en went on wuss 'n he did de night befo'. De nex' day his little eyes 'mence' ter lose dey shine, en he wouldn' eat nuffin, en he 'mence' ter look so peaked dat Aun' Nancy tuk 'n kyared 'im up ter de big house, en showed 'im ter her ole missis, en her ole missis gun her some med'cine fer 'im, en 'lowed ef he didn' git no better she sh'd fetch 'im up ter de big house ag'in, en dey'd hab a doctor, en nuss little Mose up dere. Fer Aun' Nancy's ole missis 'lowed he wuz a lackly little nigger en wu'th raisin'.

"But Aun' Nancy had l'arn' ter lack little Mose, en she didn' wanter hab 'im tuk up ter de big house. En so w'en he didn' git no better, she gethered a mess er green peas, and tuk de peas en de baby, en went ter see ole Aun' Peggy, de cunjuh 'oman down by de Wim'l'ton Road. She gun Aun' Peggy de mess er peas, en tol' her all 'bout Sis' Becky en little Mose.

"'Dat is a monst'us small mess er peas you is fotch' me,' sez Aun' Peggy, sez she.

"'Yas, I knows,' 'lowed Aun' Nancy, 'but dis yere is a monst'us small pickaninny.'

"'You'll hafter fetch me sump'n mo',' sez Aun' Peggy, 'fer you can't 'spec' me ter was'e my time diggin' roots en wukkin' cunj'ation fer nuffin.'

"'All right,' sez Aun' Nancy, 'I'll fetch you sump'n mo' nex' time.'

"'You bettah,' sez Aun' Peggy, 'er e'se dey'll be trouble. W'at dis yer little pickaninny needs is ter see his mammy. You leabe 'im heah 'tel ebenin' en I'll show 'im his mammy.'

"So w'en Aun' Nancy had gone 'way, Aun' Peggy tuk 'n wukked her roots, en tu'nt little Mose ter a hummin'-bird, en sont 'im off fer ter fin' his mammy.

"So little Mose flewed, en flewed, en flewed away, 'tel bimeby he got ter de place whar Sis' Becky b'longed. He seed his mammy wukkin' roun' de ya'd, en he could tell fum lookin' at her dat she wuz trouble' in her min' 'bout sump'n, en feelin' kin' er po'ly. Sis' Becky heared sump'n hummin' roun' en roun' her, sweet en low. Fus' she 'lowed it wuz a hummin'-bird; den she thought it sounded lack her little Mose croonin' on her breas' way back yander on de ole plantation. En she des 'magine' it wuz her little Mose, en it made her feel bettah, en she went on 'bout her wuk pearter 'n she'd done sence she'd be'n down dere. Little Mose stayed roun' 'tel late in de ebenin', en den flewed back ez hard ez he could ter Aun' Peggy. Ez fer Sis' Becky, she dremp all dat night dat she wuz holdin' her pickaninny in her arms, en kissin' him, en nussin' him, des lack she useter do back on de ole plantation whar he wuz bawn. En fer th'ee er fo' days Sis' Becky went 'bout her wuk wid mo' sperrit dan she'd showed sence she'd be'n down dere ter dis man's plantation.

"De nex' day atter he come back, little Mose wuz mo' pearter en better 'n he had be'n fer a long time. But to'ds de een' er de week he 'mence' ter git res'less ag'in, en stop' eatin', en Aun' Nancy kyared 'im down ter Aun' Peggy once mo', en she tu'nt 'im ter a mawkin'-bird dis time, en sont 'im off ter see his mammy ag'in.

"It didn' take him long fer ter git dere, en w'en he did, he seed his mammy standin' in de kitchen, lookin' back in de d'rection little Mose wuz comin' fum. En dey wuz tears in her eyes, en she look' mo' po'ly en peaked 'n she had w'en he wuz down dere befo'. So little Mose sot on a tree in de ya'd en sung, en sung, en sung, des fittin' ter split his th'oat. Fus' Sis' Becky didn' notice 'im much, but dis mawkin'-bird kep' stayin' roun' de house all day, en bimeby Sis' Becky des 'magine' dat mawkin'-bird wuz her little Mose crowin' en crowin', des lack he useter do w'en his mammy would come home at night fum de cotton-fiel'. De mawkin'-bird stayed roun' dere 'mos' all day, en w'en Sis' Becky went out in de ya'd one time, dis yer mawkin'-bird lit on her shoulder en peck' at de piece er bread she wuz eatin', en fluttered his wings so dey rub' up agin de side er her head. En w'en he flewed away 'long late in de ebenin', des 'fo' sundown, Sis' Becky felt mo' better 'n she had sence she had heared dat hummin'-bird a week er so pas'. En dat night she dremp 'bout ole times ag'in, des lack she did befo'.

"But dis yer totin' little Mose down ter ole Aun' Peggy, en dis yer gittin' things fer ter pay de cunjuh 'oman, use' up a lot er

Aun' Nancy's time, en she begun ter git kinder ti'ed. 'Sides dat, w'en Sis' Becky had be'n on de plantation, she had useter he'p Aun' Nancy wid de young uns ebenin's en Sundays; en Aun' Nancy 'mence' ter miss 'er monst'us, 'speshly sence she got a tech er de rheumatiz herse'f, en so she 'lows ter ole Aun' Peggy one day:—

" 'Aun' Peggy, ain' dey no way you kin fetch Sis' Becky back home?'

" 'Huh!' sez Aun' Peggy, 'I dunno 'bout dat. I'll hafter wuk my roots en fin' out whuther I kin er no. But it'll take a monst'us heap er wuk, en I can't was'e my time fer nuffin. Ef you'll fetch me sump'n ter pay me fer my trouble, I reckon we kin fix it.'

"So nex' day Aun' Nancy went down ter see Aun' Peggy ag'in.

" 'Aun' Peggy,' sez she, 'I is fotch' you my bes' Sunday head-hankercher. Will dat do?'

"Aun' Peggy look' at de head-hankercher, en run her han' ober it, en sez she:—

" 'Yas, dat'll do fus'-rate. I's be'n wukkin' my roots sence you be'n gone, en I 'lows mos' lackly I kin git Sis' Becky back, but it's gwine take fig'rin' en studyin' ez well ez cunj'in'. De fus' thing ter do'll be ter stop fetchin' dat pickaninny down heah, en not sen' 'im ter see his mammy no mo'. Ef he gits too po'ly, you lemme know, en I'll gib you some kin' er mixtry fer ter make 'im fergit Sis' Becky fer a week er so. So 'less'n you comes fer dat, you neenter come back ter see me no mo' 'tel I sen's fer you.'

"So Aun' Peggy sont Aun' Nancy erway, en de fus' thing she done wuz ter call a hawnet fum a nes' unner her eaves.

" 'You go up ter Kunnel Pen'leton's stable, hawnet,' sez she, 'en sting de knees er de race hoss name' Lightnin' Bug. Be sho' en git de right one.'

"So de hawnet flewed up ter Kunnel Pen'leton's stable en stung Lightnin' Bug roun' de laigs, en de nex' mawnin' Lightnin' Bug's knees wuz all swoll' up, twice't ez big ez dey oughter be. W'en Kunnel Pen'leton went out ter de stable en see de hoss's laigs, hit would 'a' des made you trimble lack a leaf fer ter heah him cuss dat hoss trader. Howsomeber, he cool' off bimeby en tol' de stable boy fer ter rub Lightnin' Bug's laigs wid some lini-mum. De boy done ez his marster tol' 'im, en by de nex' day de swellin' had gone down consid'able. Aun' Peggy had sont a sparrer, w'at had a nes' in one er de trees close ter her cabin, fer ter watch w'at wuz gwine on 'roun' de big house, en w'en dis yer sparrer tol' 'er de hoss wuz gittin' ober de swellin', she sont de hawnet back fer ter sting 'is knees some mo', en de nex' mawnin' Lightnin' Bug's laigs wuz swoll' up wuss 'n befo'.

"Well, dis time Kunnel Pen'leton wuz mad th'oo en th'oo, en all de way 'roun', en he cusst dat hoss trader up en down, fum *A* ter *Izzard.* He cusst so ha'd dat de stable boy got mos' skeered ter def, en went off en hid hisse'f in de hay.

"Ez fer Kunnel Pen'leton, he went right up ter de house en got out his pen en ink, en tuk off his coat en roll' up his sleeves, en writ a letter ter dis yer hoss trader, en sezee:—

"'You is sol' me a hoss w'at is got a ringbone er a spavin er sump'n, en w'at I paid you fer wuz a soun' hoss. I wants you ter sen' my nigger 'oman back en take yo' ole hoss, er e'se I'll sue you, sho's you bawn.'

"But dis yer man wa'n't skeered a bit, en he writ back ter Kunnel Pen'leton dat a bahg'in wuz a bahg'in; dat Lightnin' Bug wuz soun' w'en he sol' 'im, en ef Kunnel Pen'leton didn' knowed ernuff 'bout hosses ter take keer er a fine racer, dat wuz his own fune'al. En he say Kunnel Pen'leton kin sue en be cusst fer all he keer, but he ain' gwine ter gib up de nigger he bought en paid fer.

"W'en Kunnel Pen'leton got dis letter he wuz madder 'n he wuz befo', 'speshly 'ca'se dis man 'lowed he didn' know how ter take keer er fine hosses. But he couldn' do nuffin but fetch a lawsuit, en he knowed, by his own 'spe'ience, dat lawsuits wuz slow ez de seben-yeah eetch and cos' mo' d'n dey come ter, en he 'lowed he better go slow en wait awhile.

"Aun' Peggy knowed w'at wuz gwine on all dis time, en she fix' up a little bag wid some roots en one thing en ernudder in it, en gun it ter dis sparrer er her'n, en tol' 'im ter take it 'way down yander whar Sis' Becky wuz, en drap it right befo' de do' er her cabin, so she'd be sho' en fin' it de fus' time she come out'n de do'.

"One night Sis' Becky dremp' her pickaninny wuz dead, en de nex' day she wuz mo'nin' en groanin' all day. She dremp' de same dream th'ee nights runnin', en den, de nex' mawnin' atter de las' night, she foun' dis yer little bag de sparrer had drap' in front her do'; en she 'lowed she'd be'n cunju'd, en wuz gwine ter die, en ez long ez her pickaninny wuz dead dey wa'n't no use tryin' ter do nuffin nohow. En so she tuk 'n went ter bed, en tol' her marster she'd be'n cunju'd en wuz gwine ter die.

"Her marster lafft at her, en argyed wid her, en tried ter 'suade her out'n dis yer fool notion, ez he called it,—fer he wuz one er dese yer w'ite folks w'at purten' dey doan b'liebe in cunj'in',—but hit wa'n't no use. Sis' Becky kep' gittin' wusser en wusser, 'tel fin'lly dis yer man 'lowed Sis' Becky wuz gwine ter die, sho' 'nuff. En ez he knowed dey hadn' be'n nuffin de matter wid Lightnin' Bug w'en he traded 'im, he 'lowed mebbe he could kyo' 'im en fetch 'im roun' all right, leas'ways good 'nuff ter sell ag'in. En anyhow, a lame hoss wuz better 'n a dead nigger. So he sot down en writ Kunnel Pen'leton a letter.

"'My conscience,' sezee, 'has be'n troublin' me 'bout dat ringbone' hoss I sol' you. Some folks 'lows a hoss trader ain' got no conscience, but dey doan know me, fer dat is my weak spot, en de reason I ain' made no mo' money hoss tradin'. Fac' is,' sezee, 'I is got so I can't sleep nights fum studyin' 'bout dat spavin' hoss; en I is made up my min' dat, w'iles a bahg'in is a bahg'in, en you seed Lightnin' Bug befo' you traded fer 'im, principle is wuth mo' d'n money er hosses er niggers. So ef you'll sen' Lightnin' Bug down heah, I'll sen' yo' nigger 'oman back, en we'll call de trade off, en be ez good frien's ez we eber wuz, en no ha'd feelin's.'

"So sho' 'nuff, Kunnel Pen'leton sont de hoss back. En w'en de man w'at come ter bring Lightnin' Bug tol' Sis' Becky her pickaninny wa'n't dead, Sis' Becky wuz so glad dat she 'lowed she wuz gwine ter try ter lib 'tel she got back whar she could see little Mose once mo'. En w'en she retch' de ole plantation en seed her baby kickin' en crowin' en holdin' out his little arms to'ds her, she wush' she wuzn' cunju'd en didn' hafter die. En w'en Aun' Nancy tol' 'er all 'bout Aun' Peggy, Sis' Becky went down ter see de cunjuh 'oman, en Aun' Peggy tol' her she had cunju'd her. En den Aun' Peggy tuk de goopher off'n her, en she got well, en stayed on de plantation, en raise' her pickaninny. En w'en little Mose growed up, he could sing en whistle des lack a mawkin'-bird, so dat de w'ite folks useter hab 'im come up ter de big house at night, en whistle en sing fer 'em, en dey useter gib 'im money en vittles en one thing er ernudder, w'ich he alluz tuk home ter his mammy; fer he knowed all 'bout w'at she had gone th'oo. He tu'nt out ter be a sma't man, en l'arnt de blacksmif trade; en Kunnel Pen'leton let 'im hire his time. En bimeby he bought his mammy en sot her free, en den he bought hisse'f, en tuk keer er Sis' Becky ez long ez dey bofe libbed."

My wife had listened to this story with greater interest than she had manifested in any subject for several days. I had watched her furtively from time to time during the recital, and had observed the play of her countenance. It had expressed in turn sympathy, indignation, pity, and at the end lively satisfaction.

"That is a very ingenious fairy tale, Julius," I said, "and we are much obliged to you."

"Why, John!" said my wife severely, "the story bears the stamp of truth, if ever a story did."

"Yes," I replied, "especially the humming-bird episode, and the mocking-bird digression, to say nothing of the doings of the hornet and the sparrow."

"Oh, well, I don't care," she rejoined, with delightful animation; "those are mere ornamental details and not at all essential. The story is true to nature, and might have happened half a hundred times, and no doubt did happen, in those horrid days before the war."

"By the way, Julius," I remarked, "your story doesn't establish what you started out to prove,—that a rabbit's foot brings good luck."

"Hit's plain 'nuff ter me, suh," replied Julius. "I bet young missis dere kin 'splain it herse'f."

"I rather suspect," replied my wife promptly, "that Sis' Becky had no rabbit's foot."

"You is hit de bull's-eye de fus' fire, ma'm," assented Julius. "Ef Sis' Becky had had a rabbit foot, she nebber would 'a' went th'oo all dis trouble."

I went into the house for some purpose, and left Julius talking to my wife. When I came back a moment later, he was gone.

My wife's condition took a turn for the better from this very day, and she was soon on the way to ultimate recovery. Several weeks later, after she had resumed her afternoon drives, which had been interrupted by her illness, Julius brought the rockaway round to the front door one day, and I assisted my wife into the carriage.

"John," she said, before I had taken my seat, "I wish you would look in my room, and bring me my handkerchief. You will find it in the pocket of my blue dress."

I went to execute the commission. When I pulled the handkerchief out of her pocket, something else came with it and fell on the floor. I picked up the object and looked at it. It was Julius's rabbit's foot.

THE GRAY WOLF'S HA'NT

It was a rainy day at the vineyard. The morning had dawned bright and clear. But the sky had soon clouded, and by nine o'clock there was a light shower, followed by others at brief intervals. By noon the rain had settled into a dull, steady downpour. The clouds hung low, and seemed to grow denser instead of lighter as they discharged their watery burden, and there was now and then a muttering of distant thunder. Outdoor work was suspended, and I spent most of the day at the house, looking over my accounts and bringing up some arrears of correspondence.

Towards four o'clock I went out on the piazza, which was broad and dry, and less gloomy than the interior of the house, and composed myself for a quiet smoke. I had lit my cigar and opened the volume I was reading at that time, when my wife, whom I had left dozing on a lounge, came out and took a rocking-chair near me.

"I wish you would talk to me, or read to me—or something," she exclaimed petulantly. "It's awfully dull here today."

"I'll read to you with pleasure," I replied, and began at the point where I had found my bookmark:—

"'The difficulty of dealing with transformations so many-sided as those which all existences have undergone, or are undergoing, is such as to make a complete and deductive interpretation almost hopeless. So to grasp the total process of redistribution of matter and motion as to see simultaneously its several necessary results in their actual interdependence is scarcely possible. There is, however, a mode of rendering the process as a whole tolerably comprehensible. Though the genesis of the rearrangement of every evolving aggregate is in itself one, it presents to our intelligence'"—

"John," interrupted my wife, "I wish you would stop reading that nonsense and see who that is coming up the lane."

I closed my book with a sigh. I had never been able to interest my wife in the study of philosophy, even when presented in the simplest and most lucid form.

Some one was coming up the lane; at least, a huge faded cotton umbrella was making progress toward the house, and beneath it a pair of nether extremities in trousers was discernible. Any doubt in my mind as to whose they were was soon resolved when Julius reached the steps and, putting the umbrella down, got a good dash of the rain as he stepped up on the porch.

"Why in the world, Julius," I asked, "didn't you keep the umbrella up until you got under cover?"

"It's bad luck, suh, ter raise a' umbrella in de house, en w'iles I dunno whuther it's bad luck ter kyar one inter de piazzer er no, I 'lows it's alluz bes' ter be on de safe side. I didn' s'pose you en young missis 'u'd be gwine on yo' dribe ter-day, but bein' ez it's my pa't ter take you ef you does, I 'lowed I'd repo't fer dooty, en let you say whuther er no you wants ter go."

"I'm glad you came, Julius," I responded. "We don't want to go driving, of course, in the rain, but I should like to consult you about another matter. I'm thinking of taking in a piece of new ground. What do you imagine it would cost to have that neck of woods down by the swamp cleared up?"

The old man's countenance assumed an expression of unwonted seriousness, and he shook his head doubtfully.

"I dunno 'bout dat, suh. It mought cos' mo', en it mought cos' less, ez fuh ez money is consarned. I ain' denyin' you could cl'ar up dat trac' er lan' fer a hund'ed er a couple er hund'ed dollahs,—ef you wants ter cl'ar it up. But ef dat 'uz my trac' er lan', I wouldn' 'sturb it, no, suh, I wouldn'; sho's you bawn, I wouldn'."

"But why not?" I asked.

"It ain' fittin' fer grapes, fer noo groun' nebber is."

"I know it, but"—

"It ain' no yeathly good fer cotton, 'ca'se it's too low."

"Perhaps so; but it will raise splendid corn."

"I dunno," rejoined Julius deprecatorily. "It's so nigh de swamp dat de 'coons'll eat up all de cawn."

"I think I'll risk it," I answered.

"Well, suh," said Julius, "I wushes you much joy er yo' job. Ef you has bad luck er sickness er trouble er any kin', doan blame *me*. You can't say ole Julius didn' wa'n you."

"Warn him of what, Uncle Julius?" asked my wife.

"Er de bad luck w'at follers folks w'at 'sturbs dat trac' er lan'. Dey is snakes en sco'pions in dem woods. En ef you manages ter 'scape de p'isen animals, you is des boun' ter hab a ha'nt ter settle wid,—ef you doan hab two."

"Whose haunt?" my wife demanded, with growing interest.

"De gray wolf's ha'nt, some folks calls it,—but I knows better."

"Tell us about it, Uncle Julius," said my wife. "A story will be a godsend to-day."

It was not difficult to induce the old man to tell a story, if he were in a reminiscent mood. Of tales of the old slavery days he seemed indeed to possess an exhaustless store,—some weirdly grotesque, some broadly humorous; some bearing the stamp of truth, faint, perhaps, but still discernible; others palpable inventions, whether his own or not we never knew, though his fancy doubtless embellished them. But even the wildest was not without an element of pathos,—the tragedy, it might be, of the story itself; the shadow, never absent, of slavery and of ignorance; the sadness, always, of life as seen by the fading light of an old man's memory.

"Way back yander befo' de wah," began Julius, "ole Mars Dugal' McAdoo useter own a nigger name' Dan. Dan wuz big en strong en hearty en peaceable en good-nachu'd most er de time, but dange'ous ter aggervate. He alluz done his task, en nebber had no trouble wid de w'ite folks, but woe be unter de nigger w'at 'lowed he c'd fool wid Dan, fer he wuz mos' sho' ter git a good lammin'. Soon ez eve'ybody foun' Dan out, dey didn' many un 'em 'temp' ter 'sturb 'im. De one dat did would 'a' wush' he hadn', ef he could 'a' libbed long ernuff ter do any wushin'.

"It all happen' dis erway. Dey wuz a cunjuh man w'at libbed ober t' other side er de Lumbe'ton Road. He had be'n de only cunjuh doctor in de naberhood fer lo! dese many yeahs, 'tel ole Aun' Peggy sot up in de bizness down by de Wim'l'ton Road. Dis cunjuh man had a son w'at libbed wid 'im, en it wuz dis yer son w'at got mix' up wid Dan,—en all 'bout a 'oman.

"Dey wuz a gal on de plantation name' Mahaly. She wuz a monst'us lackly gal,—tall en soopl', wid big eyes, en a small foot, en a lively tongue, en w'en Dan tuk ter gwine wid 'er eve'ybody 'lowed dey wuz well match', en none er de yuther nigger men on de plantation das' ter go nigh her, fer dey wuz all feared er Dan.

"Now, it happen' dat dis yer cunjuh man's son wuz gwine 'long de road one day, w'en who sh'd come pas' but Mahaly. En de minute dis man sot eyes on Mahaly, he 'lowed he wuz gwine ter hab her fer hisse'f. He come up side er her en 'mence' ter talk ter her; but she didn' paid no 'tention ter 'im, fer she wuz studyin' 'bout Dan, en she did n' lack dis nigger's looks nohow. So w'en she got ter whar she wuz gwine, dis yer man wa'n't no fu'ther 'long dan he wuz w'en he sta'ted.

"Co'se, atter he had made up his min' fer ter git Mahaly, he 'mence' ter 'quire 'roun', en soon foun' out all 'bout Dan, en w'at a dange'ous nigger he wuz. But dis man 'lowed his daddy wuz a cunjuh man, en so he'd come out all right in de een'; en he kep' right on atter Mahaly. Meanw'iles Dan's marster had said dey could git married ef dey wanter, en so Dan en Mahaly had tuk up wid one ernudder, en wuz libbin' in a cabin by deyse'ves, en wuz des wrop' up in one ernudder.

"But dis yer cunjuh man's son didn' 'pear ter min' Dan's takin' up wid Mahaly, en he kep' on hangin' 'roun' des de same, 'tel fin'lly one day Mahaly sez ter Dan, sez she:—

" 'I wush you'd do sump'n ter stop dat free nigger man fum follerin' me 'roun'. I doan lack him nohow, en I ain' got no time fer ter was'e wid no man but you.'

"Co'se Dan got mad w'en he heared 'bout dis man pest'rin' Mahaly, en de nex' night, w'en he seed dis nigger comin' 'long de road, he up en ax' 'im w'at he mean by hangin' 'roun' his 'oman. De man didn' 'spon' ter suit Dan, en one wo'd led ter ernudder, 'tel bimeby dis cunjuh man's son pull' out a knife en

97

sta'ted ter stick it in Dan; but befo' he could git it drawed good, Dan haul' off en hit 'im in de head so ha'd dat he nebber got up. Dan 'lowed he'd come to atter a w'ile en go 'long 'bout his bizness, so he went off en lef' 'im layin' dere on de groun'.

"De nex' mawnin' de man wuz foun' dead. Dey wuz a great 'miration made 'bout it, but Dan didn' say nuffin, en none er de yuther niggers hadn' seed de fight, so dey wa'n't no way ter tell who done de killin'. En bein' ez it wuz a free nigger, en dey wa'n't no w'ite folks 'speshly int'rusted, dey wa'n't nuffin done 'bout it, en de cunjuh man come en tuk his son en kyared 'im 'way en buried 'im.

"Now, Dan hadn' meant ter kill dis nigger, en w'iles he knowed de man hadn' got no mo' d'n he desarved, Dan 'mence' ter worry mo' er less. Fer he knowed dis man's daddy would wuk his roots en prob'ly fin' out who had killt 'is son, en make all de trouble fer 'im he could. En Dan kep' on studyin' 'bout dis 'tel he got so he didn' ha'dly das' ter eat er drink fer fear dis cunjuh man had p'isen' de vittles er de water. Fin'lly he 'lowed he'd go ter see Aun' Peggy, de noo cunjuh 'oman w'at had moved down by de Wim'l'ton Road, en ax her fer ter do sump'n ter pertec' 'im fum dis cunjuh man. So he tuk a peck er 'taters en went down ter her cabin one night.

"Aun' Peggy heared his tale, en den sez she:—

"'Dat cunjuh man is mo' d'n twice't ez ole ez I is, en he kin make monst'us powe'ful goopher. W'at you needs is a life-cha'm, en I'll make you one ter-morrer; it's de on'y thing w'at'll do you any good. You leabe me a couple er ha'rs fum yo' head, en fetch me a pig ter-morrer night fer ter roas', en w'en you come I'll hab de cha'm all ready fer you.'

"So Dan went down ter Aun' Peggy de nex' night,—wid a young shote,—en Aun' Peggy gun 'im de cha'm. She had tuk de ha'rs Dan had lef' wid 'er, en a piece er red flannin, en some roots en yarbs, en had put 'em in a little bag made out'n 'coon-skin.

"'You take dis cha'm,' sez she, 'en put it in a bottle er a tin box, en bury it deep unner de root er a live-oak tree, en ez long ez it stays dere safe en soun', dey ain' no p'isen kin p'isen you, dey ain' no rattlesnake kin bite you, dey ain' no sco'pion kin sting you. Dis yere cunjuh man mought do one thing er 'nudder ter you, but he can't kill you. So you neenter be at all skeered, but go 'long 'bout yo' bizness en doan bother yo' min'.'

"So Dan went down by de ribber, en 'way up on de bank he buried de cha'm deep unner de root er a live-oak tree, en kivered it up en stomp' de dirt down en scattered leaves ober de spot, en den went home wid his min' easy.

"Sho' 'nuff, dis yer cunjuh man wukked his roots, des ez Dan had 'spected he would, en soon l'arn' who killt his son. En co'se he made up his min' fer ter git eben wid Dan. So he sont a rattle-snake fer ter sting 'im, but de rattlesnake say de nigger's heel wuz so ha'd he couldn' git his sting in. Den he sont his jay-bird fer ter put p'isen in Dan's vittles, but de p'isen didn' wuk. Den de cunjuh man 'low' he'd double Dan all up wid de rheumatiz, so he couldn' git 'is han' ter his mouf ter eat, en would hafter sta've ter def; but Dan went ter Aun' Peggy, en she gun 'im a' 'intment ter kyo de rheumatiz. Den de cunjuh man 'lowed he'd bu'n Dan up wid a fever, but Aun' Peggy tol' 'im how ter make some yarb tea fer dat. Nuffin dis man tried would kill Dan, so fin'lly de cunjuh man 'lowed Dan mus' hab a life-cha'm.

"Now, dis yer jay-bird de cunjuh man had wuz a monst'us sma't creeter,—fac', de niggers 'lowed he wuz de ole Debbil hisse'f, des settin' roun' waitin' ter kyar dis ole man erway w'en he'd retch' de een' er his rope. De cunjuh man sont dis jay-bird fer ter watch Dan en fin' out whar he kep' his cha'm. De jay-bird hung roun' Dan fer a week er so, en one day he seed Dan go down by de ribber en look at a live-oak tree; en den de jay-bird went back ter his marster, en tol' 'im he 'spec' de nigger kep' his life-cha'm under dat tree.

"De cunjuh man lafft en lafft, en he put on his bigges' pot, en fill' it wid his stronges' roots, en b'iled it en b'iled it, 'tel bimeby de win' blowed en blowed, 'tel it blowed down de live-oak tree. Den he stirred some more roots in de pot, en it rained en rained 'tel de water run down de ribber bank en wash' Dan's life-cha'm inter de ribber, en de bottle went bobbin' down de current des ez onconsarned ez ef it wa'n't takin' po' Dan's chances all 'long wid it. En den de cunjuh man lafft some mo', en 'lowed ter hisse'f dat he wuz gwine ter fix Dan now, sho' 'nuff; he wa'n't gwine ter kill 'im des yet, fer he could do sump'n ter 'im w'at would hu't wusser 'n killin'.

"So dis cunjuh man 'mence' by gwine up ter Dan's cabin eve'y night, en takin' Dan out in his sleep en ridin' 'im roun' de roads en fiel's ober de rough groun'. In de mawnin' Dan would be ez ti'ed ez ef he hadn' be'n ter sleep. Dis kin' er thing kep' up fer a week er so, en Dan had des 'bout made up his min' fer ter go en see Aun' Peggy ag'in, w'en who sh'd he come across, gwine 'long de road one day, to'ds sundown, but dis yer cunjuh man. Dan felt kinder skeered at fus'; but den he 'membered 'bout his life-cha'm, w'ich he hadn' be'n ter see fer a week er so, en 'lowed wuz safe en soun' unner de live-oak tree, en so he hilt up 'is head en walk' 'long, des lack he didn' keer nuffin 'bout dis man no mo' d'n any yuther nigger. W'en he got close ter de cunjuh man, dis cunjuh man sez, sezee:—

"'Hoddy, Brer Dan? I hopes you er well?'

"W'en Dan seed de cunjuh man wuz in a good humor en didn' 'pear ter bear no malice, Dan 'lowed mebbe de cunjuh man hadn' foun' out who killt his son, en so he 'termine' fer ter let on lack he didn' know nuffin, en so sezee:—

"'Hoddy, Unk' Jube?'—dis ole cunjuh man's name wuz Jube. 'I's p'utty well, I thank you. How is you feelin' dis mawnin'?'

"'I's feelin' ez well ez a' ole nigger could feel w'at had los' his only son, en his main 'pen'ence in 'is ole age.

"'But den my son wuz a bad boy,' sezee, 'en I couldn' 'spec' nuffin e'se. I tried ter l'arn him de arrer er his ways en make him go ter chu'ch en pra'r-meetin'; but it wa'n't no use. I dunno who killt 'im, en I doan wanter know, fer I'd be mos' sho' ter fin' out dat my boy had sta'ted de fuss. Ef I'd 'a' had a son lack you, Brer Dan, I'd 'a' be'n a proud nigger; oh, yas, I would, sho's you bawn. But you ain' lookin' ez well ez you oughter, Brer Dan. Dey's sump'n de matter wid you, en w'at's mo', I 'spec' you dunno w'at it is.'

"Now, dis yer kin' er talk nach'ly th'owed Dan off'n his gya'd, en fus' thing he knowed he wuz talkin' ter dis ole cunjuh man des lack he wuz one er his bes' frien's. He tol' 'im all 'bout not feelin' well in de mawnin', en ax' 'im ef he could tell w'at wuz de matter wid 'im.

"'Yas,' sez de cunjuh man. 'Dey is a witch be'n ridin' you right 'long. I kin see de marks er de bridle on yo' mouf. En I'll des bet yo' back is raw whar she's be'n beatin' you.'

"'Yas,' 'spon' Dan, 'so it is.' He hadn' notice it befo', but now he felt des lack de hide had be'n tuk off'n 'im.

"'En yo' thighs is des raw whar de spurrers has be'n driv' in you,' sez de cunjuh man. 'You can't see de raw spots, but you kin feel 'em.'

"'Oh, yas,' 'lows Dan, 'dey does hu't pow'ful bad.'

"'En w'at's mo',' sez de cunjuh man, comin' up close ter Dan en whusp'in' in his yeah, 'I knows who it is be'n ridin' you.'

"'Who is it?' ax' Dan. 'Tell me who it is.'

"'It's a' ole nigger 'oman down by Rockfish Crick. She had a pet rabbit, en you cotch' 'im one day, en she's been squarin' up wid you eber sence. But you better stop her, er e'se you'll be rid ter def in a mont' er so.'

"'No,' sez Dan, 'she can't kill me, sho'.'

"'I dunno how dat is,' said de cunjuh man, 'but she kin make yo' life mighty mis'able. Ef I wuz in yo' place, I'd stop her right off.'

"'But how is I gwine ter stop her?' ax' Dan. 'I dunno nuffin 'bout stoppin' witches.'

"'Look a heah, Dan,' sez de yuther; 'you is a good young man. I lacks you monst'us well. Fac', I feels lack some er dese days I mought buy you fum yo' marster, ef I could eber make money ernuff at my bizness dese hard times, en 'dop' you fer my son. I lacks you so well dat I'm gwine ter he'p you git rid er dis yer witch fer good en all; fer des ez long ez she libs, you is sho' ter hab trouble, en trouble, en mo' trouble.'

"'You is de bes' frien' I got, Unk' Jube,' sez Dan, 'en I'll 'member yo' kin'ness ter my dyin' day. Tell me how I kin git rid er dis yer ole witch w'at's be'n ridin' me so ha'd.'

"'In de fus' place,' sez de cunjuh man, 'dis ole witch nebber comes in her own shape, but eve'y night, at ten o'clock, she tu'ns herse'f inter a black cat, en runs down ter yo' cabin en bridles you, en mounts you, en dribes you out th'oo de chimbly, en rides you ober de roughes' places she kin fin'. All you got ter do is ter set fer her in de bushes 'side er yo' cabin, en hit her in de head wid a rock er a lighterd-knot w'en she goes pas'.'

"'But,' sez Dan, 'how kin I see her in de da'k? En s'posen I hits at her en misses her? Er s'posen I des woun's her, en she gits erway,—w'at she gwine do ter me den?'

"'I is done studied 'bout all dem things,' sez de cunjuh man, 'en it 'pears ter me de bes' plan fer you ter foller is ter lemme tu'n you ter some creetur w'at kin see in de da'k, en w'at kin run des ez fas' ez a cat, en w'at kin bite, en bite fer ter kill; en den you won't hafter hab no trouble atter de job is done. I dunno whuther you'd lack dat er no, but dat is de sho'es' way.'

"'I doan keer,' 'spon' Dan. 'I'd des ez lief be anything fer a' hour er so, ef I kin kill dat ole witch. You kin do des w'at you er mineter.'

"'All right, den,' sez de cunjuh man, 'you come down ter my cabin at half-past nine o'clock ter-night, en I'll fix you up.'

"Now, dis cunjuh man, w'en he had got th'oo talkin' wid Dan, kep' on down de road 'long de side er de plantation, 'tel he met Mahaly comin' home fum wuk des atter sundown.

"'Hoddy do, ma'm,' sezee; 'is yo' name Sis' Mahaly, w'at b'longs ter Mars Dugal' McAdoo?'

"'Yas,' 'spon' Mahaly, 'dat's my name, en I b'longs ter Mars Dugal'.'

"'Well,' sezee, 'yo' husban' Dan wuz down by my cabin dis ebenin', en he got bit by a spider er sump'n, en his foot is swoll' up so he can't walk. En he ax' me fer ter fin' you en fetch you down dere ter he'p 'im home.'

"Co'se Mahaly wanter see w'at had happen' ter Dan, en so she sta'ted down de road wid de cunjuh man. Ez soon ez he got her inter his cabin, he shet de do', en sprinkle' some goopher mixtry on her, en tu'nt her ter a black cat. Den he tuk'n put her in a bairl, en put a bo'd on de bairl, en a rock on de bo'd, en lef' her dere 'tel he got good en ready fer ter use her.

"'Long 'bout half-pas' nine o'clock Dan come down ter de cunjuh man's cabin. It wuz a wa'm night, en de do' wuz stan'in' open. De cunjuh man 'vited Dan ter come in, en pass' de time er day wid 'im. Ez soon ez Dan 'mence' talkin', he heared a cat miauin' en scratchin' en gwine on at a tarrable rate.

"'W'at's all dat fuss 'bout?' ax' Dan.

"'Oh, dat ain' nuffin but my ole gray tomcat,' sez de cunjuh man. 'I has ter shet 'im up sometimes fer ter keep 'im in nights, en co'se he doan lack it.'

"'Now,' 'lows de cunjuh man, 'lemme tell you des w'at you is got ter do. W'en you ketches dis witch, you mus' take her right by de th'oat en bite her right th'oo de neck. Be sho' yo' teef goes th'oo at de fus' bite, en den you won't nebber be bothe'd no mo' by dat witch. En w'en you git done, come back heah en I'll tu'n you ter yo'se'f ag'in, so you kin go home en git yo' night's res'.'

"Den de cunjuh man gun Dan sump'n nice en sweet ter drink out'n a new go'd, en in 'bout a minute Dan foun' hisse'f tu'nt ter a gray wolf; en soon ez he felt all fo' er his noo feet on de groun', he sta'ted off fas' ez he could fer his own cabin, so he could be sho' en be dere time ernuff ter ketch de witch, en put a' een' ter her kyarin's-on.

"Ez soon ez Dan wuz gone good, de cunjuh man tuk de rock off'n de bo'd, en de bo'd off'n de bairl, en out le'p' Mahaly en sta'ted fer ter go home, des lack a cat er a 'oman er anybody e'se would w'at wuz in trouble; en it wa'n't many minutes befo' she wuz gwine up de path ter her own do'.

"Meanw'iles, w'en Dan had retch' de cabin, he had hid hisse'f in a bunch er jimson weeds in de ya'd. He hadn' wait' long befo' he seed a black cat run up de path to'ds de do'. Des ez soon ez she got close ter 'im, he le'p' out en ketch' her by de th'oat, en got a grip on her, des lack de cunjuh man had tol' 'im ter do. En lo en behol'! no sooner had de blood 'mence' ter flow dan de black cat tu'nt back ter Mahaly, en Dan seed dat he had killt his own wife. En w'iles her bref wuz gwine she call' out:

"'*O* Dan! *O* my husban'! come en he'p me! come en sabe me fum dis wolf w'at's killin' me!'

"W'en po' Dan sta'ted to'ds her, ez any man nach'ly would, it des made her holler wuss en wuss; fer she didn' knowed dis yer wolf wuz her Dan. En Dan dés had ter hide in de weeds, en grit his teef en hol' hisse'f in, 'tel she passed out'n her mis'ry, callin' fer Dan ter de las', en wond'rin' w'y he didn' come en he'p her. En Dan 'lowed ter hisse'f he'd ruther 'a' be'n killt a dozen times 'n ter 'a' done w'at he had ter Mahaly.

"Dan wuz mighty nigh 'stracted, but w'en Mahaly wuz dead en he got his min' straighten' out a little, it didn' take 'im mo' d'n a minute er so fer ter see th'oo all de cunjuh man's lies, en how de cunjuh man had fooled 'im en made 'im kill Mahaly, fer ter git eben wid 'im fer killin' er his son. He kep' gittin' madder en madder, en Mahaly hadn' much mo' d'n drawed her' las' bref befo' he sta'ted back ter de cunjuh man's cabin ha'd ez he could run.

"W'en he got dere, de do' wuz stan'in' open; a lighterd-knot wuz flick'rin' on de h'a'th, en de ole cunjuh man wuz settin' dere noddin' in de corner. Dan le'p' in de do' en jump' fer dis man's th'oat, en got de same grip on 'im w'at de cunjuh man had tol' 'im 'bout half a' hour befo'. It wuz ha'd wuk dis time, fer de ole man's neck wuz monst'us tough en stringy, but Dan hilt on long ernuff ter be sho' his job wuz done right. En eben den he didn' hol' on long ernuff; fer w'en he tu'nt de cunjuh man loose en he fell ober on de flo', de cunjuh man rollt his eyes at Dan, en sezee:—

"'I's eben wid you, Brer Dan, en you er eben wid me; you killt my son en I killt yo' 'oman. En ez I doan want no mo' d'n w'at's fair 'bout dis thing, ef you'll retch up wid yo' paw en take down dat go'd hangin' on dat peg ober de chimbly, en take a sip er dat mixtry, it'll tu'n you back ter a nigger ag'in, en I kin die mo' sad'sfied 'n ef I lef' you lack you is.'

"Dan nebber 'lowed fer a minute dat a man would lie wid his las' bref, en co'se he seed de sense er gittin' tu'nt back befo' de cunjuh man died; so he clumb on a chair en retch' fer de go'd, en tuk a sip er de mixtry. En ez soon ez he'd done dat de cunjuh man lafft his las' laf, en gapsed out wid 'is las' gaps:—

"'Uh huh! I reckon I's square wid you now fer killin' me, too; fer dat goopher on you is done fix' en sot now fer good, en all de cunj'in' in de worl' won't nebber take it off.

'Wolf you is en wolf you stays,
All de rest er yo' bawn days.'

"Co'se Brer Dan couldn' do nuffin. He knowed it wa'n't no use, but he clumb up on de chimbly en got down de go'ds en bottles en yuther cunjuh fixin's, en tried 'em all on hisse'f, but dey didn' do no good. Den he run down ter ole Aun' Peggy, but she didn' know de wolf langwidge, en couldn't 'a' tuk off dis yuther goopher nohow, eben ef she'd 'a' unnerstood w'at Dan wuz sayin'. So po' Dan wuz bleedgd ter be a wolf all de rest er his bawn days.

"Dey foun' Mahaly down by her own cabin nex' mawnin', en eve'ybody made a great 'miration 'bout how she'd be'n killt. De niggers 'lowed a wolf had bit her. De w'ite folks say no, dey ain' be'n no wolves 'roun' dere fer ten yeahs er mo'; en dey didn' know w'at ter make out'n it. En w'en dey couldn' fin' Dan

nowhar, dey 'lowed he'd quo'lled wid Mahaly en killt her, en
run erway; en dey didn' know w'at ter make er dat, fer Dan
en Mahaly wuz de mos' lovin' couple on de plantation. Dey put
de dawgs on Dan's scent, en track' 'im down ter ole Unk' Jube's
cabin, en foun' de ole man dead, en dey didn' know w'at ter
make er dat; en den Dan's scent gun out, en dey didn' know
w'at ter make er dat. Mars Dugal' tuk on a heap 'bout losin' two
er his bes' han's in one day, en ole missis 'lowed it wuz a jedg-
ment on 'im fer sump'n he'd done. But dat fall de craps wuz
monst'us big, so Mars Dugal' say de Lawd had temper' de win'
ter de sho'n ram, en make up ter 'im fer w'at he had los'.

"Dey buried Mahaly down in dat piece er low groun' you er
talkin' 'bout cl'arin' up. Ez fer po' Dan, he didn' hab nowhar e'se
ter go, so he des stayed 'roun' Mahaly's grabe, w'en he wa'n't
out in de yuther woods gittin' sump'n ter eat. En sometimes,
w'en night would come, de niggers useter heah him howlin' en
howlin' down dere, des fittin' ter break his hea't. En den some
mo' un 'em said dey seed Mahaly's ha'nt dere 'bun'ance er times,
colloguin' wid dis gray wolf. En eben now, fifty yeahs sence,
long atter ole Dan has died en dried up in de woods, his ha'nt
en Mahaly's hangs 'roun' dat piece er low groun', en eve'body
w'at goes 'bout dere has some bad luck er 'nuther; fer ha'nts
doan lack ter be 'sturb' on dey own stompin'-groun'."

The air had darkened while the old man related this harrow-
ing tale. The rising wind whistled around the eaves, slammed
the loose window-shutters, and, still increasing, drove the rain
in fiercer gusts into the piazza. As Julius finished his story and
we rose to seek shelter within doors, the blast caught the angle
of some chimney or gable in the rear of the house, and bore to
our ears a long, wailing note, an epitome, as it were, of remorse
and hopelessness.

"Dat 's des lack po' ole Dan useter howl," observed Julius, as
he reached for his umbrella, "en w'at I be'n tellin' you is de
reason I doan lack ter see dat neck er woods cl'ared up. Co'se it
b'longs ter you, en a man kin do ez he choose' wid 'is own. But
ef you gits rheumatiz er fever en agur, er ef you er snake-bit er
p'isen' wid some yarb er 'nuther, er ef a tree falls on you, er a
ha'nt runs you en makes you git 'stracted in yo' min', lack some
folks I knows w'at went foolin' 'roun' dat piece er lan', you can't

say I neber wa'ned you, suh, en tol' you w'at you mought look fer en be sho' ter fin'."

When I cleared up the land in question, which was not until the following year, I recalled the story Julius had told us, and looked in vain for a sunken grave or perhaps a few weather-bleached bones of some denizen of the forest. I cannot say, of course, that some one had not been buried there; but if so, the hand of time had long since removed any evidence of the fact. If some lone wolf, the last of his pack, had once made his den there, his bones had long since crumbled into dust and gone to fertilize the rank vegetation that formed the undergrowth of this wild spot. I did find, however, a bee-tree in the woods, with an ample cavity in its trunk, and an opening through which convenient access could be had to the stores of honey within. I have reason to believe that ever since I had bought the place, and for many years before, Julius had been getting honey from this tree. The gray wolf's haunt had doubtless proved useful in keeping off too inquisitive people, who might have interfered with his monopoly.

HOT-FOOT HANNIBAL

I hate you and despise you! I wish never to see you or speak to you again!"

"Very well; I will take care that henceforth you have no opportunity to do either."

These words—the first in the passionately vibrant tones of my sister-in-law, and the latter in the deeper and more restrained accents of an angry man—startled me from my nap. I had been dozing in my hammock on the front piazza, behind the honeysuckle vine. I had been faintly aware of a buzz of conversation in the parlor, but had not at all awakened to its import until these sentences fell, or, I might rather say, were hurled upon my ear. I presume the young people had either not seen me lying there,—the Venetian blinds opening from the parlor windows upon the piazza were partly closed on account of the heat,—or else in their excitement they had forgotten my proximity.

I felt somewhat concerned. The young man, I had remarked, was proud, firm, jealous of the point of honor, and, from my observation of him, quite likely to resent to the bitter end what he deemed a slight or an injustice. The girl, I knew, was quite as high-spirited as young Murchison. I feared she was not so just, and hoped she would prove more yielding. I knew that her affections were strong and enduring, but that her temperament was capricious, and her sunniest moods easily overcast by some small cloud of jealousy or pique. I had never imagined, however, that she was capable of such intensity as was revealed by these few words of hers. As I say, I felt concerned. I had

learned to like Malcolm Murchison, and had heartily consented
to his marriage with my ward; for it was in that capacity that I
had stood for a year or two to my wife's younger sister, Mabel.
The match thus rudely broken off had promised to be another
link binding me to the kindly Southern people among whom I
had not long before taken up my residence.

Young Murchison came out of the door, cleared the piazza
in two strides without seeming aware of my presence, and went
off down the lane at a furious pace. A few moments later Mabel
began playing the piano loudly, with a touch that indicated
anger and pride and independence and a dash of exultation, as
though she were really glad that she had driven away forever
the young man whom the day before she had loved with all the
ardor of a first passion.

I hoped that time might heal the breach and bring the two
young people together again. I told my wife what I had overheard. In return she gave me Mabel's version of the affair.

"I do not see how it can ever be settled," my wife said. "It is
something more than a mere lovers' quarrel. It began, it is true,
because she found fault with him for going to church with that
hateful Branson girl. But before it ended there were things said
that no woman of any spirit could stand. I am afraid it is all
over between them."

I was sorry to hear this. In spite of the very firm attitude taken
by my wife and her sister, I still hoped that the quarrel would
be made up within a day or two. Nevertheless, when a week had
passed with no word from young Murchison, and with no sign
of relenting on Mabel's part, I began to think myself mistaken.

One pleasant afternoon, about ten days after the rupture, old
Julius drove the rockaway up to the piazza, and my wife, Mabel,
and I took our seats for a drive to a neighbor's vineyard, over
on the Lumberton plank-road.

"Which way shall we go," I asked, "the short road or the
long one?"

"I guess we had better take the short road," answered my
wife. "We will get there sooner."

"It's a mighty fine dribe roun' by de big road, Mis' Annie,"
observed Julius, "en it doan take much longer to git dere."

"No," said my wife, "I think we will go by the short road.

There is a bay-tree in blossom near the mineral spring, and I wish to get some of the flowers."

"I 'spec's you'd fin' some bay-trees 'long de big road, ma'm," suggested Julius.

"But I know about the flowers on the short road, and they are the ones I want."

We drove down the lane to the highway, and soon struck into the short road leading past the mineral spring. Our route lay partly through a swamp, and on each side the dark, umbrageous foliage, unbroken by any clearing, lent to the road solemnity, and to the air a refreshing coolness. About half a mile from the house, and about half-way to the mineral spring, we stopped at the tree of which my wife had spoken, and reaching up to the low-hanging boughs, I gathered a dozen of the fragrant white flowers. When I resumed my seat in the rockaway, Julius started the mare. She went on for a few rods, until we had reached the edge of a branch crossing the road, when she stopped short.

"Why did you stop, Julius?" I asked.

"I didn', suh," he replied. "'T wuz de mare stop'. G' 'long dere, Lucy! W'at you mean by dis foolis'ness?"

Julius jerked the reins and applied the whip lightly, but the mare did not stir.

"Perhaps you had better get down and lead her," I suggested. "If you get her started, you can cross on the log and keep your feet dry."

Julius alighted, took hold of the bridle, and vainly essayed to make the mare move. She planted her feet with even more evident obstinacy.

"I don't know what to make of this," I said. "I have never known her to balk before. Have you, Julius?"

"No, suh," replied the old man, "I neber has. It's a cu'ous thing ter me, suh."

"What's the best way to make her go?"

"I 'spec's, suh, dat ef I'd tu'n her 'roun', she'd go de udder way."

"But we want her to go this way."

"Well, suh, I 'low ef we des set heah fo' er fibe minutes, she'll sta't up by herse'f."

"All right," I rejoined; "it is cooler here than any place I have struck to-day. We'll let her stand for a while, and see what she does."

We had sat in silence for a few minutes, when Julius suddenly ejaculated, "Uh huh! I knows w'y dis mare doan go. It des flash' 'cross my recommemb'ance."

"Why is it, Julius?" I inquired.

" 'Ca'se she sees Chloe."

"Where is Chloe?" I demanded.

"Chloe's done be'n dead dese fo'ty years er mo'," the old man returned. "Her ha'nt is settin' ober yander on de udder side er de branch, unner dat willer-tree, dis blessed minute."

"Why, Julius!" said my wife, "do you see the haunt?"

"No'm," he answered, shaking his head, "I doan see 'er, but de mare sees 'er."

"How do you know?" I inquired.

"Well, suh, dis yer is a gray hoss, en dis yer is a Friday; en a gray hoss kin alluz see a ha'nt w'at walks on Friday."

"Who was Chloe?" said Mabel.

"And why does Chloe's haunt walk?" asked my wife.

"It's all in de tale, ma'm," Julius replied, with a deep sigh. "It's all in de tale."

"Tell us the tale," I said. "Perhaps, by the time you get through, the haunt will go away and the mare will cross."

I was willing to humor the old man's fancy. He had not told us a story for some time; and the dark and solemn swamp around us; the amber-colored stream flowing silently and sluggishly at our feet, like the waters of Lethe; the heavy, aromatic scent of the bays, faintly suggestive of funeral wreaths,—all made the place an ideal one for a ghost story.

"Chloe," Julius began in a subdued tone, "use' ter b'long ter ole Mars' Dugal' McAdoo,—my ole marster. She wuz a lackly gal en a smart gal, en ole mis' tuk her up ter de big house, en l'arnt her ter wait on de w'ite folks, 'tel bimeby she come ter be mis's own maid, en 'peared ter 'low she run de house herse'f, ter heah her talk erbout it. I wuz a young boy den, en use' ter wuk 'bout de stables, so I knowed eve'ythin' dat wuz gwine on 'roun' de plantation.

"Well, one time Mars' Dugal' wanted a house boy, en sont down ter de qua'ters fer ter hab Jeff en Hannibal come up ter

de big house nex' mawnin'. Ole marster en ole mis' look' de
two boys ober, en 'sco'sed wid deyse'ves fer a little w'ile, en den
Mars' Dugal' sez, sezee:—

"'We lacks Hannibal de bes', en we gwine ter keep him.
Heah, Hannibal, you'll wuk at de house fum now on. En ef you er a
good nigger en min's yo' bizness, I'll gib you Chloe fer a wife
nex' spring. You other nigger, you Jeff, you kin go back ter de
qua'ters. We ain' gwine ter need you.'

"Now Chloe had be'n stan'in' dere behin' ole mis' dyoin' all
er dis yer talk, en Chloe made up her min' fum de ve'y fus'
minute she sot eyes on dem two dat she didn' lack dat nigger
Hannibal, en wa'n't neber gwine keer fer 'im, en she wuz des ez
sho' dat she lack' Jeff, en wuz gwine ter set sto' by 'im, whuther
Mars' Dugal' tuk 'im in de big house er no; en so co'se Chloe
wuz monst'us sorry w'en ole Mars' Dugal' tuk Hannibal en sont
Jeff back. So she slip' roun' de house en waylaid Jeff on de way
back ter de qua'ters, en tol' 'im not ter be down-hea'ted, fer she
wuz gwine ter see ef she couldn' fin' some way er 'nuther ter
git rid er dat nigger Hannibal, en git Jeff up ter de house in
his place.

"De noo house boy kotch' on monst'us fas', en it wa'n't no
time ha'dly befo' Mars' Dugal' en ole mis' bofe 'mence' ter 'low
Hannibal wuz de bes' house boy dey eber had. He wuz peart en
soopl', quick ez lightnin', en sha'p ez a razor. But Chloe didn'
lack his ways. He wuz so sho' he wuz gwine ter git 'er in de
spring, dat he didn' 'pear ter 'low he had ter do any co'tin', en
w'en he'd run 'cross Chloe 'bout de house, he'd swell roun' 'er
in a biggity way en say:—

"'Come heah en kiss me, honey. You gwine ter be mine in de
spring. You doan 'pear ter be ez fon' er me ez you oughter be.'

"Chloe didn' keer nuffin fer Hannibal, en hadn' keered nuffin fer 'im, en she sot des ez much sto' by Jeff ez she did de
day she fus' laid eyes on 'im. En de mo' fermilyus dis yer Hannibal got, de mo' Chloe let her min' run on Jeff, en one ebenin'
she went down ter de qua'ters en watch', 'tel she got a chance
fer ter talk wid 'im by hisse'f. En she tol' Jeff fer ter go down
en see ole Aun' Peggy, de cunjuh 'oman down by de Wim'l'ton
Road, en ax her ter gib 'im sump'n ter he'p git Hannibal out'n
de big house, so de w'ite folks 'u'd sen' fer Jeff ag'in. En bein' ez

Jeff didn' hab nuffin ter gib Aun' Peggy, Chloe gun 'im a silber dollah en a silk han'kercher fer ter pay her wid, fer Aun' Peggy neber lack ter wuk fer nobody fer nuffin.

"So Jeff slip' off down ter Aun' Peggy's one night, en gun 'er de present he brung, en tol' 'er all 'bout 'im en Chloe en Hannibal, en ax' 'er ter he'p 'im out. Aun' Peggy tol' 'im she'd wuk 'er roots, en fer 'im ter come back de nex' night, en she'd tell 'im w'at she c'd do fer 'im.

"So de nex' night Jeff went back, en Aun' Peggy gun 'im a baby doll, wid a body made out'n a piece er co'n-stalk, en wid splinters fer a'ms en laigs, en a head made out'n elderberry peth, en two little red peppers fer feet.

"'Dis yer baby doll,' sez she, 'is Hannibal. Dis yer peth head is Hannibal's head, en dese yer pepper feet is Hannibal's feet. You take dis en hide it unner de house, on de sill unner de do', whar Hannibal 'll hafter walk ober it eve'y day. En ez long ez Hannibal comes anywhar nigh dis baby doll, he'll be des lack it is,—light-headed en hot-footed; en ef dem two things doan git 'im inter trouble mighty soon, den I'm no cunjuh 'oman. But w'en you git Hannibal out'n de house, en git all th'oo wid dis baby doll, you mus' fetch it back ter me, fer it's monst'us powerful goopher, en is liable ter make mo' trouble ef you leabe it layin' roun'.'

"Well, Jeff tuk de baby doll, en slip' up ter de big house, en whistle' ter Chloe, en w'en she come out he tol' 'er w'at ole Aun' Peggy had said. En Chloe showed 'im how ter git unner de house, en w'en he had put de cunjuh doll on de sill, he went 'long back ter de qua'ters—en des waited.

"Nex' day, sho' 'nuff, de goopher 'mence' ter wuk. Hannibal sta'ted in de house soon in de mawnin' wid a armful er wood ter make a fire, en he hadn' mo' d'n got 'cross de do'-sill befo' his feet begun ter bu'n so dat he drap' de armful er wood on de flo' en woke ole mis' up a' hour sooner 'n yushal, en co'se ole mis' didn' lack dat, en spoke sha'p erbout it.

"W'en dinner-time come, en Hannibal wuz help'n' de cook kyar de dinner f'm de kitchen inter de big house, en wuz gittin' close ter de do' whar he had ter go in, his feet sta'ted ter bu'n en his head begun ter swim, en he let de big dish er chicken en dumplin's fall right down in de dirt, in de middle er de ya'd, en de w'ite folks had ter make dey dinner dat day off'n col' ham en sweet'n' 'taters.

"De nex' mawnin' he overslep' hisse'f, en got inter mo' trouble. Atter breakfus', Mars' Dugal' sont 'im ober ter Mars' Marrabo Utley's fer ter borry a monkey wrench. He oughter be'n back in ha'f a' hour, but he come pokin' home 'bout dinner-time wid a screw-driver stidder a monkey wrench. Mars' Dugal' sont ernudder nigger back wid de screw-driver, en Hannibal didn' git no dinner. 'Long in de afternoon, ole mis' sot Hannibal ter weedin' de flowers in de front gya'den, en Hannibal dug up all de bulbs ole mis' had sont erway fer, en paid a lot er money fer, en tuk 'em down ter de hawg-pen by de ba'nya'd, en fed 'em ter de hawgs. W'en ole mis' come out in de cool er de ebenin', en seed w'at Hannibal had done, she wuz mos' crazy, en she wrote a note en sont Hannibal down ter de oberseah wid it.

"But w'at Hannibal got fum de oberseah didn' 'pear ter do no good. Eve'y now en den 'is feet'd 'mence ter torment 'im, en 'is min' 'u'd git all mix' up, en his conduc' kep' gittin' wusser en wusser, 'tel fin'lly de w'ite folks couldn' stan' it no longer, en Mars' Dugal' tuk Hannibal back down ter de qua'ters.

"'Mr. Smif,' sez Mars' Dugal' ter de oberseah, 'dis yer nigger has done got so triflin' yer lately dat we can't keep 'im at de house no mo', en I's fotch' 'im ter you ter be straighten' up. You's had 'casion ter deal wid 'im once, so he knows w'at ter expec'. You des take 'im in han', en lemme know how he tu'ns out. En w'en de han's comes in fum de fiel' dis ebenin' you kin sen' dat yaller nigger Jeff up ter de house. I'll try 'im, en see ef he's any better 'n Hannibal.'

"So Jeff went up ter de big house, en pleas' Mars' Dugal' en ole mis' en de res' er de fambly so well dat dey all got ter lackin' 'im fus'rate; en dey'd 'a' fergot all 'bout Hannibal, ef it hadn' be'n fer de bad repo'ts w'at come up fum de qua'ters 'bout 'im fer a mont' er so. Fac' is, dat Chloe en Jeff wuz so int'rusted in one ernudder sence Jeff be'n up ter de house, dat dey fergot all 'bout takin' de baby doll back ter Aun' Peggy, en it kep' wukkin' fer a w'ile, en makin' Hannibal's feet bu'n mo' er less, 'tel all de folks on de plantation got ter callin' 'im Hot-Foot Hannibal. He kep' gittin' mo' en mo' triflin', 'tel he got de name er bein' de mos' no 'countes' nigger on de plantation, en Mars' Dugal' had ter th'eaten ter sell 'im in de spring, w'en bimeby de goopher quit wukkin', en Hannibal 'mence' ter pick up some en make folks set a little mo' sto' by 'im.

"Now, dis yer Hannibal was a monst'us sma't nigger, en w'en he got rid er dem so' feet, his min' kep' runnin' on 'is udder troubles. Heah th'ee er fo' weeks befo' he'd had a' easy job, waitin' on de w'ite folks, libbin' off'n de fat er de lan', en promus' de fines' gal on de plantation fer a wife in de spring, en now heah he wuz back in de co'n-fiel', wid de oberseah a-cussin' en a-r'arin' ef he didn' get a ha'd tas' done; wid nuffin but co'n bread en bacon en merlasses ter eat; en all de fiel'-han's makin' rema'ks, en pokin' fun at 'im 'ca'se he'd be'n sont back fum de big house ter de fiel'. En de mo' Hannibal studied 'bout it de mo' madder he got, 'tel he fin'lly swo' he wuz gwine ter git eben wid Jeff en Chloe, ef it wuz de las' ac'.

"So Hannibal slipped 'way fum de qua'ters one Sunday en hid in de co'n up close ter de big house, 'tel he see Chloe gwine down de road. He waylaid her, en sezee:—

"'Hoddy; Chloe?'

"'I ain' got no time fer ter fool wid fiel'-han's,' sez Chloe, tossin' her head; 'w'at you want wid me, Hot-Foot?'

"'I wants ter know how you en Jeff is gittin' 'long.'

"'I 'lows dat's none er yo' bizness, nigger. I doan see w'at 'casion any common fiel'-han' has got ter mix in wid de 'fairs er folks w'at libs in de big house. But ef it'll do you any good ter know, I mought say dat me en Jeff is gittin' 'long mighty well, en we gwine ter git married in de spring, en you ain' gwine ter be 'vited ter de weddin' nuther.'

"'No, no!' sezee, 'I wouldn' 'spec' ter be 'vited ter de weddin',—a common, low-down fiel'-han' lack *I* is. But I's glad ter heah you en Jeff is gittin' 'long so well. I didn' knowed but w'at he had 'mence' ter be a little ti'ed.'

"'Ti'ed er me? Dat's rediklus!' sez Chloe. 'W'y, dat nigger lubs me so I b'liebe he'd go th'oo fire en water fer me. Dat nigger is des wrop' up in me.'

"'Uh huh,' sez Hannibal, 'den I reckon it mus' be some udder nigger w'at meets a 'oman down by de crick in de swamp eve'y Sunday ebenin', ter say nuffin 'bout two er th'ee times a week.'

"'Yas, hit is ernudder nigger, en you is a liah w'en you say it wuz Jeff.'

"'Mebbe I is a liah, en mebbe I ain' got good eyes. But 'less'n I *is* a liah, en 'less'n I *ain'* got good eyes, Jeff is gwine ter meet dat 'oman dis ebenin' 'long 'bout eight o'clock right down dere by de crick in de swamp 'bout half-way betwix' dis plantation en Mars' Marrabo Utley's.'

"Well, Chloe tol' Hannibal she didn' b'liebe a wo'd he said, en call' 'im a low-down nigger, who wuz tryin' ter slander Jeff 'ca'se he wuz mo' luckier 'n he wuz. But all de same, she couldn' keep her min' fum runnin' on w'at Hannibal had said. She 'membered she'd heared one er de niggers say dey wuz a gal ober at Mars' Marrabo Utley's plantation w'at Jeff use' ter go wid some befo' he got 'quainted wid Chloe. Den she 'mence' ter figger back, en sho' 'nuff, dey wuz two er th'ee times in de las' week w'en she'd be'n he'pin' de ladies wid dey dressin' en udder fixin's in de ebenin', en Jeff mought 'a' gone down ter de swamp widout her knowin' 'bout it at all. En den she 'mence' ter 'member little things w'at she hadn' tuk no notice of befo', en w'at 'u'd make it 'pear lack Jeff had sump'n on his min'.

"Chloe set a monst'us heap er sto' by Jeff, en would 'a' done mos' anythin' fer 'im, so long ez he stuck ter her. But Chloe wuz a mighty jealous 'oman, en w'iles she didn' b'liebe w'at Hannibal said, she seed how it *could* 'a' be'n so, en she 'termine' fer ter fin' out fer herse'f whuther it *wuz* so er no.

"Now, Chloe hadn' seed Jeff all day, fer Mars' Dugal' had sont Jeff ober ter his daughter's house, young Mis' Ma'g'ret's, w'at libbed 'bout fo' miles fum Mars' Dugal's, en Jeff wuzn' 'spected home 'tel ebenin'. But des atter supper wuz ober, en w'iles de ladies wuz settin' out on de piazzer, Chloe slip' off fum de house en run down de road,—dis yer same road we come; en w'en she got mos' ter de crick—dis yer same crick right befo' us—she kin' er kep' in de bushes at de side er de road, 'tel fin'lly she seed Jeff settin' on de bank on de udder side er de crick,—right unner dat ole willer-tree droopin' ober de water yander. En eve'y now en den he'd git up en look up de road to'ds Mars' Marrabo's on de udder side er de swamp.

"Fus' Chloe felt lack she'd go right ober de crick en gib Jeff a piece er her min'. Den she 'lowed she better be sho' befo' she done anythin'. So she helt herse'f in de bes' she could, gittin' madder en madder eve'y minute, 'tel bimeby she seed a 'oman comin' down de road on de udder side fum to'ds Mars' Marrabo

Utley's plantation. En w'en she seed Jeff jump up en run to'ds dat 'oman, en th'ow his a'ms roun' her neck, po' Chloe didn' stop ter see no mo', but des tu'nt roun' en run up ter de house, en rush' up on de piazzer, en up en tol' Mars' Dugal' en ole mis' all 'bout de baby doll, en all 'bout Jeff gittin' de goopher fum Aun' Peggy, en 'bout w'at de goopher had done ter Hannibal.

"Mars' Dugal' wuz monst'us mad. He didn' let on at fus' lack he b'liebed Chloe, but w'en she tuk en showed 'im whar ter fin' de baby doll, Mars' Dugal' tu'nt w'ite ez chalk.

"'W'at debil's wuk is dis?' sezee. 'No wonder de po' nigger's feet eetched. Sump'n got ter be done ter l'arn dat ole witch ter keep her han's off'n my niggers. En ez fer dis yer Jeff, I'm gwine ter do des w'at I promus', so de darkies on dis plantation 'll know I means w'at I sez.'

"Fer Mars' Dugal' had warned de han's befo' 'bout foolin' wid cunju'ation; fac', he had los' one er two niggers hisse'f fum dey bein' goophered, en he would 'a' had ole Aun' Peggy whip' long ago, on'y Aun' Peggy wuz a free 'oman, en he wuz 'feard she'd cunjuh him. En w'iles Mars' Dugal' say he didn' b'liebe in cunj'in' en sich, he 'peared ter 'low it wuz bes' ter be on de safe side, en let Aun' Peggy alone.

"So Mars' Dugal' done des ez he say. Ef ole mis' had ple'd fer Jeff, he mought 'a' kep' 'im. But ole mis' hadn' got ober losin' dem bulbs yit, en she neber said a wo'd. Mars' Dugal' tuk Jeff ter town nex' day en sol' 'im ter a spekilater, who sta'ted down de ribber wid 'im nex' mawnin' on a steamboat, fer ter take 'im ter Alabama.

"Now, w'en Chloe tol' ole Mars' Dugal' 'bout dis yer baby doll en dis udder goopher, she hadn' ha'dly 'lowed Mars' Dugal' would sell Jeff down Souf. Howsomeber, she wuz so mad wid Jeff dat she 'suaded herse'f she didn' keer; en so she hilt her head up en went roun' lookin' lack she wuz rale glad 'bout it. But one day she wuz walkin' down de road, w'en who sh'd come 'long but dis yer Hannibal.

"W'en Hannibal seed 'er, he bus' out laffin' fittin' fer ter kill: 'Yah, yah, yah! ho, ho, ho! ha, ha, ha! Oh, hol' me, honey, hol' me, er I'll laf myse'f ter def. I ain' nebber laf' so much sence I be'n bawn.'

"'W'at you laffin' at, Hot-Foot?'

"'Yah, yah, yah! W'at I laffin' at? W'y, I's laffin' at myse'f, tooby sho',—laffin' ter think w'at a fine 'oman I made.'

"Chloe tu'nt pale, en her hea't come up in her mouf.

"'W'at you mean, nigger?' sez she, ketchin' holt er a bush by de road fer ter stiddy herse'f. 'W'at you mean by de kin' er 'oman you made?'

"'W'at do I mean? I means dat I got squared up wid you fer treatin' me de way you done, en I got eben wid dat yaller nigger Jeff fer cuttin' me out. Now, he's gwine ter know w'at it is ter eat co'n bread en merlasses once mo', en wuk fum daylight ter da'k, en ter hab a oberseah dribin' 'im fum one day's een' ter de udder. I means dat I sont wo'd ter Jeff dat Sunday dat you wuz gwine ter be ober ter Mars' Marrabo's visitin' dat ebenin', en you want 'im ter meet you down by de crick on de way home en go de rest er de road wid you. En den I put on a frock en a sun-bonnet, en fix' myse'f up ter look lack a 'oman; en w'en Jeff seed me comin', he run ter meet me, en you seed 'im,—fer I'd be'n watchin' in de bushes befo' en 'skivered you comin' down de road. En now I reckon you en Jeff bofe knows w'at it means ter mess wid a nigger lack me.'

"Po' Chloe hadn' heared mo' d'n half er de las' part er w'at Hannibal said, but she had heared 'nuff to l'arn dat dis nigger had fooled her en Jeff, en dat po' Jeff hadn' done nuffin, en dat fer lovin' her too much en goin' ter meet her she had cause' 'im ter be sol' erway whar she'd neber, neber see 'im no mo'. De sun mought shine by day, de moon by night, de flowers mought bloom, en de mawkin'-birds mought sing, but po' Jeff wuz done los' ter her fereber en fereber.

"Hannibal hadn' mo' d'n finish' w'at he had ter say, w'en Chloe's knees gun 'way unner her, en she fell down in de road, en lay dere half a' hour er so befo' she come to. W'en she did, she crep' up ter de house des ez pale ez a ghos'. En fer a mont' er so she crawled roun' de house, en 'peared ter be so po'ly dat Mars' Dugal' sont fer a doctor; en de doctor kep' on axin' her questions 'tel he foun' she wuz des pinin' erway fer Jeff.

"W'en he tol' Mars' Dugal', Mars' Dugal' lafft, en said he'd fix dat. She could hab de noo house boy fer a husban'. But ole mis' say, no, Chloe ain' dat kin'er gal, en dat Mars' Dugal' sh'd buy Jeff back.

"So Mars' Dugal' writ a letter ter dis yer spekilater down ter Wim'l'ton, en tol' ef he ain' done sol' dat nigger Souf w'at he bought fum 'im, he'd lack ter buy 'im back ag'in. Chloe 'mence' ter pick up a little w'en ole mis' tol' her 'bout dis letter. Howsomeber, bimeby Mars' Dugal' got a' answer fum de spekilater, who said he wuz monst'us sorry, but Jeff had fell ove'boa'd er jumped off 'n de steamboat on de way ter Wim'l'ton, en got drownded, en co'se he couldn' sell 'im back, much ez he'd lack ter 'bleedge Mars' Dugal'.

"Well, atter Chloe heared dis, she wa'n't much mo' use ter nobody. She pu'tended ter do her wuk, en ole mis' put up wid her, en had de doctor gib her medicine, en let 'er go ter de circus, en all so'ts er things fer ter take her min' off 'n her troubles. But dey didn' none un 'em do no good. Chloe got ter slippin' down here in de ebenin' des lack she 'uz comin' ter meet Jeff, en she'd set dere unner dat willer-tree on de udder side, en wait fer 'im, night atter night. Bimeby she got so bad de w'ite folks sont her ober ter young Mis' Ma'g'ret's fer ter gib her a change; but she runned erway de fus' night, en w'en dey looked fer 'er nex' mawnin', dey foun' her co'pse layin' in de branch yander, right 'cross fum whar we're settin' now.

"Eber sence den," said Julius in conclusion, "Chloe's ha'nt comes eve'y ebenin' en sets down unner dat willer-tree en waits fer Jeff, er e'se walks up en down de road yander, lookin' en lookin', en waitin' en waitin', fer her sweethea't w'at ain' neber, neber come back ter her no mo'."

There was silence when the old man had finished, and I am sure I saw a tear in my wife's eye, and more than one in Mabel's.

"I think, Julius," said my wife, after a moment, "that you may turn the mare around and go by the long road."

The old man obeyed with alacrity, and I noticed no reluctance on the mare's part.

"You are not afraid of Chloe's haunt, are you?" I asked jocularly.

My mood was not responded to, and neither of the ladies smiled.

"Oh, no," said Annie, "but I've changed my mind. I prefer the other route."

When we had reached the main road and had proceeded

along it for a short distance, we met a cart driven by a young negro, and on the cart were a trunk and a valise. We recognized the man as Malcolm Murchison's servant, and drew up a moment to speak to him.

"Who's going away, Marshall?" I inquired.

"Young Mistah Ma'colm gwine 'way on de boat ter Noo Yo'k dis ebenin', suh, en I'm takin' his things down ter de wharf, suh."

This was news to me, and I heard it with regret. My wife looked sorry, too, and I could see that Mabel was trying hard to hide her concern.

"He's comin' 'long behin', suh, en I 'spec's you'll meet 'im up de road a piece. He's gwine ter walk down ez fur ez Mistah Jim Williams's, en take de buggy fum dere ter town. He 'spec's ter be gone a long time, suh, en say prob'ly he ain' neber comin' back."

The man drove on. There were a few words exchanged in an undertone between my wife and Mabel, which I did not catch. Then Annie said: "Julius, you may stop the rockaway a moment. There are some trumpet-flowers by the road there that I want. Will you get them for me, John?"

I sprang into the underbrush, and soon returned with a great bunch of scarlet blossoms.

"Where is Mabel?" I asked, noting her absence.

"She has walked on ahead. We shall overtake her in a few minutes."

The carriage had gone only a short distance when my wife discovered that she had dropped her fan.

"I had it where we were stopping. Julius, will you go back and get it for me?"

Julius got down and went back for the fan. He was an unconscionably long time finding it. After we got started again we had gone only a little way, when we saw Mabel and young Murchison coming toward us. They were walking arm in arm, and their faces were aglow with the light of love.

I do not know whether or not Julius had a previous understanding with Malcolm Murchison by which he was to drive us round by the long road that day, nor do I know exactly what motive influenced the old man's exertions in the matter. He was fond of Mabel, but I was old enough, and knew Julius well enough, to be skeptical of his motives. It is certain that a most excellent understanding existed between him and Murchison after the reconciliation, and that when the young people set up housekeeping over at the old Murchison place, Julius had an opportunity to enter their service. For some reason or other, however, he preferred to remain with us. The mare, I might add, was never known to balk again.

RELATED TALES

DAVE'S NECKLISS

ave some dinner, Uncle Julius?" said my wife.

It was a Sunday afternoon in early autumn. Our two women-servants had gone to a camp-meeting some miles away, and would not return until evening. My wife had served the dinner, and we were just rising from the table, when Julius came up the lane, and, taking off his hat, seated himself on the piazza.

The old man glanced through the open door at the dinner-table, and his eyes rested lovingly upon a large sugar-cured ham, from which several slices had been cut, exposing a rich pink expanse that would have appealed strongly to the appetite of any hungry Christian.

"Thanky, Miss Annie," he said, after a momentary hesitation, "I dunno ez I keers ef I does tas'e a piece er dat ham, ef yer'll cut me off a slice un it."

"No," said Annie, "I won't. Just sit down to the table and help yourself; eat all you want, and don't be bashful."

Julius drew a chair up to the table, while my wife and I went out on the piazza. Julius was in my employment; he took his meals with his own family, but when he happened to be about our house at meal-times, my wife never let him go away hungry.

I threw myself into a hammock, from which I could see Julius through an open window. He ate with evident relish, devoting his attention chiefly to the ham, slice after slice of which disappeared in the spacious cavity of his mouth. At first the old man ate rapidly, but after the edge of his appetite had been taken off he proceeded in a more leisurely manner. When he had cut the sixth slice of ham (I kept count of them from a lazy curiosity to see how much he *could* eat) I saw him lay it on his plate; as he adjusted the knife and fork to cut it into smaller pieces, he paused, as if struck by a sudden thought, and a tear rolled down his rugged cheek and fell upon the slice of ham before him. But the emotion, whatever the thought that caused it, was transitory, and in a moment he continued his dinner. When he was through eating, he came out on the porch, and resumed his seat with the satisfied expression of countenance that usually follows a good dinner.

"Julius," I said, "you seemed to be affected by something, a moment ago. Was the mustard so strong that it moved you to tears?"

"No, suh, it wa'n't de mustard; I wuz studyin' 'bout Dave."

"Who was Dave, and what about him?" I asked.

The conditions were all favorable to story-telling. There was an autumnal languor in the air, and a dreamy haze softened the dark green of the distant pines and the deep blue of the Southern sky. The generous meal he had made had put the old man in a very good humor. He was not always so, for his curiously undeveloped nature was subject to moods which were almost childish in their variableness. It was only now and then that we were able to study, through the medium of his recollection, the simple but intensely human inner life of slavery. His way of looking at the past seemed very strange to us; his view of certain sides of life was essentially different from ours. He never indulged in any regrets for the Arcadian joyousness and irresponsibility which was a somewhat popular conception of slavery; his had not been the lot of the petted house-servant, but that of the toiling field-hand. While he mentioned with a warm appreciation the acts of kindness which those in authority had shown to him and his people, he would speak of a cruel deed, not with the indignation of one accustomed to quick feeling and spontaneous expression, but with a furtive disapproval which suggested to us a doubt in his own mind as to whether he had a right to think or to feel, and presented to us the curious psychological spectacle of a mind enslaved long after the shackles had been struck off from the limbs of its possessor. Whether the sacred name of liberty ever set his soul aglow with a generous fire; whether he had more than the most elementary ideas of love, friendship, patriotism, religion,—things which are half, and the better half, of life to us; whether he even realized, except in a vague, uncertain way, his own degradation, I do not know. I fear not; and if not, then centuries of repression had borne their legitimate fruit. But in the simple human feeling, and still more in the undertone of sadness, which pervaded his stories, I thought I could see a spark which, fanned by favoring breezes and fed by the memories of the past, might become in his children's children a glowing flame of sensibility, alive to every thrill of human happiness or human woe.

"Dave use' ter b'long ter my ole marster," said Julius; "he wuz raise' on dis yer plantation, en I kin 'member all erbout 'im, fer I wuz ole 'nuff ter chop cotton w'en it all happen'. Dave wuz a tall man, en monst'us strong: he could do mo' wuk in a day dan any yuther two niggers on de plantation. He wuz one er dese yer solemn kine er men, en nebber run on wid much foolishness, like de yuther darkies. He use' ter go out in de woods en pray; en w'en he hear de han's on de plantation cussin' en gwine on wid dere dancin' en foolishness, he use' ter tell 'em 'bout religion en jedgmen'-day, w'en dey would haf ter gin account fer eve'y idle word en all dey yuther sinful kyarin's-on.

"Dave had l'arn' how ter read de Bible. Dey wuz a free nigger boy in de settlement w'at wuz monst'us smart, en could write en cipher, en wuz alluz readin' books er papers. En Dave had hi'ed dis free boy fer ter l'arn 'im how ter read. Hit wuz 'g'in' de law, but co'se none er de niggers didn' say nuffin ter de w'ite folks 'bout it. Howsomedever, one day Mars Walker—he wuz de oberseah—foun' out Dave could read. Mars Walker wa'n't nuffin but a po'bockrah, en folks said he couldn' read ner write hisse'f, en co'se he didn' lack ter see a nigger w'at knowed mo' d'n he did; so he went en tole Mars Dugal'. Mars Dugal' sont fer Dave, en ax' 'im 'bout it.

"Dave didn't hardly knowed w'at ter do; but he couldn' tell no lie, so he 'fessed he could read de Bible a little by spellin' out de words. Mars Dugal' look' mighty solemn.

" 'Dis yer is a se'ious matter,' sezee; 'it's 'g'in' de law ter l'arn niggers how ter read, er 'low 'em ter hab books. But w'at yer l'arn oui'n dat Bible, Dave?'

"Dave wa'n't no fool, ef he wuz a nigger, en sezee:—

"'Marster, I l'arns dat it's a sin fer ter steal, er ter lie, er fer ter want w'at doan b'long ter yer; en I l'arns fer ter love de Lawd en ter 'bey my marster.'

"Mars Dugal' sorter smile' en laf' ter hisse'f, like he 'uz might'ly tickle' 'bout sump'n, en sezee:—

"'Doan 'pear ter me lack readin' de Bible done yer much harm, Dave. Dat's w'at I wants all my niggers fer ter know. Yer keep right on readin', en tell de yuther han's w'at yer be'n tellin' me. How would yer lack fer ter preach ter de niggers on Sunday?'

"Dave say he'd be glad fer ter do w'at he could. So Mars Dugal' tole de oberseah fer ter let Dave preach ter de niggers, en tell 'em w'at wuz in de Bible, en it would he'p ter keep 'em fum stealin' er runnin' erway.

"So Dave 'mence' ter preach, en done de han's on de plantation a heap er good, en most un 'em lef' off dey wicked ways, en 'mence' ter love ter hear 'bout God, en religion, en de Bible; en dey done dey wuk better, en didn' gib de oberseah but mighty little trouble fer ter manage 'em.

"Dave wuz one er dese yer men w'at didn' keer much fer de gals,—leastways he didn' 'tel Dilsey come ter de plantation. Dilsey wuz a monst'us peart, good-lookin', gingybread-colored gal,—one er dese yer high-steppin' gals w'at hol's dey heads up, en won' stan' no foolishness fum no man. She had b'long' ter a gemman over on Rockfish, w'at died, en whose 'state ha' ter be sol' fer ter pay his debts. En Mars Dugal' had be'n ter de oction, en w'en he seed dis gal a-cryin' en gwine on 'bout bein' sol' erway fum her ole mammy, Aun' Mahaly, Mars Dugal' bid 'em bofe in, en fotch 'em ober ter our plantation.

"De young nigger men on de plantation wuz des wil' atter Dilsey, but it didn' do no good, en none un 'em couldn' git Dilsey fer dey junesey,[1] 'tel Dave 'mence' fer ter go roun' Aun' Mahaly's cabin. Dey wuz a fine-lookin' couple, Dave en Dilsey wuz, bofe tall, en well-shape', en soopl'. En dey sot a heap by one ernudder. Mars Dugal' seed 'em tergedder one Sunday, en de nex' time he seed Dave atter dat, sezee:—

"'Dave, w'en yer en Dilsey gits ready fer ter git married, I ain' got no rejections. Dey's a poun' er so er chawin'-terbacker up

1 Sweetheart.

at de house, en I reckon yo' mist'iss kin fine a frock en a ribbin er two fer Dilsey. Youer bofe good niggers, en yer neenter be feared er bein' sol' 'way fum one ernudder long ez I owns dis plantation; en I 'spec's ter own it fer a long time yit.'

"But dere wuz one man on de plantation w'at didn' lack ter see Dave en Dilsey tergedder ez much ez ole marster did. W'en Mars Dugal' went ter de sale whar he got Dilsey en Mahaly, he bought ernudder han', by de name er Wiley. Wiley wuz one er dese yer shiny-eyed, double-headed little niggers, sha'p ez a steel trap, en sly ez de fox w'at keep out'n it. Dis yer Wiley had be'n pesterin' Dilsey 'fo' she come ter our plantation, en had nigh 'bout worried de life out'n her. She didn' keer nuffin fer 'im, but he pestered her so she ha' ter th'eaten ter tell her marster fer ter make Wiley let her 'lone. W'en he come ober to our place it wuz des ez bad, 'tel bimeby Wiley seed dat Dilsey had got ter thinkin' a heap 'bout Dave, en den he sorter hilt off aw'ile, en purten' lack he gin Dilsey up. But he wuz one er dese yer 'ceitful niggers, en w'ile he wuz laffin' en jokin' wid de yuther han's 'bout Dave en Dilsey, he wuz settin' a trap fer ter ketch Dave en git Dilsey back fer hisse'f.

"Dave en Dilsey made up dere min's fer ter git married long 'bout Christmas time, w'en dey'd hab mo' time fer a weddin'. But 'long 'bout two weeks befo' dat time ole mars 'mence' ter lose a heap er bacon. Eve'y night er so somebody 'ud steal a side er bacon, er a ham, er a shoulder, er sump'n, fum one er de smoke-'ouses. De smoke-'ouses wuz lock', but somebody had a key, en manage' ter git in some way er 'nudder. Dey's mo' ways 'n one ter skin a cat, en dey's mo' d'n one way ter git in a smoke-'ouse,—leastways dat's w'at I hearn say. Folks w'at had bacon fer ter sell didn' hab no trouble 'bout gittin' rid un it. Hit wuz 'g'in' de law fer ter buy things fum slabes; but Lawd! dat law didn' 'mount ter a hill er peas. Eve'y week er so one er dese yer big covered waggins would come 'long de road, peddlin' terbacker en w'iskey. Dey wuz a sight er room in one er dem big waggins, en it wuz monst'us easy fer ter swop off bacon fer sump'n ter chaw er ter wa'm yer up in de winter-time. I s'pose de peddlers didn' knowed dey wuz breakin' de law, caze de niggers alluz went at night, en stayed on de dark side er de waggin; en it wuz mighty hard fer ter tell *w'at* kine er folks dey wuz.

"Atter two er th'ee hund'ed er meat had be'n stole', Mars

Walker call all de niggers up one ebenin', en tol' 'em dat de fus' nigger he cot stealin' bacon on dat plantation would git sump'n fer ter 'member it by long ez he lib'. En he say he'd gin fi' dollars ter de nigger w'at 'skiver' de rogue. Mars Walker say he s'picion' one er two er de niggers, but he couln' tell fer sho, en co'se dey all 'nied it w'en he 'cuse em un it.

"Dey wa'n't no bacon stole' fer a week er so, 'tel one dark night w'en somebody tuk a ham fum one er de smoke-'ouses. Mars Walker des cusst awful w'en he foun' out de ham wuz gone, en say he gwine ter sarch all de niggers' cabins; w'en dis yer Wiley I wuz tellin' yer 'bout up'n say he s'picion' who tuk de ham, fer he seed Dave comin' 'cross de plantation fum to'ds de smoke-'ouse de night befo'. W'en Mars Walker hearn dis fum Wiley, he went en sarch' Dave's cabin, en foun' de ham hid under de flo'.

"Eve'ybody wuz 'stonish'; but dere wuz de ham. Co'se Dave 'nied it ter de las', but dere wuz de ham. Mars Walker say it wuz des ez he 'spected: he didn' b'lieve in dese yer readin' en prayin' niggers; it wuz all 'pocrisy, en sarve' Mars Dugal' right fer 'lowin' Dave ter be readin' books w'en it wuz 'g'in' de law.

"W'en Mars Dugal' hearn 'bout de ham, he say he wuz might'ly 'ceived en disapp'inted in Dave. He say he wouldn' nebber hab no mo' conferdence in no nigger, en Mars Walker could do des ez he wuz a mineter wid Dave er any er de res' er de niggers. So Mars Walker tuk 'n tied Dave up en gin 'im forty; en den he got some er dis yer wire clof w'at dey uses fer ter make sifters out'n, en tuk'n wrap' it roun' de ham en fasten it tergedder at de little een'. Den he tuk Dave down ter de blacksmif-shop, en had Unker Silas, de plantation blacksmif, fasten a chain ter de ham, en den fasten de yuther een' er de chain roun' Dave's neck. En den he says ter Dave, sezee:—

"'Now, suh, yer'll wear dat neckliss fer de nex' six mont's; en I 'spec's yer ner none er de yuther niggers on dis plantation won' steal no mo' bacon dyoin' er dat time.'

"Well, it des 'peared ez if fum dat time Dave didn' hab nuffin but trouble. De niggers all turnt ag'in' 'im, caze he be'n de 'casion er Mars Dugal' turnin' 'em all ober ter Mars Walker. Mars Dugal' wa'n't a bad marster hisse'f, but Mars Walker wuz hard ez a rock. Dave kep' on sayin' he didn' take de ham, but none un 'em didn' b'lieve 'im.

"Dilsey wa'n't on de plantation w'en Dave wuz 'cused er stealin' de bacon. Ole mist'iss had sont her ter town fer a week er so fer ter wait on one er her darters w'at had a young baby, en she didn' fine out nuffin 'bout Dave's trouble 'tel she got back ter de plantation. Dave had patien'ly endyoed de finger er seawn, en all de hard words w'at de niggers pile' on 'im caze he wuz sho' Dilsey would stan' by 'im, en wouldn' b'lieve he wuz a rogue, ner none er de yuther tales de darkies wuz tellin' 'bout 'im.

"W'en Dilsey come back fum town, en got down fum behine de buggy whar she b'en ridin' wid ole mars, de fus' nigger 'ooman she met says ter her,—

" 'Is yer seed Dave, Dilsey?'

" 'No, I ain' seed Dave,' says Dilsey.

" 'Yer des oughter look at dat nigger; reckon yer wouldn' want 'im fer yo' junesey no mo'. Mars Walker cotch 'im stealin' bacon, en gone en fasten' a ham roun' his neck, so he can't git it off 'n hisse'f. He sut'nly do look quare.' En den de 'ooman bus' out laffin' fit ter kill hers'f. W'en she got thoo laffin' she up'n tole Dilsey all 'bout de ham, en all de yuther lies w'at de niggers be'n tellin' on Dave.

"W'en Dilsey started down ter de quarters, who should she meet but Dave, comin' in fum de cotton-fiel'. She turnt her head ter one side, en purten' lack she didn' seed Dave.

" 'Dilsey!' sezee.

"Dilsey walk' right on, en didn' notice 'im.

" '*Oh*, Dilsey!'

"Dilsey didn' paid no 'tention ter 'im, en den Dave knowed some er de niggers be'n tellin' her 'bout de ham. He felt monst'us bad, but he 'lowed ef he could des git Dilsey fer ter listen ter 'im fer a minute er so, he could make her b'lieve he didn' stole de bacon. It wuz a week er two befo' he could git a chance ter speak ter her ag'in; but fine'ly he cotch her down by de spring one day, en sezee:—

" 'Dilsey, w'at fer yer won' speak ter me, en purten' lack yer doan see me? Dilsey, yer knows me too well fer ter b'lieve I'd steal, er do dis yuther wick'ness de niggers is all layin' ter me,— yer *knows* I wouldn' do dat, Dilsey. Yer ain' gwine back on yo' Dave, is yer?'

"But w'at Dave say didn' hab no 'fec' on Dilsey. Dem lies folks b'en tellin' her had p'isen' her min' 'g'in' Dave.

"'I doan wanter talk ter no nigger,' says she, 'w'at be'n whip' fer stealin', en w'at gwine roun' wid sich a lookin' thing ez dat hung roun' his neck. I's a 'spectable gal, *I* is. W'at yer call dat, Dave? Is dat a cha'm fer ter keep off witches, er is it a noo kine er neckliss yer got?'

"Po' Dave didn' knowed w'at ter do. De las' one he had 'pended on fer ter stan' by 'im had gone back on 'im, en dey didn' 'pear ter be nuffin mo' wuf libbin' fer. He couldn' hol' no mo' pra'r-meetin's, fer Mars Walker wouldn' 'low 'im ter preach, en de darkies wouldn' 'a' listen' ter 'im ef he had preach'. He didn' eben hab his Bible fer ter comfort hisse'f wid, fer Mars Walker had tuk it erway fum 'im en burnt it up, en say ef he ketch any mo' niggers wid Bibles on de plantation he'd do 'em wuss'n he done Dave.

"En ter make it still harder fer Dave, Dilsey tuk up wid Wiley. Dave could see him gwine up ter Aun' Mahaly's cabin, en settin' out on de bench in de moonlight wid Dilsey, en singin' sinful songs en playin' de banjer. Dave use' ter scrouch down behine de bushes, en wonder w'at de Lawd sen' 'im all dem tribberlations fer.

"But all er Dave's yuther troubles wa'n't nuffin side er dat ham. He had wrap' de chain roun' wid a rag, so it didn' hurt his neck; but w'eneber he went ter wuk, dat ham would be in his way; he had ter do his task, howsomedever, des de same ez ef he didn' hab de ham. W'eneber he went ter lay down, dat ham would be in de way. Ef he turn ober in his sleep, dat ham would be tuggin' at his neck. It wuz de las' thing he seed at night, en de fus' thing he seed in de mawnin'. W'eneber he met a stranger, de ham would be de fus' thing de stranger would see. Most un 'em would 'mence' ter laf, en whareber Dave went he could see folks p'intin' at him, en year 'em sayin':—

"'W'at kine er collar dat nigger got roun' his neck?' er, ef dey knowed 'im, 'Is yer stole any mo' hams lately?' er 'W'at yer take fer yo' neckliss, Dave?' er some joke er 'nuther 'bout dat ham.

"Fus' Dave didn' mine it so much, caze he knowed he hadn' done nuffin. But bimeby he got so he couldn' stan' it no longer, en he'd hide hisse'f in de bushes w'eneber he seed anybody comin', en alluz kep' hisse'f shet up in his cabin atter he come in fum wuk.

"It wuz monst'us hard on Dave, en bimeby, w'at wid dat ham eberlastin' en etarnally draggin' roun' his neck, he 'mence' fer ter do en say quare things, en make de niggers wonder ef he wa'n't gittin' out'n his mine. He got ter gwine roun' talkin' ter hisse'f, en singin' corn-shuckin' songs, en laffin' fit ter kill 'bout nuffin. En one day he tole one er de niggers he had 'skivered a noo way fer ter raise hams,—gwine ter pick 'em off'n trees, en save de expense er smoke-'ouses by kyoin' 'em in de sun. En one day he up'n tole Mars Walker he got sump'n pertickler fer ter say ter 'im; en he tuk Mars Walker off ter one side, en tole 'im he wuz gwine ter show 'im a place in de swamp whar dey wuz a whole trac' er lan' covered wid ham-trees.

"W'en Mars Walker hearn Dave talkin' dis kine er fool-talk, en w'en he seed how Dave wuz 'mencin' ter git behine in his wuk, en w'en he ax' de niggers en dey tole 'im how Dave be'n gwine on, he 'lowed he reckon' he'd punish' Dave ernuff, en it mou't do mo' harm dan good fer ter keep de ham on his neck any longer. So he sont Dave down ter de blacksmif-shop en had de ham tuk off. Dey wa'n't much er de ham lef' by dat time, fer de sun had melt all de fat, en de lean had all swivel' up, so dey wa'n't but th'ee er fo' poun's lef'.

"W'en de ham had be'n tuk off'n Dave, folks kinder stopped talkin' 'bout 'im so much. But de ham had be'n on his neck so long dat Dave had sorter got use' ter it. He look des lack he'd los' sump'n fer a day er so atter de ham wuz tuk off, en didn' 'pear ter know w'at ter do wid hisse'f; en fine'ly he up 'n tuk 'n tied a lighterd-knot ter a string, en hid it under de flo' er his cabin, en w'en nobody wuzn' lookin' he'd take it out en hang it roun' his neck, en go off in de woods en holler en sing; en he allus tied it roun' his neck w'en he went ter sleep. Fac', it 'peared lack Dave done gone clean out'n his mine. En atter a w'ile he got one er de quarest notions you eber hearn tell un. It wuz 'bout dat time dat I come back ter de plantation fer ter wuk,—I had be'n out ter Mars Dugal's yuther place on Beaver Crick for a mont' er so. I had hearn 'bout Dave en de bacon, en 'bout w'at wuz gwine on on de plantation; but I didn' b'lieve w'at dey all say 'bout Dave, fer I knowed Dave wa'n't dat kine er man. One day atter I come back, me'n Dave wuz choppin' cotton tergedder, w'en Dave lean' on his hoe, en motion' fer me ter come ober close ter 'im; en den he retch' ober en w'ispered ter me.

" 'Julius', sezee, 'did yer knowed yer wuz wukkin' long yer wid a ham?'

"I couldn' 'magine w'at he meant. 'G'way fum yer, Dave.' says I. 'Yer ain' wearin' no ham no mo'; try en fergit 'bout dat; 't ain' gwine ter do yer no good fer ter 'member it.'

" 'Look a-yer, Julius,' sezee, 'kin yer keep a secret?'

" 'Co'se I kin, Dave.' says I. 'I doan go roun' tellin' people w'at yuther folks says ter me.'

" 'Kin I trus' yer, Julius? Will yer cross yo' heart?'

"I cross' my heart. 'Wush I may die ef I tells a soul,' says I.

"Dave look' at me des lack he wuz lookin' thoo me en 'way on de yuther side er me, en sezee:—

" 'Did yer knowed I wuz turnin' ter a ham, Julius?'

"I tried ter 'suade Dave dat dat wuz all foolishness, en dat he oughtn't ter be talkin' dat-a-way,—hit wa'n't right. En I tole 'im ef he'd des be patien', de time would sho'ly come w'en eve'ything would be straighten' out, en folks would fine out who de rale rogue wuz w'at stole de bacon. Dave 'peared ter listen ter w'at I say, en promise' ter do better, en stop gwine on dat-a-way; en it seem lack he pick' up a bit w'en he seed dey wuz one pusson didn' b'lieve dem tales 'bout 'im.

"Hit wa'n't long atter dat befo' Mars Archie McIntyre, ober on de Wimbleton road, 'mence' ter complain 'bout somebody stealin' chickens fum his hen-'ouse. De chickens kep' on gwine, en at las' Mars Archie tole de han's on his plantation dat he gwine ter shoot de fus' man he ketch in his hen-'ouse. In less'n a week atter he gin dis warnin', he cotch a nigger in de hen-'ouse, en fill' 'im full er squir'l-shot. W'en he got a light, he 'skivered it wuz a strange nigger; en w'en he call' one er his own sarven's, de nigger tole 'im it wuz our Wiley. W'en Mars Archie foun' dat out, he sont ober ter our plantation fer ter tell Mars Dugal' he had shot one er his niggers, en dat he could sen' ober dere en git w'at wuz lef' un 'im.

"Mars Dugal' wuz mad at fus'; but w'en he got ober dere en hearn how it all happen', he didn' hab much ter say. Wiley wuz

shot so bad he wuz sho' he wuz gwine ter die, so he up'n says
ter ole marster:—

"'Mars Dugal',' sezee, 'I knows I's be'n a monst'us bad nigger,
but befo' I go I wanter git sump'n off'n my mine. Dave didn'
steal dat bacon w'at wuz tuk out'n de smoke-'ouse. *I* stole it all,
en I hid de ham under Dave's cabin fer ter th'ow de blame on
him—en may de good Lawd fergib me fer it.'

"Mars Dugal' had Wiley tuk back ter de plantation, en sont fer
a doctor fer ter pick de shot out'n 'im. En de ve'y nex' mawnin'
Mars Dugal' sont fer Dave ter come up ter de big house; he felt
kinder sorry fer de way Dave had be'n treated. Co'se it wa'n't
no fault er Mars Dugal's, but he wuz gwine ter do w'at he could
fer ter make up fer it. So he sont word down ter de quarters fer
Dave en all de yuther han's ter 'semble up in de yard befo' de
big house at sun-up nex' mawnin'.

"Yearly in de mawnin' de niggers all swarm' up in de yard.
Mars Dugal' wuz feelin' so kine dat he had brung up a bairl er
cider, en tole de niggers all fer ter he'p deyselves.

"All de han's on de plantation come but Dave; en bimeby,
w'en it seem lack he wa'n't comin', Mars Dugal' sont a nigger
down ter de quarters ter look fer 'im. De sun wuz gittin' up, en
dey wuz a heap er wuk ter be done, en Mars Dugal' sorter got
ti'ed waitin'; so he up'n says:—

"'Well, boys en gals, I sont fer yer all up yer fer ter tell yer
dat all dat 'bout Dave's stealin' er de bacon wuz a mistake, ez I
s'pose yer all done hearn befo' now, en I's mighty sorry it happen'. I wants ter treat all my niggers right, en I wants yer all
ter know dat I sets a heap by all er my han's w'at is hones' en
smart. En I want yer all ter treat Dave des lack yer did befo'
dis thing happen', en mine w'at he preach ter yer; fer Dave is
a good nigger, en has had a hard row ter hoe. En de fus' one
I ketch sayin' anythin' 'g'in' Dave, I'll tell Mister Walker ter gin
'im forty. Now take ernudder drink er cider all roun', en den
git at dat cotton, fer I wanter git dat Persimmon Hill trac' all
pick' ober ter-day.'

"W'en de niggers wuz gwine 'way, Mars Dugal' tole me fer ter
go en hunt up Dave, en bring 'im up ter de house. I went down
ter Dave's cabin, but couldn' fine 'im dere. Den I look' roun' de
plantation, en in de aidge er de woods, en 'long de road; but I

couldn' fine no sign er Dave. I wuz 'bout ter gin up de sarch, w'en I happen' fer ter run 'cross a foot-track w'at look' lack Dave's. I had wukked 'long wid Dave so much dat I knowed his tracks: he had a monst'us long foot, wid a holler instep, w'ich wuz sump'n skase 'mongs' black folks. So I follered dat track 'cross de fiel' fum de quarters 'tel I got ter de smoke-'ouse. De fus' thing I notice' wuz smoke comin' out'n de cracks: it wuz cu'ous, caze dey hadn' be'n no hogs kill' on de plantation fer six mont' er so, en all de bacon in de smoke-'ouse wuz done kyoed. I couldn' 'magine fer ter sabe my life w'at Dave wuz doin' in dat smoke-'ouse. I went up ter de do' en hollered:—

"'Dave!'

"Dey didn' nobody answer. I didn' wanter open de do', fer w'ite folks is monst'us pertickler 'bout dey smoke-'ouses; en ef de oberseah had a-come up en cotch me in dere, he mou't not wanter b'lieve I wuz des lookin' fer Dave. So I sorter knock at de do' en call' out ag'in:—

"'O Dave, hit's me—Julius! Doan be skeered. Mars Dugal' wants yer ter come up ter de big house,—he done 'skivered who stole de ham.'

"But Dave didn' answer. En w'en I look' roun' ag'in en didn' seed none er his tracks gwine way fum de smoke-'ouse, I knowed he wuz in dere yit, en I wuz 'termine' fer ter fetch 'im out; so I push de do' open en look in.

"Dey wuz a pile er bark burnin' in de middle er de flo', en right ober de fier, hangin' fum one er de rafters, wuz Dave; dey wuz a rope roun' his neck, en I didn' haf ter look at his face mo' d'n once fer ter see he wuz dead.

"Den I knowed how it all happen'. Dave had kep' on gittin' wusser en wusser in his mine, 'tel he des got ter b'lievin' he wuz all done turnt ter a ham; en den he had gone en built a fier, en tied a rope roun' his neck, des lack de hams wuz tied, en had hung hisse'f up in de smoke-'ouse fer ter kyo.

"Dave wuz buried down by de swamp, in de plantation buryin'-groun'. Wiley didn' died fum de woun' he got in Mars McIntyre's hen-'ouse; he got well atter a w'ile, but Dilsey wouldn' hab nuffin mo' ter do wid 'im, en 't wa'n't long 'fo' Mars Dugal' sol' 'im ter a spekilater on his way souf,—he say he didn' want no sich a nigger on de plantation, ner in de county, ef he could he'p it. En w'en de een' er de year come, Mars Dugal' turnt Mars Walker off, en run de plantation hisse'f atter dat.

"Eber sence den," said Julius in conclusion, "w'eneber I eats ham, it min's me er Dave. I lacks ham, but I nebber kin eat mo' d'n two er th'ee poun's befo' I gits ter studyin' 'bout Dave, en den I has ter stop en leab de res' fer ernudder time."

There was a short silence after the old man had finished his story, and then my wife began to talk to him about the weather, on which subject he was an authority. I went into the house. When I came out, half an hour later, I saw Julius disappearing down the lane, with a basket on his arm.

At breakfast, next morning, it occurred to me that I should like a slice of ham. I said as much to my wife.

"Oh, no, John," she responded, "you shouldn't eat anything so heavy for breakfast."

I insisted.

"The fact is," she said, pensively, "I couldn't have eaten any more of that ham, and so I gave it to Julius."

A Deep Sleeper

I t was four o'clock on Sunday afternoon, in the month of July. The air had been hot and sultry, but a light, cool breeze had sprung up, and occasional cirrus clouds overspread the sun, and for a while subdued his fierceness. We were all out on the piazza—as the coolest place we could find—my wife, my sister-in-law and I. The only sounds that broke the Sabbath stillness were the hum of an occasional vagrant bumble-bee, or the fragmentary song of a mocking-bird in a neighboring elm, who lazily trolled a stave of melody, now and then, as a sample of what he could do in the cool of the morning, or after a light shower, when the conditions would be favorable to exertion.

"Annie," said I, "suppose, to relieve the deadly dulness of the afternoon, that we go out and pull the big watermelon, and send for Colonel Pemberton's folks to come over and help us eat it."

"Is it ripe, yet?" she inquired sleepily, brushing away a troublesome fly that had impudently settled on her hair.

"Yes, I think so. I was out yesterday with Julius, and we thumped it, and concluded it would be fully ripe by to-morrow or next day. But I think it is perfectly safe to pull it to-day."

"Well, if you are sure, dear, we'll go. But how can we get it up to the house? It's too big to tote."

"I'll step round to Julius's cabin and ask him to go down with the wheelbarrow and bring it up," I replied.

Julius was an elderly colored man who worked on the plantation and lived in a small house on the place, a few rods from my own residence. His daughter was our cook, and other members of his family served us in different capacities.

As I turned the corner of the house I saw Julius coming up the lane. He had on his Sunday clothes, and was probably returning from the afternoon meeting at the Sandy Run Baptist Church, of which he was a leading member and deacon.

"Julius," I said, "we are going out to pull the big watermelon, and we want you to take the wheelbarrow and go with us, and bring it up to the house."

"Does yer reckon dat watermillun's ripe yit, sah?" said Julius. "Didn' 'pear ter me it went quite plunk enuff yistiddy fer ter be pull' befo' termorrer."

"I think it is ripe enough, Julius."

"Mawnin' 'ud be a better time fer ter pull it, sah, w'en de night air an' de jew's done cool' it off nice."

"Probably that's true enough, but we'll put it on ice, and that will cool it; and I'm afraid if we leave it too long, some one will steal it."

"I 'spec's dat so," said the old man, with a confirmatory shake of the head. "Yer takes chances w'en yer pulls it, en' yer takes chances w'en yer don't. Dey's a lot er po' w'ite trash roun' heah w'at ain' none too good fer ter steal it. I seed some un' 'em loafin' long de big road on mer way home fum chu'ch jes' now. I has ter watch mer own chicken-coop ter keep chick'ns 'nuff fer Sunday eatin'. I'll go en' git de w'eelborrow."

Julius had a profound contempt for poor whites, and never let slip an opportunity for expressing it. He assumed that we shared this sentiment, while in fact our feeling toward this listless race was something entirely different. They were, like Julius himself, the product of a system which they had not created and which they did not know enough to resist.

As the old man turned to go away he began to limp, and put his hand to his knee with an exclamation of pain.

"What's the matter, Julius?" asked my wife.

Yes, Uncle Julius, what ails you?" echoed her sweet young sister. "Did you stump your toe?"

"No, miss, it's dat mis'able rheumatiz. It ketches me now an' den in de lef' knee, so I can't hardly draw my bref. O Lawdy!"

he added between his clenched teeth, "but dat do hurt. Ouch! It's a little better now," he said, after a moment, "but I doan' b'lieve I kin roll dat w'eelborrow out ter de watermillun-patch en' back. Ef it's all de same ter yo', sah, I'll go roun' ter my house en' sen' Tom ter take my place, w'iles I rubs some linimum on my laig."

"That'll be all right, Julius," I said, and the old man, hobbling, disappeared round the corner of the house. Tom was a lubberly, sleepy-looking negro boy of about fifteen, related to Julius's wife in some degree, and living with them.

The old man came back in about five minutes. He walked slowly, and seemed very careful about bearing his weight on the afflicted member.

"I sont 'Liza Jane fer ter wake Tom up," he said. "He's down in de orchard asleep under a tree somewhar. 'Liza Jane knows whar he is. It takes a minute er so fer ter wake 'im up. 'Liza Jane knows how ter do it. She tickles 'im in de nose er de yeah wid a broomstraw; hollerin' doan' do no good. Dat boy is one er de Seben Sleepers. He's wuss'n his gran'daddy used ter be."

"Was his grandfather a deep sleeper, Uncle Julius?" asked my wife's sister.

"Oh, yas, Miss Mabel," said Julius, gravely. "He wuz a monst'us pow'ful sleeper. He slep' fer a mont' once."

"Dear me, Uncle Julius, you must be joking," said my sister-in-law incredulously. I thought she put it mildly.

"Oh, no, ma'm, I ain't jokin'. I never jokes on ser'ous subjec's. I wuz dere w'en it all happen'. Hit wuz a monst'us quare thing."

"Sit down, Uncle Julius, and tell us about it," said Mabel; for she dearly loved a story, and spent much of her time "drawing out" the colored people in the neighborhood.

The old man took off his hat and seated himself on the top step of the piazza. His movements were somewhat stiff and he was very careful to get his left leg in a comfortable position.

"Tom's gran'daddy wuz name' Skundus," he began. "He had a brudder name' Tushus en' ernudder name Cottus en' ernudder name' Squinchus." The old man paused a moment and gave his leg another hitch.

My sister-in-law was shaking with laughter. "What remarkable names!" she exclaimed. "Where in the world did they get them?"

"Dem names wuz gun ter 'em by ole Marse Dugal' McAdoo, wat I use' ter b'long ter, en' dey use' ter b'long ter. Marse Dugal' named all de babies w'at wuz bawn on de plantation. Dese young un's mammy wanted ter call 'em sump'n plain en' simple, like 'Rastus' er 'Caesar' er 'George Wash'n'ton'; but ole Marse say no, he want all de niggers on his place ter hab diffe'nt names, so he kin tell 'em apart. He'd done use' up all de common names, so he had ter take sump'n else. Dem names he gun Skundus en' his brudders is Hebrew names en' wuz tuk out'n de Bible."

"Can you give me chapter and verse?" asked Mabel.

"No, Miss Mabel, I doan know 'em. Hit ain' my fault dat I ain't able ter read de Bible. But ez I wuz a-sayin', dis yer Skundus growed up ter be a peart, lively kind er boy, en' wuz very well liked on de plantation. He never quo'lled wid de res' er de han's en' alluz behaved 'isse'f en' tended ter his wuk. De only fault he had wuz his sleep'ness. He'd haf ter be woke up ev'y mawnin' ter go ter his wuk, en' w'enever he got a chance he'd fall ersleep. He wuz might'ly nigh gittin' inter trouble mod'n once fer gwine ter sleep in de fiel'. I never seed his beat fer sleepin'. He could sleep in de sun er sleep in de shade. He could lean upon his hoe en' sleep. He went ter sleep walk'n' 'long de road oncet, en' mighty nigh bus't his head open 'gin' a tree he run inter. I did heah he oncet went ter sleep while he wuz in swimmin'. He wuz floatin' at de time, en' come mighty nigh gittin' drownded befo' he woke up. Ole Marse heared 'bout it en' ferbid his gwine in swimmin' enny mo', fer he said he couldn't 'ford ter lose 'im.

"When Skundus wuz growed up he got ter lookin' roun' at de gals, en' one er de likeliest un 'em tuk his eye. It was a gal name' Cindy, w'at libbed wid 'er mammy in a cabin by deyse'ves. Cindy tuk ter Skundus ez much ez Skundus tuk ter Cindy, en' bimeby Skundus axed his marster ef he could marry Cindy. Marse Dugal' b'long' ter de P'isbytay'n Chu'ch en' never 'lowed his niggers ter jump de broomstick, but alluz had a preacher fer ter marry 'em. So he tole Skundus ef him en' Cindy would 'ten' ter dey wuk good dat summer till de crap was laid by, he'd let 'em git married en' hab a weddin' down ter de quarters.

"So Skundus en' Cindy wukked hahd as dey could till 'bout a mont' er so befo' layin' by, w'en Marse Dugal's brudder, Kunnel Wash'n'ton McAdoo, w'at libbed down in Sampson County, 'bout a hunderd mile erway, come fer ter visit Marse Dugal'.

Dey wuz five er six folks in de visitin' party, en' our w'ite folks needed a new gal fer ter he'p wait on 'em. Dey picked out de likeliest gal dey could fine 'mongs' de fiel'-han's, en' 'cose dat wuz Cindy. Cindy wuz might'ly tickled fer ter be tuk in de house-sarvice, fer it meant better vittles en' better clo's en' easy wuk. She didn' seed Skundus quite as much, but she seed 'im w'eneber she could. Prospe'ity didn' spile Cindy; she didn' git stuck up en' 'bove 'sociatin' wid fiel'-han's, lack some gals in her place 'ud a done.

"Cindy wuz sech a handy gal 'roun' de house, en' her marster's relations lacked her so much, dat w'en dey visit wuz ober, dey wanted ter take Cindy 'way wid 'em. Cindy didn' want ter go en' said so. Her marster wuz a good-natured kind er man, en' would 'a' kep' her on de plantation. But his wife say no, it 'ud nebber do ter be lett'n' de sarvants hab dey own way, er dey soon wouldn' be no doin' nuthin' wid 'em. Ole marster tole 'er he done promus ter let Cindy marry Skundus.

"'O, well,' sez ole Miss, 'dat doan' cut no figger. Dey's too much er dis foolishness 'bout husban's en' wibes 'mongs' de niggers now-a-days. One nigger man is de same as ernudder, en' dey'll be plenty un 'em down ter Wash'n'ton's plantation.' Ole Miss wuz a mighty smart woman, but she didn' know ev'ything.

"'Well,' says ole Marse, 'de craps'll be laid by in a mont' now, 'en den dey won't be much ter do fer ernudder mont' er six weeks. So we'll let her go down dere an' stay till cotton-pickin' time; I'll jes' len' 'er ter 'em till den. Ef dey wants ter keep 'er en' we finds we doan need 'er, den we'll talk furder 'bout sellin' 'er. We'll tell her dat we jes' gwine let her go down dere wid de chil'en a week er so en' den come back, en' den we won't hab no fuss 'bout it.'

"So dey fixed it dat erway, en' Cindy went off wid 'em, she 'spectin' ter be back in a week er so, en' de w'ite folks not hahdly 'lowin' she'd come back at all. Skundus didn' lack ter hab Cindy go, but he couldn' do nuthin'. He wuz wukkin' off in ernudder part er de plantation w'en she went erway, en' had ter tell her good-by de night befo'.

"Bimeby, w'en Cindy didn' come back in two or th'ee weeks, Skundus 'mence ter git res'less. En' Skundus wuz diff'ent f'um udder folks. Mos' folks w'en dey gits res'less can't sleep good, but de mo' res'lesser Skundus got, de mo' sleepier he 'peared ter git. W'eneber he wuz'n wukkin' er eatin', he'd be sleepin'. W'en de yuther niggers 'ud be skylarkin' 'roun' nights en' Sundays, Skundus 'ud be soun' asleep in his cabin. Things kep' on dis way fer 'bout a mont' atter Cindy went away, w'en one mawnin' Skundus didn't come ter wuk. Dey look' fer 'im 'roun' de plantation, but dey couldn' fin' 'im, en' befo' de day wuz gone, ev'ybody wuz sho' dat Skundus had runned erway.

"Cose dey wuz a great howdydo 'bout it. Nobody hadn' nebber runned erway fum Marse Dugal' befo', an' dey hadn' b'en a runaway nigger in de neighbo'hood fer th'ee er fo' years. De w'ite folks wuz all wukked up, en' dey wuz mo' ridin' er hosses en' mo' hitchin up er buggies d'n a little. Ole Marse Dugal' had a lot er papers printed en' stuck up on trees 'long de roads, en' dey wuz sump'n put in de noospapers—a free nigger f'um down on de Wim'l'ton Road read de paper ter some er our han's—tellin' all 'bout how high Skundus wuz, en' w'at kine er teef he had, en' 'bout a skyah he had on his lef' cheek, en' how sleepy he wuz, en' off'rin' a reward er one hunder' dollars fer whoeber 'ud ketch 'im. But none of 'em eber cotch 'im.

"W'en Cindy fus' went away she wuz kinder down in de mouf fer a day er so. But she went to a fine new house, de folks treated her well en' dere wuz sich good comp'ny 'mongs' her own people, dat she made up 'er min' she might's well hab a good time fer de week er two she wuz gwine ter stay down dere. But w'en de time roll' on en' she didn' heared nothin' 'bout gwine back, she 'mence' ter git kinder skeered she wuz'n nebber gwine ter see her mammy ner Skundus no mo'. She wuz monst'us cut up 'bout it, an' los' 'er appetite en' got so po' en' skinny, her mist'ess sont 'er down ter de swamp fer ter git some roots fer ter make some tea fer 'er health. Her mist'ess sont her 'way 'bout th'ee o'clock en' Cindy didn' come back till atter sundown; en' she say she b'en lookin' fer de roots, dat dey didn' 'pear ter be none er dem kin' er roots fer a mile er so 'long de aidge er de swamp.

"Cindy 'mence' ter git better jes' ez soon as she begun ter drink de root-tea. It wuz a monst'us good med'cine, leas'ways in her case. It done Cindy so much good dat her mist'ess 'cluded she'd take it herse'f en' gib it ter de chil'en. De fus' day Cindy went atter de roots dey wuz some lef' ober, en' her mist'ess tol' 'er fer ter use dat fer de nex' day. Cindy done so, but she tol' 'er mist'ess hit didn' hab no strenk en' didn' do 'er no good. So ev'y day atter dat Marse Wash'n'ton's wife 'ud sen' Cindy down by de aidge er de swamp fer ter git fresh roots.

" 'Cindy,' said one er de fiel'-han's one day, 'yer better keep 'way fum dat swamp. Dey's a ha'nt walkin' down dere.'

" 'Go way fum yere wid yo' foolishness,' said Cindy. 'Dey ain' no ha'nts. W'ite folks doan' b'lieve in sich things, fer I heared 'em say so; but yer can't 'spec' nothin' better fum fiel'-han's.'

"Dey wuz one man on de plantation, one er dese yer dandy niggers w'at 'uz alluz runnin' atter de wimmen folks, dat got ter pest'rin' Cindy. Cindy didn' paid no 'tention ter 'im, but he kep' on tryin' fer ter co't her w'en he could git a chance. Fin'ly Cindy tole 'im fer ter let her 'lone, er e'se sump'n' might happen ter 'im. But he didn' min' Cindy, en' one ebenin' he followed her down ter de swamp. He los' track un er, en' ez he wuz a-startin' back out'n de swamp, a great big black ha'nt 'bout ten feet high, en' wid a fence-rail in its han's jump out'n de bushes en' chase 'im cl'ar up in de co'n fiel'. Leas'ways he said it did; en' atter dat none er de niggers wouldn't go nigh de swamp, 'cep'n Cindy, who said it wuz all foolishness—it wuz dis nigger's guilty conscience dat skeered 'im—she hadn' seed no ha'nt en' wuz'n skeered er nuffin' she didn't see.

"Bimeby, w'en Cindy had be'n gone fum home 'bout two mont's, harves'-time come on, en' Marse Dugal' foun' hisse'f short er han's. One er de men wuz down wid de rheumatiz, Skundus wuz gone, en' Cindy wuz gone, en' Marse Dugal tole ole Miss dey wuz no use talkin', he couldn' 'ford ter buy no new han's, en' he'd ha' ter sen' fer Cindy, 'en put her in de fiel'; fer de cotton-crap wuz a monst'us big 'un dat year, en' Cindy wuz one er de bes' cotton-pickers on de plantation. So dey wrote a letter to Marse Wash'n'ton dat day fer Cindy, en' wanted Cindy by de 'een er de mont', en' Marse Wash'n'ton sont her home. Cindy didn't 'pear ter wanter come much. She said she'd got kinder use' ter her noo home; but she didn' hab no mo' ter say 'bout comin' dan she did 'bout goin'. Howsomedever, she went down ter de swamp fer ter git roots fer her mist'ess up ter de las' day she wuz dere.

"W'en Cindy got back home, she wuz might'ly put out 'ca'se Skundus wuz gone, en' hit didn' 'pear ez ef anythin' anybody said ter 'er 'ud comfort 'er. But one mawnin' she said she'd dreamp' dat night dat Skundus wuz gwine ter come back; en' sho' 'nuff, de ve'y nex' mawnin' who sh'd come walkin' out in de fiel' wid his hoe on his shoulder but Skundus, rubbin' his eyes ez ef he hadn' got waked up good yit.

"Dey wuz a great 'miration mongs' de niggers, en' somebody run off ter de big house fer ter tell Marse Dugal'. Bimeby here come Marse Dugal' hisse'f, mad as a hawnit, a-cussin' en' gwine on like he gwine ter hurt somebody; but anybody w'at look close could' 'a' seed he wuz 'mos' tickled ter def fer ter git Skundus back ergin.

"'Whar yer be'n run erway ter, yer good-fer-nuthin', lazy, black nigger?' sez 'e. 'I'm gwine ter gib yer fo' hunderd lashes. I'm gwine ter hang yer up by yer thumbs en' take ev'y bit er yer black hide off'n yer, en' den I'm gwine ter sell yer ter de fus' specilater w'at comes' long buyin' niggers fer ter take down ter Alabam'. W'at yer mean by runnin' er way fum yer good, kin' marster, yer good-fer-nuthin', wool-headed, black scound'el?'

"Skundus looked at 'im ez ef he didn' understan'. 'Lawd, Marse Dugal',' sez 'e, 'I doan' know w'at youer talkin' 'bout. I ain' runned erway; I ain' be'n nowhar.'

"'Whar yer be'n fer de las' mon'?' said Marse Dugal'. 'Tell me de truf, er I'll hab yer tongue pulled out by de roots. I'll tar yer all ober yer en' set yer on fiah. I'll—I'll'—Marse Dugal' went on at a tarrable rate, but eve'ybody knowed Marse Dugal' bark uz wuss'n his bite.

"Skundus look lack 'e wuz skeered mos' ter def fer ter heah Marse Dugal' gwine on dat erway, en' he couldn' 'pear to un'erstan' w'at Marse Dugal' was talkin' erbout.

"'I didn' mean no harm by sleep'n in de barn las' night, Marse Dugal',' sez 'e, 'en' ef yer'll let me off dis time, I won' nebber do so no mo'.'

"Well, ter make a long story sho't, Skundus said he had gone ter de barn dat Sunday afternoon befo' de Monday w'en he couldn't be foun', fer ter hunt aigs, en' wiles he wuz up dere de hay had 'peared so sof' en' nice dat he had laid down fer take a little nap; dat it wuz mawnin' w'en he woke en' foun' hisse'f all covered up whar de hay had fell over on 'im. A hen had built a nes' right on top un 'im, en' it had half-a-dozen aigs in it. He said he hadn't stop fer ter git no brekfus', but had jes' suck' one or two er de aigs en' hurried right straight out in de fiel', fer he seed it wuz late en' all de res' er de han's wuz gone ter wuk.

" 'Youer a liar,' said Marse Dugal', 'en' de truf ain't in yer. Yer b'en run erway en' hid in de swamp somewhar ernudder.' But Skundus swo' up en' down dat he hadn' b'en out'n dat barn, en' fin'lly Marse Dugal' went up ter de house en' Skundus went on wid his wuk.

"Well, yer mought know dey wuz a great 'miration in de neighbo'hood. Marse Dugal' sont fer Skundus ter cum up ter de big house nex' day, en' Skundus went up 'spect'n' fer ter ketch forty. But w'en he got dere, Marse Dugal' had fetched up ole Doctor Leach fum down on Rockfish, 'en another young doctor fum town, en' dey looked at Skundus's eyes en' felt of his wris' en' pulled out his tongue, en' hit 'im in de chis', en' put dey yeahs ter his side fer ter heah 'is heart beat; en' den dey up 'n made Skundus tell how he felt w'en 'e went ter sleep en' how he felt w'en 'e woke up. Dey stayed ter dinner, en' w'en dey got thoo' talkin' en' eatin' en' drinkin', dey tole Marse Dugal' Skundus had had a catacornered fit, en' had be'n in a trance fer fo' weeks. En' w'en dey l'arned about Cindy, en' how dis yer fit had come on gradg'ly atter Cindy went away, dey 'lowed Marse Dugal' 'd better let Skundus en' Cindy git married, er he'd be liable ter hab some mo' er dem fits. Fer Marse Dugal' didn' want no fittified niggers ef 'e could he'p it.

"Atter dat, Marse Dugal' had Skundus up ter de house lots er times fer ter show 'im off ter folks w'at come ter visit. En' bein' as Cindy wuz back home, en' she en' Skundus wukked hahd, en' he couldn' 'ford fer ter take no chances on dem long trances, he 'lowed em ter got married soon ez cotton-pickin' wuz ober, en' gib 'em a cabin er dey own ter lib in down in de quarters. En' sho' 'nuff, dey didn' had no trouble keep'n' Skundus wak f'm dat time fo'th, fer Cindy turned out ter hab a temper of her own, en' made Skundus walk a chalk-line.

"Dis yer boy Tom," said the old man, straightening out his leg carefully, preparatory to getting up, "is jes' like his gran'daddy. I b'lieve ef somebody didn' wake 'im up he'd sleep till jedgmen' day. Heah 'e comes now. Come on heah wid dat w'eelborrow, yer lazy, good-fer-nuthin' rascal."

Tom came slowly round the house with the wheelbarrow, and stood blinking and rolling his eyes as if he had just emerged from a sound sleep and was not yet half awake.

We took our way around the house, the ladies and I in front, Julius next and Tom bringing up the rear with the wheelbarrow. We went by the well-kept grape-vines, heavy with the promise of an abundant harvest, through a narrow field of yellowing corn, and then picked our way through the watermelon-vines to the spot where the monarch of the patch had lain the day before, in all the glory of its coat of variegated green. There was a shallow concavity in the sand where it had rested, but the melon itself was gone.

LONESOME BEN

There had been some talk among local capitalists about building a cotton mill on Beaver Creek, a few miles from my place on the sand hills in North Carolina, and I had been approached as likely to take an interest in such an enterprise. While I had the matter under advisement it was suggested, as an inducement to my co-operation, that I might have the brick for the mill made on my place—there being clay there suitable for the purpose—and thus reduce the amount of my actual cash investment. Most of my land was sandy, though I had observed several outcroppings of clay along the little creek or branch forming one of my boundaries.

One afternoon in summer, when the sun was low and the heat less oppressive than it had been earlier in the day, I ordered Julius, our old colored coachman, to harness the mare to the rockaway and drive me to look at the clay-banks. When we were ready, my wife, who wished to go with me for the sake of the drive, came out and took her seat by my side.

We reached our first point of destination by a road running across the plantation, between a field of dark-green maize on the one hand and a broad expanse of scuppernong vines on the other. The road led us past a cabin occupied by one of my farm-hands. As the carriage went by at a walk, the woman of the house came to the door and curtsied. My wife made some inquiry about her health, and she replied that it was poor. I noticed that her complexion, which naturally was of a ruddy brown, was of a rather sickly hue. Indeed, I had observed a greater sallowness among both the colored people and the poor whites thereabouts than the hygienic conditions of the neighborhood seemed to justify.

After leaving this house our road lay through a cotton field for a short distance, and then we entered a strip of woods, through which ran the little stream beside which I had observed the clay. We stopped at the creek, the road by which we had come crossing it and continuing over the land of my neighbor, Colonel Pemberton. By the roadside, on my own land, a bank of clay rose in almost a sheer perpendicular for about ten feet, evidently extending back some distance into the low, pine-clad hill behind it, and having also frontage upon the creek. There were marks of bare feet on the ground along the base of the bank, and the face of it seemed freshly disturbed and scored with finger marks, as though children had been playing there.

"Do you think that clay would make good brick, Julius?" I asked the old man, who had been unusually quiet during the drive. He generally played with the whip, making little feints at the mare, or slapping her lightly with the reins, or admonishing her in a familiar way; but on this occasion the heat or some other cause had rendered him less demonstrative than usual.

"Yas, suh, I knows it would," he answered.

"How do you know? Has it ever been used for that purpose?"

"No, suh; but I got my reasons fer sayin' so. Ole Mars Dugal useter hab a brickya'd fu'ther up de branch—I dunno as yer noticed it, fer it's all growed ober wid weeds an' grass. Mars Dugal said dis-yer clay wouldn' make good brick, but I knowed better."

I judged from the appearance of the clay that it was probably deficient in iron. It was of a yellowish-white tint and had a sort of greasy look.

"Well," I said, "we'll drive up to the other place and get a sample of that clay, and then we'll come back this way."

"Hold on a minute, dear," said my wife, looking at her watch, "Mabel has been over to Colonel Pemberton's all the afternoon. She said she'd be back at five. If we wait here a little while she'll be along and we can take her with us."

"All right," I said, "we'll wait for her. Drive up a little farther, Julius, by that jessamine vine."

While we were waiting, a white woman wearing a homespun dress and slat-bonnet, came down the road from the other side of the creek, and lifting her skirts slightly, waded with bare feet across the shallow stream. Reaching the clay-bank she stooped and gathered from it, with the aid of a convenient stick, a quantity of the clay which she pressed together in the form of a ball. She had not seen us at first, the bushes partially screening us; but when, having secured the clay, she turned her face in our direction and caught sight of us watching her, she hid the lump of clay in her pocket with a shamefaced look, and hurried away by the road she had come.

"What is she going to do with that, Uncle Julius?" asked my wife. We were Northern settlers, and still new to some of the customs of the locality, concerning which we often looked to Julius for information. He had lived on the place many years and knew the neighborhood thoroughly.

"She's gwineter eat it, Miss Annie," he replied, "w'en she gits outer sight."

"Ugh!" said my wife with a grimace, "you don't mean she's going to eat that great lump of clay?"

"Yas'm I does; dat's jes' w'at I means—gwineter eat eve'y bit un it, an' den come back bimeby fer mo'."

"I should think it would make them sick," she said.

"Dey gits use' ter it," said Julius. "Howsomeber, ef dey eats too much it does make 'em sick; an' I knows w'at I'm er-talkin' erbout. I doan min' w'at dem kinder folks does," he added, looking contemptuously after the retreating figure of the poor-white woman, "but w'eneber I sees black folks eat'n' clay of'n dat partic'lar clay-bank, it alluz sets me ter studyin' 'bout po' lonesome Ben."

"What was the matter with Ben?" asked my wife. "You can tell us while we're waiting for Mabel."

Old Julius often beguiled our leisure with stories of plantation life, some of them folk-lore stories, which we found to be in general circulation among the colored people; some of them tales of real life as Julius had seen it in the old slave days; but the most striking were, we suspected, purely imaginary, or so colored by old Julius's fancy as to make us speculate at times upon how many original minds, which might have added to the world's wealth of literature and art, had been buried in the ocean of slavery.

"W'en ole Mars Marrabo McSwayne owned dat place ober de branch dere, w'at Kunnel Pembe'ton owns now," the old man began, "he useter hab a nigger man name' Ben. Ben wuz one er dese yer big black niggers—he was mo' d'n six foot high an' black ez coal. He wuz a fiel'-han' an' a good wukker, but he had one little failin'—he would take a drap er so oncet in a w'ile. Co'se eve'ybody laks a drap now an' den, but it 'peared ter 'fec' Ben mo' d'n it did yuther folks. He didn' hab much chance dat-a-way, but eve'y now an' den he'd git holt er sump'n' somewahr, an' sho's he did, he'd git out'n de narrer road. Mars Marrabo kep' on wa'nin' 'm 'bout it, an' fin'lly he tol' 'im ef he eber ketch 'im in dat shape ag'in he 'uz gwineter gib 'im fo'ty. Ben knowed ole Mars Marrabo had a good 'memb'ance an' alluz done w'at he said, so he wuz monst'us keerful not ter gib 'm no 'casion fer ter use his 'memb'ance on him. An' so fer mos' a whole yeah Ben 'nied hisse'f an' nebber teched a drap er nuffin'.

"But it's ha'd wuk ter larn a ole dog new tricks, er ter make him fergit de ole uns, an' po' Ben's time come bimeby, jes' lak ev'ybody e'se's does. Mars Marrabo sent 'im ober ter dis yer plantation one day wid a bundle er cotton-sacks fer Mars Dugal', an' wiles he wuz ober yere, de ole Debbil sent a' 'oman w'at had cas' her eyes on 'im an' knowed his weakness, fer ter temp' po' Ben wid some licker. Mars Whiskey wuz right dere an' Mars Marrabo wuz a mile erway, an' so Ben minded Mars Whiskey an' fergot 'bout Mars Marrabo. W'en he got back home he couldn' skasely tell Mars Marrabo de message w'at Mars Dugal' had sent back ter 'im.

"Mars Marrabo listen' at 'im 'temp' ter tell it; and den he says, kinder col' and cuttin'-like—he didn' 'pear ter get mad ner nuffin':

"'Youer drunk, Ben.'

"De way his marster spoke sorter sobered Ben, an' he 'nied it of co'se.

"'Who? Me, Mars Marrabo? *I* ain' drunk; no, marster, *I* ain' drunk. I ain' teched a drap er nuffin' sence las' Chris'mas, suh'.

"'Youer drunk, Ben, an' don't you dare ter 'spute my wo'd, er I'll kill you in yo' tracks! I'll talk ter you Sad'day night, suh, w'en you'll be sober, an' w'en you'll hab Sunday ter 'flect over ou' conve'sation, an' 'nuss yo' woun's.'

"W'en Mars Marrabo got th'oo talkin' Ben wuz mo' sober dan he wuz befo' he got drunk. It wuz Wednesday w'en Ben's marster tol 'im dis, an' 'twix' den and Friday night Ben done a heap er studyin'. An' de mo' he studied de mo' he didn' lak de way Mars Marrabo talked. He hadn' much trouble wid Mars Marrabo befo', but he knowed his ways, an' he knowed dat de longer Mars Marrabo waited to do a thing de wusser he got 'stid er gittin' better lak mos' folks. An' Ben fin'lly made up his min' he wa'n't gwineter take dat cowhidin'. He 'lowed dat ef he wuz little, like some er de dahkies on de plantation, he wouldn' min' it so much; but he wuz so big dey'd be mo' groun' fer Mars Marrabo ter cover, an' it would hurt dat much mo'. So Ben 'cided ter run erway.

"He had a wife an' two chil'en, an' dey had a little cabin ter deyse'ves down in de quahters. His wife Dasdy wuz a good-lookin', good-natu'd 'oman, an' 'peared ter set a heap er sto' by Ben. De little boy wuz name' Pete; he wuz 'bout eight er nine years ole, an' had already 'menced ter go out in de fiel' an' he'p his mammy pick cotton, fer Mars Marrabo wuz one er dese yer folks w'at wants ter make eve'y aidge cut. Dis yer little Pete wuz a mighty soople dancer, an' w'en his daddy would set out in de yahd an' pick de banjo fer 'im, Pete could teach de ole folks noo steps—dancin' jes seemed to come nachul ter 'im. Dey wuz a little gal too; Ben didn' pay much 'tention ter de gal, but he wuz monst' us fond er Dasdy an' de boy. He wuz sorry ter leab 'em, an' he didn' tell 'em nuffin' 'bout it fer fear dey'd make a fuss. But on Friday night Ben tuk all de bread an' meat dey wuz in de cabin an' made fer de woods.

"W'en Sad'day come an' Ben didn' 'pear, an' nobody didn' know nuffin' 'bout 'im, Mars Marrabo 'lowed of co'se dat Ben had runned erway. He got up a pahty an' tuk de dawgs out an' follered de scen' down ter de crick an' los' it. Fer Ben had tuk a go'd-full er tar 'long wid' 'im, an' w'en he got ter de crick he had 'n'inted his feet wid tar, an' dat th'owed de houns' off'n de scent. Dey sarched de woods an' follered de roads an' kep' watchin' fer a week, but dey couldn' fin' no sign er Ben. An' den Mars Marrabo got mo' stric', an' wuked his niggers hahder'n eber, ez ef he wanted ter try ter make up fer his loss.

"W'en Ben stahted out he wanted ter go ter de No'th. He didn' know how fur it wuz, bet he 'lowed he retch dar in fo' er five days. He knowed de No'th Stah, an' de fus night he kep' gwine right straight to'ds it. But de nex' night it was rainin', an' fer two er th'ee nights it stayed cloudy, an' Ben couldn' see de No'th Stah. Howsomeber, he knowed he had got stahted right' an' he kep' gwine right straight on de same way fer a week er mo' 'spectin' ter git ter de No'th eve'y day, w'en one mawin' early, atter he had b'en walkin' all night, he come right smack out on de crick jes whar he had stahted f'om.

"Co'se Ben wuz monst'us disapp'inted. He had been wond'rin' w'y he hadn' got ter de No'th befo', an' behol', heah he wuz back on de ole plantation. He couldn' un'erstan' it at fus', but he wuz so hongry he didn' hab time ter study 'bout nuffin' fer a little w'ile but jes' ter git sump'n' ter eat; fer he had done eat up de bread an' meat he tuk away wid 'im, an' had been libbin' on roas'n-ears an' sweet'n taters he'd slip out'n de woods an' fin' in co'n fiel's 'an 'tater-patches. He look 'cross de crick, an' seed dis yer clay-bank, an' he waded ober an' got all he could eat, an' den tuk a lump wid 'im, an' hid in de woods ag'in 'til he could study de matter ober some.

"Fus' he 'lowed dat he better gib hiss'ef up an' take his lammin'. But jes' den he 'membered de way Mars Marrabo looked at 'im an' w'at he said 'bout Sad'day night; an' den he 'lowed dat ef Mars Marrabo ketch 'im now, he'd wear 'im ter a frazzle an' chaw up de frazzle, so de wouldn' be nuffin' lef' un 'im at all, an' dat Mars Marrabo would make a' example an' a warnin' of 'im fer all de niggers in de naberhood. Fac' is Mars Marrabo prob'ly wouldn' a' done much ter 'im fer it 'ud be monst'us po' 'couragement fer runaway niggers ter come back, ef dey gwineter git killed w'en dey come. An' so Ben waited 'til night, an' den he went back an' got some mo' clay an' eat it an' hid hisse'f in de woods ag'in.

"Well, hit wuz quare 'bout Ben, but he stayed roun' heah fer a mont', hidin' in de woods in de daytime, an' slippin' out nights an' gittin' clay ter eat an' water 'fom de crick yanker ter drink. De water in dat crick wuz cl'ar in dem days, stidder bein' yallar lak it is now."

We had observed that the water, like that of most streams that take their rise in swamps, had an amber tint to which the sand

and clay background of the bed of the stream imparted an even yellower hue.

"What did he do then, Julius?" asked my wife, who liked to hear the end of a story.

"Well, Miss, he made up his min' den dat he wuz gwineter staht fer de No'th ag'in. But wiles he b'en layin' roun' in de woods he had 'mence ter feel monst'us lonesome, an' it 'peared ter him dat he jes' couldn' go widout seein' Dasdy an' little Pete. Fus' he 'lowed he'd go up ter de cabin, but he thought 'bout de dogs 'roun' de yahd, an' dat de yuther dahkies mought see 'im, and so he 'cided he'd better watch fer 'em 'til dey come long de road—it wuz dis yer same road—w'en he could come out'n de woods an' talk ter 'em. An' he eben 'lowed he mought 'suade 'em ter run erway wid 'im an' dey could all get ter de No'th, fer de nights wuz cl'ar now, an' he couldn' lose de No'th Stah.

"So he waited two er th'ee days, an' sho' nuff long come Dasdy one mornin', comin' over to Mars Dugal's fer ter fetch some things fer her missis. She wuz lookin' kinder down in de mouf, fer she thought a heap er Ben, an' wuz monst'us sorry ter lose 'im, w'iles at de same time she wuz glad he wuz free, fer she 'lowed he'd done got ter de Norf long befo'. An' she wuz studyin' 'bout Ben, w'at a fine-lookin' man he wuz, an' wond'rin' ef she'd eber see 'im any mo'.

"W'en Ben seed her comin' he waited 'til she got close by, an' den he stepped out'n de woods an' come face ter face wid her. She didn' 'pear to know who he wuz, an' seem kinder skeered.

"'Hoddy, Dasdy honey,' he said.

"'Huh!' she said, 'pears ter me you'er mighty fermilyer on sho't acquaintance.'

"'Sho't acquaintance.' Why, doan' yer know me, Dasdy?'

"'No. I doan know yer f'om a skeercrow. I never seed yer befo' in my life, an' nebber wants ter see yer ag'in. Whar did yer com f'om anyhow? Whose nigger is yer? Er is yer some low-down free nigger dat doan b'long ter nobody an' doan own nobody?'

"'W'at fer you talk ter me like dat, honey? I's Ben, yo' Ben. Why doan you know yo' own man?'

"He put out his ahms fer ter draw her ter 'im, but she jes' gib one yell, an' stahted ter run. Ben wuz so 'stonish' he didn' know w'at ter do, an' he stood dere in de road 'til he heared somebody e'se comin', w'en he dahted in de woods ag'in.

"Po' Ben wuz so 'sturbed in his min' dat he couldn' hahdly eat any clay dat day. He couldn' make out w'at wuz de matter wid Dasdy but he 'lowed maybe she'd heared he wuz dead er sump'n', an' thought he wuz a ha'nt, an' dat wuz w'y she had run away. So he watch' by de side er de road, an' nex' mornin' who should come erlong but little Pete, wid a reed over his shoulder, an' a go'd-full er bait, gwine fishin' in de crick.

"Ben called 'im; 'Pete, O Pete! *Little* Pete.'

"Little Pete cocked up his ears an' listened. 'Peared lak he'd heared dat voice befo'. He stahted fer de woods fer ter see who it wuz callin' 'im, but befo' he got dere Ben stepped out an' retched fer im.

"'Come heah, honey, an' see yo' daddy, who ain' seenyer fer so long.'

"But little Pete tuk one look at 'im, an' den 'menceter holler an squeal an' kick an' bite an' scratch. Ben wuz so 'stonish' dat he couldn' hol' de boy, who slipped out'n his han's an run to'ds de house ez fas' ez his legs would tote 'im.

"Po' Ben kep' gittin' wus an' wus mixed up. He couldn' make out fer de life er 'im w'at could be de matter. Nobody didn' 'pear ter wanter own 'im. He felt so cas' down dat he didn' notice a nigger man comin' long de road 'til he got right close up on 'im, an' didn' heah dis man w'en he said 'Hoddy' ter 'im.

"'W'at's de matter wid yer?' said de yuther man w'en Ben didn' 'spon'. 'W'at jedge er member er de legislater er hotel-keeper does you b'long ter dat you can't speak ter a man w'en he says hoddy ter yer?'

"Ben kinder come ter hisse'f an' seed it wuz Primus, who b'long ter his marster an' knowed 'im as well as anybody. But befo' he could git de words out'n his mouf Primus went on talkin'.

"'Youer de mos' mis'able lookin' merlatter I eber seed. Dem rags look lak dey be'n run th'oo a sawmill. My marster doan 'low no strange niggers roun' dis yer plantation, an' yo' better take yo' yaller hide 'way f'um yer as fas' as yo' kin.'

"Jes den somebody hollered on de yuther side er de crick, an' Primus stahted off on a run, so Ben didn' hab no chance ter say no mo' ter 'im.

"Ben almos' 'lowed he wuz gwine out'n' his min', he wuz so

'stonished an' mazed at none er dese yer folks reco'nizin' 'im. He went back in de woods ag'in an' stayed dere all day, wond'rin' w'at he wuz gwineter do. Oncet er twicet he seed folks comin' 'long de road, an' stahted out ter speak ter 'em, but changed his min' an' slip' back ag'in.

"Co'se ef Mars Marrabo had been huntin' Ben he would 'a' foun' 'im. But he had long sence los' all hope er seein' im ag'in, an' so nobody didn' 'sturb Ben in de woods. He stayed hid a day er two mo' an' den he got so lonesome an' homesick fer Dasdy an' little Pete an' de yuther dahkies,—somebody ter talk ter— dat he jes' made up his min' ter go right up ter de house an' gib hisse'f up an' take his med'cine. Mars Marrabo couldn' do nuffin' mo' d'n kill 'im an' he mought's well be dead as hidin' in de woods wid nobody ter talk ter er look at ner nuffin'. He had jes' come out'n de woods an' stahted up dis ve'y road, w'en who sh'd come 'long in a hoss 'n buggy but ole Mars Marrabo, drivin' ober ter dat yuther brickyahd youer gwinter see now. Ben run out'n de woods, and fell down on his knees in de road right in front er Mars Marrabo. Mars Marrabo had to pull on de lines an' hol' de hoss up ter keep 'im f'um runnin' ober Ben.

"'Git out'n de road, you fool nigger,' says Mars Marrabo, 'does yer wanter git run ober? Who's nigger is you, anyhow?'

"'I's yo' nigger, Mars Marrabo; doan yer know Ben, w'at runned erway?'

"'Yas, I knows my Ben w'at runned erway. Does you know whar he is?'

"'Why, I's yo' Ben, Mars Marrabo. Doan yer know me, marster?'

"'No, I doan know yer, yer yaller rascal! W'at de debbil yer mean by tellin' me sich a lie? Ben wuz black ez a coal an' straight ez an' arrer. Youer yaller ez dat clay-bank, an' crooked ez a bair'l-hoop. I reckon youer some 'stracted nigger, tun't out by some marster w'at doan wanter take keer er yer. You git off'n my plantation, an' doan show yo' clay-cullud hide aroun' yer no more, er I'll hab yer sent ter jail an' whip.'

"Mars Marrabo drove erway an' lef' po' Ben mo' dead 'n alive. He crep' back in de bushes an' laid down an' wep' lak a baby. He didn' hab no wife, no chile, no frien's, no marster—he'd be'n willin ernuff to git 'long widout a marster, w'en he had one, but it 'peared lak a sin fer his own marster ter 'ny 'im an' cas' 'im off dat-a-way. It 'peared ter 'im he mought jes' ez well be dead ez livin', fer he wuz all alone in de worl', wid nowhar ter go, an' nobody didn' hab nuffin' ter say ter 'im but ter 'buse 'im an' drive 'im erway.

"Atter he got ober his grievin' spell he 'mence ter wonder w'at Mars Marrabo meant by callin' 'im yaller, an' ez long ez nobody didn' seem ter keer whuther dey seed 'im er not, he went down by de crick in broad daylight, an' kneel down by de water an' looked at his face. Fus' he didn' reco'nize hisse'f an' glanshed back ter see ef dey wa'n't somebody lookin' ober his shoulder—but dey wa'n't. An' w'en he looked back in de water he seed de same thing—he wa'n't black no mo', but had turnt ter a light yaller.

"Ben didn' knowed w'at ter make er it fer a minute er so. Fus' he 'lowed he must hab de yaller fever, er de yaller janders, er sump'n lak dat'! But he had knowed rale dark folks ter hab janders befo', and it hadn't nebber 'fected 'em dat-a-way. But bimeby he got up o'ff'n 'is han's an' knees an' wuz stan'in' lookin' ober de crick at de clay-bank, an' wond'rin' ef de clay he'd b'en eat'n' hadn' turnt 'im yaller w'en he heard sump'n say jes' ez plain ez wo'ds.

"'Turnt ter clay! turnt ter clay! turnt ter clay!'

"He looked all roun', but he couldn' see nobody but a big bullfrog settin' on a log on de yuther side er de crick. An' w'en he turnt roun' an' sta'ted back in de woods, he heared de same thing behin' 'im.

"'Turnt ter clay! turnt ter clay! turnt ter clay!'

"Dem wo'ds kep' ringin' in 'is yeahs 'til he fin'lly 'lowed dey wuz boun' ter be so, er e'se dey wouldn' a b'en tol' ter 'im, an' dat he had libbed on clay so long an' had eat so much, dat he must 'a' jes' nach'ly turnt ter clay!"

> "Imperious Caesar, turned to clay,
> Might stop a hole to keep the wind away,"

I murmured parenthetically.

"Yas, suh," said the old man, "turnt ter clay. But you's mistook in de name, suh; hit wuz Ben, you 'member, not Caesar.

155

Ole Mars Marrabo did hab a nigger name' Caesar, but dat wuz anudder one."

"Don't interrupt him, John," said my wife impatiently. "What happened then, Julius?"

"Well, po' Ben didn' know w'at ter do. He had be'n lonesome ernuff befo', but now he didn' eben hab his own se'f ter 'so'ciate wid, fer he felt mo' lak a stranger 'n he did lak Ben. In a day er so mo' he 'mence ter wonder whuther he wuz libbin' er not. He had hearn 'bout folks turnin' ter clay w'en dey wuz dead, an' he 'lowed maybe he wuz dead an' didn' knowed it, an' dat wuz de reason w'y eve'body run erway f'm 'im an' wouldn' hab nuffin' ter do wid 'im. An' ennyhow, he 'lowed ef he wa'n't dead, he mought's well be. He wande'ed roun' a day er so mo', an' fin'lly de lonesomeness, an' de sleepin' out in de woods, 'mongs' de snakes an' sco'pions, an' not habbin' nuffin' fit ter eat, 'mence ter tell on him, mo' an' mo', an' he kep' gittin' weakah an' weakah 'til one day, w'en he went down by de crick fer ter git a drink er water, he foun' his limbs gittin' so stiff hit 'uz all he could do ter crawl up on de bank an' lay down in de sun. He laid dere 'til he died, an' de sun beat down on 'im, an' beat down on 'im, an' beat down on 'im, fer th'ee er fo' days, 'til it baked 'im as ha'd as a brick. An' den a big win' come erlong an' blowed a tree down, an' it fell on 'im an' smashed 'im all ter pieces, an' groun' 'im ter powder. An' den a big rain come erlong, an' washed 'im in de crick, 'an eber sence den de water in dat crick's b'en jes' as yer sees it now. An dat wuz de een' er po' lonesome Ben, an' dat's de reason w'y I knows dat clay'll make brick an' w'y I doan nebber lak ter see no black folks eat'n it."

My wife came of a family of reformers, who could never contemplate an evil without seeking an immediate remedy. When I decided that the bank of edible clay was not fit for brickmaking, she asked me if I would not have it carted away, suggesting at the same time that it could be used to fill a low place in another part of the plantation.

"It would be too expensive," I said.

"Oh, no," she replied, "I don't think so. I have been talking with Uncle Julius about it, and he says he has a nephew who is out of employment, and who will take the contract for ten dollars, if you will furnish the mule and cart, and board him while the job lasts."

As I had no desire to add another permanent member to my household, I told her it would be useless; that if the people did not get clay there they would find it elsewhere, and perhaps an inferior quality which might do greater harm, and that the best way to stop them from eating it was to teach them self-respect, when she had opportunity, and those habits of industry and thrift whereby they could get their living from the soil in a manner less direct but more commendable.

THE DUMB WITNESS

The old Murchison place was situated on the Lumberton plank road, about two miles from my vineyard on the North Carolina sandhills. Old Julius, our colored coachman, had driven me over one spring morning to see young Murchison, the responsible manager of the property, about some walnut timber I wished to purchase from him for shipment. I had noticed many resources of the country that the easy-going Southerners had not thought of developing; and I took advantage of them when I found it convenient and profitable to do so.

We entered the lane leading to the house by passing between two decaying gateposts. This entrance had evidently once possessed some pretensions to elegance, for the massive posts had been faced with dressed lumber and finished with ornamental tops, some fragments of which still remained; and the one massive hinge, hanging by a slender rust-eaten nail, had been wrought into a fantastic shape. As we drove through the gateway, a green lizard scampered down from the top of one of the posts, where he had been sunning himself, and a rattlesnake lying in the path lazily uncoiled his motley brown length, and, sounding his rattle the meanwhile, wriggled slowly off into the rank grass and weeds.

The house stood well back from the road, on the crest of one of the regular undulations of the sandhill country. It was partly concealed, when approached from the road, by intervening trees and shrubbery, which had once formed a well ordered pleasaunce, but now grew in wild and tangled profusion, so that it was difficult to distinguish one bush or tree from another. The lane itself was partially overgrown, and the mare's fetlocks swept the dew from the grass, where it had not yet been dried by the morning sun.

As we drew nearer, the house stood clearly revealed. It was apparently of more ancient date than any I had seen in the neighborhood. It was a large two-story frame house, built in the colonial style, with a low-pitched roof, and a broad piazza along the front, running the full length of both stories and supported by huge round columns, and suggesting distantly, in its general effect, the portico of a Greek temple. The roof had sunk on one side, and the shingles were old and cracked and moss-grown; while several of the windows in the upper part of the house were boarded up, and others filled with sash from which the glass had apparently long since been broken.

For a space of several rods on each side of the house the ground was bare of grass and shrubbery, and scarcely less forbidding than the road we had traveled. It was rough and uneven, lying in little hillocks and hollows, as though it had been dug over at hazard, or explored by some vagrant drove of hogs. At one side, beyond this barren area, lay an enclosed kitchen garden, in which a few collards and okra-plants and tomato-vines struggled desperately against neglect and drought and poverty of soil.

A casual glance might have led one not informed to the contrary, to believe the place untenanted, so lonely and desolate did it seem. But as we approached we became aware of two figures on the long piazza. At one end of it, in a massive arm-chair of carved oak, a man was seated—apparently a very old man, for he was bent and wrinkled. His thin white hair hung down upon his shoulders. His face was of a high-bred and strongly marked type, with something of the hawk-like contour usually associated with extreme acquisitiveness. His eyes were turned toward the opposite end of the piazza, where a woman was also seated. She seemed but little younger than the man, and her face was enough like his, in a feminine way, to suggest that they might be related in some degree, unless this inference was negatived by the woman's complexion, which disclosed a strong infusion of darker blood. She wore a homespun frock and a muslin cap and sat bolt upright, with her hands folded on her lap, looking toward her *vis-à-vis* at the other end of the piazza.

As we drew up a short distance from the door, the old man rose, as we supposed, to come forward and greet us. But, instead of stopping at the steps and facing outward, he continued his course to the other end of the piazza and halted before the woman.

"Viney," he said, in a sharply imperative voice, "my uncle says you will tell me where he put the papers. I am tired of this nonsense. I insist upon knowing immediately."

The woman made no reply, but her faded eyes seemed to glow for a moment, like the ashes of a dying fire fanned by some random breath of air.

"Why do you not answer me?" he continued, with increasing vehemence. "I tell you I insist upon knowing. It is imperative that I should know, and know at once. My interests are suffering for every day's delay. The papers—where are the papers?"

Still the woman sat silent, though her figure seemed to stiffen as she leaned slightly toward him. He grew visibly more impatient at her silence, and began to threaten her.

"Tell me immediately, you hussy, or you will have reason to regret it. You take liberties that cannot be permitted. I will not put up with it," he said, shaking his fist as he spoke. "I shall have to have you whipped."

The slumbrous fire in the woman's eyes flamed up for a moment. She rose from her seat, and drawing herself up to her full height—she was a tall woman, though bowed somewhat with years—began to speak, I thought at first in some foreign tongue. But after a moment I knew that no language or dialect, at least none of European origin, could consist of such a discordant jargon, such a meaningless cacophony as that which fell from the woman's lips. And as she went on, pouring out a flood of sounds that were not words, and which yet seemed now and then vaguely to suggest words, as clouds suggest the shapes of mountains and trees and strange beasts, the old man seemed to bend like a reed before a storm, and began to expostulate, accompanying his words with deprecatory gestures.

"Yes, Viney, good Viney," he said in soothing tones, "I know it was wrong, and I've always regretted it—always from the very day I did it. But you shouldn't bear malice, Viney, it isn't Christian. The Bible says you should bless them that curse you, and do good to them that despitefully use you. But I was good to you before, Viney, and I was good to you afterwards, and I know you have forgiven me—good Viney, noble-hearted Viney!— and you are going to tell me. Now, *do* tell me where the papers are," he added, pleadingly, offering to take her hand, which lay on the arm of the chair.

She drew her hand away, as she muttered something in the same weird tones she had employed before. The old man bent toward her, in trembling eagerness, but seemed disappointed.

"Try again, Viney," he said, "that's a good girl. Your old master thinks a great deal of you, Viney. He is your best friend."

Again she made an inarticulate response. He seemed to comprehend, and turning from her, came down the steps, muttering to himself, took up a spade that stood at one end of the steps, passed by us without seeming conscious of our presence, and hastening with tottering footsteps to one side of the yard began digging furiously.

I had been so much interested in this curious drama that I had forgotten for the time being the business that brought me there. The old woman, however, when the man had gone, rose from her seat and went into the house, without giving us more than a look.

"What's the matter with them, Julius?" I said, returning with a start to the world of reality.

The old man pointed to his head.

"Dey's bofe 'stracted, suh," he said, "out'n dey min'. Dey's be'n dat-a-way fer yeahs an' yeahs."

At that moment the young man of the house came out to the door, and greeted us pleasantly. He asked me to alight from the carriage and led me to the chair the old man had occupied. It was a massive oak affair, with carved arms and back and a wooden seat, and looked as though it might be of ancient make, perhaps an heirloom. I found young Murchison was a frank and manly young fellow, and quite capable of looking out for his own interests. I struck a bargain with him, on terms that were fair to both. When I had concluded my business and invited him to call and see me sometime, I got into the carriage, and Julius drove down the lane and out into the road again. In going out, we passed near the old man, who was still muttering to himself and digging rapidly, but with signs of weariness. He did not look up as we went by, but seemed entirely absorbed in his strange pursuit.

In the evening, after supper, Julius came up to the house. We sat out on the porch, my wife and her sister and Julius and I. We cut a large watermelon, and when Julius had eaten the half we gave to him, he told us the story of old man Murchison's undoing. The air was cool, the sky was clear, the stars shone with a brightness unknown in higher latitudes. The voices of the night came faintly from the distant woods, and there could have been no more romantic setting for the story of jealousy, revenge and disappointment which the old white-haired negro told us, in his own quaint dialect—a story of things possible only in an era which, happily, has passed from our history, as, in God's own time—and may it be soon!—it will from all the earth. Some of the facts in this strange story—circumstances of which Julius was ignorant, though he had the main facts correct—I learned afterwards from other sources, but I have woven them all together here in orderly sequence.

The Murchison family had occupied their ancestral seat on the sandhills for a hundred years or more. There were not many rich families in that part of North Carolina, and this one, by reason of its wealth and other things, was easily the most conspicuous in several counties. The first great man of the family, General Arthur Murchison, had won distinction in the war of independence, and during all the Revolutionary period had been one of the most ardent of the Carolina patriots. After peace was established he had taken high place in the councils of the State. Elected a delegate to the Constitutional Convention at Philadelphia in 1787, it was largely due to his efforts that North Carolina adopted the Federal Constitution the following year. His son became a distinguished jurist, whose name is still a synonym for legal learning and juridical wisdom in North Carolina. Roger Murchison, the son of Judge Murchison—the generations had followed one another rapidly in a country of warm skies and early marriages—was the immediate predecessor of Malcolm Murchison, the demented old man who was nominal owner of the estate at the time of my visit to the house. In Roger Murchison the family may be said to have begun to decline from the eminence it had attained in the career of Judge Murchison. In the first place, Roger Murchison did not marry, thus seemingly indicating a lack of the family pride which would have made him wish to continue the name in the direct line. Again, though his career in college had been brilliant; though the wealth and standing of the family gave him social and political prestige; and though he had held high office under the State and National governments, he had never while in public life especially distinguished himself for eloquence or statesmanship, but had, on the contrary, enjoyed a life of ease and pleasure and had wasted what his friends thought rare gifts. He was fond of cards, of fast horses, of rare wines, and of gay society. It is not surprising, therefore, that he spent very little time on his property, preferring the life of cities to the comparative dullness of plantation life with such colorless distractions as a neighboring small town could offer.

He had inherited a large estate, including several plantations, and numerous slaves. During his frequent absences from home, in the last fifteen years of his life, he left his property under the management of a nephew, Malcolm Murchison, the orphan son of a younger brother, and his own prospective heir. Young Malcolm was a youth of unusual strength of character and administrative capacity, and even before he had attained his majority showed himself a better manager than his uncle had ever been. So well, indeed, did he manage the estate that his uncle left it for ten years practically in his hands, looking to him only for the means he required to lead his own life in other places. It is true he appeared periodically and assumed the role of proprietor, but Malcolm was the man to whom the community and the slaves looked as both the present and the future master.

Young Murchison kept bachelor's hall in the great house. The only women about the establishment were an old black cook, and the housekeeper, a tall, comely young quadroon—she had too a dash of Indian blood, which perhaps gave her straighter and blacker hair than she would otherwise have had, and also

perhaps endowed her with some other qualities which found
their natural expression in the course of subsequent events—if
indeed her actions needed anything more than common human
nature to account for them.[1] The duties of young Murchison's
housekeeper were not onerous; compared with a toiling field
hand she led a life of ease and luxury. The one conspicuous vice
of Malcolm Murchison was avarice. If he had other failings,
they were the heritage of the period, and he shared them with
his contemporaries of the same caste. Perhaps it was his avarice
that kept him from marrying; it was cheaper to have his clothing and his table looked after by a slave than by a woman who
would not have been content with her food and clothing. At
any rate, for ten or fifteen years he remained single, and ladies
never set foot in the Murchison house. Men sometimes called
and smoked and drank, played cards, bought and sold produce or slaves, but the foot of a white woman had not touched
the floor for fifteen years, when Mrs. Martha Todd came from
Pennsylvania to the neighboring town of Patesville to visit a
cousin living there, who had married a resident of the town.

Malcolm Murchison met Mrs. Todd while she was driving
on the road one day. He knew her companion, in response to
whose somewhat distant bow he lifted his hat. Attracted by the
stranger's appearance, he made inquiries about her in the town,
and learned that she was a widow and rich in her own right.
He sought opportunities to meet her, courted her, and after a
decent interval of hesitation on her part—she had only just put
off mourning for her first husband—received her promise to
be his wife.

He broke the news to his housekeeper by telling her to make
the house ready for a mistress. The housekeeper had been in
power too long to yield gracefully, or perhaps she foresaw and
dreaded the future. Some passionate strain of the mixed blood
in her veins—a very human blood—broke out in a scene of hys-
terical violence. She pleaded, remonstrated, raged. He listened

1 A cancelled passage here reads: We like to speak of Negro cunning, of Indian
revengefulness, of the low morality of inferior races, when, alas! our own race
excels in all of these things, when it wishes, because it lends to evil purposes a
higher intelligence and a wider experience than inferior races can command.

calmly through it all—he had anticipated some such scene—and at the end said to her:

"You had better be quiet and obedient. I have heard what you have to say—this once—and it will be useless for you to repeat it, for I shall not listen again. If you are reasonable, I will send you to the other plantation. If not, I will leave you here, with your new mistress."

She was silent for the time being, but raged inwardly. The next day she stole away from home, went to the town, sought out the new object of Murchison's devotion, and told her something—just what she told no one but herself and the lady ever knew.

When Murchison called in the evening, Mrs. Todd sent down word that she was not at home. With the message came a note: "I have had my wedded happiness spoiled once. A burnt child dreads the fire—I do not care to go twice through the same experience. I have learned some things about you that will render it impossible for me ever to marry you. It is needless to seek an explanation."

He went away puzzled and angry. His housekeeper wore an anxious look, which became less anxious as she observed his frame of mind. He had been wondering where Mrs. Todd had got the information—he could not doubt what it was—that had turned her from him. Suddenly a suspicion flashed into his mind. He went away early the next morning and made investigations. In the afternoon he came home with all the worst passions of weak humanity, clad with irresponsible power, flaming in his eyes.

"I will teach you," he said to his housekeeper, who quailed before him, "to tell tales about your master. I will put it out of your power to dip your tongue in where you are not concerned."

There was no one to say him nay. The law made her his. It was a lonely house, and no angel of mercy stayed his hand.

About a week later he received a letter,—a bulky envelope. On breaking the seal, he found the contents to consist of two papers, one of which was a letter from a friend and political associate of his uncle. It was dated at Washington, and announced the death of his Uncle Roger as the result of an accident. A team of spirited horses had run away with him and thrown him out of the carriage, inflicting a fatal injury. The letter stated that his uncle had lingered for a day, during which he had dictated a letter to his nephew; that his body had been embalmed and placed in a vault, to await the disposition of his relatives or representatives. His uncle's letter was enclosed with the one above and ran as follows:

"My dear Malcolm: This is the last communication I shall ever make to you, I am sorry to say—though I don't know that I ought to complain, for I have always been a philosopher, and have had a good time to boot. There must be an end to all things, and I cannot escape the common fate.

"You have been a good nephew and a careful manager, and I have not forgotten the fact. I have left a will in which you are named as my sole heir, barring some small provision for my sister Mary. With the will you will find several notes, and mortgages securing them, on plantations in the neighborhood—I do not need to specify, as they explain themselves; also some bonds and other securities of value and your grandmother's diamond necklace. I do not say here where they are, lest this letter might fall into the wrong hands; but your housekeeper Viney knows their hiding place. She is devoted to you and to the family—she ought to be, for she is of our blood—and she only knows the secret. I would not have told her, of course, had I not thought of just some such chance as this which has befallen me. She does not know the value of the papers, but simply that they are important.

"And now, Malcolm, my boy, goodbye. I am crossing the river and I reach back to clasp your hand once more—just once.

"Your dying Uncle,
"Roger Murchison"

Malcolm Murchison took this letter to Viney. She had been banished from the house to a cabin in the yard, where she was waited on by the old black cook. He felt a little remorseful as he looked at her; for, after all, she was a woman, and there had been excuses for what she had done; and he had begun to feel, in some measure, that there was no sufficient excuse for what he had done.

She looked at him with an inscrutable face as he came in, and he felt very uncomfortable under the look.

"Viney," he said, not unkindly, "I'm sorry I went so far, and I'm glad you're getting better." Her expression softened, a tear rolled down her cheek, and he felt correspondingly relieved. It is so easy to forgive our own sins against others. "Your old Master Roger is dead. I have just received a letter telling me how it happened. He was thrown from a buggy in a runaway and injured so badly that he died the same day. He had time to write me a letter, in which he says you can tell me where he put certain papers that you know about. Can you tell"—he remembered her condition—"can you show me where they are?"

A closer observer than Malcolm Murchison might have detected at this moment another change in the woman's expression. Perhaps it was in her eyes more than elsewhere; for into their black depths there sprang a sudden fire. Beyond this, however, and a slight quickening of her pulse, of which there was no visible manifestation, she gave no sign of special feeling; and even if these had been noticed they might have been attributed to the natural interest felt at hearing of her old master's death.

The only answer Viney made was to lift her hand and point it to her mouth.

"Yes, I know," he said hastily, "you can't tell me—not now at least, but you can surely point out the place to me."

She shook her head and pointed again to her mouth.

"Is it hidden in some place that you can't lead me to when you are able to get up?"

She nodded her head.

"Will it require words to describe it so that I can find it?"

Again she nodded affirmatively.

He reflected a moment. "Is it in the house?" he asked.

She shook her head.

"In the yard?"

Again she made a negative sign.

"In the barn?"

No.

"In the fields?"

No.

He tried for an hour, naming every spot he could think of as a possible hiding-place for the papers, but with no avail. Every question was answered in the negative.

When he had exhausted his ingenuity in framing questions he went away very much disappointed. He had been patiently waiting for his reward for many years, and now when it should be his, it seemed to elude his grasp.

"Never mind," he said, "we will wait until you are better, and then perhaps you may be able to speak intelligibly. In the meantime you shall not want for anything."

He had her removed to the house and saw that she received every attention. She was fed with dainty food, and such care as was possible was given to her wound. In due time it healed. But she did not even then seem able to articulate, even in whispers, and all his attempts to learn of her the whereabouts of the missing papers, were met by the same failure. She seemed willing enough, but unable to tell what he wished to know. There was apparently some mystery which only words could unravel.

It occurred to him more than once how simple it would be for her to write down the few words necessary to his happiness. But, alas! She might as well have been without hands, for any use she could make of them in that respect. Slaves were not taught to write, for too much learning would have made them mad. But Malcolm Murchison was a man of resources—he would have her taught to write. So he employed a teacher—a free colored man who had picked up some fragments of learning, and who could be trusted to hold his tongue, to teach Viney to read and write. But somehow she made poor progress. She was handicapped of course by her loss of speech.[2] It was unfamiliar work too for the teacher, who would not have been expert with a pupil equipped with all the normal faculties. Perhaps she had begun too old; or her mind was too busily occupied with other thoughts to fix it on the tedious and painful steps by which the art of expression in writing is acquired. Whatever the reason, she manifested a remarkable stupidity while seemingly anxious to learn; and in the end Malcolm was compelled to abandon the attempt to teach her.

2 The earlier version reads: "Ignorant people learn with their voices as well as with their minds."

Several years passed in vain efforts to extract from Viney in some way the wished-for information. Meantime Murchison's affairs did not prosper. Several other relatives claimed a share in his uncle's estate; on the ground that he had died intestate. In the absence of the will, their claims could not be successfully disputed. Every legal means of delay was resorted to, and the authorities were disposed, in view of the remarkable circumstances of the case, to grant every possible favor. But the law fixed certain limits to delay in the settlement of an estate, and in the end he was obliged either to compromise the adverse claims or allow them to be fixed by legal process. And while certain of what his own rights were, he was compelled to see a large part of what was rightfully his go into hands where it would be difficult to trace or recover it if the will were found. Some of the estates against which he suspected the hidden notes and mortgages were held, were sold and otherwise disposed of. His worry interfered with proper attention to his farming operations, and one crop was almost a failure. The factor to whom he shipped his cotton went bankrupt owing him a large balance, and he fell into debt and worried himself into a fever. The woman Viney nursed him through it, and was always present at his side, a mute reproach for his cruelty, a constant reminder of his troubles. Her presence was the worst of things for him, and yet he could not bear to have her out of his sight; for in her lay the secret he longed for and which he hoped at some time in some miraculous way to extract from her.

When he rose from his sick-bed after an illness of three months, he was but the wreck of the strong man he had once been. His affairs had fallen into hopeless disorder. His slaves, except Viney, were sold to pay his debts, and there remained to him of the almost princely inheritance he had expected, only the old place on the sandhills and his slave, Viney, who still kept house for him. His mind was vacant and wandering, except on the one subject of the hidden will, and he spent most of the time in trying to extract from Viney the secret of its hiding-place. A young nephew came and lived with him and did what was necessary to hold the remnant of the estate together.

When the war came Viney was freed, with the rest of her brethren in bondage. But she did not leave the old place. There was some gruesome attraction in the scene of her suffering, or perhaps it was the home instinct. The society of humankind did not possess the same attraction for her as if she had not been deprived of the power of speech. She stayed on and on, doing the simple housework for the demented old man and his nephew, until the superstitious negroes and poor whites of the neighborhood said that she too shared the old man's affliction. Day after day they sat on the porch, when her indoor work was done, the old man resting in the carved oaken arm-chair, and she in her splint-bottom chair; or the old man commanding, threatening, expostulating, entreating her to try, just once more, to tell him his uncle's message—she replying in the meaningless inarticulate mutterings that we had heard; or the old man digging, digging furiously, and she watching him from the porch, with the same inscrutable eyes, though dulled somewhat by age, that had flashed upon him for a moment in the dimly lighted cabin where she lay on her bed of pain.

The summer following the visit I made to the old Murchison place I accompanied my wife North on a trip to our former home. On my return several weeks later I had occasion again to visit young Murchison, and drove over one morning to the house. As we drove up the lane I noticed a surprising change in the surroundings. A new gate had been hung, upon a pair of ugly cast-iron hinges. The grass in the path had been mowed, and the weeds and shrubs bordering it had been cut down. The neglected pleasure-garden had been reduced to some degree of order, and the ground around the house had been plowed and harrowed, and the young blades of grass were shooting up and covering the surface with a greenish down. The house itself had shared in the general improvement. The roof had been repaired and the broken windows mended, and from certain indications in the way of ladders and pails in the yard, I inferred that it was intended to paint the house. This however was merely a supposition, for house-painting is an art that languishes in the rural districts of the South.

Julius had been noticing my interest in these signs of prosperity, with a pleased expression that boded further surprises.

"What's been going on here, Julius?" I asked.

"Ole Mars Murchison done dead, suh—died las' mont', an'

eve'ything goes ter young Mistah Roger. He's done 'mence' ter fix de ole place up. He be'n ober ter yo' place lookin' 'roun', an' he say he's gwineter hab his'n lookin' lak yo'n befo' de yeah's ober."

We stopped the rockaway in front of the house. As we drew up, an old woman came out of the front door, in whom I recognized one of the strange couple I had seen on the piazza on my former visit. She seemed intelligent enough, and I ventured to address her.

"Is Mr. Murchison at home?"

"Yas, suh," she answered, "I'll call 'im."[3]

Her articulation was not distinct, but her words were intelligible. I was never more surprised in my life.

"What does this mean, Julius?" I inquired, turning to the old man, who was grinning and chuckling to himself in great glee at my manifest astonishment. "Has she recovered her speech?"

"She'd nebber lost it, suh. Ole Viney could 'a' talked all de time, ef she'd had a min' ter. Atter ole Mars Ma'colm wuz dead, she tuk an' showed Mistah Roger whar de will an' de yuther papers wuz hid. An' whar yer reckon dey wuz, zuh?"

"I give it up, Julius. Enlighten me."

"Dey wa'n't in de house, ner de yah'd, ner de ba'n, ner de fiel's. Dey wuz hid in de seat er dat ole oak a'm-cheer on de piazza yander w'at ole Mars Ma'colm be'n settin' in all dese yeahs."

3 Chesnutt apparently hesitated as to whether Viney should speak "perfect" English or black dialect English. In the first version she replies, "Yes, sir, I'll call him."—ED.

A Victim of Heredity; or, Why the Darkey Loves Chicken

I went to North Carolina a few years after the war with some hopeful views in regard to the colored people. It was my idea that with the larger opportunities of freedom they would improve gradually and learn in due time to appreciate the responsibilities of citizenship. This opinion, based on simple faith in human nature, which is much the same the world over, I never saw any good reason to change.

There were a few of my dusky neighbors, however, who did not shake off readily the habits formed under the old system, and I suffered more or less, from time to time, from petty thievery. So long as it was confined to grapes on the vine, or roasting-ears, or hanging fruit, or an occasional watermelon, I did not complain so much; but one summer, after several raids upon my hen-house, I determined to protect my property. I therefore kept close watch one night, and caught a chicken-thief in the very act. I locked him up in a strongly-built smokehouse, where I thought he would be safe until morning.

I made up my mind, before I went to sleep, that an example must be made of this miscreant. Knowing that the law in North Carolina, as elsewhere, was somewhat elastic, and the degree of punishment for crime largely dependent upon the vigor of the prosecution, I decided that five years in the penitentiary would be about right for this midnight marauder. It would give him time to break off the habit of stealing, and would strike terror to the hearts of other evil-doers.

In the morning I went down to the smokehouse to inspect my captive. He was an insignificant looking fellow, and seemed very much frightened. I sent him down something to eat, and told him I was going to have him taken to jail.

During breakfast I turned the matter over in my mind, and concluded that five years' imprisonment would be a punishment rather disproportioned to the offence, and that perhaps two years in the penitentiary would be an equally effective warning.

One of my servants was going to town toward noon with a load of grapes for shipment to the nearest market, and I wrote a note to the sheriff, Mr. Weems, requesting him to send a constable out to take charge of the thief. The ink was scarcely dry before it occurred to me that over-severity in the punishment of crime was often productive of harm, and had seldom resulted in any good, and that in all probability, taking everything into consideration, a year in jail in the neighborhood would be ample punishment, and a more impressive object-lesson than a longer term in the more distant penitentiary.

During the afternoon I learned, upon inquiry, that my captive had a large family and a sick wife; that because of a trifling disposition he was without steady employment, and therefore dependent upon odd jobs for a livelihood. But while these personal matters might be proper subjects of consideration for the humanitarian, I realized that any false sentiment on my part would be dangerous to social order; and that property must be protected, or soon there would be no incentive to industry and thrift. I determined that the thief should have at least six months in jail, if I had to support his family during his incarceration.

I was sitting on the front piazza, indulging in a quiet smoke during the hot part of the afternoon, just after having arrived at this final conclusion, when old Julius came around the house, and, touching his hat, asked at what time my wife wished the rockaway brought round for our afternoon drive.

"I hardly think we shall go to-day," I replied, "until the constable has come and taken that thief to jail. By the way, Julius," I added with some severity, "why is it that your people can't let chickens alone?"

The old man shook his head sadly.

"It's a myst'ry, suh," he answered with a sigh, "dat ev'ybody doan understan'. Ef dey did, some un 'em mought make mo' 'lowance."

My wife came out of the house and took a seat in an armchair near me, behind the honeysuckle vine.

"I am asking Julius to explain," I said, "why his people are so partial to chickens."

"I think it unkind, John," returned my wife, "to charge upon a whole race the sins of one worthless individual. There are thieves wherever there is portable property, and I don't imagine colored people like chicken better than other people."

Old Julius shook his head dissentingly. "I is bleedzd ter differ fum you dere, ma'm," he said, with as much positiveness as he was capable of in conversation with white people; "cullud folks is mo' fonder er chick'n 'n w'ite folks. Dey can't he'p but be."

"Why so?" I asked. "Is it in the blood?"

"You's hit it, suh, de fus' sta't-off. Yas, suh, dat is de fac', tooby sho', en no mistake erbout it."

"Why, Uncle Julius!" exclaimed my wife with some show of indignation. "You ought to be ashamed to slander your race in that way."

"I begs yo' pardon, ma'm, ef it hu'ts yo' feelin's, but I ain' findin' no fault wid *dem. Dey* ain' 'sponsible fer dey tas'e fer chick'n-meat. A w'ite man's ter blame fer dat."

"Well," I said, "that statement is interesting. Sit down and tell us all about it."

Julius took a seat on the top step, and laying his ragged straw hat beside him, began:

"Long yeahs befo' de wah dey wuz a monst'us rich w'ite gent'eman, name' Mars Donal' McDonal', w'at useter lib down on de yuther side er de Wim'l'ton Road. He hadn' alluz be'n rich, fer w'en he fus' come ter dis county he wuz po', en he wukked fer a yeah er so as oberseah fer anudder w'ite man, 'tel he had save' money 'nuff ter buy one er two niggers, en den he rented a place on sheers, en bimeby he had bought a plantation en bought some mo' niggers en raise' some, 'tel he 'mence' ter be so well-off dat folks mos' fergot he had eber be'n a nigger-driber. He kep' on gittin' richer en richer, 'tel fin'lly he wuz one er de riches' men in de county.

"But he wa'n't sat'sfied. He had a neffy, name' Tom, en Mars Donal' had be'n lef' gyardeen fer dis yer neffy er his'n, en he had manage' so dat w'en young Mars Tom growed up dey wa'n't nuffin at all lef' er de fine proputty w'at young Mars Tom's daddy had own' w'en he died.

"Folks said Mars Donal' had rob' his neffy, but dey wa'n't no way ter prove it. En mo' d'n dat, Mars Donal' didn' 'pear ter lak Mars Tom a-tall atter he growed up, en turnt 'im out in de worl' ter shif' fer hisse'f widout no money ner nuffin.

"Mars Tom had be'n co'tin' fer lo! dese many yeahs his secon' cousin, young Miss 'Liza M'Guire, who useter lib on de yuther side er de ribber, en young Mars Tom wanter ter marry Miss 'Liza monst'us bad. But w'en Mars Tom come er age, en Mars Donal' say all his proputty done use' up on his edication, Miss 'Liza's daddy say he wouldn' 'low her ter marry Mars Tom 'tel he make some money, er show her daddy how he wuz gwine ter suppo't Miss 'Liza ef he married her.

"De young folks wa'n't 'lowed ter see one ernudder ve'y often, but Mars Tom had a batteau down on de ribber en he useter paddle ober sometimes ter meet Miss 'Liza whuther er no.

"One eb'nin' Mars Tom went down ter de ribber en ontied his batteau en wuz startin' ter cross w'en he heared somebody holler. He looked roun' en he see hit wuz a' ole nigger 'oman had fell in de ribber. She had sunk once, en wuz gwine down ag'in, w'en Mars Tom cotch 'er en pull't' er out, en gin er a drink er sump'n he had in a flas', en den tied his boat en he'ped 'er up de bank ter de top, whar she could git 'long by herse'f.

"Now, dis yer 'oman w'at Mars Tom pull't out'n de ribber des happen' ter be ole Aun' Peggy, de free-nigger cunjuh 'oman w'at libbed down by de Wim'l'ton Road. She had be'n diggin' roots fer her cunj'in', en had got too close ter de ribber, en had fell in whar de water wuz deep en strong, en had come monst'us close ter bein' drownded. Aun' Peggy knowed all 'bout Mars Tom en his uncle ole Mars Donal', en his junesey Miss 'Liza, en she made up her min' dat she wuz gwine ter do sump'n fer young Mars Tom de fus' chanst she got. She wuz wond'rin' wot kinder goopher she could wuk fer Mars Tom, w'en who should come ter see her one day but ole Mars Donal' hisse'f.

"Now, w'y Mars Donal' come ter go ter see ole Aun' Peggy

wuz dis erway. Mars Donal' had be'n gittin' richer en richer, en closeter en closeter, 'tel he'd got so he'd mos' skin a flea fer his hide en taller. But he wa'n't sat'sfied, en he kep' on projickin' wid one thing en fig'rin' on ernudder, fer ter see how he could git mo' en mo'. He wuz a'ready wukkin' his niggers ez ha'd ez dey could stan', but he got his 'count-book out one day en 'mence' ter cackilate w'at it cos' 'im ter feed his niggers, en it 'peared ter be a monst'us sum. En he 'lowed ter hiss'f dat ef he could feed his niggers fer 'bout half er w'at it had be'n costin' 'im, he'd save a heap er money ev'y yeah.

"Co'se ev'ybody knowed, en Mars Donal' knowed, dat a fiel'-han' had ter hab so much bacon en so much meal and so much merlasses a week ter make 'im fittin' ter do his wuk. But Mars Donal' 'lowed dey mought be some way ter fool de niggers, er sump'n; so he tuk a silber dollar en went down ter see ole Aun' Peggy.

"Aun' Peggy laid de silber dollar on de mantelpiece en heared w'at he had to say, en den she 'lowed she'd wuk her roots, en he'd hafter come back nex' day en fetch her ernudder silber dollar, en she'd tell 'im w'at he sh'd do.

"Mars Donal' sta'ted out, en bein' ez Aun' Peggy's back wuz tu'nt, he 'lowed he'd take dat silber dollar 'long wid 'im, bein' ez she hadn' tole 'im nuffin, en he'd gin it ter her nex' day. But w'en he pick' up de silber dollar, it wuz so hot it bu'nt 'is han', he laid it down rale quick en went off rubbin' his han' en cussin' kinder sof' ter hisse'f.

"De nex' day he went back, en Aun' Peggy gun 'im a goopher mixtry in a bottle.

" 'You take dis yer mixtry,' sez she, 'en put it on yo' niggers' rashuns de nex' time you gibs 'em out, en den stidder 'lowin' yo' han's a poun' er bacon en a peck er meal en a qua't er merlasses, you gin 'em half a poun' er bacon en half a peck er meal en a pint er merlasses, en dey won' know de diffe'nce. Fac', dis yer goopher mixtry'll make de half look des lak de whole, en atter de niggers has once eat some er dat conju'd meat en meal en merlasses, it's gwine ter take dey ap'tites erway so dey'll be des ez well sat'sfied ez ef dey had a side a bacon en a bairl er flour.'

"W'en Mars Donal' sta'ted erway Aun' Peggy sez, sez she:

" 'You done fergot dat yuther dollar, ain' you, Mars Donal'?'

" 'Oh, yes, Peggy,' sezee, 'but heah it is.' En Mars Donal' retch' down in his pocket en pull 't out a han'ful er gol' en silber, en picked out a lead dollar en handed it ter Aun' Peggy. Aun' Peggy seed de dollar wuz bad, but she tuk it en didn' let on. But ez Mars Donal' wuz turnin' ter go 'way, Aun' Peggy sprinkle' sump'n on dat lead dollar, en sez she:

" 'O Mars Donal' kin I get you ter change a twenty-dollar gol' piece fer me?'

" 'Yas, I reckon,' sezee.

"Aun' Peggy handed him de lead dollar, en he looked at it en bit it en sounded it on de table, en it 'peared ter be a bran'-noo gol' piece; so he tuk'n pull't out his pu'se en gun Aun' Peggy th'ee five-dollar gol' pieces en five good silber dollars, en den he tuk his goopher mixtry en went 'long home wid it.

"W'en Mars Donal' had gone, Aun' Peggy sont a mawkin'-bird fer ter tell young Mars Tom ter came en see her.

"Mars Tom wuz gwine 'long de road one eb'nin' w'en he heared a mawkin'-bird singin' right close ter 'im, en de mawkin'-bird seem' ter be a-sayin':

" 'Go see ole Aun' Peggy,
      She wants ter see you bad,
      She'll show you how ter git back
      De lan' yo' daddy had.'

"Mars Tom wuz studyin' 'bout sump'n e'se, en he did n' pay no 'tention ter w'at de mawkin'-bird say. So pretty soon he heahs de mawkin'-bird ag'in:

" 'Go en see Aun' Peggy,
      She wants ter see you bad,
      She's gwine ter he'p you git back
      The gol' yo' daddy had.'

"But Mars Tom had sump'n e'se on his min', en he wuz gwine on down de road right pas' whar Aun' Peggy lib' w'en de mawkin'-bird come up en mos' pe'ched on his shoulders, en sez, des ez plain ez ef he wuz talkin':

" 'Go see ole Aun' Peggy,
      Er e'se you'll wush you had;
      She'll show you how ter marry
      De gal you wants so bad.'

"Dat happen' ter be des w'at Mars Tom wuz studyin' erbout,

en he 'mence' ter 'low dey mought be sump'n in w'at dis yer mawkin'-bird say, so he up' n' goes ter see Aun' Peggy.

"Aun' Peggy say how glad she wuz ter see 'im, en tol 'im how she'd be'n wantin' ter do sump'n fer 'im. En den she 'splained 'bout Mars Donal', en tole Mars Tom sump'n w'at he mus' go en do.

"'But I ain' got no money, Aun' Peggy,' sezee.

"'Nemmine,' sez Aun' Peggy, 'You borry all de money you kin rake en scrape, en you git all de credit you kin; en I ain' be'n cunj'in' all dese yeahs fer nuffin, en I'll len' you some money. But you do des ez I tell you, en doan git skeert, en ev'ything'll tu'n out des exac'ly ez I say.'

"Ole Mars Donal' sprinkle' de goopher mixtry on his niggers' rashuns, nex' Sunday mawnin', en den sarved out half rashuns, des ez Aun' Peggy say, en sho' 'nuff, de niggers didn' 'pear ter notice no diffe'nce, des ez Aun' Peggy say. En all de week none er de han's didn' say nuffin 'bout not habbin' 'nuff ter eat, en dey 'peared ter be des ez well sat'sfied ez ef dey'd got dey reg'lar rashuns.

"Mars Donal' figgered up his books at de een' er a week er so en foun' he had sabe' so much money dat he 'mence' ter wonder ef he couldn' sabe some mo'. En bein' ez de niggers wuz all gittin' 'long so nice, en de cotton had be'n laid by, en de fiel'-han's wouldn' hab ter wuk so tarrable ha'd fer a mont' er so, Mars Donal' 'lowed he'd use Aun' Peggy's goopher some mo', en so he tuk 'n sprinkle' some mo' er de mixtry on de nex' week's rashuns en den cut de rashuns in two once mo'; stidder givin' de han's a half a peck er meal en a pint er merlasses en half a poun' er bacon, he gun 'em a qua'ter er a peck er meal en half a pint er merlasses en fo' ounces er meat fer a week's rashuns. De goopher wukked des de same ez it had befo', en de niggers didn' 'pear ter notice no diffe'nce. Mars Donal' wuz tickle' mos' ter def, en kep' dis up right along fer th'ee er fo' weeks.

"But Mars Donal' had be'n so busy fig'rin' up his profits en countin' his money, dat he hadn' be'n payin' ez close 'tention ter his niggers ez yushal, en fus' thing he knowed, w'en de ha'd wuk begun ag'in, he 'skivered dat mos' er his niggers wuz so weak en feeble dat dey couldn' ha'dly git 'roun' de plantation; 'peared ez ef dey had des use' up all de strenk dey had, en den des all gun out at once.

"Co'se Mars Donal' got skeert, en 'mence' ter gib' em dey reg'lar rashuns. But somehow er nuther dey didn' 'pear ter hab no ap'tite, en dey wouldn' come fer dey rashuns w'en dey week wuz up, but 'lowed dey had 'nuff ter las' 'em fer a mont'. En meanw'iles dey kep' on gittin po'er an po'er, en weaker en weaker, 'tel Mars Donal' got so skeert he hasten' back ter see ole Aun' Peggy en ax' her ter take dat goopher off'n his niggers.

"Aun' Peggy knowed w'at Mars Donal' had done 'bout cuttin' down de rashuns, but she wa'n't ready to finish up wid Mars Donal' yit; so she didn' let on, but des gun 'im ernudder mixtry, en tol' 'im fer to sprinkle dat on de niggers' nex' rashuns.

"Mars Donal' sprinkle' it on, but it didn' do no good, en nex' week he come back ag'in.

" 'Dis yer mixtry ain' got no power, Peggy,' sezee. 'It ain' 'sturb' de yuther goopher a-tall.'

" 'I doan unnerstan' dis,' sez Aun' Peggy; 'how did you use dat fus' mixtry I gun you?'

"Well, den Mars Donal' 'lowed how he had sprinkle' it on de fus' time, en how it wukked so good dat he had sprinkle' it on de nex' time en cut de rashuns in two ag'in.

" 'Uh huh, uh huh!' 'spon' Aun' Peggy, 'look w'at you gone en done! You wa'n't sat'sfied wid w'at I tol' you, en now you gone en got ev'ything all mess' up. I knows how to take dat fus' goopher off, but now you gone en double de strenk, en I doan know whuther I kin fin' out how to take it off er no. Anyhow, I got ter wuk my roots fer a week er so befo' I kin tell. En w'ile's I is wukkin', you mought gib yo' niggers sump'n a little better ter eat, en dey mought pick up a little. S'posen you tries roas' po'k?'

"So Mars Donal' killt all 'is hawgs en fed his niggers on roas' po'k fer a week; but it didn' do 'em no good, en at de een' er de week he went back ter Aun' Peggy ag'in.

" 'I's monst'us sorry,' she sez, 'but it ain' my fault. I's wukkin' my roots ez ha'd ez I kin, but I ain' foun' out how ter take de goopher off yit. S'pos'n you feed yo' han's on roas' beef fer a week er so?'

"So Mars Donal' killt all 'is cows en fed de niggers on roas' beef fer a week, but dey didn' pick up. En all dis time dey wa'n' wukkin', en Mars Donal's craps wuz gittin 'way behin', en he wuz gwine mos' 'tracted fer fear he wuz bleedzd ter lose dem five hund'ed niggers w'at he sot so much sto' by. So he goes back ter ole Aun' Peggy ag'in.

" 'Peggy,' sezee, 'you is got ter do sump'n fer me, er e'se I'll be in de po'-house fus' thing I know.'

" 'Well, suh,' sez Aun' Peggy, 'I's be'n doin' all I knows how, but dey's a root I's bleedzd ter hab, en it doan grow nowhar but down in Robeson County. En I got ter go down dere en gether it on a Friday night in de full er de moon. En I won't be back yer fer a week or ten days.'

"Mars Donal' wuz mos' out'n his min' wid waitin' en losin' money. 'But s'posen dem niggers dies on my han's w'iles you er gone,' sezee, 'w'at is I gwine ter do?'

"Aun' Peggy studied en studied, en den she up en sez, sez she: " 'Well, ef dey dies I reckon you'll hatter bury 'em. Dey is one thing you mought try, en I s'pec's its 'bout de only thing w'at'll keep yo' niggers alibe 'tel I gits back. You mought see ef dey won' eat chick'n.'

"Well, Mars Donal' wanted ter sabe his niggers. Dey wuz all so po' en so skinny en so feeble dat he couldn' sell 'em ter nobody, en dey wouldn' eat nuffin' e'se, so he des had ter feed 'em on chick'n. W'en he had use' up all de chick'ns on his place, he went roun' ter his nabers ter buy chick'ns, en dey say dey wuz sorry, but dey'd sol' all dey chick'ns ter a man in town. Mars Donal' went ter dis yer man, en he say dem chick'ns doan b'long ter him but ter ernudder man w'at wuz geth'in' chick'ns fer ter ship ter Wim'l'ton, er de No'f, er some'ers. Mars Donal' say he des bleedzd ter hab chick'ns, en fer dat man to see de yuther gent'eman en ax 'im w'at he'd take fer dem chick'ns. De nex' day de man say Mars Donal' could hab de chick'ns fer so much, w'ich wuz 'bout twicet ez much ez chick'ns had be'n fetchin' in de market befo'. It mos' broke Mars Donal's hea't, but he 'lowed dem chick'ns would las' 'tel Aun' Peggy come back en tuk de goopher off'n de niggers.

"But w'en de een' er de week wuz retch', ole Aun' Peggy hadn' come back, en Mars Donal' had ter hab mo' chick'ns, fer chick'n-meat des barely 'peared ter keep de niggers alibe; en so he went out in de country fer ter hunt fer chick'ns. En ev'ywhar he'd go, dis yuther man had be'n befo' 'im en had bought up all de chick'ns, er contracted fer 'em all, en Mars Donal' had ter go back ter dis man in town en pay two prices ter git chick'ns ter feed his niggers.

"De nex' week it wuz de same way, en Mars Donal' 'mence' ter git desp'rit. He sont way off in two er th'ee counties, fer ter hunt chick'ns, but high er low, no matter whar, dis yuther man had be'n befo', 'tel it 'peared lak he had bought up all de chick'ns in No'f Ca'lina.

"But w'at wuz dribin' Mars Donal' mos' crazy wuz de money he had ter spen' fer dese chick'ns. It has mos' broke his hea't fer ter kill all his hawgs, en he had felt wuss w'en he hatter kill all his cows. But w'en dis yer chick'n business begun, it come mighty nigh ruinin' 'im. Fus', he spen' all de money he had saved feedin' de niggers. Den he spent all de money he had in de bank, er sto'ed away. Den he borried all de money he could on his notes, en he des 'bout retch' de pint whar he'd hatter mawgidge his plantation fer ter raise mo' money ter buy chick'ns fer his niggers, w'en one day Aun' Peggy come back fum Robeson County en tol' Mars Donal' she had foun' de root she 'uz lookin' fer, en gun 'im a mixtry fer ter take de goopher off'n de niggers.

"'Dis yer mixtry,' sez she, "ll fetch yo' niggers ap'tites back en make 'em eat dey rashuns en git dey strenk ag'in. But you is use' dat yuther mixtry so strong, en put dat goopher on so ha'd, dat I 'magine its got in dey blood, en I's feared dey ain' nobody ner nuffin kin eber take it all off'n 'em. So I 'spec's you'll hatter gib yo' niggers chick'n at leas' oncet a week ez long ez dey libs, ef you wanter git de wuk out'n 'em dat you oughter.

"Dey wuz so many niggers on ole Mars Donal's plantation," continued Julius, "en dey got scattered roun' so befo' de wah en sence, dat dey ain' ha'dly no cullu'd folks in No'f Ca'lina but w'at's got some er de blood er dem goophered niggers in dey vames. En so eber sence den, all de niggers in No'f Ca'lina has ter hab chick'n at leas' oncet er week fer ter keep dey healt' en strenk. En dat's w'y cullu' folks laks chick'n mo' d'n w'ite folks."

"What became of Tom and his sweetheart?" asked my wife.

"Yas'm," said Julius, "I wuz a-comin' ter dat. De nex' week atter de goopher wuz tuk off'n de niggers, Mars Tom come down ter Aun' Peggy en paid her back de money he borried. En he tol' Aun' Peggy he had made mo' money buyin' chick'ns en sellin' 'em ter his Uncle Donal' dan his daddy had lef' 'im w'en he died, en he say he wuz gwine ter marry Miss 'Liza en buy a big plantation en a lot er niggers en hol' up his head 'mongs' de big w'ite folks des lak he oughter. En he tol' Aun' Peggy he wuz much bleedzd ter her, en ef she got ti'ed cunj'in' en wanter res' en lib easy, she could hab a cabin on his plantation en a stool by his kitchen fiah, en all de chick'n en wheat-bread she wanter eat, en all de terbacker she wanter smoke ez long ez she mought stay in dis worl' er sin en sorrer."

I had occasion to visit the other end of the vineyard shortly after Julius had gone shambling down the yard toward the barn. I left word that the constable should be asked to wait until my return. I was detained longer than I expected, and when I came back I asked if the officer had arrived.

"Yes," my wife replied, "he came."

"Where is he?" I asked.

"Why, he's gone."

"Did he take the chicken-thief?"

"I'll tell you, John," said my wife, with a fine thoughtful look, "I've been thinking more or less about the influence of heredity and environment, and the degree of our responsibility for the things we do, and while I have not been able to get everything reasoned out, I think I can trust my intuitions. The constable came awhile after you left, but I told him that you had changed your mind, and that he might send in his bill for the time lost and you would pay for it."

"And what am I going to do with Sam Jones?" I asked.

"Oh," she replied, "I told Julius he might unlock the smoke-house and let him go."

TOBE'S TRIBULATIONS

About half a mile from our house on the North Carolina sand-hills there lay, at the foot of a vine-clad slope, and separated from my scuppernong vineyard by a rail fence, a marsh of some extent. It was drained at a somewhat later date, but at the time to which I now refer spread for half a mile in length and a quarter of a mile in breadth. Having been planted in rice many years before, it therefore contained no large trees, but was grown up chiefly in reeds and coarse grasses, with here and there a young sycamore or cypress. Though this marsh was not visible from our house, nor from any road that we used, it was nevertheless one of the most prominent features of our environment. We might sometimes forget its existence in the day-time, but it never failed to thrust itself upon our attention after night had fallen.

It may be that other localities in our neighborhood were infested with frogs; but if so, their vocal efforts were quite overborne by the volume of sound that issued nightly from this particular marsh. As soon as the red disk of the sun had set behind the pines the performance would begin, first perhaps with occasional shrill pipings, followed by a confused chattering; then, as the number of participants increased, growing into a steady drumming, punctuated every moment by the hoarse bellowing note of some monstrous bull-frog. If the day had perchance been rainy, the volume of noise would be greater. For a while after we went to live in the neighborhood, this ceaseless, strident din made night hideous, and we would gladly have dispensed with it. But as time wore on we grew accustomed to our nocturnal concert; we began to differentiate its notes and to distinguish a sort of rude harmony in these voices of the night; and after we had become thoroughly accustomed to it, I doubt whether we could have slept comfortably without their lullaby. But I had not been living long in the vicinity of this frog-pond before its possibilities as a source of food-supply suggested themselves to my somewhat practical mind. I was unable to learn that any of my white neighbors indulged in the delicate article of diet which frogs' legs might be made to supply; and strangely enough, among the negroes, who would have found in the tender flesh of the batrachian a toothsome and bountiful addition to the coarse food that formed the staple of their diet, its use for that purpose was entirely unknown.

One day I went frog-fishing and brought home a catch of half a dozen. Our colored cook did not know how to prepare them, and looked on the whole proceeding with ill-concealed disgust. So my wife, with the aid of a cook-book, dressed the hind legs quite successfully in the old-fashioned way, and they were served at supper. We enjoyed the meal very much, and I determined that thereafter we would have the same dish often.

Our supper had been somewhat later than usual, and it was dusk before we left the table and took our seats on the piazza. We had been there but a little while when old Julius, our colored coachman, came around the house and approaching the steps asked for some instructions with reference to the stable-work. As the matter required talking over, I asked him to sit down.

When we had finished our talk the old man did not go away immediately, and we all sat for a few moments without speaking. The night was warm but not sultry; there was a sort of gentle melancholy in the air, and the chorus from the distant frog-pond seemed pitched this night in something of a minor key.

"Dem frogs is makin' dey yuzh'al racket ternight," observed the old man, breaking the silence.

"Yes," I replied, "they are very much in evidence. By the way, Annie, perhaps Julius would like some of those frogs' legs. I see Nancy hasn't cleared the table yet."

"No ma'm," responded Julius quickly, "I's much obleedzd, but I doan eat no frog-laigs; no, *suh*, no *ma'm*, I doan eat no frog-laigs, not ef I knows w'at I's eatin'!"

"Why not, Julius?" I asked. "They are excellent eating."

"You listen right close, suh," he answered, "en you'll heah a pertic'ler bull-frog down yander in dat ma'sh. Listen! Dere he goes now—callin', callin', callin'! sad en mo'nful, des lak somebody w'at's los' somewhar, en can't fin' de way back."

"I hear it distinctly," said my wife after a moment. "It sounds like the lament of a lost soul."

I had never heard the vocal expression of a lost soul, but I tried, without success, to imagine that I could distinguish one individual croak from another.

"Well, what is there about that frog, Julius," I inquired, "that makes it any different from the others?"

"Dat's po' Tobe," he responded solemnly, "callin' Aun' Peggy —po' ole Aun' Peggy w'at's dead en gone ter de good Marster, yeahs en yeahs ago."

"Tell us about Tobe, Julius," I asked. I could think of no more appropriate time for one of the old man's stories. His views of life were so entirely foreign to our own, that for a time after we got acquainted with him his conversations were a never-failing source of novelty and interest. He had seen life from what was to us a new point of view—from the bottom, as it were; and there clung to his mind, like barnacles to the submerged portion of a ship, all sorts of extravagant beliefs. The simplest phenomena of life were to him fraught with hidden meaning,— some prophesy of good, some presage of evil. The source of these notions I never traced, though they doubtless could be easily accounted for. Some perhaps were dim reflections of ancestral fetishism; more were the superstitions, filtered through the negro intellect, of the Scotch settlers who had founded their homes on Cape Fear at a time when a kelpie haunted every Highland glen, and witches, like bats, darkened the air as they flew by in their nocturnal wanderings. But from his own imagination, I take it—for I never heard quite the same stories from anyone else—he gave to the raw material of folk-lore and superstition a fancifulness of touch that truly made of it, to borrow a homely phrase, a silk purse out of a sow's ear. And if perhaps, at times, his stories might turn out to have a purpose apart from any esthetic or didatic end, he probably reasoned, with a philosophy for which there is high warrant, that the laborer was worthy of his hire.

"'Bout fo'ty years ago," began Julius, "ole Mars Dugal McAdoo—*my* ole marster—useter own a man name' Tobe. Dis yer Tobe wuz a slow kind er nigger, en w'iles he'd alluz git his tas' done, he'd hafter wuk harder 'n any yuther nigger on de place ter do it. One time he had a monst'us nice 'oman fer a wife, but she got bit by a rattlesnake one summer en died, en dat lef' Tobe kind er lonesome. En mo' d'n dat, Tobe's wife had be'n cook at de big house, en eve'y night she'd fetch sump'n down ter her cabin fer Tobe; en he foun' it mighty ha'd ter go back ter bacon and co'n-bread atter libbin' off 'n de fat er de lan' all dese yeahs.

"Des 'bout a mont' er so atter Tobe's wife died, dey wuz a nigger run 'way fum ole Mars Marrabo McSwayne's—de nex' plantation—en in spite er all de w'ite folks could do, dis yer nigger got clean off ter a free state in de Norf, en bimeby he writ a sassy letter back ter Mars Marrabo, en sont 'im a bill fer de wuk he done fer 'im fer twenty yeahs er mo', at a dollah en a half a day—w'at he say he wuz gittin' at de Norf. One er de gals w'at wukked roun' de big house heared de w'ite folks gwine on 'bout it, en she say Mars Marrabo cusst en swo' des tarrable, en ole missis 'mos' wep' fer ter think how ongrateful dat nigger wuz, not on'y ter run 'way, but to write back sich wick'niss ter w'ite folks w'at had alluz treated 'im good, fed 'im en clothed 'im, en nussed 'im w'en he wuz sick, en nebber let 'im suffer fer nuffin all his life.

"But Tobe heared 'bout dis yer nigger, en he tuk a notion he'd lak ter run 'way en go ter de Norf en be free en git a dollah en a half a day too. But de mo' he studied 'bout it, de ha'der it 'peared ter be. In de fus' place, de Norf wuz a monst'us long ways off, en de dawgs mought track 'im, er de patteroles mought ketch 'im, er he mought sta've ter def ca'se he couldn' git nuffin ter eat on de way; en ef he wuz cotch' he wuz lakly ter be sol' so fur souf dat he'd nebber hab no chance ter git free er eber see his ole frien's nuther.

"But Tobe kep' on studyin' 'bout runnin 'way 'tel fin'lly he 'lowed he'd go en see ole Aun' Peggy, de cunjuh 'oman down by de Wim'l'ton Road, en ax her w'at wuz de bes' way fer him ter sta't. So he tuk a pa'r er pullets down ter Aun' Peggy one night en tol' her all 'bout his hank'in's en his longin's, en ax' her w'at he'd hafter do fer ter run 'way en git free.

"'W'at you wanter be free fer?' sez Aun' Peggy. "Doan you git ernuff ter eat?'

"'Yas, I gits ernuff ter eat, but I'll hab better vittles w'en I's free.'

"'Doan you git ernuff sleep?'

"'Yas, but I'll sleep mo' w'en I's free.'

"'Does you wuk too ha'd?'

"'No, I doan wuk too ha'd fer a slabe nigger, but ef I wuz free I wouldn' wuk a-tall 'less'n I felt lak it.'

"Aun' Peggy shuck her head. 'I dunno, nigger,' sez she, 'whuther you gwine ter fin' w'at you er huntin' fer er no. But w'at is it you wants me ter do fer you?'

"'I wants you ter tell me de bes' en easies' way fer ter git ter de Norf en be free.'

"'Well,' sez Aun' Peggy, 'I's feared dey ain' no easy way. De bes' way fer you ter do is ter fix yo' eye on de Norf Stah en sta't. You kin put some tar on yo' feet ter th'ow de houn's off'n de scent, en ef you come ter a crick you mought wade 'long fer a mile er so. I sh'd say you bettah sta't on Sad'day night, fer den mos' lakly you won' be miss' 'tel Monday mawnin', en you kin git a good sta't on yo' jou'ney. En den maybe in a mont' er so you'll retch de Norf en you'll be free, en whar you kin eat all you want, ef you kin git it, en sleep ez long ez you mineter, ef you kin 'ford it, en whar you won't hafter wuk ef you'd ruther go to jail.'

"'But w'at is I gwine ter eat dyo'in' er dis yer mont' I's trabblin'?' ax' Tobe. 'It makes me sick ef I doan git my reg'lar meals.'

"'Doan ax me,' sez Aun' Peggy. 'I ain' nebber seed de nigger yit w'at can't fin' sump'n ter eat.'

"Tobe scratch' his head. 'En whar is I gwine to sleep dyo'in' er dat mont'? I'll hafter hab my reg'lar res'.'

"'Doan ax me,' sez Aun' Peggy. 'You kin sleep in de woods in de daytime, en do yo' trabblin' at night.'

"'But s'pose'n a snake bites me?'

"'I kin gib you a cha'm fer ter kyo snake-bite.'

"'But s'pose'n' de patteroles ketch me?'

"'Look a heah, nigger,' sez Aun' Peggy, 'I's ti'ed er yo' s'pose'n', en I's was'e all de time on you I's gwine ter fer two chick'ns. I's feared you wants ter git free too easy. I s'pose you des wants ter lay down at night, do yo' trabblin' in yo' sleep, en

187

wake free in de mawn'in. You wants ter git a thousan' dollah nigger fer nuffin' en dat's mo' d'n anybody but de sma'test w'ite folks kin do. Go 'long back ter yo' wuk, man, en doan come back ter me 'less'n you kin fetch me sump'n mo'.'

"Now, Tobe knowed well ernuff dat ole Aun' Peggy'd des be'n talkin' ter heah herse'f talk, en so two er th'ee nights later he tuk a side er bacon en kyared it down ter her cabin.

" 'Uh huh,' sez Aun' Peggy, 'dat is sump'n lak it. I s'pose you still 'lows you'd lak ter be free, so you kin eat w'at you mineter, en sleep all you wanter, en res' w'eneber you feels dat erway?'

" 'Yas'm, I wants ter be free, en I wants you ter fix things so I kin be sho' ter git ter de Norf widout much trouble; fer I sho'ly does hate en 'spise trouble.'

"Aun' Peggy studied fer a w'ile, en den she tuk down a go'd off'n de she'f, en sez she:—

" 'I's got a goopher mixtry heah w'at 'll tu'n you ter a b'ar. You know dey use'ter be b'ars roun' heah in dem ole days.'

"Den she tuk down ernudder go'd. 'En,' she went on, 'ef I puts some er dis yuther mixtry wid it, you'll tu'n back ag'in in des a week er mont' er two mont's, 'cordin' ter how much I puts in. Now, ef I tu'ns you ter a b'ar fer, say a mont', en you is keerful en keeps 'way fum de hunters, you kin feed yo'se'f ez you goes 'long, en by de een' er de mont' you'll be ter de Norf; en w'en you tu'ns back you'll tu'n back ter a free nigger, whar you kin do w'at you wanter, en go whar you mineter, en sleep ez long ez you please.'

"So Tobe say all right, en Aun' Peggy mix' de goopher, en put it on Tobe en turn't 'im ter a big black b'ar.

"Tobe sta'ted out to'ds de Norf, en went fifteen er twenty miles widout stoppin'. Des befo' day in de mawnin' he come ter a 'tater patch, en bein' ez he wuz feelin' sorter hongry, he stop' fer a hour er so 'tel he got all de 'taters he could hol'. Den he sta'ted out ag'in, en bimeby he run 'cross a bee-tree en eat all de honey he could. 'Long to'ds ebenin' he come ter a holler tree, en bein' ez he felt kinder sleepy lak, he 'lowed he'd crawl in en take a nap. So he crawled in en went ter sleep.

"Meanw'ile, Monday mawn'in' w'en de niggers went out in de fiel' ter wuk, Tobe wuz missin'. All de niggers 'nied seein' 'im, en ole Mars Dugal sont up ter town en hi'ed some dawgs, en gun 'em de scent, en dey follered it ter ole Aun' Peggy's cabin. Aun' Peggy 'lowed yas, a nigger had be'n ter her cabin Sad'day night, en she had gun 'im a cha'm fer ter keep off de rheumatiz, en he had sta'ted off down to'ds de ribber, sayin' he wuz ti'ed wukkin' en wuz gwine fishin' fer a mont' er so. De w'ite folks hunted en hunted, but co'se dey did'n fin' Tobe.

"Bout a mont' atter Tobe had run 'way, en w'en Aun' Peggy had mos' fergot 'bout im, she wuz sett'n' in her cabin one night, wukkin' her roots, w'en somebody knock' at her do'.

" 'Who dere?' sez she.

" 'It's me, Tobe; open de do', Aun' Peggy.'

"Sho' 'nuff, w'en Aun' Peggy tuk down de do'-bar, who sh'd be stan'in' dere but Tobe.

" 'Whar is you come fum, nigger?' ax' Aun' Peggy, 'I 'lowed you mus' be ter de Norf by dis time, en free, en libbin' off'n de fat er de lan'.'

" 'You must 'a s'pected me ter trabbel monst'us fas' den,' sez Tobe, 'fer I des sta'ted fum heah yistiddy mawnin', en heah I is turnt back ter a nigger ag'in befo' I'd ha'dly got useter walkin' on all-fours. Dey's sump'n de matter wid dat goopher er y'n, fer yo' cunj'in' ain' wuk right dis time. I crawled in a holler tree 'bout six o'clock en went ter sleep, en w'en I woke up in de mawnin' I wuz tu'nt back ag'in, en bein' ez I hadn' got no fu'ther 'n Rockfish Crick, I des 'lowed I'd come back en git dat goopher w'at I paid fer fix' right.'

"Aun' Peggy scratched her head en studied a minute, en den sez she:—

" 'Uh huh! I sees des w'at de trouble is. I is tu'nt you ter a b'ar heah in de fall, en w'en you come ter a holler tree you crawls in en goes ter sleep fer de winter, des lak any yuther b'ar 'd do; en ef I hadn' mix' dat yuther goopher in fer ter tu'n you back in a mont', you'd a slep' all th'oo de winter. I had des plum' fergot 'bout dat, so I reckon I'll hafter try sumpin' diff'ent. I 'spec' I better tu'n you ter a fox. En bein' ez a fox is a good runner, you oughter git ter de Norf in less time dan a b'ar, so I'll fix dis yer goopher so you'll tu'n back ter a nigger en des th'ee weeks, en you'll be able ter enjoy yo' freedom a week sooner.'

"So Aun' Peggy tu'nt Tobe ter a fox, en he sta'ted down de road in great has'e, en made mo' d'n ten miles, w'en he 'mence' ter feel kinder hongry. So w'en he come ter a hen-house he tuk a hen en eat it, en lay down in de woods ter git his night's res'. In de mawnin', w'en he woke up, he 'lowed he mought 'swell hab ernudder chick'n fer breakfus', so he tuk a fat pullet en eat dat.

"Now, Tobe had be'n monst's fon' er chick'n befo' he wuz tu'nt ter a fox, but he hadn' nebber had ez much ez he could eat befo.' En bein' ez dere wuz so many chick'ns in dis naberhood, en dey mought be ska'se whar he wuz gwine, he 'lowed he better stay 'roun' dere 'tel he got kinder fat, so he could stan' bein' hongry a day er so ef he sh'd fin' slim pickin's fu'ther 'long. So he dug hisse'f a nice hole under a tree in de woods, en des stayed dere en eat chick'n fer a couple er weeks er so. He wuz so comf'table, eatin' w'at he laked, en restin' w'en he wa'n't eatin', he des kinder los' track er de time, 'tel befo' he notice' it his th'ee weeks wuz mos' up.

"But bimeby de people w'at own dese yer chick'ns 'mence' ter miss 'em, en dey 'lowed dey wuz a fox som'ers roun'. So dey got out dey houn's en dey hawns en dey hosses, en sta'ted off fer a fox-hunt. En sho' nuff de houn's got de scent, en wuz on po' Tobe's track in a' hour er so.

"W'en Tobe heared 'em comin' he wuz mos' skeered ter def, en he 'mence' ter run ez ha'd ez he could, en bein' ez de houn's wuz on de norf side, he run to'ds de souf, en soon foun' hisse'f back in de woods right whar he wuz bawn en raise'. He jumped a crick en doubled en twisted, en done ev'ything he could fer ter th'ow de houn's off'n de scent but 't wa'n't no use, fer dey des kep' gittin' closeter, en closeter, en closeter.

"Ez soon ez Tobe got back to'ds home en 'skivered whar he wuz, he sta'ted fer ole Aun' Peggy's cabin fer te git her ter he'p 'im, en des ez he got ter her do', lo en behol'! he tu'nt back ter a nigger ag'in, fer de th'ee weeks wuz up des ter a minute. He knock' at de do', en hollered:—

"'Lemme in, Aun' Peggy, lemme in! De dawgs is atter me.'

"Aun' Peggy open' de do'.

"'Fer de Lawd sake! nigger, whar is you come fum dis time?' sez she. 'I 'lowed you wuz done got ter de Norf, en free long ago. W'at's de matter wid you now?'

"So Tobe up'n' tol' her 'bout how he had been stop' by dem

chick'ns, en how ha'd it wuz ter git 'way fum 'em. En w'iles he wuz talkin' ter Aun' Peggy dey heared de dawgs comin' closeter, en closeter, en closeter.

"'Tu'n me ter sump'n e'se, Aun' Peggy,' sez Tobe, 'fer dat fox scent runs right up ter de do', en dey'll be 'bleedzd ter come in, en dey'll fin' me en kyar me back home, en lamb me, en mos' lakly sell me 'way. Tu'n me ter sump'n, quick, I doan keer w'at, fer I doan want dem dawgs ner dem w'ite folks ter ketch me.'

"Aun' Peggy look' 'roun' de cabin, en sez she, takin' down a go'd fum de chimbly:—

"'I ain' got no goopher made up ter-day, Tobe, but dis yer bull-frog mixtry. I'll tu'n you ter a bull-frog, en I'll put in ernuff er dis yuther mixtry fer ter take de goopher off in a day er so, en meanw'iles you kin hop down yander ter dat ma'sh en stay, en w'en de dawgs is all gone en you tu'ns back, you kin come ter me en I'll tu'n you ter a sparrer er sump'n' w'at kin fly swif', en den maybe you'll be able ter git 'way en be free widout all dis yer foolishness you's be'n goin' th'oo.'

"By dis time de dawgs wuz scratchin' at de do' en howlin', en Aun' Peggy en Tobe could heah de hawns er de hunters blowin' close behin'. All dis yer racket made Aun' Peggy sorter narvous, en w'en she went ter po' dis yuther mixtry in fer ter lif' 'de bull-frog goopher off'n Tobe in a day er so, her han' shuck so she spilt it ober de side er de yuther go'd en didn' notice dat it hadn' gone in. En Tobe wuz so busy lis'nin' en watchin' de do', dat he didn' notice nuther, en so w'en Aun' Peggy put de goopher on Tobe en tu'nt 'im inter a bull-frog, dey wa'n't none er dis yuther mixtry in it w'atsomeber.

"Tobe le'p' out'n a crack 'twix' de logs, en Aun' Peggy open' de do', en de dawgs run 'roun', en de w'ite folks come en inqui'ed, en w'en dey seed Aun' Peggy's roots en go'ds en snake-skins en yuther cunjuh-fixin's, en a big black cat wid yaller eyes, settin' on de h'a'th, dey 'lowed dey wuz wastin' dey time, so dey des cusst a little en run 'long back home widout de fox dey had come atter.

"De nex' day Aun' Peggy stayed roun' home all day, makin' a mixtry fer ter tu'n Tobe ter a sparrer, en 'spectin' 'im eve'y minute fer ter come in. But he nebber come. En bein' ez he didn' 'pear no mo', Aun' Peggy 'lowed he'd got ti'ed er dis yer animal bizness en w'en he had tu'nt back fum de bull-frog had runned 'way on his own 'sponsibility, lak she 'vised 'im at fus'. So Aun' Peggy went on 'bout her own bizness en didn' paid no mo' tention ter Tobe.

"Ez fer po' Tobe, he had hop' off down ter dat ma'sh en had jump' in de water, en had waited fer hisse'f ter tu'n back. But w'en he didn' tu'n back de fus' day, he 'lowed Aun' Peggy had put in too much er de mixtry, en bein' ez de ma'sh wuz full er minners en snails en crawfish en yuther things w'at bull-frogs laks ter eat, he 'lowed he mought's well be comf'table en enjoy hisse'f 'tel his bull-frog time wuz up.

"But bimeby, w'en a mont' roll' by, en two mont's, en th'ee mont's, en a yeah, Tobe kinder 'lowed dey wuz sump'n wrong 'bout dat goopher, en so he 'mence' ter go up on de dry lan' en look fer Aun' Peggy. En one day w'en she came 'long by de ma'sh, he got in front er her, en croak' en croak'; but Aun' Peggy wuz studyin' 'bout sump'n e'se; en 'sides, she 'lowed Tobe wuz done gone 'way en got free long, long befo', so she didn' pay no 'tention ter de big bull-frog she met in de path, 'cep'n ter push him out'n de road wid her stick.

"So Tobe went back ter his ma'sh, en dere he's be'n eber sence. It's be'n fifty yeahs er mo', en Tobe mus' be 'bout ten yeahs older 'n I is. But he ain' nebber got ti'ed er wantin' ter be tu'nt back ter hisse'f, er ter sump'n w'at could run erway ter de Norf. Co'se ef he had waited lak de res' un us he'd a be'n free long ago; but he didn' know dat, en he doan know it yet. En eve'y night, w'en de frogs sta'ts up, dem w'at knows 'bout Tobe kin reco'nize his voice en heah 'im callin', callin', callin' ole Aun' Peggy fer ter come en tu'n 'im back, des ez ef Aun' Peggy hadn' be'n restin' in Aberham's bosom fer fo'ty yeahs er mo'. Oncet in a w'ile I notices dat Tobe doan say nuffin fer a night er so, en so I 'lows he's gittin' ole en po'ly, en trouble' wid hoa'seness er rheumatiz er sump'n er 'nuther, fum bein' in de water so long. I doan 'spec' he's gwine to be dere many mo' yeahs; but w'iles he is dere, it 'pears ter me he oughter be 'lowed ter lib out de res' er his days in peace.

"Dat's de reason w'y," the old man concluded, "I doan lak ter see nobody eat'n frogs' laigs out 'n dat ma'sh. Ouch!" he added suddenly, putting his hand to the pit of his stomach, "Ouch!"

"What's the matter, Uncle Julius?" my wife inquired with solicitude.

"Oh, nuffin, ma'm, nuffin wuf noticin'—des a little tech er mis'ry in my innards. I s'pose talkin' 'bout po' old Tobe, in dat col', wet ma'sh, wid nobody ter 'sociate wid but frogs en crawfish en water-moccasins en sich, en wid nuffin fittin' ter eat, is des sorter upsot me mo' er less. If you is anyways int'rusted in a ole nigger's feelin's, I ruther 'spec' a drap er dem bitters out'n dat little flat jimmyjohn er yo'n git me shet er dis mis'ry quicker'n anything e'se I knows."

THE MARKED TREE

I had been requested by my cousin, whose home was in Ohio, to find for him, somewhere in my own neighborhood in the pine belt of North Carolina, a suitable place for a winter residence. His wife was none too strong; his father, who lived with him, was in failing health; and he wished to save them from the raw lake winds which during the winter season take toll of those least fitted to resist their rigor. My relative belonged to the fortunate class of those who need take no thought today for tomorrow's needs. The dignity of labor is a beautiful modern theory, in which no doubt many of the sterner virtues find their root, but the dignity of ease was celebrated at least as long ago as the days of Horace, a gentleman and philosopher, with some reputation as a poet.

Since my cousin was no lover of towns, and the term neighborhood is very elastic when applied to rural life, I immediately thought of an old, uncultivated—I was about to say plantation, but its boundaries had long since shrunk from those which in antebellum times would have justified so pretentious a designation. It still embraced, however, some fifteen or twenty acres of diversified surface—part sand-hill, part meadow; part overgrown with scrubby shortleaf pines and part with a scraggy underbrush. Though the soil had been more or less exhausted by the wasteful methods of slavery, neglected grapevines here and there, and gnarled and knotted fruit-trees, smothered by ruder growths about them, proved it to have been at one time in a high state of cultivation.

I had often driven by the old Spencer place, as it was called, from the name of the family whose seat it had been. It lay about five miles from my vineyard and was reached by a drive down the Wilmington Road and across the Mineral Spring swamp. Having brought with me to North Carolina a certain quickness of decision and promptness of action which the climate and *laissez-faire* customs of my adopted state had not yet overcome, upon receipt of my cousin's letter I ordered old Julius to get out the gray mare and the rockaway and drive me over to the old Spencer place.

When we reached it, Julius left his seat long enough to take down the bars which guarded the entrance and we then drove up a short lane to the cleared space, surrounded by ragged oaks and elms, where the old plantation house had once stood. It had been destroyed by fire many years before and there were few traces of it remaining—a crumbling brick pillar here and there, on which the sills of the house had rested, and the dilapidated, ivy-draped lower half of a chimney, of which the yawning, blackened fireplace bore mute witness of the vanished generations which had lived and loved—and perchance suffered and died, within the radius of its genial glow.

Not far from where the house had stood, there was a broad oak stump, in a good state of preservation, except for a hole in the center, due, doubtless, to a rotten heart, in what had been in other respects a sound and perfect tree. I had seated myself upon the top of the stump—the cut had been made with the axe, almost as smoothly as though with a saw—when old Julius, who was standing near me, exclaimed, with some signs of concern.

"Excuse me, suh, I know you come from de No'th, but did any of yo' folks, way back yonder, come from 'roun' hyuh?"

"No," I returned, "they were New England Yankees, with no Southern strain whatever. But why do you ask?" I added, observing that he had something on his mind, and having often found his fancies quaint and amusing, from the viewpoint of one not Southern born.

"Oh, nothin', suh, leas'ways nothin' much—only I seed you settin' on dat ol' stump, an' I wuz kind er scared fer a minute."

"I don't see anything dangerous about the stump," I replied. "It seems to be a very well preserved oak stump."

"Oh, no, suh," said Julius, "dat ain' no oak stump."

It bore every appearance of an oak stump. The grain of the wood was that of oak. The bark was oak bark, and the spreading base held the earth in the noble grip of the king of trees.

"It is an oak, Julius—it is the stump of what was once a fine oak tree."

"Yas, suh, I know it 'pears like oak wood, and it 'pears like oak bahk, an' it looked like a oak tree w'en it wuz standin' dere, fifty feet high, fohty years ago. But it wa'n't—no, suh, it wa'n't."

"What kind of a tree was it, if not an oak?"

"It was a U-pass tree, suh; yes, sah, dat wuz de name of it—a U-pass tree."

"I have never heard of that variety," I replied.

"No, suh, it wuz a new kind er tree roun' hyuh. I nevah heard er any but dat one."

"Where did you get the name?" I asked.

"I got it from ol' Marse Aleck Spencer hisse'f, fohty years ago—fohty years ago, suh. I was lookin' at dat tree one day, aftuh I'd heared folks talkin' 'bout it, an' befo' it wuz cut down, an' ole Marse Aleck come erlong, an' sez I, 'Marse Aleck, dat is a monst'us fine oak tree.' An' ole Marse Aleck up an sez, sezee, 'No, Julius, dat ain' no oak-tree—dat is a U-pass tree.' An' I've 'membered the name evuh since, suh—de U-pass tree. Folks useter call it a' oak tree, but Marse Aleck oughter a knowd;—it 'us his tree, an' he had libbed close to it all his life."

It was evident that the gentleman referred to had used in a figurative sense the name which Julius had remembered so literally—the Upas tree, the fabled tree of death. I was curious to know to what it owed this sinister appellation. It would be easy, I knew, as it afterwards proved, to start the old man on a train of reminiscence concerning the family and the tree. How much of it was true I cannot say; I suspected Julius at times of a large degree of poetic license—he took the crude legends and vague superstitions of the neighborhood and embodied them in stories as complete, in their way, as the Sagas of Iceland or the primitive tales of ancient Greece. I have saved a few of them. Had Julius lived in a happier age for men of his complexion, the world might have had a black Aesop or Grimm or Hoffman—as it still may have, for who knows whether our civilization has yet more than cut its milk teeth, or humanity has even really begun to walk erect?

Later in the day, in the cool of the evening, on the front piazza, left dark because of the mosquitoes, except for the light of the stars, which shone with a clear, soft radiance, Julius told my wife and me his story of the old Spencer oak. His low, mellow voice rambled on, to an accompaniment of night-time sounds— the deep diapason from a distant frog-pond, the shrill chirp of the cicada, the occasional bark of a dog or cry of an owl, all softened by distance and merging into a melancholy minor which suited perfectly the teller and the tale.

"Marse Aleck Spencer uster be de riches' man in all dis neighborhood. He own' two thousan' acres er lan'—de ole place ovuh yonduh is all dat is lef'. Dere wus ovuh a hund'ed an' fifty slaves on de plantation. Marse Aleck was a magist'ate an a politician, an' eve'ybody liked him. He kep' open house all de time, an' had company eve'y day in de yeah. His hosses wuz de fastes' an' his fox-hounds de swiftes', his game-cocks de fierces', an' his servants de impidentes' in de county. His wife wuz de pretties' an' de proudes' lady, an' wo' de bes' clo's an' de mos' finguhrings, an' rid in de fines' carriage. Fac', day alluz had de best er eve'ything, an' nobody didn' 'spute it wid 'em.

"Marse Aleck's child'en wuz de apples er his eye—dere wuz a big fambly—Miss Alice an' Miss Flora, an' young Marse Johnny, an' den some yeahs latuh, little Marse Henry an' little Marse Tom, an' den dere wuz ol' Mis' Kathu'n, Marse Aleck's wife, an' de chilen's mammy.

"When young Marse Johnny was bawn, and Aunt Dasdy, who had nussed all de child'en, put de little young marster in his pappy's arms, Marse Aleck wuz de happies' man in de worl'; for it wuz his fus' boy, an' he had alluz wanted a boy to keep up de fambly name an' de fambly rep'tation. An' eve'ybody on de plantation sheered his joy, fer when de marster smile, it's sunshine, an' when de marster frown, it's cloudy weather.

"When de missis was well enough, an' de baby was ol' enough, de christenin' come off; an' nothing would do fer Marse Aleck but to have it under de fambly tree—dat wuz de stump of it ovuh yonduh, suh, dat you was setting on dis mawnin'.

" 'Dat tree,' said Marse Aleck, 'wuz planted when my great-gran'daddy wuz bawn. Under dat tree eve'y fus'-bawn son er dis fambly since den has be'n christen'. Dis fambly has growed an' flourish' wid dat tree, an' now dat my son is bawn, I wants ter hab him christen' under it, so dat he kin grow an' flourish 'long wid it. An' dis ole oak'—Marse Aleck useter 'low it wuz a oak, befo' he give it de new name—'dis ole oak is tall an' stout an' strong. It has weathe'd many a sto'm. De win' cant blow it down, an' de lightnin' ain't nevuh struck it, an' nothin' but a prunin' saw has ever teched it, ner ever shill, so long as dere is a Spencer lef' ter pertec' it.'

"'An' so my son John, my fus'-bawn, is gwineter grow up tall an' strong, an' be a big man' an' a good man; an' his child'en and his child'en's child'en an' dem dat follers shall be as many as de leaves er dis tree, an' dey shill keep de name er Spencer at de head er de roll as long as time shall las'.'"

"De same day Marse Johnny wuz bawn, which wuz de fu'st er May—anudder little boy, a little black boy, wuz bawn down in de quahtahs. De mammy had worked 'roun' de big house de yeah befo', but she had give er mist'iss some impidence one day, an' er mist'iss had made Marse Aleck sen' her back ter de cotton-fiel'. An' when little Marse Johnny wuz christen', Phillis, dis yuther baby's mammy, wuz standin' out on de edge, 'long wid de yuther fiel'-hands, fuh dey wuz all 'vited up ter take part, an' ter eat some er de christenin' feas'. Whils' de white folks wuz eatin' in de house, de cullud folks all had plenty er good things pass 'roun' out in de yahd—all dey could eat an' all they could drink, fuh dem wuz de fat yeahs er de Spencers—an' all famblies, like all folks, has deir fat yeahs an' deir lean yeahs. De lean yeahs er de Spencers wuz boun' ter come sooner er later.

"Little Marse Johnny growed an' flourish' just like the fambly tree had done, an' in due time growed up to be a tall an' straight an' smart young man. But as you sca'cely evuh sees a tree widout a knot, so you nevuh sees a man widout his faults. Marse Johnny wuz so pop'lar and went aroun' so much wid his frien's that he tuck ter drinkin' mo' dan wuz good for him. Southe'n gent'emen all drunk them days, suh—nobody had never dremp' er dis yer foolishness 'bout pro'bition dat be'n gwine roun' er late yeahs. But as a gin'ral rule, dey drunk like gent'emen—er else dey could stan mo' liquor dan folks kin dese days. An' young Marse Johnny had a mighty quick temper, which mo' d'n once got 'im inter quarrels which it give 'im mo' or less trouble to make up.

"Marse Johnny wuz mighty fond er de ladies, too, an' wuz de pet of 'em all. But he wuz jus' passin' de time wid 'em, 'tel he met Miss Mamie Imboden—de daughter er de Widder Imboden, what own' a plantation down on ole Rockfish. Ole Mis' Imboden didn' spen' much time on huh place, but left it tuh a overseah, whils' she an' Miss Mamie wuz livin' in de big towns, er de wat'rin-places, er way up yonduh in de No'th, whar you an' yo' lady come fum.

"When de Widder Imboden come home one winter wid huh daughter, Marse Johnny fell dead in lub wid Miss Mamie. He couldn' ha'dly eat ner sleep fuh a week or so, an' he jus' natch'ly couldn' keep way fum Rockfish, an' jus' wo' out Marse Aleck's ridin' hosses comin' an' going', day, night an' Sunday. An' wharevuh she wuz visitin' he'd go visitin'; an' when she went tuh town he'd go tuh town. An' Marse Johnny got mo' religious dan he had evuh be'n befo' an' went tuh de Prisbyte'ian Chu'ch down tuh Rockfish reg'lar. His own chu'ch wuz 'Piscopal, but Miss Iboden wuz a Prisbyte'ian.

"But Marse Johnny wa'n't de only one. Anudder young gentleman, Marse Ben Dudley, who come fum a fine old fambly, but wuz monst'us wild an' reckless, was payin' co't tuh Miss Mamie at de same time, an' it was nip an' tuck who should win out. Some said she favored one, and some said de yuther, an' some 'lowed she didn' knowed w'ich tuh choose.

"Young Marse Johnny kinder feared fuh a while dat she like de yuther young gentleman bes'. But one day Marse Ben's daddy, ole Marse Amos Dudley, went bankrup', an' his plantation and all his slaves wuz sol', an' he shot hisse'f in de head, and young Marse Ben wuz lef' po'. An' bein' too proud tuh work, an' havin' no relations ter live on, he tuck ter bettin' an' dicin' an' kyard-playin', an' went on jes' scan'lous. An' it wuz soon whispered 'roun' dat young Mistah Dudley wuz livin' on his winin's at kyards, an' dat he wa'n't partic'lar who he played wid, er whar er how he played. But I is ahead er my tale, fuh all dis hyuh 'bout Marse Ben happen' after Marse Johnny had cut Marse Ben out an' ma'ied Miss Mamie.

"Ol' Marse Aleck wuz monst'us glad when he heared Marse Johnny wuz gwineter git ma'ied, for he wanted de fambly kep' up, an' he 'lowed Marse Johnny needed a wife fuh tuh he'p stiddy him. An' Miss Mamie wuz one of dese hyuh sweet-nachu'd, kin'-hearted ladies dat noboddy could he'p lovin'. An, mo'over, Miss Mamie's Mammy wuz rich, an' would leave huh well off sume day.

"Fuh de lean yeahs er de Spencers wuz comin', an' Marse Aleck 'spicioned it. De cotton crop had be'n po' de yeah befo', de cawn had ben wuss, glanders had got in the hosses an most of 'em had had ter be killed; an' old Marse Aleck wuz mo' sho't of money dan he'd be'n fur a long, long time. An' when he tried tuh make it up by spekilatin', he jus' kep' on losin' mo' an' mo' an' mo'.

"But young Marse Johnny had ter hab money for his weddin', an' the house had to be fix' up fuh 'im an' his wife, an' dere had ter be a rich weddin' present an' a fine infair, an' all dem things cos' money. An' sence he didn' wanter borry de money, Marse Aleck 'lowed he s'posed he'd hafter sell one er his han's. An' ole Mis' Spencer say he should sell Phillis's Isham. Marse Aleck didn' wanter sell Isham, fur he 'membered Isham wuz de boy dat wuz bawn on de same day Marse Johnny wuz. But ole Mis' Spencer say she didn' like dat boy's looks nohow, an' dat his mammy had be'n impident tuh huh one time, an ef Marse Aleck gwine sell anybody he sh'd sell Isham.

"Prob'bly ef old Marse Aleck had knowed jus' what wuz gwineter happen he mought not 'a' sol' Isham—he'd 'a' ruther gone inter debt, er borried de money. But den nobody nevuh knows whats gwineter happen; an' what good would it do 'em ef dey did? It'd only make 'em mizzable befo' han', an' ef it wuz gwineter happen, how could dey stop it? So Marse Aleck wuz bettuh off dan ef he had knowed.

"Now, dis hyuh Isham had fell in love, too, wid a nice gal on de plantation, an' wuz jus' 'bout making up his min' tuh ax Marse Aleck tuh let 'im marry her an' tuh give 'em a cabin tuh live in by deyse'ves, when one day Marse Aleck tuck Isham ter town, an' sol' 'im to another gent'eman, fuh tuh git de money fuh de expenses er his own son's weddin'.

"Isham's mammy wuz workin' in de cotton-fiel' way ovuh at

de fah end er de plantation dat day, an' when she went home at night an' foun' dat Marse Aleck had sol' huh Isham, she run up to de big house an' wep' an' hollered an' went on terrible. But Marse Aleck tol huh it wuz all right, dat Isham had a good marster, an' wa'n't many miles erway, an' could come an' see his mammy whenevuh he wanter.

"When de young ma'ied folks came back f'm dey weddin' tower, day had de infair, an' all de rich white folks wuz invited. An' dat same night, whils' de big house wuz all lit up, an' de fiddles wuz goin', an' dere wuz eatin' an' drinkin' an' dancin' an' sky-larkin' an' eve'body wuz jokin' de young couple an' wushin' 'em good luck, Phillis wuz settin' all alone in huh cabin, way at de fah end er de quarters, studyin' 'bout huh boy, who had be'n sol' to pay fer it all. All de other cullud folks wuz up 'round' de big house, some waitin' on de white folks, some he'pin in de kitchen, some takin' keer er de guest's hosses, an de res' swa'min' 'round de yahd, gittin' in one anudder's way, an' waitin' 'tel de white folks got thoo, so dey could hab somethin' tuh eat too; fuh Marse Aleck had open' de big blade, an' wanted eve'body to have a good time.

"'Bout time de fun wuz at de highes' in de big house, Phillis heared somebody knockin' at huh cabin do'. She didn' know who it could be, an' bein' as dere wa'nt nobody e'se 'roun', she sot still an' didn' say nary word. Den she heared somebody groan, an' den dere wuz anudder knock, a feeble one dis time, an' den all wuz still.

"Phillis wait' a minute, an' den crack' de do', so she could look out, an' dere wuz somebody layin' all crumple' up on de do'-step. An' den somethin' wahned huh what it wuz, an' she fetched a lighterd to'ch fum de ha'th. It wuz huh son Isham. He wuz wownded an' bleedin'; his feet wuz so' wid walkin'; he wuz weak from loss er blood.

"Phillis pick' Isham up an' laid 'im on huh bed an' run an' got some whiskey an' give 'im a drap, an' den she helt camphire tuh his nost'ils, meanwhile callin' his name an' gwine on like a wild 'oman. An' bimeby he open' his eyes an' look' up an' says—'I'se come home, mammy,'—an' den died. Dem wuz de only words he spoke, an' he nevuh drawed anudder bref.

"It come tuh light nex' day, when de slave-ketchers come

aftuh Isham wid deir dawgs an' deir guns, dat he had got in a 'spute wid his marster, an' had achully *hit his marster!* An' realizin' what he had done, he had run erway; natch'ly to'ds his mammy an' de ole plantation. Dey had wounded 'im an' had mos' ketched him, but he had 'scaped ag'in an' had reach' home just in time tuh die in his mammy's ahms.

"Phillis laid Isham out wid her own han's—dere wa'n't nobody dere tuh he'p her, an' she didn' want no he'p nohow. An' when it wuz all done, an' she had straighten' his lim's an' fol' his han's an' close his eyes, an' spread a sheet ovuh him, she shut de do' sof'ly, and stahted up ter de big house.

"When she drawed nigh, de visituhs wuz gittin' ready tuh go. De servants wuz bringin' de hosses an' buggies an' ca'iges roun'; de white folks wuz laffin' an gwine on an' sayin' good-bye. An' whils' Phillis wuz standin' back behin' a bunch er rose-bushes in de yahd, listenin' an' waitin', ole Marse Aleck come out'n de house wid de young couple an' stood unduh de ole fambly tree. He had a glass er wine in his han', an' a lot er de yuthers follered:

"'Frien's,' says he, 'drink a toas' wid me tuh my son an' his lady, hyuh under dis ole tree. May it last anudder hund'ed yeahs, an' den anudder, an' may it fetch good luck tuh my son an' his wife, an' tuh deir child'en an' deir child'en's child'en.'

"De toas' wuz drunk, de gues's depahted; de slaves went back tuh de quahtuhs, an' Phillis went home tuh huh dead boy.

"But befo' she went, she *marked de Spencer tree!*

"Young Marse Johnny an' his wife got 'long mighty well fuh de fust six mont's er so, an' den trouble commence' betwix' 'em. Dey wus at a pahty one night, an' young Marse Johnny seen young Marse Ben Dudley talking in a cawnuh wid Miss Mamie. Marse Johnny wuz mighty jealous-natu'ed, an didn' like dis at all. Endoyin' de same evenin' he overheard somebody say that Miss Mamie had th'owed Marse Ben ovuh beca'se he was po' an' married Marse Johnny beca'se he wuz rich. Marse Johnny didn' say nothin', but he kep' studyin' an studyin' 'bout dese things. An' it didn' do him no good to let his min' run on 'em.

"Marse Ben Dudley kep' on gwine from bad ter wuss, an' one day Marse Johnny foun' a letter from Marse Ben in his wife's bureau drawer.

"'You used ter love me' says Marse Ben in dis hyuh letter—

'you know you did, and you love me yit—I know you does. I am in trouble. A few hun'ed dollahs'll he'p me out. Youer totin' mo' d'n dat 'roun' on yo' pretty little fingers. Git the money fuh me—it'll save my honor an' my life. I swear I'll pay it back right soon.'

"Den' all Marse Johnny's jealousy b'iled up at once, an' he seed eve'ything red. He went straight to Miss Mamie an' shuck de lettuh in her face an' 'cused her er gwine on wid Marse Ben. Co'se she denied it. Den he ax' huh what had become er huh di'mon' 'gagement ring dat he had give huh befo' dey wuz ma'ied.

"Miss Mamie look' at huh han' an' turn' white as chalk, fer de ring wa'n't dere.

"'I tuck it off las' night, when I went tuh bed, an' lef' it on de bureau, an' I fuhgot tuh put it on dis mawnin'.'

"But when she look' fer it on de bureau it wuz gone. Marse Johnny swo' she had give' it tuh Marse Ben, an' she denied it tuh de las'. He showed her de letter. She said she hadn' answered it, an' hadn't meant to answer it, but had meant to bu'n it up. One word led to another. Dere wuz a bitter quarrel, an' Marse Johnny swo' he'd never speak to his wife ag'in 'tel de di'mond ring wuz foun'. And he didn'.

"Ole Marse Aleck wuz 'way from home dat winter, to congress or de legislator, or somewhar, an' Marse Johnny wuz de boss er de plantation whils' he wuz gone. He wuz busy all day, on de plantation, or in his office, er in town. He tuck moster his meals by hisself, an' when he et wid Miss Mamie he manage' so as nevuh to say nothin'. Ef she spoke, he purten' not to hear her, an' so she didn' try mo' d'n once er twice. Othe'wise, he alluz treated her like a lady—'bout a mile erway.

"Miss Mamie tuck it mighty ha'd. Fuh she was tenduh as well as proud. She jus' 'moped an' pined erway. One day in de springtime, when Marse Johnny wuz in town all day, she wuz tuck ill sudden, an' her baby wuz bawn, long befo' its time. De same day one er de little black child'en clum up in de ole Spencer tree an' fetch' down a jaybird's nes', an' in de nes' dey foun' Miss Mamie's ring, whar de jaybird had stole it an' hid it. When Marse Johnny come home dat night he found his wife an' his chile bofe dead, an' de ring on Miss Mamie's finger.

"Well, suh, you nevuh seed a man go on like Marse Johnny

did; an' folks said dat ef he could 'a' foun' Marse Ben Dudley
he sho' would a' shot 'im; but lucky fer Marse Ben he had gone
away. Aftuh de fune'al, Marse Johnny shet hisse'f up in his room
fer two er three days; an' as soon as Marse Aleck come home,
Marse Johnny j'ind de ahmy an' went an' fit in de Mexican Wah
an' wuz shot an' kill'.

"Ole Marse Aleck wuz so' distress' by dese yer troubles, an'
grieve' migh'ly over de loss er his fus' bawn son. But he got ovuh
it after a while. Dere wuz still Marse Henry an Marse Tom, bofe
un' 'em good big boys, ter keep up de name, an' Miss Alice an'
Miss Flora who wuz bofe ma'ied an' had child'en, ter see dat
de blood didn' die out. An' in spite er dis hyuh thievin' jaybird,
nobody 'lowed dat de ole tree had anything ter do wid Marse
Johnny's troubles, fer 'co'se nobody but Phillis knowed dat it
had evuh been mark'.

"But dis wuz only de beginnin'.

"Next year, in the spring, Miss Alice, Marse Aleck's oldes'
daughter, wuz visitin' the fambly wid her nuss an' chile—she
had ma'ied sev'al yeahs befo' Marse Johnny—an' one day de
nuss wuz settin' out in de yahd, wid de chile, under de ole tree,
when a big pizen spider let hisse'f down from a lim' when de
nuss wa'n't lookin', an' stung the chile. The chile swoll up, an'
dey sent fer de doctuh, but de doctuh couldn' do nothin', an'
the baby died in spasms dat same night, an' de mammy went
inter a decline fum grief an' died er consumption insid' er six
mont's.

"Of co'se de tree wuz watched close fer spiders aftah dis, but
none er de white folks thought er blamin' de tree—a spider
mought 'a' come from de ceiling' er from any other tree; it
wuz jes' one er dem things dat couldn' be he'ped. But de servants commence' ter whisper 'mongs' deyse'ves dat de tree wuz
conju'ed an' dere'd be still mo' trouble from it.

"It wa'n't long coming. One day young Marse Henry, de nex'
boy ter Marse Johnny, went fishin' in de ribber, wid one er de
naber boys, an' he clumb out too fah on a log, an' tip' de log up,
an' fell in de ribber an' got drownded. Nobody could see how de
ole tree wuz mix' up wid little Marse Henry's drowndin', 'tel one
er de house servants 'membered he had seed de boys diggin'
bait in de shade er de ole tree. An' whils' they didn' say nothin'
ter de white folks, leas'ways not jes' den, dey kep' it in min' an'

waited tuh see what e'se would happen. Dey didn' know den dat Phillis had mark' de tree, but dey mo' den half s'picioned it.

"Sho' 'nuff, one day de next' fall, Mis' Flora, Marse Aleck's secon' daughter, who wuz ma'ied an' had a husban', come home to visit her folks. An' one day whils' she wuz out walkin' wid her little boy, a sto'm come up, an' it stahted ter rain, an' dey didn' hab no umbreller, an' wuz runnin' ter de house, when jes' as dey got under de ole tree, de lightnin' struck it, broke a limb off 'n de top, skun a little strip off 'n de side all de way down, an' jump off an' hit Mis' Flora an' de boy, an' killt 'em bofe on de spot—dey didn't have time ter draw anudder bref.

"Still de white folks didn' see nuthin wrong wid de tree. But by dis time de cullud folks all knowed de tree had be'en conju'd. One un 'em said somethin' 'bout it one day ter old Marse Aleck, but he tol' 'em ter go 'long wid deir foolishness; dat it wuz de will er God; dat de lightnin' mought's well 'a' struck any yuther tree dey'd be'en under as dat one; an' dat dere wouldn' be no danger in de future, fer lightnin' nebber struck twice in de same place nohow.

"It wus 'bout a yeah after dat befo' anything mo' happen', an' de cullud folks 'lowed dat mo' likely dey had be'n mistaken an' dat maybe de tree hadn' be'n mark', er e'se de goopher wuz all wo' off, when one day little Marse Tom, de only boy dat wuz lef', wuz ridin' a new hoss Marse Aleck had give 'm, when a rabbit jump 'cross de road in front er him, an' skeered dis hyuh young hoss, an' de hoss run away an' thowed little Marse Tom up 'gins' de ole Spencer tree, an' bu'st his head in an' killt 'im.

"Marse Aleck wuz 'mos' heartbroken, fer Marse Tom wuz do only son he had lef'; dere wa'n't none er his child'en lef' now but Miss Alice, whose husban' had died, an' who had come wid her little gal ter lib wid her daddy and mammy.

"But dere wuz so much talk 'bout de ole tree 'tel it fin'lly got ter ole Miss Katherine's yeahs, an' she tol' Marse Aleck. He didn' pay no 'tention at fu'st, jes' 'lowed it 'uz all foolishness. But he kep' on hearin' so much of it, dat bimeby he wuz 'bleege' ter listen. An' he fin'lly 'lowed dat whether de tree was conju'd or not, it had never brought nuthin' but bad luck evuh sence Marse Johnny's weddin', an' he made up his min' ter git rid of it, in hopes er changin' de fambly luck.

"So one day he ordered a couple er han's ter come up ter de

house wid axes an' cut down de ole tree. He tol' 'em jes' how ter chop it, one on' one side an' one on de yuther, so's ter make it fall a partic'lar way. He stood off ter one side, wid his head bowed down, 'tel de two cuts had 'mos' met, an' den he tu'ned his eyes away, fer he did n' wanter see de ole tree fall—it had meant so much ter him fer so long. He heared de tree commence crackin', an' he heared de axemen holler, but he didn' know dey wuz hollerin' at him, an' he didn' look round'—he didn't wanter see de ole Spencer tree fall. But stidder fallin' as he had meant it ter, an' as by rights it couldn' he'p fallin', it jes' twisted squar' roun' sideways to'ds ole Marse Aleck an' ketched 'im befo' he could look up, an' crushed 'im ter de groun'.

"Well, dey buried Marse Aleck down in de fambly buryin'-groun'—you kin see it over at de ole place, not fur from de house; it's all growed up now wid weeds an' briars, an' most er de tombstones is fell down and covered wid green moul'. It wuz already pretty full, an' dere wa'n't much room lef'. After de fune'al, de ole tree wuz cut up inter firewood an' piled up out in de yard.

"Ole Miss' Kathun an' her daughter, Mis' Alice, an' Mis' Alice's little gal, went inter mo'nin' an' stayed home all winter.

"One col' night de house-boy toted in a big log fum de old Spencer tree, an' put it on de fire, an' when ole Miss' Kathun an' her daughter an' her gran' daughter went to bed, dey lef' de log smoulderin' on de ha'th. An' 'long 'bout midnight, when eve'ybody wuz soun' asleep, dis hyuh log fell out'n de fireplace an' rolled over on de flo' an' sot de house afire an' bu'nt it down ter de groun', wid eve'ybody in it.

"Dat, suh, wuz de end er de Spencer fambly. De house wuz nebber rebuil'. De war come erlong soon after, an' nobody had no money no mo' ter buil' houses. De lan', or what little wuz lef' after de mogages an' de debts wuz paid off, went ter dis hyuh young gentleman, Mistuh Brownlow, down to Lumberton, who wuz some kinder fo'ty-secon' cousin er nuther, an' I reckon he'd be only too glad ter sell it."

I wrote to young Mr. Brownlow, suggesting an appointment for an interview. He replied that he would call on me the following week, at an hour stated, if he did not hear from me beforehand that some other time would be more convenient.

I awaited him at the appointed hour. He came in the morning and stayed to luncheon. He was willing to sell the old place and we agreed upon a price at which it was to be offered to my cousin. He was a shallow, amiable young fellow, unmarried, and employed as a clerk in a general store. I told him the story of the Spencer oak, as related by old Julius. He laughed lightly.

"I believe the niggers did have some sort of yarn about the family and the old tree," he said, "but of course it was all their silly superstition. They always would believe any kind of foolishness their crazy imaginations could cook up. Well, sir, let me know when you hear from your friend. I reckon I'll drive past the old place on my way home, and take a last look at it, for the sake of the family, for it was a fine old family, and it was a pity the name died out."

An hour later there was an agitated knock at my library door. When I opened it old Julius was standing there in a state of great excitement.

"What is the matter, Julius?"

"It's done gone an' happen', suh, it's done gone an' happen'!"

"What has done gone and happened?"

"De tree, suh, de U-pass tree—de ole Spencer tree."

"Well, what about it?"

"Young Mistuh Brownlow lef' here an' went ovuh tuh de old place, an' sot down en de ole stump, an' a rattlesnake come out'n de holler an' stung 'im, an' killt 'im, suh. He's layin' ovuh dere now, all black in de face and swellin' up fas'."

I closed my deal for the property through Mr. Brownlow's administrator. My cousin authorized me to have the land cleared off, preparatory to improving it later on. Among other things, I had the stump of the Spencer oak extracted. It was a difficult task even with the aid of explosives, but was finally accomplished without casualty, due perhaps to the care with which I inquired into the pedigree of the workmen, lest perchance among them there might be some stray offshoot of this illustrious but unfortunate family.

Charles W. Chesnutt was an American novelist and
essayist at the turn of the twentieth century. He wrote
*The Conjure Woman, The House Behind the Cedars, The
Marrow of Tradition, The Wife of His Youth and Other
Stories,* and *The Colonel's Dream.*

Richard H. Brodhead is Housum Professor of English at
Yale University and Dean of Yale College. He is author
of *Hawthorne, Melville and the Novel, The School of
Hawthorne,* and *Cultures of Letters: Scenes of Reading and
Writing in Nineteenth Century America,* and is editor of
*William Faulkner: New Perspectives, New Essays on Melville's
Moby Dick,* and *The Journals of Charles W. Chesnutt.*

Library of Congress Cataloging-in-Publication Data
Chesnutt, Charles Waddell, 1858–1932.
The conjure woman, and other conjure tales / by
Charles W. Chesnutt ; edited and with an introduction
by Richard H. Brodhead.
Includes bibliographical references.
ISBN 0-8223-1378-2 (cloth).
ISBN 0-8223-1387-1 (paper)
1. Afro-Americans—Southern States—Fiction.
I. Brodhead, Richard H., 1947– . II. Title.
PS1292.C6A6 1993
813'.4—dc20   93-4215 CIP